THE WISDOM OF ESAU

THE
WISDOM OF ESAU

BY

R. L. OUTHWAITE

AND

C. H. CHOMLEY

Biography of C. H. Chomley

Charles Henry Chomley was born on 28th April 1868 in Sale, Victoria, Australia. He was the son of banker, Henry Baker Chomley and his wife Eliza (daughter of lawyer and politician, Thomas Turner à Beckett). The second of four children, Chomley attended Trinity College, University of Melbourne, graduating with a BA in 1888, and an LL.B in 1889, consequently being accepted to the Victorian Bar in 1891. Chomley left the legal profession two years later however, and established a farming partnership in Australia with his cousin, Frank Chomley. With a group of friends, he settled in the King River Valley in northeast Victoria.

Chomley returned to Melbourne due to heart problems in 1900 - a move which signalled the launch of his journalistic career. Here, he took up editorship of the illustrated weekly *Arena*. Dedicated to the arts, politics, and society gossip, the magazine also demonstrated strong support of both the suffragette movement and free trade. Over the following few years, Chomley wrote and co-wrote several works, before setting sail for London in 1907. In 1908 he became editor of the *British Australasian*, a weekly tabloid that provided Antipodeans in London a link to news, markets, weather, and society information from home. Under Chomley's editorship, the magazine developed a distinctly more artistic tone, with some summer numbers featuring sketches, poetry, short stories and interviews with prominent members of the Australasian arts community in London. He remained editor of the paper until his death in 1942.

Chomley was heavily interested in both Australian and British politics, and published his novel, *Mark Meredith: A Tale of Socialism* in 1905. It is an important work in the Australian literary canon as it provides not only an insight into the political sphere, but also the emotions of the Australian people at this changeable time. It depicts a fictitious period in Australian history where socialism has been in place for numerous years, according to Chomley, an entirely negative development. Another politically inspired work is *Protection in Canada and Australasia* (1904), discussing the federations of the British Empire in relation to free trade and protectionist battles. He maintained his early interest in the law though and wrote *The True Story of the Kelly Gang of Bushrangers* (1900), a highly researched biography utilising court documents, police records and court evidence. This was followed by *The Wisdom of Esau* in 1901, another fictional work examining land laws within Australia.

Chomley died on 21st October 1942, in London, England, aged seventy four.

CONTENTS

THE WISDOM OF ESAU

BOOK I

CHAPTER I

ON an evening of early summer in the year 1863 two bronzed and bearded men sat by a camp fire on a three-chain road in the north-eastern district of Victoria. Their clothes were rough, and the shine upon leggings and riding-breeches bore witness to many days in the saddle, for it was a fortnight before that John Toland and his younger mate, George Scott, had met and fraternised on the road which both were travelling to Thomas Harlin's Kumbarra run, just thrown open for selection under the Gavan Duffy Land Act. Their horses grazed among a mob of others near by, whence came the sound of jingling hobble-chains. Fires flickered at intervals down the wide sweep of the road, and the murmur of many voices was heard when the breeze rustled towards them through the forest.

'I'm afraid we'll have little chance at the ballot to-morrow,' said Toland, a man of fine physique, with quick eyes and resolute face, as he glanced towards a dimly-lighted building among the trees. 'The dummies are rolling up by the dozen.'

'Yes; Harlin's got that wizen-faced slip of a lawyer

A

that come up from Melbourne along with him at the shanty. They say the blackguards Mallock has picked up are signing agreements to transfer any lot they get to Harlin, and he's to pay them ten pound a head when they do it.'

' It's a damned swindle, and a disgrace that makes my blood boil, for my own sake and every honest man's ! '

Toland's voice was strenuous with anger. His words needed no expressed assent, and the men smoked for a time in sympathetic silence.

' It will be just the Warrooma estate business over again,' said Toland, presently. 'I rode down there, a couple of hundred miles, and spent a week on the land to see what lots were worth having ; but I might have saved myself the trouble. The place just stank of dummies, and they got all the best of the run back for M'Gubbin. One chap had a nice block, but M'Gubbin threatened to cut him off from water and see the storekeepers sold him nothing, so he funked and slung it up for a few pounds. I'd have cut my throat—or the squatter's—rather than be done out of my rights like that.'

' Well, if I get a bit of that open country on the flats, it will take something to shift me,' said Scott. ' I wouldn't take five pound an acre for it.'

' Oh, the dummies will get all the pick of that, and if there's anything left for us it will be away back in the stringy bark country that Harlin doesn't think worth paying for. Will you select there if you have the chance ? '

' I suppose so. A man can't waste all his little savings going from ballot to ballot. It's not bad land,'

'No,' said Toland, reflectively, 'but a man's heart will have to be in the right place to clear it.'

'It will that,' agreed Scott, 'but I mean to have a bit of land of my own somewhere and be as free as any man.'

'That's what brings me here,' replied Toland. 'In a way I wasn't doing so bad in the old country, where my people were tenant farmers, but I've seen enough of slaving for the landlord, and, by Heaven, I'll stick to any land I get, spite of squatters and their dummies, if I have to live on possum and kangaroo, and work till I drop—for this is going to be a great country some day.'

'It is so,' assented Scott, 'and I reckon that any man that will work will be able to earn a living.'

The two men lapsed into silence again, and Scott went in·search of more wood, while Toland, deep in reverie, gazed into the glowing embers, pursuing further the thoughts he had just uttered. Presently his look grew sterner, and he muttered to himself as he rose from the ground, 'Yes, thank God! There's no poorhouse in this land.'

Then Scott returned with some sticks, and, lighting their pipes, he and Toland strolled away to see what the other men were doing.

Camp fires glowed around them on both sides of the main road to Melbourne, which followed the narrowing valley no further, but turned at a sharp angle to the left, a few chains from Toland's camp, to cross a gap in the hills to a mining town beyond. At the corner of the road stood Mallock's shanty, grandiloquently called the 'Morning Star' Hotel. As a changing station for Cobb & Co.'s mail coaches, and the only house on the road for miles, it was a

place of some importance. There the land ballot
was to be held on the morrow, and at that moment
its neighbourhood was the scene of much activity.
Outside, the road was thronged with men, divided
instinctively into two hostile groups. In the smaller
were comprised miners, artisans, mechanics and
farmers—all men who had come for the purpose of
trying to obtain land for themselves at the ballot.
The other and larger group consisted of men gathered
together by Mallock from the nearest townships to
dummy for Harlin, whose run, held now as leasehold,
was to be thrown open for selection under the Act
passed only a few months previously, with the
nominal object of 'unlocking the lands' and making
them available in smaller holdings for agriculture.

Mallock's time as agent for Harlin was fully
occupied that night. In a room off the bar, Harlin,
and Wise, the lawyer, were taking the signatures of
the dummies, whom Mallock introduced one by one,
going out to the group each time to secure his man,
and leaving his bar meanwhile in charge of a frowsy
Hebe whom he had engaged for the occasion at a
distant township. It was evident that he took a pride
in his work and regarded each dummy whom he led
into the sitting-room as a trophy of his prowess.

Though, like Toland, a powerfully - built man,
Mallock was in other respects of a strikingly different
stamp. In the midst of a black bushy beard was set
a thick-lipped, gluttonous mouth, overhung by a large
hooked nose. His eyes were keen and cruel, his
eyebrows thick and black, and his whole appearance
suggested power and unscrupulousness.

He had come to the end of his list; and when the
last of the dummies left the room, Harlin, a short,

fair-bearded man with a phenomenally red face, went to the door. 'Come in, Mallock,' he said, 'and bring a bottle of brandy and glasses.'

'Well, you have done very fairly,' he continued when the shanty keeper had returned with the liquor. 'I wanted two hundred and you have got me a hundred and eighty; but I think that will be enough.'

'Oh, plenty,' said Mallock. 'And if any of the other rascals should get a block you want you'll be able to shift him all right.'

'I think so,' replied Harlin. 'Of course I shall take up the river frontages first, and then I shall be fairly right. The back country is a God-forsaken wilderness that should frighten any man who wants to put a plough in it. But confound the rascally Government for not letting me buy the land at the pound an acre they are trying to get rid of it for to all the penniless blackguards who think they are going to have a landed estate and be gentlemen.'

Wise laughed at Harlin's vehemence. 'But, my dear fellow, the Government is not trying to sell the land to the people—only pretending to do so in deference to popular clamour. You ought to thank your stars that your run is thrown open for selection while you can dummy it into your hands as freehold before the farce is howled off the political stage. Now, as I am a little exhausted by my part in it, I propose that we swallow our poison to the health of Gavan Duffy.'

'Well,' said Harlin, grudgingly, as he poured out the spirit, 'things might be worse. But, after all, it's a confounded expense.'

'Expense?' queried Wise, with sarcastically-raised

eyebrows. 'You call it expense to pay ten pounds for the services of a dummy who puts into your hand a block worth thousands in a few years' time if not to-day. Truly this is an ungrateful and a stiff-necked generation.'

'Perhaps everything is for the best,' laughed Harlin. 'Anyhow, business is done, so we may as well get back to the station. Tell Bill to bring our horses round, Mallock. What I think annoys me most,' he continued, glancing after Mallock as he left the room, 'is that nearly all my good money will go to that scoundrel, who I should like to see out of the district. There'll be a glorious drunk here to-morrow night after the dummies get their cheques.'

'I suppose he'll keep them sufficiently sober till then.'

'Yes; he doesn't give tick, and I don't suppose there's the price of a drink all round amongst them. I can't say I like this business much, and I shall be glad when it's all over.'

Harlin got up, yawning, and handed his cigar-case to Wise, and by the time the lawyer had collected his papers Mallock returned to say the horses were ready.

With a parting injunction, as they stepped into the fresh air, to take care of the dummies and have them on hand early in the morning, the two men mounted and rode away.

'It looks quite picturesque, don't it?' said Wise, glancing lazily down the road.

The camp fires were burning more dimly now, for it was after midnight, but every one of them showed up a surrounding patch of spectral forest. Voices sounded from some of the camps; in others men slept in their blankets on the ground, dreaming, perhaps, of good fortune at the ballot which should give them a footing on the soil. And Harlin, as he rode along the line, thought of the dummies with contempt, and the selectors with bitterness, as enemies who had come to rob him of his own, for it was war to the knife in those days between the squatter and the 'cockie.' Therefore Harlin, no better and no worse than his neighbours, thought all means to hold their land justified in the owners of the flocks and herds—the pioneers who had made the country what it was.

He had no sympathy for the selectors' aspirations, nor scruples about defeating them, but it was annoying that he had to employ such a dirty tool as Mallock. In spite of what Wise might say, the whole thing was a confounded expense ; and he nursed a feeling of injury at the hands of the law.

Mallock stood at the door for some time and watched the others well on their way down the road before going back into the bar parlour to wrestle with a legal problem of some complexity. Then seating himself at the rickety table, in an atmosphere reeking with spirits and fumes of a tallow dip— fashioned of twisted worsted in a pannikin of melted fat—he spread a piece of paper before him and proceeded to painfully decipher its contents.

The document was a blank form of transfer of land, which the lawyer had carelessly dropped beneath the table when gathering up his papers before leaving—one of many for to-morrow's use, to be signed by the successful dummies in accordance with the agreements they had made.

Mallock pondered over it for a long time. At

length, saying to himself, 'It may be of use. I don't
see why I mightn't play their own game,' he folded
it carefully and put it in his pocket. Then he took
the dip and went into the bar.

A few men were still there in a rather maudlin
condition, and these he turned out, whilst a drunken
man, snoring in the corner, he hauled into the road
and left to be sobered by the cool night air. After
dismissing his bar help he locked the entrance door,
and, evidently well pleased with himself and the
world in general, retired to his rough, uninviting couch,
which consisted of a wooden stretcher with a wool
pack for mattress.

Having taken off his boots, by way of undressing,
he drew over himself a dirty blanket and soon slept
as placidly as an innocent child.

CHAPTER II

THE laughing jackasses were merry over the first joke of the day, and the magpies still warbling their matin song, when the camp began to stir. From all sides came voices and whistling, the barking of dogs, neighing of horses, and snatches of time-honoured ballads.

Toland rose at dawn and made up the fire, after which he strolled along the road past Mallock's shanty to a point whence an extensive view could be obtained. The sun was just rising over the hills into a cloudless sky and filling the valleys with light. The mists were curling up like incense from the shrine of the god of day, and in the distance the waters of the Tonga glinted here and there amid the dark red gums as it took its course through the fertile flats of Kumbarra.

No prospect could have been more alluring to a strong man hungry for a home than this glimpse of Australia Felix, and Toland, stretching out his hand, as if in anticipation of ownership, said to himself, 'This is the promised land.' After dreaming for a while he strolled back to the camp and found the unimaginative Scott intent upon breakfast. The cold meat and damper were soon disposed of, and, lighting their pipes, the two men began once more to discuss the absorbing topic of the ballot and their chances of securing a portion of the 6000 acres of river flats which Harlin had determined to obtain for himself.

The hours dragged slowly till ten o'clock, when Harlin and Wise drove by to the 'Morning Star,' followed shortly afterwards by Archer, the land officer, and Watterson, his clerk. Then the selectors began to gather at the shanty, forming a group apart from the dummies, and soon the officials, with Harlin and Wise, appeared upon the verandah, smoking cigars and chatting together. 'These are the would-be country gentlemen, I presume,' said Archer, with a sneer. 'They are an elegant-looking lot, and the other crowd beyond look, if anything, worse.'

'Those are the gentlemen Mr Harlin hopes to see provided with estates to-day,' said Wise.

'Ah, I am glad to see Mr Harlin has not left much to chance,' commented Archer, opening his watch with a yawn. 'Shall we make a start now? It's about half-past ten.'

Harlin agreed, and Watterson, placing the ballot-box on the verandah, took a plan of the estate, marked off in selections, into a room behind. Then Archer announced that the ballot was about to begin, and the men in the road pressed close to him, but the troopers pushed their horses among the crowd till a space was cleared before the verandah, when the land officer produced a paper from which, in a weary voice, he read the conditions of the ballot.

The procedure was simple enough. Numbers corresponding with those on the application forms had been placed in the box, to be taken out, one by one, by the land officer, who would call aloud the number drawn and summon its owner to step into the room and choose a block.

Watterson, followed by Harlin and Wise, went into the shanty, and Archer turned the crank handle of the box in an ostentatious manner to mix up the numbers and indicate that no manipulation was possible. Then he turned back his sleeve to still further advertise the honesty of the proceedings, and, putting his hand into the box, drew out a number and glanced at it. ' I call on No. 60 to come forward and select,' he said.

A dissolute-looking ruffian stepped out from the crowd, and there was a murmur from the selectors as he was seen to be one of Harlin's dummies.

'There goes the pick of the land back to the squatter,' muttered one.

' Harlin's got his ten pounds' worth there all right,' said another ; and many low-breathed curses followed the man on to the verandah.

'Go in, my good fellow, and select,' said Archer, lighting a fresh cigar and sitting down to wait.

The man on entering the room gave his application to Watterson, who, having noted it as correct, placed the plan before him and told him to point out the block he desired to select. Harlin stepped alongside to direct the man in his choice.

' I'll take this here block,' said the dummy, with a wink ; and Watterson, having made an entry in his book, struck out the block upon the plan.

' I suppose that's very satisfactory to you, Mr Harlin,' he said as the man retired.

'Very,' was the reply. ' It's worth two thousand pounds to me.'

' The Duffy Act isn't such a bad thing for the squatters after all,' meditatively commented Wise.

As soon as the first applicant reappeared on the

verandah the land officer drew another number, which again was that of a dummy, and again from the selectors came angry mutterings. The man selected under Harlin's orders as before, and dummies' numbers followed one another until the seventh call. 'No. 101,' said Archer.

'Here, sir,' answered a cheerful voice, and George Scott stepped forward, radiant, his comrades congratulating him as he went.

'Good luck to you, George!' said Toland, clapping him on the back.

'Just in time for a bit of the flats,' said one.

'Don't let Harlin jockey you,' advised another.

'Spoil his block, old man,' added a third.

Scott stepped into the room tremulous with excitement.

'Show me your form,' said the clerk, coldly, 'and hurry up, as we have no time to lose.'

However, Scott was too pleased with himself to be flustered, and Watterson was now quite an insignificant person in his eyes. 'All right, I reckon,' he said cheerily as he laid the paper on the table.

'You may select on that plan,' said the clerk, while Harlin looked on by no means pleased.

'I'll take this block,' said Scott, indicating an excellent area on the edge of dummy selections.

'All right, you can go,' said Watterson as he marked it off.

'Wait a minute, my man,' interrupted Harlin, stepping forward. 'I want to see you after the ballot is over.'

'What for?' asked Scott, bluntly.

'I thought we might arrange a sale,' answered Harlin, rather taken aback.

'Not much!' said Scott, jauntily. 'And you needn't bother to try.'

Harlin glanced angrily at the retreating figure.

'By G—! I'll make him change his tune before long,' he muttered, but the appearance of five dummies in succession mollified him, and he turned to Wise with a sigh of satisfaction. 'I'm right now,' he said. 'I've got back all the flats except the block of that fellow Scott, and I'll have that in time.'

So it went on, five or six blocks going to the dummies for every one to a man eager to make a home, and forty blocks had gone when No. 120 was called.

In response Toland stepped on to the verandah, but not the Toland of the hopeful morning. Watching fraud destroy his fondest hopes had roused in him an anger that he found difficult to control. He strode with a savage look into the room and flung his paper to the clerk. Watterson pointed to the plan and told him to select.

Harlin was leaning over it.

'On one side!' said Toland gruffly.

Harlin drew back in astonishment. 'You might be more civil, my man!' he exclaimed angrily.

'And you more honest,' retorted Toland, turning his back on Harlin, who muttered something about handing him over to the police.

Toland slowly scrutinised the plan. All the best land was gone. Only the heavily-timbered country remained and it was difficult to make a choice.

'Hurry up,' said the clerk, snappishly.

'The day is young,' replied Toland.

'Is that man going to take all day? What's keeping him?' called Archer from the verandah.

Toland walked to the door with the plan in his hand. 'I'm trying to find,' he called out, 'if those rascals of dummies and the man that bought them have left a decent piece of ground for an honest man to select, but, by God! sir, they've collared the lot.'

Then he turned back into the room, marked off a block, and shoved his way roughly through a group of dummies to join Scott on the outskirts of the crowd.

Meanwhile the ballot proceeded, and fifty blocks had been disposed of, including one secured by Mallock on the main road near his shanty, when No. 200 was drawn.

'Is No. 200 here?' called Archer, as no one spoke.

'Yes,' said a gruff voice, and a burly fellow stepped forward. 'I'm here all right, but I'm not goin' to select. Harlin can keep his scrub. I don't want it.'

A laugh went round the crowd ; Archer called irritably to Watterson and drew another slip. Later on the dummies, acting under instructions from Harlin, who did not think the land worth the Government price, declined to select. Some of the other men, too, refused to have it, but the bulk went to would-be farmers, and the Kumbarra ballot resulted, as so many before it, in the allotment of rich land to the rich man and poor land to the poor.

As soon as it was over Harlin and Wise began taking the signatures of the dummies to the transfers of the various blocks they had secured, and one by one these worthy selectors filed into the bar parlour to assign their land to the squatter, each one receiving a £10 cheque in payment for his dishonesty.

When the last one had been dealt with Harlin turned to Wise. 'We had better get away as soon as we can,' he said. 'There's going to be an unholy orgie here, and I've asked Watterson and Archer to stay the night at the station. The troopers have gone back to Tongalong and Mallock will have the field to himself.'

'I am sure I have no desire to dispute it with him,' answered Wise. 'Let us go at once.'

Archer and Watterson were waiting on the verandah. The buggies were soon brought round and the party left the 'Morning Star,' not before an uproar rising in the bar gave promise of what was to come.

Scott and Toland were already sitting in their camp, with a damper on the fire, when the buggies passed them, and shortly afterwards Bill Briggs, Mallock's stableman, appeared on the scene.

'Good evening, mates,' he said. 'Is one of you named Scott?'

'I'm the man,' replied Scott.

'Well, I've just come down to say as how Mr Archer, the land hofficer, wants to see you at onst. You've forgotten to fix up one of them papers an' he says you've to come straight aways.'

'All right, I'll come at once,' said Scott, alarmed at the very suggestion of there being anything wrong. 'I'll be back in a jiffy, mate.'

'Hurry up, then,' said Toland, as he turned the damper, 'and steer clear of the grog.'

'I'll see he don't go wrong,' said Bill, patronisingly, and the two departed. Bill was most friendly. He congratulated Scott heartily on getting a good block of land, and when they reached the shanty invited him to have a glass on the strength of it. Not liking to appear churlish, Scott agreed, and though the bar was crowded they managed to squeeze into a corner near the wall, and Bill asked his guest what he fancied.

'Dark brandy?' said Mallock, with a wink. 'I've the very thing for you, sir—something real good.'

'Mine's a taste of gin,' said Bill.

Mallock, after a little delay, handed them the bottles and Scott and Bill helped themselves.

'Well, here's luck,' said Bill, emptying his glass at a draught.

'Same to you,' said Scott, following suit.

Bill looked regretfully at the empty tumbler. 'I'm powerful dry to-day,' he said meaningly.

Scott smacked his lips like a connoisseur. He was on fire from his mouth to the bottom of his stomach, and yet he felt a craving for more.

'My shout this time,' he said, after leaning against the wall a second to consider. 'By Gosh, I've a thirst on me too!'

'Same again?' asked Mallock.

Bill and Scott nodded.

'I thought you'd like this stuff,' said Mallock, sympathetically. 'I sized you up as a gent what knew brandy from tobacco juice.'

Bill grinned wickedly, and Scott, who seldom drank spirits, felt flattered. 'Won't you join us, Mr Mallock?' he said.

'Thank you, sir,' said Mallock, 'I'm sorry I can't drink brandy. I 'ave to go in for something softer · myself.'

Number two nobbler went down, and Scott leaned more heavily against the wall.

'I don't know the gentleman's name,' said Mallock to Bill,

'Oh, beg pardon, this is Mr Scott what got that block of land Mr Harlin 'ad 'is 'eart on.'

'What! You're the Mr Scott the land officer was askin' after.' Mallock leaned over the counter and shook Scott warmly by the hand. 'He went away a moment before you came,' he continued, 'but he's left a paper here for you to sign and leave with me.'

'I'll do it now,' said Scott, trying to raise himself, though instinctively he felt it would not be safe to leave the wall.

'Wait; you must have one more glass for luck,' objected Mallock. 'I never drinks with a man without he drinks with me.'

Scott hesitated, but it was too late. He had been hocussed; power and volition had gone. All he knew was that his throat was parched, his brain reeled, his knees shook and his stomach burned.

They raised their glasses and drank together.

'Bill, show Mr Scott round to the parlour,' said Mallock. Scott heard the voice somewhere far away and started to go, leaning heavily on Bill, who dragged him through the crowd. He lurched against a selector also leaving the bar, who looked round with anger that changed to surprise as he recognised the drunken man in Bill's charge. They stumbled somehow along the verandah and at last reached the parlour, which Mallock entered at the same time by another door.

Bill dropped Scott into a chair, and with a wink to Mallock left the room.

'Here's the paper, Mr Scott,' said Mallock, placing it on the table before him and handing him a pen. 'And here's where you have to sign.' Scott looked at him blankly as he took the pen and dropped it.

B

' Here's where the land officer said you have to sign,' repeated Mallock, in an irritated tone.

' Can't read'sh,' mumbled Scott, looking helplessly at the paper.

' What the blazes does that matter ?   Mr Archer said to sign here.   I reckon you'd better hurry up.'

' Give me 'nother drink.'

' No ; not till you've signed it.'

' Sign n'other day—too tired to-day—han' shaky to-day.'

' Oh, it's all right, man !—and Mr Archer said if you didn't sign to-day you'd lose the land.'

' Wa'sh-you-say ? ' cried Scott, fiercely.

' Sign, or you'll likely lose the land.'

' Gim'me th' pensh.'

Mallock gave it him again.   With some difficulty he got it fixed between his fingers and the point was on the paper when he looked up and said with a feeble smile, ' What *ish* my name ? '

' Damn it ! ' said Mallock, whose eyes had grown expectant, ' your name's Scott—George Scott—G. Scott—any blasted Scott ! '

Scott again prepared himself, fortified by this information, and resolved to accomplish the great feat.   He wrote the G slowly but fairly well.   The S was an even greater success, as its curly nature suited his condition, and with infinite care the signature was finished.   He gazed at it for a moment with stupid complacency, and then, stretching his arms out on the table and laying his head upon them, he immediately fell asleep.

' That's all right, old chap,' said Mallock, soothingly. He patted Scott on the head, and picking up the document put it into his pocket with a sinister smile.

'Say, boss,' interrupted Bill, thrusting his head through the doorway, 'you'd better hurry up. Toland's in the bar asking for his mate. A chap told him at the camp he was here drunk. What'll I say?'

'All right, Bill, I'm coming,' answered Mallock, with an appropriate oath. He roughly shook Scott, who raised his head and half opened his eyes, blurred with drunkenness, which overcame him again immediately. His head fell back on the table, and Mallock, lifting him from his chair, laid him at full length upon the floor before joining Bill on the verandah.

As they reached the bar Toland came out with a savage look on his face. 'Look here, you,' he said roughly, 'can you tell me where my mate Scott is?'

'I can that,' answered Mallock, virtuously indignant. 'The fool came down here, signed a paper for Mr Archer, and then went on the drunk—drank a bottle of brandy right off, didn't 'e, Bill?'

'He did,' replied Bill, shaking his head. 'I never seen the likes of it.'

'He's sleepin' it off in the parlour,' added Mallock; 'and if I was you I'd just let him be till he comes round a bit.'

By way of reply Toland strode past them into the parlour. The ghastly look on his mate's face, as he lay with it upturned upon the floor, shocked him, and but for the stertorous breathing he might have supposed him dead. He knelt down, spoke to him and tried to rouse him without effect. Then he lifted him on to his shoulders, and, regaining his feet with an effort, strode out of the shanty along the road to their camp. Mallock and Bill stood on the verandah watching him.

'That chap's got some muscle all right,' said Mallock.

'I reckon his mate'll lose some of his liquor if 'e don't keep his 'ead up,' grinned Bill. 'But I say, boss, I was goin' to tell you I seen those girls take a couple of cheques in the bar, an' it might be as well if you got in and looked after things. They're gettin' a bit sudden, I tell you.'

Mallock was immediately roused to a sense of duty, and hurrying into the bar possessed himself of the cheques. It was a red-letter day in his career. He had laid himself out to make a big haul, and when Harlin instructed him to procure dummies he took care to get men who might be trusted not to carry their cheques away from the shanty ; and considering the presence of lovely woman essential to human happiness, he engaged two houris from a drinking den in Tongalong to do the honours of his establishment on this great occasion. Consequently, now that the time had come, everything went with a verve entirely to his satisfaction. The bar that had at first been merely a babel gradually became, as night wore on, a scene of horrible debauchery, over which Mallock worthily presided, growing more and more elated as cheque after cheque found its way into his pocket. Soon, however, he noticed that some of the men still kept their heads and their cheques, and in order to stir their sluggish veins he had the parlour cleared of its scanty furniture and told Bill to start a dance to the music of his fiddle. The women left the bar to attend the revel, which gained immediate popularity notwithstanding that the atmosphere was stifling—unwashed humanity, bad spirits and flaring tallow dips each contributing a quota.

Most of the men danced together. The two women, who only favoured the more sober of the crew, danced with them till their brains whirled, when they led them to the bar, drank with them, ogled and kissed them, and finally filched away their money. Soon all were drunk and the foul air was full of fouler ravings, and when the fighting over the women began the shanty became a perfect pandemonium.

By midnight Mallock had about fifty ten-pound cheques in his possession, but pleasure at the success of his venture was tinctured with alarm, for matters were getting far beyond his control. As time wore on and the mad devilry of the men increased, the sense of personal danger completely took possession of him. Consequently, when the coach stopped after midnight for a change of horses, he called the driver aside. 'Look here, Alick,' he said, 'I want you to take word to the police-station at Tongalong as soon as you get in. Tell them I want the troopers sent out as I have a lot of fellows here smashing up the place and putting me in fear of my life.'

'All right; it looks as if you had a rough time ahead,' replied the driver, consolingly, as he turned away. Passing the bar he caught sight of a young fellow he knew and warned him that Mallock was sending for the police. As the coach rumbled off the meaning of the driver's words appealed to the man, and after some unsuccessful attempts he clambered on to the counter. 'I say, mates,' he shouted from this point of vantage, 'Mallock has sent for the traps!'

There was a volley of more or less coherent oaths, and at this inauspicious moment Mallock appeared behind the bar.

Alick's confidant turned on him savagely. 'Why have you sent for the traps, you hound?' he cried.

Mallock winced. 'Who said I had?' he replied evasively.

'You have, you cur! Alick told me.'

'You'd better be civil,' retorted Mallock, fiercely, 'or I'll have you marched off pretty quick when they do come.'

'Will you—you damned thief! Then I'll break your neck first and get our cheques back.'

He leapt from the bar counter, but Mallock drew back, and snatching up an empty bottle struck his assailant a blow on the head that stretched him on the floor.

Immediately a dozen men scrambled upon the counter, but before they were over it Mallock rushed out through a door opening into the yard behind, pursued by a frenzied mob, who poured out of the dancing-saloon to join the chase. Dodging his pursuers round the stable he was making for the bush when he saw a saddled horse hitched by his bridle to the road fence. His pursuers, yelling with drunken fury, were close upon him when he grabbed the reins. There was no time to deal with buckles. He snapped the reins with a wrench from the rail, and springing into the saddle galloped away from the eager hands outstretched to seize him. For some hundred yards he rode at breakneck speed, after which his panic subsided and he pulled up to consider the position. Nothing could be gained by going back, so he determined to reach Tongalong as soon as possible, to make his money safe and return with the police. One by one Mallock's pursuers straggled in, baffled and cursing, but his absence was not for long a check upon their merriment. More willing hands than his behind the bar distributed the liquor gratis, and the scene soon became indescribable, while nothing could be heard but foul oaths and blasphemy, the screaming of women and drunken shouting and laughter of men.

So the revels continued for a time; and then, in response to a brilliant idea engendered in some half-maddened brain, a horrible procession left the shanty. The more sober pulled out the wholly stupefied, after which all gathered in the road waiting for something to happen. Presently a man ran out laughing and hurrahing, and a thin curl of smoke followed him through the door. This was greeted with drunken cheers, renewed a few seconds later when a dense cloud streaked with red rolled forth on to the verandah, and soon there was a roar as the spirits ignited and the fire shot up through the bark, quickly wrapping the whole building in flames. In a few minutes the rafters burned through and the roof fell in, sending fountains of sparks into the sky, and a quarter of an hour sufficed to reduce the shanty to ashes.

When the fun was over and only a smoking mass remained, the company began to disperse, thoroughly satisfied with their night's entertainment. Some staggered off to where they imagined their camps to be, while others, more wisely, lay down on the ground to sleep off the effects of their intoxication. The two women found a camping-place for themselves on the hay in the stable.

Next morning, when daylight and returning consciousness enabled the men to see the result of their evening's enjoyment, it was unanimously resolved to leave as soon as possible. Horses were hurriedly saddled, swags strapped on, and when Mallock and the troopers arrived at ten o'clock, Bill and the two women alone remained to tell the tale. Mallock at first was furious and swore to have the rascals who had destroyed his property arrested, but on second thoughts he decided to do nothing in the matter, for he remembered that £500 in hand was worth many shanties in the bush, and that it was just as well for him that the rightful owners of the cheques should be fleeing from the law. So, having instructed the women to come on by coach, he rode away to prepare for a fresh start in life.

CHAPTER III

IT was nearly dark when the squatter's party left the shanty *en route* for Kumbarra homestead.

Wise was in Harlin's single-seated buggy behind a smart pair of horses, while Archer, driving a hired vehicle from Tongalong stables, hung close on his wheels, not relishing such a pace for night travelling on a bush road with which he was not acquainted.

The men, tired after their day's work, puffed at pipes or cigars in comparative silence, and the ten miles to the station were soon covered. Harlin stood waiting at the outer gate for his guests to come up.

'Thanks! That's very kind of you,' said Archer as he passed into a five-hundred-acre paddock, beyond which the house lay by the river. 'I must congratulate you on entering for the first time in your life on to your own estate.'

'Thank you,' laughed Harlin; 'but I've been driving over it for miles, chuckling to myself all the time at the way we've done the blasted cockies. Better let me take the lead again here. The track's a bit puzzling on these gum flats.'

He got into his buggy, and soon, beyond another gate, they passed the great woolshed, near the head of a reedy lagoon, giving over their horses a few minutes later to the men at the stables.

Mrs Harlin met them on the verandah of the

rambling, commodious house, and glanced with a shade of surprise at Archer and Watterson, whom she had not seen before.

'Well, Tom, did things go satisfactorily?' she asked.

'Splendidly, my dear. The landscape for miles around won't be spoilt by cockies' huts. Let me introduce Mr Archer, the land officer, and Mr. Watterson—also in the Department. They want rooms, of course. Mr Wise stays with us too, to-night—and we all want our dinner.'

The men bowed, and Archer expressed the hope that their unceremonious arrival would cause no inconvenience, wondering all the time how such a rough diamond as Harlin had become possessed of the beautiful girl, seeming, in black evening gown, almost taller than her husband.

Their arrival gave no trouble of any kind, she said. Their rooms would be ready in a minute or two, and dinner in half an hour.

When the other men had gone to dress Harlin remained in the dining-room for another drink, and spent a few minutes in getting out wine from the cellar; consequently, when the gong sounded, he was in his dressing-room, hurriedly slipping on a black coat. It was too much of a bore to struggle into dress clothes in his own house.

Mrs Harlin's eyebrows contracted slightly. She would have liked to see her husband a little less red in the face and as well groomed as the other men, but it was not worth troubling about—not in any case a thing that one could mention—and she showed her guests their places at the table.

Archer sat on her right, with a slight, fair girl of

eighteen as his neighbour on the other side. From Mrs Harlin he had only learnt when they were introduced that her name was Macfarlane.

She seemed somewhat shy and wore a walking dress, neatly made, but of some cheap material. From these data Archer, who noticed such things and always liked to know who people were in order to decide if they were anybody, had decided Miss Macfarlane's case in the negative, putting her down as a governess until Harlin spoke to her. She had arrived from Tongalong that morning with her father, she said, and he would call for her to-morrow on his way home.

Mr Macfarlane, Harlin explained, as though apologising for the girl's presence, was a Presbyterian clergyman of the district, for whom the station was a convenient halting-place on his rounds; and, determined to take his cue from the squatter's tone, Archer was presently somewhat staggered on noticing that Miss Macfarlane addressed Mrs Harlin by her Christian name.

Incidents of the ballot formed the chief subject of conversation, and the women, for some time taking little part in it, listened with interest.

When the dessert came in, the land officer, in a tone suggesting that the freehold was a gift conferred by him, congratulated Harlin again upon becoming the owner of such a magnificent property.

'And you too, Mrs Harlin,' he said, raising a glass of wine to his lips—'will you allow me to felicitate you both and to drink success to the future of Kumbarra Station—one of the finest trophies of the Duffy Land Act?'

Mrs Harlin bowed rather coldly.

'You don't look altogether pleased, Mrs Harlin,'

said Wise, glancing across the table. 'You don't entirely share Mr Archer's enthusiasm for the legislation he takes such an able part in administering.'

'I hardly know,' she said with a thoughtful frown. 'Of course I am glad the place is ours—it has always seemed that it should be. But I don't feel particularly proud of the way we have obtained it.'

'What nonsense, my dear! Everyone has done the same thing,' said Harlin, contemptuously.

'Done what?' asked Miss Macfarlane, interest in the subject triumphing over her shyness. 'I'm afraid I'm very stupid, but I haven't quite understood what you were talking about.'

Mrs Harlin laughed. 'Neither have I, Ruth,' she said, 'beyond that there has been some smart piece of trickery—part of a general scheme for saving the country which it behoves us all to be very proud of and thankful for. Your confession has emboldened me to admit it, and perhaps Mr Archer will explain.'

Archer shrugged his shoulders. 'Trickery is a nasty word,' he said; 'your husband has only made good use of a bad law.'

'Out of which you draw a handsome salary by assisting to subvert it,' put in Wise, pleasantly.

Harlin laughed. Watterson permitted himself a smile, and Archer flushed slightly.

'That remark is scarcely in good taste, or fair, Wise,' he said. You twit me with subverting the law, which is not strictly true, while you and your profession have used all your ingenuity in doing so.'

'Granted, my dear fellow! But that's what we are paid for; and you are paid for precisely the reverse.'

Archer showed decided symptoms of annoyance.

Mrs Harlin interposed. 'You are still both talking

in riddles,' she said, smiling. 'I wish you would really explain the facts for Miss Macfarlane and me, and let us assess the praise or blame where it is due.'

'Very well, Mrs Harlin,' said Wise, 'if your husband doesn't object to my taking a brief on the other side.'

'I have the land, you guarantee I have the law, so I don't care what you say about the ethics,' laughed Harlin. 'But it's like the cheek of you lawyers to turn upon the squatters, who have put thousands into your pockets.'

'I wonder what fraction of one per cent it would amount to on the thousands we have put into yours?' queried Wise, blandly. 'However, we will let that pass. You want to know what the Duffy Act was designed for, Mrs Harlin, and what it is being used for?' he continued, turning to her with some animation warming his cold, intellectual face.

Mrs Harlin nodded.

'It was meant to parcel out about four million acres of the most fertile lands of this colony, leased heretofore by the squatters, among agriculturists, who would convert them into farms and homes. And it is being used to put those millions of acres of land securely into the absolute ownership of the squatters for all time.'

'And a jolly good thing too!' commented Harlin, pouring himself out another glass of port.

'Don't interrupt, Tom. Let us hear how it is done.'

'Very simply. A squatter's run is thrown open for selection in blocks of various sizes. Applicants for land register their names. A ballot is held, whereat the first person chosen by lot has first pick of the blocks, and so on in order. The squatter who wishes

to buy his land, or any part of it, at the price of a
pound an acre, gets a number of men to apply,
nominally on their own behalf, but really on his, as
his agents—slang term "dummies." He procures a
sufficient number of these estimable people to reasonably ensure that they shall swamp the genuine
applicants, and that the greater number of blocks, by
the laws of chance—not to mention an occasional
manipulation of the ballot box—shall go to them—
that is, to their employer, the squatter.'

'That seems clear enough,' said Mrs Harlin. 'And
what do the dummies get out of it?'

'That will be clear enough too, my dear,' said
Harlin, with a rueful smile, 'if you consult my bank-
book in a day or two.'

'Mr Harlin has been unfortunate,' said Wise. 'The
dummies about here are low people and a mercenary
tribe; but in many cases—notably where a large
station was recently thrown open for selection near
Sale—the good people so dearly loved a lord that
they tumbled over each other in their anxiety to
dummy, gratis and gratefully, for the nearest approach
to it—a big landlord near the town.'

'That simply means,' said Archer, who had listened
with supercilious resignation, 'when it is shorn of
your cheap sarcasm, that decent people were willing
to give a decent man a hand against the depredations
of a lot of riff-raff upon his estate.'

'I am flattered by your detection of the sarcasm,'
replied Wise. 'I know it is a shibboleth—of our class,
shall I say?—that the large landowner is necessarily
a decent man, and the man with aspirations to become a small landowner, *ipso facto*, a scoundrel—but
I do not subscribe to it.'

'You have hidden your philanthropic light under a bushel—of fees, I presume,' sneered Archer.

'I lay claim to no light but that of common sense. But does it never occur to you that it may be a mistake for you, in a semi-judicial position, to cynically strip the liberal disguise from the Act that employs you on behalf of the people, by showing yourself so ardently a squatters' champion?'

Reddening with anger under Wise's persistent attacks, Archer snorted indignantly, unable to become effectively articulate in the presence of ladies. Harlin enjoyed the situation, too pleased with the day's success to find much personal sting in the lawyer's words. Besides, he liked anything in the nature of a fight; and a suspicion that Archer was inclined to patronise made it seem good that he should be taken down a peg or two in a duel with Wise.

'These lawyers are too smart for us stupid fellows, Archer,' he said, with a wink at the other men. 'Help yourself and pass the bottle—while you think of something to say.'

'Won't you cease lashing us poor squatters and our allies and tell us what we have really done?' interposed Mrs Harlin, smiling.

'Have I not told you?—reaped salvation from a law which was meant for your destruction.'

'And do you blame us?'

Wise shrugged his shoulders.

'I am not a moralist. But you must admit that there is humour in the position. And, as a philosopher, I find it amusing that the most wealthy and honourable men in the country should subscribe a huge fund to bribe the less wealthy and honourable men of the Legislature—for the honourable men's advantage.'

'I think we've had enough of this, Wise,' said Harlin, with a not altogether pleased laugh, and Archer muttered something about execrable taste.

'But can that be true? What do you mean?' asked Miss Macfarlane, with wide-open, troubled eyes.

Wise met her glance with a slight smile. 'I must ask Mrs Harlin's permission before I can explain.'

'Go on,' she said somewhat coldly.

'I mean simply this—that an association, called "The Victorian Association," was formed by the squatters. Its object was to prevent the breaking up of large estates. Huge sums of money passed through its hands, and it is believed that thousands were paid to obtain the insertion in the Duffy Act of one little word "assigns." It's a lawyer's word, meaning, perhaps, not much to you, but in its place in the Act it means that dummying is legal, that the genuine selector is burdened with obligations to fence and clear his land from which the squatter to whom the dummy has assigned is free—means, in fact, the wreck of the Duffy Act as a measure for settling people instead of sheep upon the land. And, as I say, the most honourable Pharisees of the country paid thousands for that little word, to prevent the riff-raff, of whom Mr Archer was speaking, from obtaining the selections which his employers pay him for pretending to sell them.'

'Did you subscribe to this association, Tom?' asked Mrs Harlin, after a pause.

'Only a hundred, my dear.'

'I am sure you would not have Mr Harlin reap its

advantages without paying something towards its expenses,' said Wise, softly. 'May I trouble you to pass me the almonds, Watterson?'

Mrs Harlin surveyed Wise with a displeased smile.

'We have to thank you for a most eloquent explanation. But do you know, I am almost inclined to endorse Mr Archer's opinion that it was not in the best possible taste.'

'Mr Archer is as fortunate as I am the reverse.'

There was an awkward pause, and Harlin, finding his signals ignored, suggested irritably that perhaps the ladies would like to go to the drawing-room.'

'Presently,' said Mrs Harlin.

Her eyebrows were knitted in unwelcome thought. 'Mr Wise,' she exclaimed, turning to him again, 'you have sneered to your satisfaction at the squatters as Pharisees and dispensers of bribes, at the people who take them, and at Mr Archer who dares to think that the land should remain with the better classes. Have you taken no part in assisting the squatters?'

'If he says he hasn't he shall return my fee,' grumbled Harlin.

Wise received the interjection with a smile and addressed himself to his hostess.

'You would not have me sneer at myself, Mrs Harlin, when there are so many people ready to save me the trouble. As to the part I have taken, it has been a lawyer's part only. I have interpreted the Act as the judges say it should be interpreted, and done such things as follow therefrom. So far I have helped the squatters, for only the dry bones of the Act are liberal; and the breath of life has been breathed into it by the Victorian Association. But I have had nothing to do with the making of a

C

sham law, or with a sham administration of it. One
thing I should like to add,' he said, after taking
breath, 'is that I regret if I have over-stepped the
bounds of good taste in my criticism. Of course, my
words had no personal application, and I beg your
forgiveness for speaking so frankly.'

Mrs Harlin smiled.

'The words have a personal application, for which
the facts are to blame. It is not palatable to be told
that one's acres are the trophy of bribery and fraud,'
she said bitterly. 'But I think your frankness must
be forgiven since I practically demanded it. Ruth,
shall we go to the drawing-room?'

'Thank you,' said Wise, bowing and holding the
door open as she swept gracefully from the room with
Miss Macfarlane. 'I shall be more careful in future.',

'You'd better,' laughed Harlin with annoyance when
Wise had closed the door. 'What made you such an
infernal firebrand? It's all very well among men, but
you ought to keep your mouth shut about bribery and
nonsense of that kind before ladies. It worries them,
you know—and the worst of it is my wife thinks.'

'Does she?' said Wise. 'I am sorry; and I vote
we drop the subject now, at anyrate.'

He put his pipe into his mouth to hide a sarcastic
smile that would come unbidden, and remained almost
as silent as Watterson, contributing to the conversation only smoke clouds and a word here and there.

His ideals were not high. He was quite willing, as
a matter of business, to assist the squatters, but the
smug complacency of the Archers who toadied them
was annoying to him. Therefore he felt the rebuff
from Mrs Harlin cheaply purchased by the seizure of
his opportunity to tell unpleasant truths. Mrs Harlin

thought! He had guessed she did, and that the other girl was also inclined to that unfeminine habit, or he would not have wasted breath upon his sarcasms. Wise was scarcely aware, however, how deeply Mrs Harlin took his words to heart.

'It's galling to one's pride, isn't it?' she asked, sitting by the drawing-room window.

'What?' asked Ruth Macfarlane.

'To think that we are only thieves of all these miles of country.'

Mrs Harlin knelt on the bow window-seat, and leaning her elbows on the sill gazed over the moonlit flats. 'That we have paid all the scum of the district to rob poor men of their chance of a living—and, I think worst of all, that we have laid ourselves open to be patronised by such men as Mr Archer and sneered at by such as Mr Wise.'

She spoke with a bitterness Ruth had never heard before, and leaving some work on her chair beneath the lamp she went over to the window.

'It is foolish to speak in that way, Margaret,' she said gently. 'You have done nothing to be ashamed of. And men don't look at these things as women do.'

'My husband and his friends don't—certainly,' she laughed. 'I wonder how those men—what were their names?—that we were making fun of to-night look upon us and our schemes.'

'Scott and Toland,' said Ruth, pensively.

She remembered the names, for her sympathies had been secretly with them when, at the dinner-table, Archer was making a good story of their boorish insolence.

'Yes; I can picture how they feel. One of them told my husband it was a pity he was not more

honest, didn't he? I wonder if it is. If we were
more honest I don't quite see what we'd do.'

'Don't be morbid,' laughed Ruth, placing her hand
on Mrs Harlin's shoulder. 'Come and give me some
coffee before it gets cold.'

Mrs Harlin left the window and Ruth took up her
work again. 'It is puzzling,' she said presently.
'My sympathies are with the selectors. My father
and I really belong more to their class, and I see
most of poor people; and yet I believe they are no
better than the rich and would do just what the
squatters have done if they had the chance.'

'I suppose so,' said Mrs Harlin, wearily. 'Perhaps
you will marry a selector some day and be able to
tell me if they are really so wicked as my husband
thinks. Will you have cream in your coffee?'

'Yes, please. I am not thinking of marrying anyone at present,' said Ruth, laughing. 'But if a
selector should be my fate I promise to tell you
exactly how wicked he is. However, I should like
someone with more money. I am tired of being poor.'

'Never mind the money; marry someone with
brains and strength of will and character, or—ah,
here they come from the dining-room.'

The seriousness faded from Mrs Harlin's face and
the note of earnestness disappeared from her tone as
she greeted the men with some pleasant words of
welcome; but a frown came for a second and
vanished again when Harlin entered behind the
others, with face flushed and a step studiously steady.
Then she took a seat beside him on the sofa.

'Poor old fellow, you are tired,' she whispered.
'You must not sit up late. Don't be cross with me for
my excursion into politics. I won't make any more.'

CHAPTER IV

THE collie raised his head from the hearth, to the discomfort of a yellow cat pillowed against him, and growled in a half interrogative, half assertive manner. 'Lie down, Toss, you old fool! It's nothing but a possum on the roof,' muttered Toland, who sat before the kitchen fire, with a candle on the table behind him and a well-thumbed volume of Scott's poems on his knee. He had left his clearing in the new cultivation patch only when it grew too dark to distinguish pick from shovel; and now, while he waited for the potatoes to boil, he snatched a few minutes with his favourite among the few authors that he knew.

Toss sank his head on his paws again and wagged his tail dutifully when his master spoke, but the possum theory evidently failed to satisfy, for he presently rose leisurely, sniffed at the door, and then barked his conviction that strangers were approaching. Wondering who it might be, Toland opened the door and followed Toss, who scampered out, barking furiously, and soon he heard the sound of voices, one of them, he fancied, a woman's. Uncertainty changed into astonishment when two riders emerged from the narrow track through the wattles. One was Mr Macfarlane, the Presbyterian minister whom he had met at the township, and whom, even in the dim light, he recognised; the other, a woman with a girlish and graceful figure, whom he had never set eyes on before. Macfarlane's greeting soon explained matters.

'Well, Mr Toland, you see I've kept my promise to descend upon you,' he said, 'and I have to ask you to be better than yours—which you'll remember was to give a night's lodging to the old man—for I've—for reasons which I will explain—brought my daughter with me. Ruth, my dear, let me make you acquainted with Mr Toland.'

With embarrassed pleasure Toland acknowledged the introduction and welcomed father and daughter to his home. At his suggestion they went to the kitchen fire while he let their horses go in the little paddock, and it was not till his return that he had a chance of studying his lady visitor. Then, when she looked up from the book he had left open, he saw that her large eyes were soft and blue, her complexion fair, and the foot peeping out from beneath a dark riding skirt seemed to him ridiculously small.

Macfarlane half turned on his chair, still holding his hands to the blaze, and explained to Toland the cause of his late arrival. He and his daughter, he said, had intended to put up at Mallock's new shanty, but the presence of some drunken bullock-drivers made it an undesirable stopping-place, and he had therefore taken the liberty of bringing his daughter on with him to seek Toland's hospitality. Toland expressed his pleasure at their arrival, only, he said, with a rueful glance at the shapeless piece of much-hacked corned beef on the table, he regretted that he had to offer such rough faring and lodging to a lady.

Ruth laughed pleasantly, declaring herself entirely

comfortable. She accepted a jug of hot water which Toland filled from the kettle on a hook above the fire, and went to the empty room which he told her was soon to be his sister's.

When she returned to the kitchen, with some appreciative remark about the house on her lips, Toland had respread the whole table with a coarse cloth, made the tea, and was dishing the potatoes, while Mr Macfarlane looked on.

'What a shame!' she exclaimed. 'You should have let me help you lay the table, Mr Toland.'

'If you are as hungry as I am you'll help him to clear it, my dear,' said the minister, laughing. 'The ride from Kumbarra has given me quite an appetite.'

The friendly manner of his visitors, and the justice they did to his simple fare, soon put Toland at his ease, and he felt a pleased pride in entertaining guests for the first time beneath his own roof. Mr Macfarlane was communicative, and from him Toland learnt much of the trials and hardships of a bush minister's life, spent in travelling large tracts of wild, sparsely-populated country — meeting sometimes with but surly welcome; sometimes forced to sleep under the sky with no other shelter than a gum tree. Ruth Macfarlane often accompanied her father, who had lost his wife some years before, and Toland conceived a wondering admiration for the delicate-looking girl who made light of journeys and hardships, from which, in less robust, self-reliant communities, many a man might shrink. With her mother's delicacy of feature, and a girlish education which had been her mother's chief care and pleasure in life, Ruth Macfarlane possessed her father's philosophical disposition, cheerfully disposed to make the best of everything; and she had early persuaded the minister to let her accompany him in his wanderings whenever it was possible.

Much of this Toland learnt when the frugal meal was over, and Macfarlane, swaying dangerously on his chair, with the Scotch accent broadening and the pulpit emphasis more marked, launched out upon the history of his church in Victoria bound up so closely with his own. Toland was interested, and by skilful comment and question drew Mr Macfarlane on, while Ruth, scarcely hearing the familiar facts and phrases, watched her host, interested in the lines of character in his face. This was the man Mr Archer had made such fun of at Kumbarra, but she fancied that he would scarcely care to indulge his humour in Toland's presence. A powerful, obstinate chin, she thought, if his eyes and mouth told the truth, must be hidden by the brown beard. There was something calling for sympathy in the mixture of eagerness and melancholy in his expression, and she noted with undefined satisfaction that his hands, though brown and scarred, were clean, as was also the striped flannel shirt showing beneath the unbuttoned coat of home-spun, with its low-cut collar, which emphasised the strength of a neck set well into a chest both deep and broad. To physical view and mental conjecture Ruth found him satisfying, and she pursued her own thoughts, heedless of what her father was saying, till Toland slowly turned his head, and as his scrutinising eyes met hers she realised that she had taken advantage of her host's apparent absorption to stare at him inexcusably. Macfarlane had waxed warm : ' —and though I say it who shouldn't, my dear little girl here has been the best, the bravest—'

'Please stop, father! Consider my feelings, if not Mr Toland's,' she cried, blushing and laughing. 'I don't know how long you have been talking about yourself and me.'

The minister stopped suddenly, looked taken aback, then laughed, and pulled out his watch.

'I'm afraid you are right, my dear,' he said. 'It has been a twenty minutes' discourse at the very least; and I ask our friend's pardon for inflicting such a thing unprofessionally upon him.'

'I've not been so interested before,' replied Toland, convincingly. 'England can give us no such life as you have told me of, that wants pluck and endurance and gives freedom—and I'm glad I've come here to share it. I have my own land that not a lifetime of work could win for me in the old country. Here I can use my brain and muscle for myself, and need call no man master—as good as any man—the equal of any man that I deserve to be!' Toland's voice had grown louder, his eyes flashed and he brought his fist heavily down upon the table, making the crockery dance, and he all at once became aware of the eyes of father and daughter turned upon him. Hers were suggestive of mingled interest and amusement that brought a faint flush to his cheek.

'I beg your pardon,' he said with an apologetic laugh. 'I must have thought I was talking to the village folk at home again. I get a bit silly when my thoughts run on the starvation and slavery I've seen and the freedom and plenty there might be. Won't you take a seat by the fire? I'll see to the rooms if you'll excuse me.'

He left the kitchen and his guests drew their chairs to the welcome blaze beneath the great rough chimney fashioned of slabs lined with stone, bedded in pipe-clay from the creek. Macfarlane glanced after Toland's retreating figure and shook his head.

' He's a thoughtful man, Ruth, a remarkable young man, conseederably above folks in his own walk of life in ideas and intelligence. But human nature's much the same, old world or new, and I fear that Mr Toland is destined to many a disillusion.' The minister sighed placidly for unregenerate mankind. ' You should not have laughed at him, Ruth. It was not kind, my dear.'

' It was only surprise, father. I wasn't expecting him to break out from his quiet seriousness like that. He is the man that told Mr Harlin—'

Toland's return checked Ruth in the middle of her sentence.

' I'll be lighting my pipe, Mr Toland, just to assure you that my daughter won't object if you do like-wise,' said Macfarlane, producing a well-seasoned briar from the tail pocket of his long black coat.

Ruth got up and went to the table, which Toland was regarding doubtfully. ' Smoke, of course,' she said. ' And please let me help you with the washing up. I can see that's what you are thinking about.'

With some scruples Toland consented, and smiled at Ruth's chatter as she wiped dry the tea things he handed from the tin of hot water between them, while Macfarlane, from the chimney corner, threw in an occasional remark. Then Toland was persuaded to smoke too, and when the little party was comfort-ably settled round the fire the minister questioned him upon his history and plans.

Silent and reserved in the society that was his as a rule, Toland was ready enough to speak of himself and his aspirations when he felt assured of intelligent sympathy, and he talked freely of his life in England. Ever since he was a boy he had hoarded every penny he earned with the view steadily before him of acquiring a home in some new country when he should have capital to make a start and his old father, whom he was loath to leave, should have need of him no more. His original idea had been to go to the States, but when his father died, a little more than a year ago, the disturbances in America had settled his determination towards Australia. His own savings and the sale of stock and implements on the farm, which his people had held for generations, gave him a little more than £500, and with this he had proceeded to realise his dream. It was now in part accomplished, and his first act, he told them, on entering into possession of his virgin acres, was to write to his sister Bess, his only relative, to come over with all speed she could and join him in the new home.

Ruth was interested in the sister of whom Toland spoke with much affection.

'I'm afraid I'm a poor hand at a woman's portrait,' he laughed, 'but she's a good lass, fair to see and brave to do. She can brew and bake, sing like a bird—and for the rest she's a fine lump of a girl, with colour in her cheeks and bonny blue eyes—much like your own, Miss Macfarlane.'

Ruth coloured a little and laughed, and Mr Macfarlane commented judicially. 'It's a very pleasing picture you have drawn, and I hope we'll be soon welcoming your sister among us. And may I ask what you're now doing on your farm, Mr Toland?'

'Clearing, sir, on a twenty-acre patch that I hope to begin ploughing by September.'

'And what will you put in it then?'

'Maize. I know nothing of it, but they tell me it's the thing for a first crop hereabouts.'

'Ay! you'll be doing right there,' nodded Macfarlane, approvingly. 'You should raise fine corn on those flats; and if you'll take my advice you'll plant some pumpkins in the rows.'

From farming the talk drifted to books, and Macfarlane found that Toland was, like himself, a keen student of Scott, while neither of them having quite the impartiality of their author, an argument provoked by Marmion and Flodden Field grew in warmth till Ruth, with the average woman's inclination to identify keen debate with quarrel, stepped in to part the border champions. She was tired after the ride, she said, and declared that her father, too, should go to bed, if not for his own sake to let Mr Toland get a good rest for his hard work next day. The old man, who was quite ready for another pipe and further argument, reluctantly consented. He had said grace over the meal uninvited, but Toland, determined not to be again found wanting, made a diffident suggestion about prayers, in response to which Macfarlane read a few verses from a pocket Bible and offered a commendably short extempore prayer, asking a special blessing on all subduers of the wilderness and tillers of the soil. Then Toland lighted his guests to their rooms. Macfarlane occupied his, and Ruth that which was to be his sister's, while he made a shakedown for himself before the kitchen fire, where he soon fell asleep, not hearing the rain which began after midnight and was descending in torrents when the dawn broke dull and late.

A glance showed him that work was out of the

question for a time—so also, he reflected with satisfaction, was the departure of his guests. He had slept late. The clock on the mantelpiece struck seven before he had dressed and stowed away his blankets, while the fire was only just lighted and the kettle filled from the creek, when there was a tap at the door and Ruth entered, to find him slicing rashers from a side of bacon.

'I hope I'm not in the way,' she said. 'Isn't it wet and cold?' She stood in the fireplace holding her hands to the blaze, and looked round at him, smiling.

'Yes; I doubt you won't be able to go on to-day—which I'm only too glad of—if you're not sorry,' he added shyly.

'Oh, I should be quite content to rest a little, but my father is in a hurry to reach Black Dog Creek. I wonder he hasn't been up for hours studying the weather.'

She refused the chair which Toland brought to the fire. 'No, I'm not going to sit down,' she said. 'You go on with your work and show me where the flour is. I'll make you some scones if you will let me.'

Toland's first impulse was to object, but she insisted, laughingly accusing him of grudging the flour and soda, and in the end he felt it very pleasant to see her, with her sleeves rolled up, mixing the dough while they talked. When the scones were in the camp-oven he called Mr Macfarlane and got out a tin of jam and some potted butter from his store to do honour to the occasion.

There was a break in the clouds after breakfast. Patches of blue sky showed in the north, and white mists gathered in fleecy masses against the hills. Between the showers the minister took a walk with Toland to see that the horses were all right, and to inspect the clearing, where he was taking out the smaller trees, leaving in each acre some twenty ringbarked monsters between which the plough was to find its way. Then they returned and Toland showed his visitors the house.

It was a four-roomed cottage with a detached kitchen, built by Toland himself with the help of his handy man, Mick M'Larty, beside a rapid pebbly creek, with a gentle slope rising beyond a dip in the ground on the one bank, and on the other a small, rich flat flanked by a range of hills. The cottage was innocent as yet of floors other than beaten earth. Boards would not be available till a promised saw-mill set up in the vicinity. The little window-sashes had been carted ready-made from Melbourne. Sheets of bark served for doors, and the bark walls were lined only with hessian; but the rooms were large, with a potentiality of comfort when papered and furnished.

Ruth complimented Toland on his work, and offered several hints; apologised for interfering with what would be his sister's domain, then excused herself again by the fact that Miss Toland would be ignorant of Melbourne shops and prices, and Toland, quite agreeing, wrote down addresses of cheap places and treasured many other of her suggestions in his memory. The minister, too, was interested in Toland's schemes, but kept his eye constantly on the weather, and as it cleared towards mid-day Toland regretfully brought in the horses. He begged his guests to come again soon when his sister would be with him, and they assured him that they would do so. Then they set out on their rough track, and Toland, after watching them disappear among the trees, went back, with a new sense of loneliness, to his interrupted work,

CHAPTER V

BESS TOLAND sat knitting on the verandah waiting for her brother's return as the dusk of Christmas Eve drew on, and her busy fingers moved with automatic skill, only stopping when she paused to listen for the sound of approaching hoofs. Her brother had ridden to the post-office at Mallock's shanty for the weekly mail, which seldom brought anything but the Melbourne paper—at long intervals a letter from the old country—and Bess was wondering if any of the friends left behind would time their Christmas greetings to reach her at the season which had no reality in this land of topsy-turvydom. There were no home letters, however—only a line from Scott saying that he would take a holiday and spend his Christmas with them, so Toland informed his sister as he cantered up to the garden gate, and flinging the paper on to the verandah, rode away to take the saddle off his horse. That Scott was coming pleased Bess, for besides being a link with the old country, he was cheery and pleasant and seemed to find her society agreeable. The paper she seldom took the trouble to look at, and without undoing the wrapper she sat a little longer on the verandah before going inside to make the tea.

A few minutes later, when they were seated at their meal in the skillion room, she discovered that her brother's good spirits were not solely owing to Scott's promised visit.

'We'll have quite a gay week, Bess,' he said, stirring his tea. 'I have a bit of a note from Mr Macfarlane to say he and his daughter will likely be here a day or two after Christmas.'

Bess glanced keenly at her brother, suspecting his tone of studied unconcern. 'That is fine now,' she said. 'Those will be the old gentleman and the pretty lass that visited you before I came out?'

'The very same—and I was thinking, Bess, if you were to ask Miss Macfarlane to spend a week here it would be a bit of company for you—not to say,' he added with a smile, 'but what it would be a pleasure to me too.'

'And it's small difference it would make if you didn't say it,' she replied drily. 'I'm very willing for my own sake and yours. But what will the minister do without her?'

'He has to go on yonder to Black Dog Creek,' said Toland, nodding vaguely towards the hills at the head of the valley; 'but in a fortnight's time he will be along through here again. Don't you think you might persuade him to leave his daughter with us between whiles?'

'It's a fortnight now,' said Bess, laughing; 'but a month or six months it would be all one to me. I'd like to have the girl, and I'll do my best to make the minister leave her here.'

Toland was satisfied. The bush began to seem quite homelike now that Bess was with him, adorning the house with curtains and cushions and frillings, while outside she had gathered round her the fowls and farmyard animals that gladdened her heart.

'If it wasn't that any moment as like as not you'd find a snake in the calf-pen, or a possum sitting grunting on the hen-roost, there were times,' she said, 'when you'd almost forget you were in this outlandish country, and imagine yourself in a real decent farmyard.'

With the house growing homelike, crops flourishing, and the prospect of a visit from his friends, Toland's spirits rose. He complimented Bess on her mince-pies and laughed at her sad tale of the wombat she had glimpsed that evening in the scrub and pursued, at imminent risk of garment and limb, under a momentary impression that their big pig was making a wild dash for the bush. Australian animals aroused in Bess an almost indignant contempt. 'It was bad ·enough,' she said, 'to have creatures with ducks' bills and fishes' fins that didn't rightly know whether they were beast or bird—not to mention that some of them, with their pouches and things, didn't even seem sure from one minute to the next whether there was two or one of them.'

Since she had seen a kangaroo pursued by the dogs calmly disencumber itself of a 'joey,' which leapt from the pouch and hopped along beside its mother, Bess had become imbued with a profound distrust for all the marsupial tribe.

Toland read her scraps of news from the paper after tea, while he smoked and she knitted socks for him. She paused now and then to figure out calculations on the market prices of pigs or eggs and poultry, and sighed forth an occasional ' Dear! dear!' of less interest than disgust, by way of comment on her brother's sonorously-read descriptions of scenes in the great drama of the American Civil War. She did not hold with late hours, and Toland still sat on reading and smoking long after she was in bed.

D

Indulging in holiday lateness, brother and sister were sitting down to an eight-o'clock breakfast on the following morning when Scott appeared in the doorway, his ruddy face wreathed in smiles.

'It's a snug little cot you're making this, Miss Toland,' he said, taking the place promptly laid for him, after Christmas greetings had been exchanged. 'Jack here's a lucky chap to have such a sister.'

'Do you hear that, John? Isn't that what I'm always telling you?' laughed Bess, not displeased.

'And am I ever disputing it with either of you? I'm glad you've come to make a day of it, George.'

'You bet,' answered Scott, with his mouth full of eggs and bacon. 'What mortal thing is there to do below? Sports and drink in Tongalong — drink without the sports, barrin' maybe a fight or two, at Mallock's shanty. Give me a good ride and a good breakfast—not to mention the best of good company at the end of it.'

'Well, we're right glad to see you any ways. Take some more tea, Mr Scott,' said Bess, avoiding the meaning glance which specialised the good company. Toland was no less aware than she of Scott's liking, which grew more evident with each of the Sunday visits—good evidence in themselves, since they had occurred only since Bess's arrival, and thenceforward with unfailing regularity. It was in the nature of things that he should lose his sister some day, and Toland contentedly watched events which made it probable that she would go not far and into good hands. He took himself off after breakfast. The pigs must be fed, and a bit of wood and water got in though it was a holiday. Then they could have a pipe and 'look round.'

Toland felt some slight surprise that Scott's horse was not with his own in the little house paddock, when, from behind a clump of wattles by the creek, he noticed the flick of an unfamiliar tail, and walked down to investigate. The owner of the tail proved to be a well-set-up, iron-grey pony, caparisoned in a bran new side saddle, gay with stitching and leather work, a scarlet saddle-cloth embroidered with yellow, and a double-reined bridle with blue forehead band, tassels and rosettes. Beside the pony stood Scott's own bay, and as Toland remembered a self-satisfied mystery in Scott's manner at breakfast, the situation explained itself. Things had gone further than he thought; for Scott, he reflected without ill-nature, was not a man to give anything for nothing, and this handsome present was either evidence of success with his sister, or a bold bid for it. Not wishing to spoil the secret, Toland crossed the creek for a stroll among the maize, and on his return, Scott and Bess, galloping over the paddock, nearly rode him down at the kitchen door. Bess was radiant with pleasure. Her bright hair fell in picturesque confusion about her cheeks, and in the hatless, daringly skirtless condition induced by impatience to mount her new property, there was no trace of her usual housewifely staidness.

'Did you ever see such a Christmas box?' she cried. 'Mr Scott brought him — saddle and bridle and all—for my very own! And I've been too excited to half thank him yet.'

Toland manifested due surprise, thanked Scott and congratulated his sister, concluding drily, ' And a habit skirt, my dear, you'd find more comfortable, not to say becoming.'

'Gracious goodness! I'd no notion,' she laughed, suddenly aware of much well-filled stocking, and glad that Scott rode upon the other side. 'Lift me down, Jack.'

Reluctantly consenting to postpone the ride she longed for till the horses were spelled, Bess accompanied the men in a walk of inspection till the cares of dinner called her home again. However, in a half-hour's gallop through the timber, behind an old man kangaroo and Scott's dogs, in the afternoon, she covered more ground and acquired more stiffness than in her longest ride on the old roan cob that had ambled with her down the north country lanes, almost as far back as she could remember. She rode fearlessly and awkwardly, keeping her brother in constant anxiety, and thoroughly enjoying herself.

They reached home without accident, bringing with them a kangaroo tail for soup; and after an evening spent in talk, Bess went off tired to bed, wonderingly conscious that this queer Christmas Day had been one of the happiest she had ever spent.

Scott took his departure at six o'clock next morning, and the Tolands started again on their daily routine of farm work. John's first task was to scare predatory cockatoos from his maize, on which the young cobs were just forming. Then he hunted up the cows, usually from the furthest corner of his two-hundred-acre paddock, chopped wood and filled the water barrel for the day, while Bess attended to housework and breakfast. After that he went out to ring the green timber that kept the sunlight from sweetening the grass, and his sister, in times free of bread and butter making, and other household duties, tended the garden Toland had enclosed near the house, hoeing or digging, and bringing buckets of water from the creek for the tomatoes, melons and cucumbers that were her especial care.

On New Year's Eve the Macfarlanes arrived, and Toland noticed with pleasure the well-stuffed valise hung by Ruth's saddle, which promised that want of clothes, at least, would not prevent her remaining for a time at the farm.

Mr Macfarlane won Bess's heart at once by saying that he had heard so much of her from her brother that he felt they were quite old friends already. Towards Ruth Macfarlane her attitude was more guarded. She was as yet imbued with the half hostile, reconnoitring spirit which actuates women's conduct towards new acquaintances who they think it possible may become the wives of sons or brothers. Accordingly, though polite, she was not effusive. She studied Ruth carefully, slightly set on edge by certain little refinements in dress and manner which rendered her suddenly conscious of deficiencies in her own; while Ruth wondered to herself how it came about that Toland seemed so far removed from his sister in the nature and scope of his ideas.

Ruth's sweet disposition, however, soon imposed its charm on the older woman. Bess half reluctantly admitted to herself that Ruth 'put on no side.' Un-willingness to disappoint John induced her to be gracious; and gradually, as constraint wore off, the essential kindliness and common sense of both girls led them into mutual liking, so that, before the minister read evening prayers, it was a genuinely-pressing invitation that Bess gave to Ruth to remain at the farm while Mr Macfarlane went on to Black Dog Creek.

'I should like it very much,' answered Ruth, 'if my father can do without me till he comes back.'

The minister turned the leaves of his Bible in search of the chapter for the day, and said he would consider the matter. Apparently he had been considering it during prayers, for at their close he said he would persuade himself to part with his little girl for a time, feeling sure that he was leaving her in good hands. So the matter was settled and Bess took Ruth off to her room, which they were to share, while Toland and the minister remained to discuss the crops and the war over a final pipe and bottle of whisky, produced by Toland with hesitation which proved quite needless.

The dawn broke in a cloudless sky with promise of January heat. Scott had made an early start, as on the Christmas Day visit, and it was quite a large party that sat down to breakfast on New Year's morning. A picnic to explore the creek and gather fern roots for Bess's garden occupied most of the day. The minister had decided that he need not push on to Black Dog Creek till the morrow—a blessing which scarcely inspired George Scott with due thankfulness, for Mr Macfarlane was an enthusiast about ferns and dilated to Bess upon the different varieties—maiden hair, stag horn, coral fern, etc.—and their old country prototypes. He found time also to display much intelligent interest in Scott's farm, and gave him many valuable hints, for which Scott thanked him— in words—with envious eyes all the time on Toland and Ruth, who wandered ahead or lagged behind, talking, he fancied, of things more interesting than botany.

The sun was hot, and with due respect for the

thermometer at ninety in the shade, the party chose
for their walk the creek bed, where sparkling water
flowed in a narrow stream through an arching thicket
of musk and hazel. Here and there were deep pools
to skirt, but for the greater part of the way the
channel that ran full in winter formed a pathway,
and they wandered contentedly along it. Toland shot
a tiger snake sunning himself on a gravel bed in
the open; also a couple of Wanga pigeons that
Macfarlane excitedly pointed out in a tall wattle;
and these, with a basket of fern roots, were material
trophies of the expedition.

Sitting long after their luncheon on a grassy bank,
they discussed experience and prospects of life in
Australia and Europe—a subject on which Ruth
was a silent listener, feeling herself strongly in sympathy with Toland's vigorous theories of manhood's
destiny and claims, to which her father gave a
qualified assent while the other two laughed at him
as a dreamer.

'If a few more in the world would dream as I do,
it's fewer men with hands and brains would fret their
hearts away looking for a job to do while their little
ones were starving, or worse—in the workhouse,' retorted Toland.

'I think so too,' ventured Ruth, timidly. 'Surely it's
a noble dream to make the world a little happier for
everybody; and I think it must come true some day.'

Toland looked up gratefully, and Scott chimed in
with a laugh, 'Well, Jack, old man, I wish you joy of
it. Things are a bit wrong in the old country, I
know, because the blessed place is overcrowded—
and they say Free Trade is ruining the farmers.
But here, what have you got to complain about?

There's lots of good land, and the man with pluck and go gets hold of it.'

'Have you more pluck and go than me?' asked Toland, drily.

Scott laughed in deprecation. 'Hang it, don't get riled, man! I had a bit of luck of course, but—'

'And has Harlin and that scoundrel Mallock more pluck and go than either of us? No—I'm sick of this cant, that you are picking up like the rest, about pluck, and energy, and foresight, when it's money and roguery that's parcelling out the land! This is a grand country, no doubt. You and I, luckier than some poor devils, have got a foot planted in it, more or less, but mark my words— if they go on the way they've been doing, with their dummying and bribery, there'll be men as good as you and me tramping the roads in rags before many years are out. And it's a crying sin. By God it is!'

'John, I'm ashamed of you!' interposed Bess, severely. 'I thought you'd give up that ranting, outrageous talk when you'd got the bit of land you'd set your heart on so bad—and before the minister, too!'

'Stow it, old man!' laughed Scott, with a little annoyance. 'This ain't a debatin' society, you know. What are you growling at now—on your own land by the tinkling brook, all among the pretty birds and flowers?'

'Not to mention snakes! I'm sure I heard one of the slimy beasts near me,' added Bess, gathering her skirts closer and peering suspiciously into a neighbouring clump of bracken.

'There's much in what our friend's been saying,'

summed up the minister, rising; 'and again, there's much on the other side. You'll be in danger of forgetting, Mr Toland, there's a leemit to human effort. "For the poor ye have always with you." We have our Lord's word for that; and I'm thinkin' that word'll aye stand against all man's contriving.' He shook his head in sorrowful acquiescence with the word, and seeing question and dissent in Toland's eyes, playfully tapped him on the shoulder. 'But it's ill work to be disputing on the first day of the year, in this lovely spot, with God's handiwork all around us.'

Toland shrugged his shoulders and was silent. How useless it seemed to argue against the injustice of the world when on one side he found complacent acquiescence, on the other feeble resignation. His heart went out yearningly to Ruth Macfarlane, for he guessed from her eyes that she sympathised and understood — ignorant she might be, but she could feel with him that a man need not be blind to justice because he had been forced to snatch what crumbs he might in the pitiful, sordid scramble; and she could understand that the clamouring voice of robbed humanity could not be forever silenced by the dreary iteration of a misquoted text. Tempers had been ruffled by the breeze which spoilt the pleasure of idling longer by the creek, and it was no use saying any more. With some constraint the party gathered up its properties and started on the homeward way, Toland again escaping from the others with Ruth, glad that she seemed naturally to find her place at his side, and aware with grim satisfaction that Scott was inwardly cursing the old gentleman who found his society so congenial.

'Dad and you would not get on,' said Ruth, musingly, after a long silence.

'Wouldn't we?' he asked. 'Why not?'

'Oh,' she said with a laugh, 'you are too—I don't know exactly how to express it—decided, strenuous —you go to extremes, you know.'

'If you think a thing it's not much good to half think it, is it?' he asked, smiling.

'No,' she sighed, 'but dad thinks there is much to be said on both sides—moderation in everything— except religion. You are Church of England, I suppose?'

'I suppose so.'

She looked at him with raised eyebrows. 'If that is your view of it, you and he would certainly not get on,' she said seriously.

'I'm sorry,' he answered, half wishing that he were a good Presbyterian, and vaguely wondering if Ruth could realise of what importance friendly relations with her father might mean to him. Apparently not. Her manner suggested that she regarded the subject as of quite impersonal interest, and presently she changed it, telling him incidents of her ride, and sketching portraits of some of the parishioners at Black Dog Creek. Soon they reached the cottage door. The others were not far behind, and Toland went after his cows, which regarded not high day or holiday.

Toland was silent during the evening, letting the minister do most of the talking, and the old man made an early start in the morning, departing in high good humour with everybody. Scott was devoutly thankful to see his back, and immediately announced his intention of remaining over Sunday.

It only meant the loss of a broken day's work, and no doubt he could be of use to Toland in more ways than one. Toland, smiling to himself, agreed, and Scott did shoulder an axe and spent the morning with him ringing the grazing paddock, but in the afternoon discovered that there was a hard patch to dig in the garden which was beyond Miss Toland's power.

In the evening the seats on the verandah seemed automatically to arrange themselves in pairs, and there were late hours in the house that night since the following day would be Sunday. When it came the four of them rode round the boundary fence, and Ruth's conscience sometimes raised the point whether her father would approve of the two-and-two arrangement of the party, or indeed of a Sunday ride at all for such a worldly purpose as inspecting cattle. But she enjoyed it, and she might fairly have dismissed the business aspect of the expedition from her mind, for when Toland did chance upon a few head of his scattered mob his thoughts seemed otherwhere, and he scarcely took the trouble to look at them.

CHAPTER VI

WITH each day of her visit Ruth Macfarlane grew more at home at Grimsby Farm, she and Bess discovering that they had much in common, and that though their ideas parted company when they soared beyond the practical, there was in everyday matters of house and garden an ample field for congenial intercourse. Toland read to them sometimes, which rather bored Bess; but she could see that Ruth liked it, and it was easy to doze or let her thoughts drift to more interesting people than the Lady of the Lake or Marmion. In fact, the living, commonplace Scott not far away was more often in her mind at such times than any of his great namesake's creations.

In the day-time Toland saw little of the women, for he stuck conscientiously to his work, to which new hopes gave an added zest and spur, for he knew, before Ruth had been at the farm a week, that his early admiration and liking had grown into a love, the strength of which could not be measured, while there was nothing to arrest its even course. And wherever he was upon his farm, hilling up the potatoes, cutting suckers from the maize, or working at his clearing, all his thoughts were of Ruth, or at least only radiated from her to other things to which her existence gave a newly vast importance.

His financial position and prospects especially

called for much consideration, for he guessed they would weigh heavily with the minister. Of the money with which he had sailed from England over £100 remained to his credit in the bank at Tongalong. The rest had gone in various ways—personal outfit and passage money; nearly £100 in the fees and first of the annual payments for his land ; another £50 in the house and scrap of furniture; the balance in living expenses, wages, stock and implements.

He lived economically and spent nothing in wages during the summer months, for while the ground lay baked like a brick it would be waste of money to keep men at the clearing, with which he was so anxious to proceed. However, he did a little himself ; and as each hardly-conquered tree came crashing down, Toland wiped the sweat from his brow with a sigh, trying to picture the time when the wilderness of straight boles, throwing not even a shadow, save where the sunlight beat in speckled patches through the overspreading boughs, should have vanished and given place to waving fields of corn. To take down one tree when there were so many left seemed hardly worth the labour, and the echo of its fall sounded like a mocking laugh from the thousand trunks surrounding. Then, with a smile at such coward fancies, he would shovel back the earth into the hole he had dug, and swing his pick about the roots of the next tree that was to follow.

There was encouragement in the thought that after next winter's rains he might afford to put on a couple of men at the grubbing, and that in the softened ground one man could do more than twice his present daily work—six times as much he might count on altogether as he was doing then. Even

that did not amount to very much ; and besides, there
would be ploughing and fencing to attend to, rainy
days when they could do no work at all, and after
the grubbing all the timber must be burnt before the
ground would be clear.

So, almost against his will, he pursued the inter-
minable calculation that never would bring out a
large enough result, until at the close of a day of
muscular toil he found himself quite brain weary.
Sometimes he would direct his mental arithmetic upon
simpler problems—the profit on his young cattle if
he sold them next month at so much per head or
kept them for another year to put so much more
beef on them ; the return from his maize at four
shillings a bushel and forty bushels to the acre, as
against more bushels of varying numbers and prices
less by a penny, twopence, and so on—until his
mind was stored like a ready reckoner with all
possible and impossible pecuniary results of his
maize crop.

The maize, with its rich, green leaves and swelling
cobs, was dear to him, not only as an evidence of work
done and more to follow, but because amongst its
stately rows were passed some of his happiest hours.
Ruth would sometimes accompany him when he was
hilling up the plants, soothingly appreciative of the
skill with which he and his draught horse manœuvred
the Hornsby plough in the narrow track, throwing a
straight black furrow on either side the stems to feed
the over-ground rootlets. Sometimes she would run
forward to lift a straying pumpkin vine out of danger.
Once she laughingly declared that Charlie, the horse,
went straight of his own accord, and insisted upon
taking the plough handles. Charlie might have gone

straight but that she tripped, pulled the off rein and
let the handle go, with the result that, before Toland
could put her on her feet again, half a chain of the
row was broken down or uprooted ; and, concluding
that all was not as it should be, Charlie had stopped
to consider the position and munch a fat, green cob
temptingly near his nose. Ruth did not plough any
more, but, useful or a hindrance, Toland found her
company equally delightful, and in his eyes there was
no picture so charming as Ruth waiting to meet him
in the leafy alley, the pinks and whites of her frock
and sun-bonnet contrasting with the rich black of
the soil and the green of the maize as, with outstretched hands grasping a stem on either side,
she laughingly pretended to bar his way.

It was an idyllic life, and mingled with his hopes of
prosperous independence in times to come, Toland
felt that no material success could bring more happiness than these too fleeting days when youth and
energy were at their height, and all his brightest
dreams before him, unrealised, but full of potential
reality.

Neither had Ruth ever experienced anything quite
like these weeks in restfulness and simplicity. Hers
was not usually a life of ease, burdened as it was
with church and household tasks in Tongalong, or
travelling through the district with her father.
Sometimes she spent a few days at Kumbarra
Station, where she enjoyed the comfort of wealth
and the society of Mrs Harlin, who was only two
or three years older than herself, and practically her
only friend ; but even at Kumbarra she was not
entirely at her ease, for she was aware that Mr
Harlin, whom she did not like, only tolerated her,

and when Melbourne visitors were there she felt
snubbed and out of it in a dozen little ways, as
belonging to a different world. It was an entirely
new and gratifying experience to be the important
person in a civilised household—to be petted and yet
deferred to by Bess, who recognised, in a way that
flattered harmless pride, her socially superior standing and education. She found a girlish pleasure and
excitement, too, in Toland's evident devotion. ' If a
selector should be her fate ! ' With a kind of nervous
feeling that the words might have been prophetic
she remembered laughing at the idea of such a
contingency with Mrs Harlin. Toland, at anyrate,
was entirely different from any picture that either of
them had formed of selectors. Quaint provincial
turns of expression, that at first had amused her or
jarred upon her, she had almost ceased to notice.
The man himself, large and strong, ideally as well
as physically, imposed himself upon her thoughts,
and she admired him. There were no elegancies
about him, but no littlenesses, and none of the
vulgarity, of which she could not entirely acquit
Bess, to hurt her fastidiousness and blind her to
his essential manliness.

Thus it was with regret almost equal to that of her
new friends that, one evening, Ruth opened a letter
from her father, who wrote that he had returned to
Tongalong and hoped to call at Grimsby Farm on
the morrow to take her home. When the morning
came Toland could think of nothing but that this
was the last day of Ruth's visit, the happiest time
he had ever spent, and he found it hard to tear
himself away from the house to work at his clearing, half a mile distant, on the flat.

A big peppermint gum had resisted all his attacks since dinner-time, and at half-past four was still standing, with a deep trench exposing severed roots all around it. 'Why don't you come, you brute?' muttered Toland, throwing all his weight against the undermined tree. For answer it swayed just enough to rustle the spreading leaves, and showed to his experienced eye a tiny crack in the bottom of the trench near his feet. Pick and shovel soon laid bare another root. His axe rang resonantly on the straining wood, and as the last tough fibre was severed Toland stepped back from the tree. With the creaking and snapping of a hundred rootlets it relinquished its grip of the soil, stood tottering for an instant, and then with a swish of spreading branches fell headlong over the bank of earth before it, flinging its great butt into the air.

'At last!' muttered Toland, aloud. 'You made a tough fight, but you've gone and the rest are going.'

He turned, hearing a laugh behind him, and saw Ruth standing there with a basket and a billy in her hands. 'I have been watching you for the last ten minutes,' she said. 'Do you always look so fierce and taunt your fallen enemies like that?'

'I think I only talk to the toughest—out loud, at least. Have you come to help me?'

Ruth smiled. 'If you like, to encourage you. Bess was making a cake she couldn't leave and asked me to take out your tea. I've brought my own too.'

Toland picked up his coat and watched her, half blessing and yet fearing the accident that had kept

E

Bess at home, while Ruth sat down on the fallen trunk and opened her basket.

'Here's your pannikin,' she said, glancing up. 'You look worried; is anything troubling you?'

'No—I was only thinking—the same old thing—what a lifetime it takes to make a home.' He sat down on the log by her side and looked at the great forest before him. 'If I get rid of five trees a day and there are a hundred to the acre, how long will it take me to clear three hundred and twenty acres?'

Ruth dipped her cup into the billy and pondered, with eyebrows knitted for the difficult calculation.

'One hundred and fifty seven years, five months, four weeks and two days, or thereabouts,' she said presently, laughing. 'It seems a longish time, doesn't it?'

'Yes; and your answer might just as well be right for all the difference it would make. There's only one thing would make the time seem short.' He checked himself and turned away his eyes from her face as hers met them in inquiry.

'What is that?' she asked, looking down at the ground and drawing patterns with her foot.

'You will learn some other day; I cannot tell you now.'

'But I want to know,' she persisted.

Toland hesitated, but the overwhelming impulse to tell his love and ask for hers proved stronger than his determination to say nothing till he should have her father's consent. Ruth could feel herself colouring beneath his gaze as he half turned towards her.

'I almost think that you must know already,' he said slowly. 'From the first hour I saw you I believe that I have loved you—you have filled my thoughts and my dreams ever since. Every day it's been harder not to tell you. I meant to speak to your father first, but I could not wait—not even till to-night—and now I have told you, Ruth. I love you with all my heart and soul, I always shall. With you beside me—if it was for you—all the toil in the world would seem just a bit of play.'

Blushing and smiling, Ruth raised her eyes again to Toland's face. Aglow with the ardour of hope and love it magnetised her strongly, and the quiet tones vibrating with sincerity and feeling made these first words of love that she had ever heard sound strangely musical and sweet.

She did not speak at first, and Toland rose and stood before her. 'Can you ever care for me, Ruth?' he asked appealingly. 'I feel you must have known that I loved you, and whatever's the answer that you give, you'll be always the only woman in the world for me.'

Rising almost unknowingly to her feet she held out both her hands and leaned away from him when he caught them.

'I might have guessed—a little,' she said timidly. 'And I am proud—and glad.' Toland's clasp of her hands tightened and she went on, smiling, 'I think I'm glad, too, that you spoke to me first after all. I wouldn't like anyone else to be told—all that, you know—before me.'

'And what are you going to answer to it? I know I'm not good enough for you—but then, who is?'

Her eyes met his for an instant, saying all that her lips refused to say. 'I mustn't give any answer yet,' she replied softly. 'When you have told my father! —and now,' pulling her hands away from him with a laugh, 'drink your tea before it gets cold. I must run home to help Bess with ever so many things in a minute.'

Toland mechanically did as he was bidden, and for the few minutes that Ruth remained with him he spoke scarcely a word, since none had any present meaning, but repetitions of, and variations on, the forbidden phrase—'I love you.' Instead of speaking, he gazed at her; and while he thought he had never seen her eyes so bright, or such colour in her cheeks, it did not occur to him that his words had anything to do with the matter. When she went away singing to herself he picked up his tools again, but he often paused to think, with his foot on the shovel, looking vaguely towards the house; and when the evening shadows told him it was time to return, the ground was scarcely broken round the next tree condemned to fall.

Mr Macfarlane met him on the track near the creek crossing. The minister had arrived some time before, and a word from Ruth had made him not quite unprepared for the confession into which Toland impetuously plunged. He listened gravely and patiently, walked back with Toland towards the bush, and the conversation that followed was a long one. Toland had to go exhaustively into his money affairs and prospects. The minister shook his head when he heard how little cash was left, but he thought well of Toland's abilities and of the place; while Ruth had little in the way of worldly wealth to enjoy by remaining with her father. He thought nothing of social differences, but he would have been better pleased, he confessed, if Ruth's affections had fallen on a wealthier man of his own denomination and less radical views. However, the world was moving, and he would not stand in the way of his daughter's happiness. Therefore, if she returned his sentiments, he would give his consent and Toland might trust him that what he did at all he did cordially and with his whole heart.

So Toland's fears were set at rest, and he felt some compunction for his hasty judgment of the old man, which had overlooked the kindliness softening the sharp lines of thought engendered by a narrow age and education.

At Toland's request nothing was said to Bess that night, and he and Ruth got no chance for a word, but their eyes signalled each other that all obstacles were removed, and in the morning, before she and the minister departed, he strolled with her down the track by the creek.

There, seated on an old log beneath the black-woods, he told his story once more, and she was free to answer as she chose, making Toland the happiest of men.

CHAPTER VII

THOUGH Bess was naturally blessed with a cheerful disposition, nevertheless she often found the hours pass but slowly, and had fits of deep depression. The novelty of her surroundings was wearing off, and the effect that the solitude of the bush has upon all but the native born was making itself felt.

One afternoon, about a month after Ruth's visit, more homesick and lonely than usual, Bess tried to occupy her thoughts with needlework, but they wandered away to scenes of her girlhood, and tears stole into her eyes. Then she began to sing an old ballad :—

> 'A north countrie maid up to London had strayed,
> Although with her nature it did not agree ;
> She wept and she sighed, and she bitterly cried,
> " I wish once again in the north I could be.
> Oh ! the oak and the ash and the bonnie ivy tree
> They flourish at home in my own countrie."'

'Yes, they're a deal better than these great withering old gum trees that only make a body sad,' commented Bess, pausing in her song and looking out of the window at the sapless giants that surrounded the cottage. Then she continued singing :—

> ' " While sadly I roam, I regret my dear home,
> Where lads and young lasses are making the hay,
> The merry bells ring and the birds sweetly sing,
> And maidens and meadows are pleasant and gay.
> Oh ! the oak and the ash," etc.'

'It'll be many a day before merry bells ring in this outlandish place,' she sighed, and then she sang again :—

> ' "No doubt did I please, I could marry with ease—
> Where maidens are fair many lovers will come,
> But he whom I wed must be north country bred,
> And carry me back to my north country home."

Bess laughed as she finished.

'Yes, what a lot of lovers I might have. There's old Mick, and—'

Before she could add to the possibilities there came a knock at the door. Bess sprang to her feet and with one swift motion of her right hand performed simultaneously a dozen functions—pressed in a hairpin, secured a stray lock, straightened out her apron, and altogether prepared herself for any eventuality. Then she said, 'Come in.'

The door opened and Scott appeared, resplendent in costume and countenance, self-important, self-conscious, and with his intentions writ large all over him.

'Oh, it's you, Mr Scott,' said Bess, with a becoming blush. 'Won't you come inside?'

'Thank you,' said Scott, shaking hands.

'Take a chair, Mr Scott.'

'Thank you, Miss Bess. I heard you singing, and bein' afraid of stoppin' you, I stepped up quietly and listened.'

'I'm afraid you've missed John,' said Bess, to gain time, as she guessed well what was coming.

'Did I say I had come to see him?' asked Scott with a knowing look, and with what was intended as an insinuating tone in his voice.

'No, you did not, but I supposed you had,' replied Bess with modest untruthfulness.

'But s'pose I had come to see you, Miss Bessie.'

'Is there anything I can do for you?' she asked.

Scott hesitated a minute, was nearly lost, and then plunged in bravely.

'Yes, Bess, you can promise to be my wife.'

Bess laughed as Scott drew close to her.

'And what would be the good of that, now?'

Scott looked taken aback, and for a moment his self-assurance deserted him, only to return on the full tide.

'Well, if you married me you wouldn't sit and sing and cry by yourself, but you'd have someone to sit by you, an' comfort you, an' kiss you—like this—'

'Go along now!' cried Bess, blushing. 'Who said you might?'

'You did.'

'Oh, I never!'

'You looked it, then.'

'Well, I never!'

She looked it again, so Scott kissed her again.

'You'd better have a care John doesn't return,' said Bess, laughing. 'He nearly killed Squire Jackson's son for once doing that to me at a merry-making, not meaning any harm.'

Scott cast an anxious glance at the door and for a moment felt his amorous ardour chilled; but he quickly recovered, and by way of comment repeated the offence.

'So you'll marry me, Bess?' he said.

'I will.'

'But you won't want me to take you back home and leave the best farm in the district?'

'No, lad. It seems a wee bit different now.'

So they sat down together, and although the

shadows were falling and the gloom of night approaching, for a considerable length of time Bess felt neither lonely nor unhappy.

'John's home late to-night,' Bess said to herself as, after Scott's departure, she stood in the doorway watching for her brother. She felt impatient to break the news to him, for she knew he liked her lover and would consent to anything that would increase her happiness. Soon she faintly caught the sound of hoof-beats, and a few minutes later Toland rode into the clearing. He let his horse go and came up to the cottage. Bess saw at a glance that he had a moody look, and divined with a woman's instinct that now was not the time.

'Better give him something to eat first,' she thought to herself.

'Been lonely, little woman?' he asked as he put his hand on her shoulder and walked with her into the kitchen.

'Not very,' she replied with an unperceived blush, 'but I'm glad to have you back. Hurry up, like a good old fellow, for supper is all ready.'

During the meal Toland was absorbed in his own reflections, and to break the silence Bess asked him what he had been doing.

'I've been riding after some steers most of the day that had broken through the fence. I got them making back towards the station. By the way, I passed Mallock's shanty and saw that old fool Mick knocking down his cheque. There was a horrible row going on. Harlin has just paid off a lot of men and they're pretty well all there, more or less drunk. Like a fool I tried to get Mick away and got into a row. A rough brute of a fellow called me a sanctimonious cockie, so I tossed him on his head and left them trying to bring him round. Altogether I've had a beastly day.'

'There must be something else, John, for that's the sort of thing that generally cheers you up.'

'Well, now, you're right, Bess. It wasn't altogether that that was worrying me. It was pretty well all about you.'

'About me, John? There's no need for that.'

'I was thinking,' he continued, 'I haven't acted fair by you, lassie. I got you out from the old country to keep house for me in this wilderness, and now I'm going to marry and bring a mistress to the place. I'm afraid it may make you feel out of things, though Ruth and I want it to be the same to you as ever.'

'But supposing I married too, John, how would it be then?'

'There's few good enough for you, Bess,' replied her brother, smiling, 'and I'm afraid this is a lonely part for lovers to come courting.'

'But there was one here to-day,' said Bess, boldly.

'Who?'

'George Scott. He asked me to marry him, and I said "yes." And you have to say "yes" too, John, dear.'

John said nothing but lifted his sister off her feet and kissed her heartily.

A month later the marriages took place in the little weatherboard church at Tongalong. There were no bridesmaids or wedding guests. Neither did the fact that two cockies from up the Tonga were being married cause any sensation in the township. Yet notwithstanding the simplicity of the ceremony, Toland felt a sensation akin to awe as he stood by Ruth's side and listened to the words that made them one forever. For a moment the glamour of love lifted, the roseate hues faded, and a tremor of guiltiness ran through him as he thought of the sacrifice she was making, of the burden she was taking up for him. Then swiftly the fibres of body and mind strengthened and his heart swelled to suffocation with joy. Scott, on the other hand, had no misgivings. He beamed on Bess and she on him, his only care being how not to let his delight derogate from the importance of the occasion.

After the ceremony was over the little party sat down to a merry meal, and then the two men went to get their buggies and their wives to prepare for the long journey.

When Toland returned, and whilst he was stowing the baggage, Ruth had to face the ordeal of parting from her father, whom she was leaving to travel alone the road they had trod so long together in happy comradeship. Consequently there were tears in her eyes and some remorse in her heart as she waved a farewell to the solitary figure on the verandah, whose smiles belied his feelings.

During the first part of the drive neither Toland nor Ruth said much, their hearts being too full of unwonted feelings for topics of conversation to suggest themselves; but Ruth's eyes showed the love-lit path along which her thought travelled, and the exalted yet almost stern look on Toland's face spoke of joy, sobered by the recognition of responsibilities incurred. The afternoon was hot, dust clouds rose in the wake of the buggy; the hoof-beats fell softly, the skirr of the locusts, a whispered word from

Ruth, with a guttural answer from Toland, alone broke the silence. Then later on they talked together and built such air-castles as only lovers can. The sun had set when they reached the gap on the hills over which the road runs to the Upper Valley of the Tonga, and Toland was glad to have some daylight left to show him the dangers of the track, the descent being a sharp grade on a narrow side cutting, with the hill to the right and a sheer drop to the left. They reached the bottom in safety as the gloom of night was deepening, with ten miles of a bush track through heavy timber between them and home. Soon, however, they caught a glimpse of the moon rising blood-red amongst the trees, and before long her rays began to throw bands of light and dark shadows across the track. Toland had to drive even more carefully now, for the multitudinous lights and shades made everything appear mystic and unreal. Time passed, and the miles that separated them from their journey's end—the resting-place that was to be theirs for life. The moon had risen ; the everyday world had disappeared, shut out by the trees that arched themselves overhead in a lofty awning on which the dew sparkled like diamonds when the night winds rustled the leaves. In front the road looked like a dark tunnel, pierced here and there with shafts of light that turned to giant ghosts the white gums that rose on either side. Here and there glimpses could be obtained of distant ranges rising to the sky—huge rugged barriers against the outer world, mute, impenetrable, everlasting. The gullies that they crossed looked like fairy dells, the fronds of the fern trees sparkled like jewelled plumes, the trickling water seemed the hushed laughter of elves. No sound of life broke the silence; the spell of some enchantment seemed to lie upon the forest.

Then Ruth, herself becoming unstrung, pressed closer to her husband, and the pressure of her body broke the spell for him. He bent and kissed her, and with that kiss fled the ghosts and the spectres. What was the wilderness now to him but the scene of conquests to come? The gaunt trees were his foes and he was to lay them low. He lived, and they must die so that his children should inherit the ground that they encumbered.

He began to sing a song of northern lands; he called to his horses and cracked the whip over their backs; he laughed low to himself, and he kissed his wife again.

'We'll soon be there,' he said presently, as they reached ringed timber and the boundary fence of his selection. 'It's a miserable home to bring you to, Ruth, on your wedding-day, without fire or light, but it couldn't be helped.'

Ruth smiled and pressed his arm.

'Never mind that, dear. It won't be very difficult to light a fire, and it will be so nice being by ourselves.'

Toland urged on his horses, and they soon were in the home paddock, and on the crest of the rise that overlooked the cottage. There it lay, softened and picturesque in the moonlight, but what riveted Toland's and Ruth's attention was the smoke that rose from the kitchen chimney, and the light that shone from the window.

'Hang it!' exclaimed Toland, angrily. 'Whoever can have had the impudence to camp there whilst I was away?'

Ruth felt almost afraid as they rattled down to the enclosure fence, and disgusted at the idea of an intruder.

Toland jumped out when he reached the little garden gate, lifted Ruth down, and, followed closely by her, strode up to the kitchen door and flung it open. No one was there, but a fire was burning cheerily, a kettle boiling, a pot of potatoes stood on the hearth, the table was set for two.

Toland looked round in astonishment. 'Someone must have done this for us,' he said at length. 'I wonder who was so kind? Well, you had better fix things up, Ruth, whilst I go and take out the horses.' He kissed his wife a welcome to home, and at the same time a tall figure unhitched a horse from amidst a clump of wattles not far distant and rode away, muttering to himself,—

'I've always been saying, "this is no place for a woman body."'

CHAPTER VIII

THE first autumn and winter of Toland's marriage were happy and busy seasons. Mick M'Larty, again in occupation of his hut, helped to build the maize bins in which were heaped piles of splendid cobs, all picked and carted in before the end of May. Ruth assisted in the work, delighting in the rich harvest as she stripped the husks from the golden core; and later, on days of pouring rain, when the maize sheller rattled in the shed from daylight till dark, she often made her husband dismiss Mick to other indoor tasks while she fed the hoppers and his untiring arms spun the handle of the machine.

Deep ruts, worn by the heavy six-horse waggons carting away his crops, marked the track to Toland's farm, for there were hundreds of bags to take, and his own horses were kept busy at ploughing and hauling the logs together for fires in the new clearing. Therefore, jealously grudging the heavy tax which distance from market imposed on him, Toland paid carriage on the maize and potatoes and stuck close to work at home.

In spite of all drawbacks the future looked bright enough, judged by the standard of his first year's progress; and it was a proud day for Toland when he opened a letter from his agents in Tongalong and drew out a cheque for £120, with the account sales of his first crop on Grimsby Farm.

'We'll be quite rich people soon, dear,' said Ruth, her eyes growing wide with pleasure and surprise. 'If you make all that from twenty acres, how much will you make from the whole farm? I'm almost afraid to think of it.'

Toland laughed. 'You needn't be afraid, little woman. We will easily find a use for all we get.'

He did not discourage her by saying that there was very little of the rich creek flat, that bad seasons and low prices would come, and that even that great cheque would be swallowed in paying his instalment on the land, wages owing and the storekeeper's bill. But she saw that he looked thoughtful, and kissed him affectionately.

'After all, John, while we have each other and the home, it doesn't matter one scrap whether we are rich or not,' she said.

He agreed that it did not, though money was a good thing all the same, he said, and he intended to work all he knew to get it.

The time slipped by like magic, each day, from dawn till dark, filled with work that seemed neither monotonous nor hard, since every stroke of the axe, and every new furrow turned, gave fuller meaning to that wonderful word 'home'; and as Ruth followed the plough and dropped the maize seed at intervals in the new land that he was breaking up, Toland could scarcely believe that a year had gone since Mick gave him his first lesson in maize sowing on the green patch beside him, where the wheat stood two feet high.

Such occasional light tasks were all that Toland would permit his wife to do. He was not going to have her face grow weather-scarred and wrinkled, her back bent, and her chest flattened, to make her look like other women down the river, who, scarcely older than she, had lost all the softness and charm of womanhood in their dreary round of toil. Ruth laughed and said that she couldn't dig potatoes or chop firewood if she tried, which she certainly was not going to do, and Toland felt that he had in her an incentive to success that should put such sordid needs beyond all possibility.

The neighbours thought the Tolands a little 'stand-offish' and proud—a different sort altogether from the Scotts down below, that didn't give themselves half the airs though they must have twice the money. Toland accepted the position philosophically. He gave himself no airs, and was very sure that Ruth did not either, but he was too careless of what others thought to go out of his way to please anybody. With men from the other farms he was on friendly terms, and sometimes exchanged visits, but Ruth and the women did not often meet, except when they needed the advice or help which it was tacitly recognised her better education enabled her to give, and which she gave ungrudgingly. Thus, though a dozen settlers had taken up land between himself and Scott, and three or four still further afield in the creek valleys, and towards the head of the river where it came down from the ranges, the Tolands seldom set foot in a social way in any other house but the Scotts'.

Things were going well with them, and Bess, still cheerfully scornful of Australian animals and ways, adapted herself readily to the latter, and got on famously with her husband and his friends. In her house, as in Ruth's, was a sitting-room, but the chairs

F

with their snowy antimacassars were seldom disturbed or sat on, and the oleographs in leather frames scarcely needed their green muslin coverings protecting them from flies, since it was only on rare occasions that the blinds were pulled up and light let in to give the room a housewifely airing. Bess's heart was in the kitchen; and Ruth and John, declining to be treated as visitors, always refused to leave it for the stiff discomfort of the parlour.

'You're a born bushwoman, Bess,' her brother said one day as he smoked with George and watched her busy herself about the tea. 'It's a different kitchen to old Grimsby, but you've got it comfortable and no mistake.'

'And small credit to me if I hadn't!' she replied. 'At least a body can get wood for a fire here that would make people open their eyes in the old country.'

The fireplace was built in reliance on this fact, accommodating itself to logs of six feet or more, and constructed on the usual district plan of slabs lined with stone and pipeclay. From a blackened sapling crossing it in the middle hung chains for water-fountain, kettle and camp-oven; and a little stool on the hearth was useful to anyone desirous of sitting in the chimney to dry damp clothes or superintend the cooking. The rough mantelpiece, whereon a mild-eyed pair of china dogs flanked a big Dutch clock, was bordered with a fringe of pinked leather over a deeper fringe of coloured paper. Hams, bladders of lard, a bag of onions, and bunched heads of amber-cane drying for seed, were suspended from the tie-beams of the rafters. A shot-gun and Lancaster rifle hung, with shot-belt and powder-flask, on one wall beside an oleograph in a smoke—blackened moss frame. Pictures from the *Illustrated London News* covered other areas of bark. Three-cornered brackets carried the small library — a Bible, prayer-books, *Pilgrim's Progress*, *Book of the Horse*, implement catalogues, and a few yellow-backed novels. A straw basket held the Melbourne papers for a week; on a nail hung a torn coat of Scott's, in suggestive proximity to Bess's work-bag. A concertina, a flute, a penny whistle and a Jews'-harp, not far away, evidenced Scott's musical taste, and the length of one wall, devoted entirely to the useful, was occupied by the dresser and shelves for pots and crockery. Pigeons, in perfect amity with two large cats, strutted about the floor, indented by heavy-nailed boots, and showing between the boards interstices filled with hard, much-swept earth. Altogether the kitchen, with its white deal table, bright crockery and multitudinous trifles, was a comfortable living-room, satisfying all the needs of the Scotts, who looked with friendly contempt on Ruth's tasteful little parlour.

The sisters-in-law liked one another and met when they could, which was a gratification to Toland, who feared the effect of loneliness on his young wife's spirits. Only this fear had induced him to give a reluctant consent to her spending a week at Kumbarra on Mrs Harlin's invitation, when her husband was absent from home looking after interests in New South Wales.

Over this invitation had arisen the nearest approach to a quarrel between Toland and his wife. With glistening eyes, but without a word, Ruth handed him Mrs Harlin's letter. He read it frowning, and said bitter things of Harlin and his class, finally declaring

that he would not let Ruth go to satisfy the patronis-
ing curiosity of the people who had done their best
to ruin him. Ruth with difficulty kept back her
tears, and the very meekness of her acquiescence
roused in him an anger of which he felt ashamed.
She ventured no further than to remind him that Mrs
Harlin had always been her friend, that she and Mr
Macfarlane had often been guests at Kumbarra before her marriage, and very probably she should meet
there her father, whom she had not seen for some
time. She did not say that she longed for a change
and the society of Mrs Harlin, which satisfied her
as that of good-hearted Bess could never do. He
felt these things, however ; and rebellious and sore
as he was at the idea that Ruth should owe any
pleasure in life to people who looked down on him,
and whom he regarded as a curse to the country, he
was too fond of her to stand in the way, and finally
Ruth went to Kumbarra.

Mrs Harlin received her affectionately, questioned
her with sympathetic interest on her farm life, and
pressed her to come again when, at the end of a
week, she left for Grimsby Farm.

But Ruth had found that her relations with Mrs
Harlin were subtly changed. There was a feeling of
constraint. Her husband was seldom mentioned
by either of them, but she felt that his people
had become her people, and proud of him as she
was, and better off in worldly goods by her
marriage, she recognised nevertheless that she had
lost caste in Mrs Harlin's eyes, and that only as
an exception, by no means to be made in favour of
her relatives, was she allowed the privileges of a
friend. The thought embittered her, and caused a

little scornful amusement too as she proudly compared John with Mr Harlin. It was a relief to be back again in her own little house with her husband. She felt that in future only his friends could be really hers, and understood better than she did his diatribes against social injustice and inequality.

Mr Macfarlane never failed to call at Grimsby Farm when his rounds brought him anywhere into the neighbourhood ; and when it was possible he spent a day or two after his own heart, inspecting the latest improvements, discussing plans with his son-in-law, and sometimes even substituting for his clerical clothes an old suit he kept at the farm, and putting in a day's work at the clearing or in the harvest field.

Toland cut his first year's wheat with a scythe and carted it all to Scott's, to be thrashed with his brother-in-law's larger crop, since the thrashing-machine would not, for any sum that he could afford to pay, tackle the rough roads and creek crossings on the way to Grimsby Farm. Thus his distance from market handicapped him once more—to the extent of sixpence a bushel on his wheat, he reckoned, as compared with Scott's—but the crop on the creek flat yielded well, and again his farming operations showed a fair profit.

After a year of married life, during which two crops had been harvested and much building, fencing and clearing done, his hundred pounds reserve was still intact in the bank, and, happy in his home life, with things promising fair, Toland was more content and hopeful than he had been since his first attempt to find land for himself in Australia. He had made few friends or enemies. Harlin, whom he disliked as much as a type as an individual, he very seldom

saw, and when he did, for his wife's sake he con-
strained himself to speak civilly.

Nicholas Mallock was the one man in the settlement who roused in him a violent antipathy which
he took little pains to conceal. He had hated him
from the day of the ballot, and discovered nothing
since to modify his opinion.

Mallock was far too keen-sighted a man not to
recognise how the land lay, and too cautious to give
the least sign that he did so; but ever since he had
visited Grimsby Farm, anxious to make advances to
a man with such a tidy little wife, and Toland, re-
strained only by the instinct of hospitality from active
rudeness, had taken care that Ruth did not appear,
Mallock had treasured a grudge against him which
lost nothing by keeping. In the meantime there
was no reason to lose Toland's custom at the store
adjoining the more substantial public-house which
the dummies' cheques had reared on the ruins of the
shanty.

Mallock's fortunes were thriving. Forty per cent.
profits at the store brought in a growing income, and
already he had advanced a few loans at ten per cent., in
addition to overdue accounts for goods supplied, on the
security of some of the embryo farms that most took
his fancy. One selector, whose land joined his own, he
had bought out cheap before a plough had been put
in the ground, and already he owned over a thousand
acres as the nucleus of an estate. He was also
friendly with the member of Parliament for his
district, and hoped shortly to be made a Justice of
the Peace.

Toland had not expected that his wife would ever
go to Kumbarra again. She corresponded occasion-

ally with Mrs Harlin, but he never asked to see the letters, and Ruth, knowing something of his feelings, never offered to show them. He was astonished therefore when, on a summer evening some fifteen months after his marriage, he found at the post-office a note in Mrs Harlin's handwriting addressed to him. He thought at first that it must be for Ruth, but on glancing over the few lines found that they asked him to do the writer the favour of calling on her at Kumbarra on the first occasion that he happened to be going into Tongalong.

He puzzled over it during the ride home. 'Ruth,' he said gently, noticing how frail she looked, 'can you tell me the meaning of this?'

She coloured as she read the note. 'I think I can if you want me to,' she said appealingly, 'but won't you go and see Mrs Harlin?'

He looked at her in puzzled silence, kissed her, and went earlier than business actually demanded to Tongalong, calling at Kumbarra on his way home. Mr Harlin was again absent and would be so for another three months. Would Ruth come to stay with her, the squatter's wife asked Toland, for at least a portion of that time?

Toland hesitated. He need explain nothing, Mrs Harlin continued quietly. She knew all the circumstances from Ruth. They had been real friends, she added, and she was sure that Toland's pride was not of the kind that would sacrifice Ruth's well-being—perhaps her very safety—to its gratification.

Toland was troubled. He felt she spoke the truth, and yet it was bitter that he and his should be tempted to accept so much at these people's hands. Sullen and hesitating, he said something about being grateful for her kindness, but there was self-respect to be consulted—no need to accept charity—and after all he could get lodgings for his wife in Tongalong.

He would of course do as he wished, she answered, with a smile, and in tones not free from sarcasm ; but she thought it would be more manly to put his wife first and his own feelings second. He need not suppose that she had any desire to force a favour upon him, but it was a little hard on Ruth that, because she had married a man in not quite the same social sphere, she should be cut off from the companionship and help of an old friend at a time when she needed it most. If she could forget that Toland had insulted her husband, surely he could forgive him for being better off—or at least not carry his resentment to the length of sacrificing his wife on the altar of class pride.

Her words were haughty, not altogether just, and they rankled. Still there was truth in what she said, which, allied with her strong personal magnetism, conquered Toland in the end.

Ruth's pleasure when she heard that he had accepted an invitation on her behalf, and that in a week's time she was to go to Kumbarra, almost reconciled him to the sacrifice of his pride; and yet it roused a galling sense of inferiority to think that his wife rejoiced in the prospect of leaving him at a critical time to enjoy other companionship and a hundred comforts he could not afford to give her in a house which he could never expect to enter as a guest.

Thus it happened that Toland's eldest child was born at Kumbarra, and the first time he set eyes on it was in the arms of Mrs Harlin, who softly brought it out from the room where the mother was asleep. He looked at the child in silence. Were these cursed squatters going to rob him not only of land that should be his, but even of sole property in his own flesh and blood?

It seemed as if his wife had conspired with them against the independence by which he set so much store.

These jaundiced thoughts came crowding into his brain, and only in a dazed way at first he saw Mrs Harlin with the baby girl in her arms, and her boy, a sturdy little fellow three years old, at her side, staring up at him with solemn, disapproving eyes.

Toland did not see his wife that day. They told him it would excite her, and he rode back to his lonely house full of bitter reflections—glad, after all, that the child was a girl. It would have been worse if a son of his had been born at Kumbarra.

But when Ruth returned to him happy and well, delighted with her baby and constantly sounding the praises of Margaret and her kindness, he said nothing of past ill feeling, which gradually dissipated under the influence of wife and child. He had not even the heart to refuse when Ruth asked if she might choose Mrs Harlin as one of the godmothers— Bess was to be the other—for she could never quite understand how he felt about these things, and he could not bear to disappoint his little wife. Thus Mabel Toland, so named after Ruth's mother, began life with yet another tie binding her to the mansion as well as to the cottage.

Harlin thought it a mistake on his wife's part to take so much interest in people of that class, and rebuked her for officiousness in terms which provoked from her curt advice not to meddle with affairs he did not understand.

Children had come to complicate the domestic economy of Scott's establishment as well as Grimsby Farm, for three months before the birth of Mabel, Bess's daughter had been born; and the two women visited each other when they could, comparing babies and offering each other, from the depths of their ignorance, much wonderful and interesting advice.

Thus, with the patter of baby feet and sound of children's laughter enlivening their homes, the young pioneers worked on, seeing each year new faces in the district, new huts nestling amid ringed trees in the clearings, creek crossings cut and swampy bottoms 'corduroyed' by the Road Board, modest headstones commencing to cluster in the graveyard reserve near Mallock's shanty—everywhere around, on their own farms and elsewhere, the signs of civilisation and progress and decay.

BOOK II

CHAPTER I

TOM JOHNSON, a neighbour of the Tolands, was hoeing in his maize crop one day when his twelve-year-old boy rode up with the mail.

'Got any letters, Bill?' asked his father.

'No, dad, only the paper.'

'That's good. I thought I might have had another letter from that lawyer chap. Chuck me the paper, and I'll see how oats are selling.'

The boy handed him the *Tongalong Banner*, the new sheet circulating in the district.

When he opened it his glance fell on the advertisement column, and something he saw made him stagger.

'My God! he's done it,' he muttered hoarsely, and dropping his hoe walked off rapidly towards his hut on the rising ground close by.

Bill followed silently, wondering what had happened.

Mrs Johnson was putting a piece of salt beef on to boil at the open fire behind the hut when her husband approached. A number of barefooted children, apparently about the same age, surrounded her.

'Read that, missis,' he said, opening the paper in front of her; 'read that!'

'I'm a bit out of practice, Tom,' she said.   'Read it out to me.'

In a husky voice he read,—

'SALE,

'By Order of the Mortgagee.

'Messrs SALAMAN & CROUCH, acting under instructions from the mortgagee, will offer for sale, by public auction, at their rooms, Tongalong, on the 3rd inst., at 3 p.m., the farm known as Tom Johnson's, situated about 8 miles from the Kumbarra P.O.   For titles, terms, etc., apply J. MAC-NAMARA, Solicitor, Tongalong.'

'What does it all mean?' asked the woman, with a dazed look on her careworn face.

'It means that that scoundrel Mallock is going to sell the place over our heads.   Curse him! curse him!   God Almighty blast him!'

He shouted his imprecations so fiercely that the terrified children slunk away round the humpy.

'Oh, Tom!' wailed the woman, miserably, the truth beginning to dawn upon her.   'He isn't going to take our bit of farm from us?   He can't, can he?'

'He's going to sell it, the paper says, because I couldn't pay up the money, and we'll have to tramp the roads.'

'There must be a law agin it,' said the little woman, trying hard not to sob.   'It ain't nat'ral, after your workin' so hard and making a decent place of it, another should get it.'

'And you changed from a girl to an old woman in the twelve years working of it,' added the man. 'You oughter curse me, missus, for being such a fool. Mallock must have had me drunk when I signed that paper.'

'It's not your fault, Tom,' said the wife, trying to comfort him in spite of her fears and her misery. 'We had to get things at the store or we'd have starved. We tried hard to live on kangaroo, but couldn't manage it, and there was no way of making money then, with all the clearing to be done. But God help us, what shall we do?'

'I don't know at all, but I was thinking that I'd ride over to see John Toland, who's a straight man, and have a talk with him.'

'Oh, isn't it dreadful!' sobbed the wife, 'the neighbours all knowing about it. It's more than I can bear.'

'They'll know all about it from the paper, and I'm not the only man about here Nick Mallock has his hand on, and Toland might see a way out of the fix. Bring me that horse you're on, Bill. I'll go at once.'

'Have a bite before you go; it's near dinner-time,' said the wife.

'I couldn't touch it,' he replied, as he lengthened the stirrup leathers.

'Come back to me soon, Tom, I feel kinder afeared,' she said beseechingly.

'All right, missis, I'll be back soon—and keep up your spirits.'

Johnson rode away and his wife went into the little cabin, bare and comfortless, but still a home, and sitting down, cried from grief and loneliness, whilst the children stole away and played with the kangaroo dogs in the bush.

Johnson found Toland hauling logs in his cultivation paddock, and, with Mick's assistance, stacking them in huge piles.

'Good-day, Mr Toland,' he said as he rode up. 'Doin' a bit of clearing?'

'Yes; I'm getting ready for a burn as soon as the grass is safe. How is that maize crop of yours getting on I hear so much about?'

'Oh, something splendid. It's about twelve foot all over. It'll be the best crop I've had yet.'

'It's a good piece of land on that creek flat,' said Toland.

'It is that, but it was a tough job clearing it single-handed. There were trees eight feet through on it, besides scrub you couldn't walk in.'

'Well, you have your reward now,' said Toland.

'Yes, I suppose so,' said Johnson, doubtfully, as he remembered with a pang who would gather the harvest when the grain was golden in the cobs.

Then they talked on various matters, Johnson all the time anxious to come to the point, but thinking it scarcely neighbourly or polite to rush into business. At last, however, when many topics had been exhausted, he said,—

'Did you see that advertisement in the last *Banner*?'

'No,' said Toland. 'I haven't got my mail yet. What was it about?'

'It was about my place. It's up for sale in a week.'

'I never heard you were selling out,' said Toland in surprise.

'I'm not selling out. I'm being sold up.'

'By Mallock?'

'Yes.'

'Damn him!' said Toland.

'To hell,' added Johnson.

'I'm real sorry,' said Toland, sympathetically. 'But can't anything be done?'

'I've just come over to have a yarn with you, thinking you might see a way out of this fix. When I try to think about it my head all gets muddled up and I feel kinder sick and dizzy like, and don't know what to do.'

'Well, I'm no hand at such matters myself,' said Toland. 'I suppose you ought to see a lawyer.'

'Not me,' said Johnson, decisively. 'They're all as great rogues as Mallock himself, and the only one in Tongalong, that chap Macnamara, has worked this swindle for him.'

'How much do you owe him?'

'Three hundred pounds.'

'I suppose you haven't been able to pay the interest?'

'No, it isn't that. I paid him fifteen pounds for the six months only a short time ago. He wants the lot —that's what it is.'

'Oh, I see, the mortgage is due. By Jove, he has the whip hand over you, then. What are you going to do?'

'I tell you I just don't know. There's one thing— the place is worth a lot more than three hundred pounds, and I suppose I'll get what's over when it's sold.'

'Don't trust to that anyhow,' said Toland. 'If Mallock wants the place he'll fix it so there isn't a bid that will do you any good.'

'Well, I want to stick to it if there's a way, for it's cruel hard to be chucked out, and the missis have got kinder fond of the place. Most of the kids have been born there and we've made it a bit better every year, and it's tough luck to be done out of it now, by heaven it is !'

'Couldn't you go and see Mallock and find out if he'd take anything to give you an extension of the mortgage, so that you'd have time to try and raise the money to pay him off ?'

'I'm afeared it won't be no use,' replied Johnson. 'I'm thinkin' he just wants to collar the farm now with the maize crop on it. But it's worth trying though I don't like going near the scoundrel.'

'I'll go with you if you like,' said Toland. 'They say "Two heads are better than one."'

'I'd be right glad if you would,' said Johnson, in a relieved tone, 'and I'm thinking that if you wouldn't mind I'd be just as well away, as I know I'd just fire up and spoil things ; besides, I'd like to get home to the missis, as she'll be taking on bad about it whilst I'm not there.'

'All right, just as you like, and I'll gladly see if I can fix up anything for you ; but, as I said before, I'm no hand at this sort of business and you mustn't expect much. All I can do is to try and get Mallock to put off the sale to give you a chance. I'm afraid it's a blue lookout, as his one idea seems to be to get hold of land by fair means or foul, and he'll likely get a dummy to bid to the amount of the mortgage and get the land that way.'

'Have a try anyhow, Mr Toland, and you'll have the thanks of a poor devil. You don't know how bad I feel on it. It's worse than when our eldest boy died and I had just to carry him out and bury him in the bush myself like a dog, and being summer time and the grave that shallow I had to drag logs over it for fear the dingoes would scratch it up. It'll be worse though, I say, to see the missis and kids turned out on the road to starve. It makes a fellow wish there was a poorhouse in this blasted country.'

'Don't be afraid of that, man,' said Toland, encouragingly. ' If the worst comes to the worst, there are plenty of folk round here will look after them till you get work. You get home to your wife and tell her Mrs Toland will be over to see her soon, and I'll go to Mallock this afternoon, and if I can't do anything else I might break his neck for you.'

'That's what I'd wish, only I'd like to do it myself,' said Johnson. 'I'll be over again to-night to find out how you got on. Good-day, and thanks to you.'

Johnson rode off, and Toland, having instructed Mick to go on hauling light stuff that he could get into piles himself, walked up to the cottage, catching his horse on the way.

Ruth was deeply sympathetic when she heard the news and wanted to go and comfort the family at once, but Toland persuaded her to postpone her visit until after his interview with Mallock. She did not altogether like the idea of her husband's visit to the 'Morning Star,' for she argued, from the stern expression on his face, that it would not be of an amicable nature.

'Don't get into a row with that horrid man,' she said pleadingly as Toland was leaving the cottage. 'You know it can do no good, and I do hate the thought of it.'

'Don't be afraid, little mother,' he said, laughing at her tone of alarm. 'Mallock won't hurt me. I'm too big and ugly for that.' He lifted her off her feet like a child and kissed her, and then rode away on his mission.

G

On his way to the township Toland had plenty of time for reflection. After deciding what course he would pursue with Mallock he turned to a consideration of the wider aspects of the case, and the more he dwelt upon them the more distressed he felt. Now for the first time in the new world he was face to face with conditions that had crazed his mind in the old and sent him forth as a wanderer in search of land where it was boasted that independence waited on toil. For the first time beneath Southern skies he had found man framing a supplication unto man for leave to enjoy the fruits of his labour—for a brief respite wherein to avert calamity. All this came the more as a shock to him because the life sounds that had vibrated in his being of late years had been the sweet music of hope and joyous contentment; but now a harsh, discordant note had been struck, and he felt as one who, from a dream of happiness, is awakened by a cry of pain. In his simple faith, toil in the fields, veritably in the sight of God, appeared as almost the only truly honest lifework for a man; and that those who sowed should not reap seemed to him an injustice before which all others paled. This sentiment had increased ever since his arrival in Australia, as a conception gathers strength in the process of realisation. On his farm he owned no master; emblem of constituted authority there was none; evidences of superior advantages conferred by birth, education or wealth were almost absent in a community where it was man to man and all together as soldiers of the same rank in an advance of the Anglo-Saxon world army marching to the conquest of Nature and the making of a nation. His individuality had developed under the conducive conditions of his free and independent life. The disavowal of any master—of obedience even to conventionality—had increased his stature, made him know himself, and had bred a fierce determination to resent anything even suggestive of dependence. Such independence he thought to be the inviolable prerogative of every man who bent his back in honest toil, earning his charter of freedom by the sweat of his brow. Yet now it all seemed a mockery. He found himself on an errand of mercy, sent by a slave to his master with a prayer for leave to enjoy the fruits of his labour. And such a master! Toland clenched his fists as he thought of it, and muttered to himself, 'Give me the landlords of the old country if such are to be those of the new.' Never had the great forest seemed so dark and gloomy, and for the first time the thought occurred to Toland that victory might in the end be with the giant trees, and that the tide of man's conquest might be rolled back after having inflicted a few wounds here and there, quickly to be healed and hidden from view. This feeling of depression brought a revelation to him. He marvelled how the aspect of all things might change, and repeated to himself again and again, 'Without hope a man would go mad in this wilderness.'

Thus he was led on to put himself in Johnson's place, and, with his heart-strings wrung, and full of pity and bitterness, ne rode on through the silent forest.

CHAPTER II

WHEN Toland reached the 'Morning Star' two bullock-teams were drawn up in the road outside. The dull, patient-looking brutes were panting in the hot sun with their heads almost in the dust, whilst the drivers, two big, uncouth-looking fellows, were drinking and talking in the bar with Mallock. Toland tied up his horse in the shade of a wattle and entered the bar.

'Good-day, Mr Toland,' said Mallock, without in any way showing the surprise he must have felt at seeing so unusual a visitor.

'Good-day,' replied Toland, somewhat curtly.

' It's my b—— shout,' said one of the bullock-drivers, throwing half a sovereign on to the counter. ' Will you join us, mate ? '

Toland acquiesced in order not to give offence, and when a round of drinks had been disposed of he shouted in accordance with recognised etiquette.

Then he turned to Mallock.

' I want to have a word with you,' he said.

Mallock called a woman to take his place.

'Come this way, then,' he said, going into the parlour opening off the bar. Toland followed him. ' Take a seat,' said Mallock, indicating a chair with his foot and sitting down himself.

Toland sat down.

' I've come to see you about a morgtage,' he began.

'Aha !' broke in Mallock. 'I thought so. Why,

damn it, when a cocky comes into the bar nowadays
I never know whether to say, "What'll you have?" or
"How much'll you have?" Well, what's yours?'

'I'm sorry to disappoint you,' replied Toland, 'but I
never said it was my own business I had come about.'

'No, you didn't,' said Mallock, sullenly, 'but I
thought you were the sort of chap that knew enough
to mind his own business and let other people mind
theirs. That's my rule.'

'Well, it's my rule,' said Toland, hotly, 'when I see
a man being swindled, to make his business my
business, and that's why I am here.'

'Then if you want to do any good I reckon you'd
better be a bit more civil.'

Toland felt conscious that there was some truth in
the remark, and not wishing to fail in the advocacy of
his friend's cause, he adopted a more conciliatory tone.

'I suppose it's no use coming to blows,' he said,
'before we know whether it is necessary or not. I'm
here because Mr Johnson asked me to come over and
see you about the difficulty he's in with you over his
mortgage.'

'Did he happen to send the money by you?' asked
Mallock, with a sneer.

'No, but he asked me to come and see if you'd put
off the sale for a bit, to give him a chance to raise it.'

'Not much,' replied Mallock, decisively. 'I've
heard that yarn before, and ain't green enough to
be had by it.'

'You don't mean to say that you will sell a man's
home over him without giving him a chance?'

'I mean what I say—just that and nothing else. I
gave Johnson notice months ago I'd come down on
him. I'm a man of my word. The place is up for

sale in a week, and sold it will be as sure as my name is Nicholas Mallock.'

'Well, what'll you take to put off the sale and give the man an extension? I suppose you'll do it for gold if you won't do it for anything else?'

'I won't take what all the scurvy cockies in the place could raise to give me. I've made up my mind on that. I want my money and I've got to get it.'

'But you won't get it at the sale. You know very well there'll most likely be no bid.'

'That's so; and Johnson will just have to pack up his traps and scoot out, and I'll perhaps try a little farming myself.'

'Then you mean to say that I am to tell Johnson that you intend to ruin him and seize his farm,' said Toland, angrily.

'You can tell him what you dam' well please,' replied Mallock, coolly, 'but that's about the length of it. Tell him, too, I'd advise him to look after his own business, and if he wants to stay on after the place is mine he'd better come and see me and I might rent it to him.'

'By God, you can tell him that yourself!' said Toland, springing to his feet. 'I'd sooner be dead than work for a low hound like you.'

Mallock rose with the grunt of a fierce boar and faced Toland, both waiting for the next word to spring at each other's throats. There was a silence for a few seconds, broken only by the passionate breathing of the two men.

Then of a sudden an uproar arose in the bar, easily heard through the hessian wall.

'You won't drink with me, won't you, you b—— toff!' shouted one of the bullock-drivers.

'No, thank you, I'd sooner drink with a pig.'
Toland's attention was riveted by the uncon-
cerned manner in which the words were uttered.

'I'll knock the b—— head off yer,' was the retort.

'There's going to be a row,' said Mallock, moving
towards the bar. 'It's that damned fool of a teacher
come for his letters, and Bullocky Bill's a bit on.'

Toland followed him, forgetting his own affair in
the fresh excitement.

In the centre of the bar floor two men were squar-
ing up at one another. One was Bullocky Bill—a
powerful-looking brute—and the other a tall, thin-
featured man, Conyngham by name.

'What's this about? Drop it, Bill!' said Mallock,
approaching the combatants.

'Leave him alone,' said his mate; 'he's got to take
down this b—— toff, who's too fine to drink with a
workin' man.'

'Come on, you ——!' cried Bill, making a fierce lunge.

Conyngham stepped back and the blow fell short.
Again the attempt was repeated, and again it failed.
Toland saw that Bullocky Bill had met a practised
boxer, and had no fear as to the result. Bill, too, recognised that there was need for care and moved
round muttering curses.

'Wire in, Bill! He's only playing with you,' said
his mate, in an aggrieved tone.

Thus exhorted, Bill rushed in again, hammer and
tongs, right and left, but never a blow got home, for
Conyngham was only playing with him and not even
deigning to strike in return, while the quiet, sarcastic
smile never left his face.

Bill's mate groaned in wrathful shame while Toland
and Mallock looked on fascinated. Bill was rapidly

getting pumped out by his furious and ineffectual
onslaughts and, recognising the fact, he nerved himself for a supreme effort. He rushed in with his head
down in an attempt to seize his opponent by the
waist and throw him. Then the end came. Conyngham's eyes for the first time flashed, and he swung in
a vicious upper cut with his left that sent Bill staggering back with his guard down, and then, springing
forward, he struck him a fearful blow under the jaw
with his right, and Bill crashed down backwards on
to the floor, an unconscious and bloody mass. His
mate ran to pick him up and Conyngham turned to
Mallock.

'Have you any letters for me, Mr Mallock?' he
said quietly, as he wiped a spot of blood off his
knuckles with his handkerchief.

'My oath, you're a cool 'un!' said Mallock,
admiringly.

'I asked you if you had any letters,' said Conyngham, in a chilling tone.

'I beg pardon, sir; no, I haven't. Won't you
have a taste after it?'

'Yes, I think I will. Give me some brandy, please.'

Mallock put a bottle and glass on the table, and
Conyngham tossed off over half a tumbler of raw
spirit.

'Chuck a bucket of water over him,' he said, indicating his still prostrate adversary, and then walked
outside and unhitched his horse from the fence.

Toland followed him.

'I know you're Mr Conyngham,' he said as he
approached. 'My name's John Toland, and I'd like
to shake hands with you for a man.'

Conyngham held out his hand with a smile. 'I'm

glad to meet you,' he said. 'I've heard about you from Mrs Scott.'

Toland noticed to his surprise that Conyngham's hand was quivering violently.

'I wish you would come over and see us sometimes, sir. My wife and I would be pleased.'

Conyngham was boarding with the Scotts, and their commentaries on the Tolands had made him desire to become acquainted with them, and he answered pleasantly that he would accept the invitation on the first opportunity.

Both men then mounted their horses.

'Don't our roads lie together for a while?' said Conyngham.

'Yes, they do,' said Toland, pleased at the idea of his companionship.

So they rode off together, and Toland related, much to Conyngham's amusement, how the latter had caused a sudden cessation of hostilities between him and Mallock.

'I must apologise,' he said gaily, 'but I wouldn't have missed that little excitement for worlds. It has braced me up and done me a lot of good. It has relieved me of the sense of the monotony of life. I'd like to ride for hours now in the cool evening air.' He took off his hat and Toland noticing how flushed the pale features had suddenly become, put it down to Mallock's brandy.

'Might I then ask you,' he said, 'to ride on with me and stay the night? To-morrow's Saturday and you will have nothing to do.'

'I think I shall,' replied Conyngham, 'if you will be so good as to have me. I seldom feel inclined to go a mile out of my way, but now I feel as if I really lived and were a man of action. Come, let's have a gallop. The ground is level.'

As Toland plunged along behind his companion he wondered if the man were mad, or really the quiet, saturnine scholar described to him by Bess, and concluded that the excitement of the fight and the fire of the ' Morning Star' brandy had wrought the change.

When they pulled up he asked Conyngham if he felt the loneliness of the bush very much.

'Yes,' replied Conyngham, 'but I like it. "The world forgetting, I wish to be by the world forgot," and after all I find more companionship in these mighty solitudes than I should on a human ant-hill.'

'Well, it's a grand thing to have a contented nature,' said Toland, wishing he could take this philosophical view of life.

'No, it's the worst,' said Conyngham, speaking excitedly and as a man taken out of himself. 'Discontent is manly—sometimes divine. It is an evidence of desire to struggle up the ladder of existence to the topmost height. The fool stands on the bottom rung and grows fat and contented, but the hero goes up and up, even though it be at the risk of breaking his neck.'

'Well, then, how is it that you are contented, for I am sure you are not a fool?'

A smile hovered over Conyngham's flushed features as he prepared to answer the question.

'No, I trust I am not wholly a fool in the narrow sense, however much in the larger. Let's see how it comes that I am not now "wearying deaf heaven with unavailing cries." Suppose we took a man and threw him into the river, swollen with winter floods.

He would struggle and struggle, shriek for aid across
the waters to his God and cast up his eyes in agonies
of despair, and battle till exhausted. Then he would
sink and rest in some still nook round which the
waters swirled. At first, before life departed, the
sensation would be one of perfect bliss. He would
see green fields and hear the songs of birds mingling
with the rippling of waters and feel how joyous it
was to rest after strife. He would feel content and
dream into death. So I suppose I feel content. The
turbid waters of life in which I once struggled do
not disturb the peace of this quiet spot in which I
now dream away the hours, ingloriously perhaps, but
not unhappily.'

Conyngham concluded in a dreamy tone, speaking
to himself more than to Toland. The latter felt attracted by the strange personality of the man, and
for a while they rode on in silence, broken only by
the dull soft beat of hoofs on the dusty road and by
the champing of the horses at their bits.

Presently Conyngham pulled up and faced the
west.

'Look there,' he said, pointing to the sunset.
' Who would live in the murk and squalor of a city
and miss such sights as that ? ; Do you see that black
range under the sunset ? How splendid it looks
with the gloom of this earth upon it, while overhead
the glories of the heavens are unfolding ! Those
clouds are like golden argosies floating across the
rose-tinted sea. That other to the right must be
the war-cloud we read of, saturated as it is with
blood.'

As he spoke the last words he gave a shudder
and rode on again with Toland, muttering to himself,

'By Heaven! Mallock's brandy must have iambic properties.'

Presently he drew in his horse.

'Mr Toland,' he said, 'if you will excuse me I shall not go any further with you to-night, but shall come and see you another day.'

'Oh, don't go back now,' said Toland, disappointed and surprised. 'We're only a few miles off. I hope you're feeling all right,' he added with concern, as he noticed the ashen hue that had displaced the flush on Conyngham's face.

'Oh, yes, I feel all right,' he said, 'only I'm a little upset after that row. One time it would have been different, but I am afraid my solitary life must be upsetting my nerves. The blood-red sky suggested that beastly sight in the bar, and I feel as if I wouldn't care to shake hands to-night with a refined woman like your wife.'

'Oh, don't let that stop you,' said Toland. 'If Ruth doesn't like a man to take care of himself I don't know why she married me, though I must say her last words to me this afternoon were not to get into a row. But we won't say anything about it. I want your advice on a matter and so would like you to come on.'

'If I can be of any use to you, of course I'll come,' said Conyngham, as he spurred his horse.

Toland related the history of Johnson's misfortune and found a sympathiser, though Conyngham could not suggest any way out of the difficulty.

'I suppose,' he said, 'Johnson had better take Mallock's offer and rent the place from him.'

'Well, I say he had better go and shoot himself than be slave to such a brute,' replied Toland.

'That,' said Conyngham, 'would be a very excellent way of getting himself out of the difficulty, but it would not benefit his family much; and, after all, it matters very little whether a man be tenant to the lord or the shanty-keeper, for in any case the uttermost farthing has to be paid. The injustice, if any there be, is not in relation to individuals but the system which causes one man to be at the disposal of another.'

'That's it,' said Toland, delighted to at least find someone of his own way of thinking, 'and that's why I am here instead of in the old country.'

'Do you think, then,' said Conyngham, 'there is any essential difference between the system here and there, or did you not rather come out here to perpetuate a wrong with the hope, however, of benefiting from it?'

'I scarcely understand,' replied Toland. 'We stop here. These are the slip-rails.' As he pulled up a man rode towards them out of the darkness. 'Hullo, Johnson, is that you?' asked Toland.

'Right, it's me! I couldn't wait down at the house, so I rode up to meet you. How did you get on?'

Toland told him the result of the interview and advised him to see Mallock himself.

'I'm much obliged to you, Mr Toland,' said Johnson, 'much obliged. I didn't expect no better. I'll just get back now and talk it over with the missis. Good-night to you!'

'Good-night, and better luck,' said Toland.

'Poor devil!' muttered Conyngham.

That night at Grimsby Farm was a pleasant one for the Tolands, who were delighted with their new

friend. At first he was reserved, though courteous
having shrunk back into himself after a fit of un
natural self-abandonment, and Toland could scarcely
believe that he was the man whose unguarded flow
of language had attracted him on their ride.

Gradually, however, he thawed under the softening influence of Ruth's gentle nature and sympathetic kindliness, though he seemed unable, under
any circumstances, to restrain a tendency towards
pessimism tinged with sardonic humour. Amongst
other subjects they discussed the difficulties of Mab's
education.

'It is too far to send her to school,' said Toland,
'and the wife hasn't much time.'

'Don't send her,' said Conyngham, looking at the
pretty child ; 'let her mother teach her. And if Mrs
Toland will let me I will help her as much as I
can.'

'I would indeed be glad,' said Ruth.

'Yes,' said Conyngham, smiling, 'we'll do our best.
We'll educate her so that she will grow up to despise
us all and be able to feed the pigs *en grande manière*,
Won't we, Mab?'

'I hate pigs,' replied the child. 'Joe can feed
them—he likes them.'

'No, I don't,' retorted brother Joe, indignantly. 'I
only like dogs and horses.'

'It's time you were in bed, children,' said their
father.

Joe marched off at once, grumbling to himself.
Mab kissed her father and mother, and then Conyngham, who she supposed was some sort of uncle.

Conyngham wondered how many years it was
since he had been kissed, and thought perhaps he

was not so hard-hearted as he had believed himself to be.

The elders sat up talking until the air was cool enough to render sleep a possibility, and then also went to bed. Conyngham did not undress, but waited until there was no sound to be heard but the heavy breathing of the sleepers and then opened the window and stole out. He walked a short distance from the cottage, and having lit his pipe, flung himself down on the grass with his face to the stars and thought for hours the thoughts of a lonely man who, having failed in life, had drifted into the back-blocks of the Australian Bush.

CHAPTER III

'I suppose you'd not care to let Mabel go to the Harlins for a day or two, John?'

Toland took his pipe out of his mouth and looked at his wife. He detected a tremble in her tone of assumed indifference, and his conscience smote him. There were threads of grey in her hair, lines too deep for her years beneath her eyes, and how different was this deprecatory appeal, with averted face, to the old, half-laughing, half-imperious commands she had been wont to lay upon him, looking into his eyes and crushing all power of resistance by the pressure of a little hand on his.

And once more he had to refuse the request that Ruth's words implied. 'No, dear.'

She sighed; her eyes grew suddenly dim, her hands dropped on her lap, and she looked through a mist of unshed tears into the past, whence she and John had seen these then distant years, full of hopeful mystery with golden faith-lit lights, shining out of the purple haze of the unknown. The mists of the future were greyer now. They hung over mountains of possibility, mere petty ranges close at hand, compared with the gorgeous distant heights that the eyes of youth look so confidently to explore, while the lights were paler and seldom pierced the clouds.

Then Ruth felt the touch of lips upon her hair; looking up, she saw her husband bending over her, and future, past disappointments, fears, all vanished before the magic of the present and the wonder of love.

Toland flung the pipe and newspaper off his chair and brought it close to hers before the fire, where he might draw her head down upon his shoulder. 'Are you ever sorry you married me, Ruth, little woman?'

There was a soft laugh; her head nestled closer against his coat, her hand, in which he noticed with a shock how blue the veins showed, tightened its grip of his fingers.

'I sometimes am,' he continued. 'How can I help seeing that this lonely bush life is wearing you—that you are growing old before your time?'

He felt the slightest little petulant shrug, and with a sudden realisation of woman and his own tactlessness curving his lips in a momentary smile, he went on, 'You have not lost your beauty, Ruth. For me you never will, for I shall love each grey hair and wrinkle as long as I have eyes to see.'

'And yet you are sorry?'

'Not for myself, God knows,' he said with a grip of her hand that almost made her cry aloud. 'Ruth, if I were to lose you that would be the end of me. When I met you first my soul was in a ferment of disappointment at finding injustice here worse than I had left behind—rage at being swindled of my rights—hatred of the blackguards that did it—longing for a home, for success, revenge—a dozen good and bad impulses—but if I had not met you the bad would have got me under.'

Ruth smiled proudly. 'But you did meet me and you have got them under.'

'Have I? I am not so sure. I thought when I

H

married you that I could succeed—make your life
bright and happy—and the black moods come back
when I see I haven't done it.'

He shook his head at her gesture of protest, and
lifting hers from his shoulder, stood looking at her.
' No, dear, I haven't, but Heaven knows I've worked
hard enough.'

His expression grew so fierce that Ruth was afraid
to face him as he moved restlessly about the room.

' No man has worked harder, but it's that cursed,
cursed blight that rests on labour. Where do they
shove me out to do it? Into a wilderness where
there's not a man or woman within ten miles of us
for you to make a friend of! Independence in the
bush or slavery in the towns—and such independence
too! Haven't we seen one miserable devil after
another go down all around us to feed the blasted
land sharks? And even I'm mortgaged now.'

Ruth looked at him anxiously.

' Oh, don't fret about that.' But in a gentler tone,
' What is there in it, Ruth, dear? A bare pleasure-
less life for you ; for the children a few lean, unlicked
cubs to play with. No amusements but a tea-meeting
once a year, or those bush races that Joe is getting
much too fond of.'

' The children are happy enough,' she said thoughtfully.

' Now, perhaps ; but what is their future? Joe
hates the land already that I've treasured so for his,
and small blame to him. He'll be a wage slave to
somebody, you'll see. What will Mabel be? And
our little baby that died—wasn't it murdered, like a
thousand others, by the rogues in power that crowd
honest men in slums, or drive them into the back-

woods, where the mothers toil and fret their infants'
lives away?'

'John, John, dear! Hush! You are talking
wildly.'

She was standing beside him, her gentle arms
around his neck and her cheek pressed to his.

'It's hard, dear, but you have me, and I have you,
and Mabel, if only you could persuade yourself to
let her—'

'No,' he interrupted almost roughly. 'Don't ask
me that again. It pains me beyond everything to
pain you and deny the girl any pleasure. Wasn't
that what started me talking to-night? You
belonged to those people by birth and sympathy,
and sometimes I hate myself for taking you from
them. But can you wonder I hate them too, for
first robbing me, and then bringing the only cloud
there ever was between you and me?'

'There is no cloud,' Ruth murmured with a sigh.

'No, no, there is none!' he cried eagerly, 'and you
will confess, dear, that I am right, won't you? Mabel
shall not go, because she is a pretty toy, to be petted
and patronised by that squatting crowd! We are
right to keep our independence if we can't keep
anything else, aren't we, Ruth?'

With the only selfishness of an unselfish woman,
who will sacrfiice the rest of the world, together with
her own dearest good, whatever it be, to please the
man she loves, Ruth gave way and returned his kiss.

'Yes, John, you are quite right,' she faltered, looking into his eyes, with the voice of conscience
whispering all the time that he was wrong and she
a coward; that she was wronging herself and
Margaret and Mabel because she loved her husband's

love too much to fight his wishes and darken his face with frowns.

Then she soothed him to hope and placidity again by tactful, enthusiastic praise of their beautiful farm and home—the materialised expression of his manly industry and courage. During their sixteen years of married life Ruth had learnt her husband better than he guessed. She knew what subjects it was wise to avoid and how best to pour oil on troubled waters. His arm was still round her waist and they started guiltily, like young lovers, when a door was opened before they had time to answer the knock.

Rising quickly, Ruth blushed and extended her hand to welcome Conyngham, while with the other she deftly twisted a straying lock of hair into place.

'It's a long time since you've been near us,' she said. 'Sit down here by the fire. What have you done with my young people?'

Conyngham shook hands gravely with Ruth and her husband, not a sign betraying the half-jealous amusement of a lonely man at this lover-like old couple.

'Mabel and Joe are coming nome when the moon rises, and they bid me tell you that they are bringing their Cousin Bess with them. It is cold to-night,' he continued. 'Winter has not quite sheathed his claws, though there's a fresh in the river that shows the snow in the hills is melting.'

Four years had passed since Conyngham had paid his first visit to the Tolands, and often since, on Saturday evenings, as now, he spent a few hours at Grimsby Farm, when he was always welcome, though the cynical theories of men and life which flowed so placidly from his lips were sometimes fuel to Toland's angry discontent. He had left his horse in the stable, and having taken an early tea he said he wanted nothing but a sight of the fire and leave to smoke.

No debatable subject had been touched when Conyngham startled Ruth from her composure by the suggestion that a great drought was impending.

'Yes, I read something of it in the papers,' said Toland, contemptuously, 'but I've never seen the crops look better. And what do astronomers know about it anyhow?'

'Not half so much as farmers, of course,' answered Conyngham. 'Have you got in much crop?'

'More than I ever had before—over two hundred acres.'

'Then for your sake I hope it will keep off a year, though if not an ear of wheat filled this season it would be a merciful providence—to use a cant phrase —for many of our friends.'

'Why?' asked Ruth.

'Because they would have to go quicker and get an early start clearing land for a new mortgagee; and they might have the luck to be sold up on the second occasion by a more estimable man than Mallock. He is a horrid cad, to whom I should really grudge handing over my land—if I were un-fortunate enough to possess any.'

'What a miserable view to take,' sighed Ruth.

Toland poked the fire viciously. 'But a true one,' he said. 'It's Mallock and Harlin have ruined this district.'

'Mallock, I grant you—with reservations,' said Conyngham, flicking a spark off his knee, 'but why Harlin?'

'You were not at the ballot or you would not ask that.'

Mrs Toland knitted on, resigning herself to one of the outbursts which the memory of the ballot, only graven deeper by years, usually provoked from her husband.

'I was not at the ballot,' said Conyngham, quietly, 'but I know what happened there. And what does it amount to after all? That Harlin got back some thousands of acres, which he is paying for and making money out of, and prevented the land going to thirty or forty poor beggars who would probably have been sold up, before they had paid the Government, by Mallock or someone of that breed. I prefer that it should remain in the hands of a comparatively decent man like Harlin.'

This view of the matter staggered Toland. 'Then do you mean to say the whole thing wasn't a low swindle?' he asked hotly.

Conyngham shrugged his shoulders. 'What does it matter? It has done no harm. Selectors who did get a chance on those flats have gone—more temptation to borrow. You who didn't are as flourishing as almost any of them, here where you've had to work a little harder.'

Ruth felt it almost a sacrilege on Conyngham's part to thus belittle the grievance which her husband had hugged so closely for all these years. Thoughts like those expressed by the schoolmaster had sometimes occurred to her, but she had not dared utter them.

'Then you, who I thought a radical, are a defender of land monopoly and fraud. We live and learn,' sneered Toland.

'Pardon me, no, but I consider it a pity to waste on an individual and an incident such healthily bitter animosity which is due to society and a system.'

'I hate Harlin,' persisted Toland, doggedly. 'Why should he grow rich by a swindle, and, being rich, sneer at us and look down on us as if he were a better man?'

Conyngham paused to re-light his pipe and took a few meditative whiffs. 'That speech, my friend,' he said, 'is an example of what we call in logic the fallacy of many questions. First, what you call a swindle was according to law, which we all make the best use of to our own ends. Second, I am not aware that he does sneer at us and look down on us. Third, the rich not only consider themselves better, but actually are better than the poor.'

'Do you really believe that?' asked Ruth, wonderingly, as a picture of what Harlin really was flashed before her.

'He doesn't, Ruth. He only wants to stir up an argument,' exclaimed Toland, rising impatiently. 'Why don't those children come home, I wonder?'

'Certainly I do, on the average, Mrs Toland,' answered Conyngham, turning to her with a smile; 'and if your good husband will only contain himself I shall try to explain why.'

Toland flung himself into his chair again with a grunt of disdain.

'I should have thought you, Toland,' continued Conyngham, with friendly sarcasm, 'were sufficiently a philosopher to pity, rather than hate, people who only thought themselves better than you. What gravels me,' he added with more warmth, 'is that they really are better, take it what way you will. I

am what is called an educated man. Is not the man
with some thousands a year and my attainments, such
as they are, a better man than I? Travel stores his
mind and trains his eye. Leisure gives him time for
thought. Books and pictures form his tastes. Wealth
gives him fearlessness, independence, good clothes,
good friends, good physique, power of usefulness to
others—everything in fact that goes to make a man.'

'Money gives means to do things,' assented Toland,
grudgingly.

'And what can be done without the means? You
are a good farmer. Will you tell me that with three
times the money you would not be a better one, besides
ridding your mind of much perilous stuff and storing
it with something more wholesome? Are some of the
poor wretches about us here, that slave from daylight
to dark, men at all? That's what I mean by saying
that the rich are better than the poor, and that they
and we are fools if we fail to recognise it.'

He paused for breath and Toland smoked on, sullen and thoughtful.

'But what about morals, Mr Conyngham?' put in
Ruth, timidly.

'They depend on physical well-being.'

'The French nobles before the Revolution were
well enough fed and clothed, weren't they?' asked
Toland, 'and yet we don't read that they were exactly
angels.'

'Well, my friend,' said Conyngham, smiling, 'the
sans-culottes gave many of them every chance to
become so. But they bear out what I have said, for
everything is a matter of comparison. The *noblesse*
were callous to suffering and bloodshed; the peasants
enjoyed it. The *noblesse* took it easy in the matter

of religion; the peasants stamped religion out. Morals were rather lax in some of the old houses —in many of the poor cottages they did not know what morals meant. And to come nearer home, do you know a harder task-master than the very poor man who gets a poorer to do a job for him?'

'But I thought you believed in the rights of man and the nobility of labour?' said Toland, puzzled, but unconvinced, and shelving the matter in dispute.

'So I do,' returned Conyngham. 'It's potential nobility, when it becomes, under fair conditions, the lot of everyone. I daresay I hate the common labourer of to-day much more than your friend Harlin, or any other of your pet tyrants, does. He washes less than is desirable—spits a great deal more. He is weak in knowledge and in aims. In fact, his language is the only strong thing about him.'

'What's the use of blackguarding him?' asked Toland. 'Wouldn't it be better to do something to help?'

'What's the use of shutting my eyes to facts? I help in what ways I can, by never concealing from him my opinion. And my opinion will be true till farmers and working men wake up a little and make use of the liberty they boast of. It's not Harlin—not even Mallock who are to blame for evictions here, but the cowardly fools—the rest of the people, including ourselves—who have allowed the Victorian land to be parcelled out into private hands at all. The time had not come for farming here, hundreds of miles from the seaboard. Your grievance, that you are not on better land, fifteen or twenty miles nearer to Tongalong—real enough in its way—is a petty one

compared with the great one you placidly swallow—
that the squatters have the land near Melbourne,
which should have been rented to them till it was
rented to men who wanted farms, when the sheep
would go further afield. Then we should have known
no evictions in the Tonga Valley. Harlin might
have been left in possession of his land, without the
temptation or the means to become the fraudulent
owner of it, until his time came—years hence,
perhaps—and you might have been driving your
plough on green hill sides near Melbourne, in sight
of the shipping in the bay.'

Toland and Ruth watched Conyngham in silence,
vaguely stirred by the fire in his eyes and the ring
in his tones as he sat up in his chair and waved
his pipe, with smoke curling from the bowl, over an
imaginary landscape dotted with smiling farms and
orchards. Ruth only half understood, but, like her
husband, she was carried back to days long ago, when
he too raised his voice, blindly, perhaps, but groping
after truth, against the gigantic robbery of men's
rights in the soil, before much dwelling on wrongs
personal to himself and neighbours had narrowed his
outlook, almost transmuting hatred of injustice and
longing for the general weal into hatred of more
prosperous men and a longing for revenge. It came
home to him that his ideals were vanishing and that
his aims of late years stood on a lower plane than
those of his hopeful youth.

'All that might be,' he said moodily, 'but what
good is it to us? What can we do? The land is
gone—jobbed away to each other by your " better
classes," and we will never get it back again.'

Conyngham laughed. 'Of course not, my dear

fellow—not till you and I are dead and fifty years have gone at least. I am afraid I was almost guilty of being in earnest just now, which was very weak of me.'

Ruth was disappointed. 'Don't say that, Mr Conyngham. Surely there is something to strive and hope for even now.'

'Yes; I should advise your husband to strive all he can to hold the land he has, and to hope for more when the other cockies go under, so that he may become a grazier and a well-thought-of man like Mallock or Harlin in time. Talking of Harlin—why don't you let Mabel go sometimes to Kumbarra? Mrs Harlin told me she had asked you.'

Ruth laughed nervously. 'Ask my husband,' she said.

'I dislike Harlin. We are in different spheres and I don't choose her to go where she can't go as an equal,' replied Toland, aggressively.

Conyngham raised his eyebrows. 'It's not my business, of course,' he said, 'but if she were my daughter I'd let her go. Not that I believe it would make much difference after all,' he laughed, 'for Miss Mabel has a will of her own and something of her father's queer notions. I overheard a remark of hers about squatters that terribly shocked her aunt.'

'What was it?' asked Ruth, smiling, glad to observe the soothing influence that the knowledge of Mabel's sympathy had upon her husband.

'I really think you'd better ask her, Mrs Toland. It would not be fair for me to tell tales.' Conyngham rose from his chair and looked at his watch. 'Do you know it's nearly ten? Time flies in discussion and I think I must go for my horse.'

'Let me get you some supper first, at least.' Mrs Toland went to a cupboard by the wall, and her husband opened the door, letting in a cold blast of frost-laden air.

'Crisp and clear,' he said; 'a grand night for a ride. Hullo! What's this in such a hurry? Joe and Mabel don't ride like that.'

Trembling from head to foot, Ruth put down the plates with a clatter and rushed out to join her husband on the verandah.

'What is it, John? What is it?' she cried, clutching nervously at his arm.

Conyngham, who had also left the room when his ear caught the ring of galloping hoofs, answered her question.

'Someone in a great haste,' he said, 'and alone.'

The little group on the verandah was silent. There seemed a premonition of evil in that furious gallop, for bad news travel fastest. Ruth clung to her husband and prayed. Toland stood sullen and dogged, awaiting a blow, ready to curse God if it should fall. Conyngham was wrapped in foreboding conjecture, and suddenly his thoughts flew to the swollen river, making the night musical with its murmur through the trees.

The horseman was further distant than he seemed. For a few seconds the hoof-beats died away in a hollow; then they sounded loud again on the upland and the listeners knew the rider was nearing the gate half a mile from the house,

'Jumped it, by Heaven!' muttered Toland, presently, realising that the time for the awaited pause had gone by. 'He's on nothing from Grimsby Farm.'

The suspense grew agonising. The gallop rang in their ears, there was a loud, brief splash. That meant the crossing at the muddy watercourse a quarter of a mile away. The shoes rang again on the frosty gravel, and then for the expectant trio sound lost its import as they fastened their eyes on the figure showing against the sky on the moonlit rise.

The schoolmaster recognised him first. 'It's young Harlin,' he said. 'I know the mare's gait —and he was at Scott's to-night.'

Toland turned sharply. 'Damn him if he brings me bad news! Curse him!' he hissed. 'Am I ever to have these people cross my path?'

'Hush, man!' said Conyngham, sternly. 'Look after your wife.'

Toland's arm went round Ruth where they stood at the garden gate, and in three strides the schoolmaster stood beside young Harlin, with his hand on the horse's foam - flecked bridle. Harlin was dripping from head to foot and panting from the stress of his furious ride. He gasped out a few sentences, but in spite of Conyngham's injunction to speak low, Ruth's straining ears had caught a word.

'Drowned!' she cried. 'Oh, my darlings!'

'Not your children,' came Conyngham's sharp, clear voice. 'It's young Bess Scott.'

'Thank God!' muttered Toland, and Ruth fainted in his arms.

Conyngham gave one glance behind him. 'Human nature,' he said to himself with a hard little laugh; aloud, 'Look here, my young friend'—addressing Harlin—'next time you are privileged to be the bearer of bad news don't be in quite such a hurry with

it. Those unfortunate people have lived through half
a dozen deaths in that theatrical gallop of yours.'

'Anyway, I saved their daughter's life in the river,'
said the boy, sulkily aggrieved.

'You're a fine fellow, then'—Conyngham's hand-
grip made Harlin wince. 'It's a pity you didn't tell
us that first and come something under thirty miles
an hour to tell it. Now, give me the details as I go
with you to the stable. Mr and Mrs Toland will be
best alone for a little while.'

They walked a few steps in silence.

'Don't by chance mention you heard Mr Toland
thank God his sister's child was drowned instead of
his,' said Conyngham, lifting the wire from the
yard gate.

'I expect he only meant thank God his own were
safe,' replied the boy. 'Anyway, he could say so.'

'I can't swear what he meant—but I expect he
wouldn't say so,' answered Conyngham, dryly. 'At
anyrate, don't give him the chance.'

CHAPTER IV

THE river babbled joyously down the long reach below the crossing where Bessie Scott had been swept from her horse only a few hours before. Sandbanks strewn with quartz pebbles washed bright by the fresh water glistened in the sunlight. A golden blaze of wattle bloom from the thickets that edged the shore gave colour to all the sombre scrub and filled the air with scent. The overhead sun forced its rays even into the thick blackwoods, finding vivid green traced with darker veins in the semi-transparency of the young leaves. Everywhere—in the black, steaming soil, the uncurling bracken fronds, the twitter of nesting birds—breathed the spirit of life and spring, while all the men folk of the Tonga Valley were gathered to search for the body.

George Scott was there, dressed in his best suit of black, a sense of importance overlying his grief as he stood beside the police constable from Tongalong on the right bank of the stream. A rope stretched over the river was fastened to the nose of a flat-bottomed boat, and a knot of men and boys, holding the cable ends, paid out more line or hauled it taut as the hands in the boat with the grappling-hooks signalled their wish to explore this part or that of the deep, swirling stream.

The search had begun with daylight and each hour added to the crowd of the sympathetic and curious

who mustered from every farm to give time and
labour for the recovery of a dead body, not one
tithe of which would the joint community have
expended on the most urgent living appeal of the
best-regarded man or woman in the valley.

It had been a solemn, serious business at first.
Men in their best clothes, straggling down in twos
and threes, said some awkward words of sympathy
to Scott, longing for a pipe but not sure whether
smoking would be respectful in the presence of
death, which, till more should be known, imbued all
the river below the ford with stimulating mystery.
Then the boat arrived on a dray from a bridge that
was building miles down the river and work really
began.   The constable came from Tongalong to
spread over the proceedings the ægis of constituted
authority, comforting in a vague way to Scott though
Constable Scanlan did nothing but loll at ease with
his helmet glinting officially in the sun, occasionally
giving a suggestion or order that few heard and none
heeded.

Soon a tobacco-loving casuist, reckoning that the
greatest stickler for etiquette could have no call to
complain if he went above the ford, for Bess's body
could by no possibility be there, squatted himself on
a moss-grown log and lit a pipe.   The scent of black
Derby found its way to the nostrils of others, who
grasped the example set without its delicate limitations, and all around blue clouds of smoke, mingling
their fragrance with the wattle blossom's, floated into
the still air.   Tongues were loosened from the idling
groups ; human laughter now and then answered the
jackasses ; advice, jocular as well as serious, was
bawled to the men in the boat ; rude chaff saluted the

rope-holders when they came to grief in their scrambles through the scrub to let the boat drift down the river, and when the grappling-irons hooked something in a dark pool by a sunken tree, and strong pairs of straining arms hauled the rope in hand over hand, only to bring to the surface a slimy, water-logged branch, the expectant silence reigning was broken by a loud guffaw.

By two o'clock there were sixty or seventy men and a sprinkling of women on the scene, which suggested rather a picnic outing than preliminaries to a funeral. Some of the smaller boys were playing at drowning, and there were gallant rescues of floating sticks in shallows where the river widened.

Rupert Harlin and Joe, as spectators of the tragedy, were constantly appealed to for the story, by the inquisitive and the helpful, till they grew weary of the telling.

It had been always a nasty crossing, and but that the moon was not high enough above the trees they would have seen that the water coming down made it unsafe to attempt. Harlin had led the way into the ford, Mabel and Bess following him, and Joe bringing up the rear. The younger boy had not left the bank when he saw Harlin sink to his waist in a great hole washed out by the force of the backed-up current, where it swept round a tree stranded by the flood above the crossing. For a confused second or two the others sat their frightened horses. Harlin called loudly to them to go back as he turned his own horse's head to the shore. Bess lost control of the nervous filly she rode. It stumbled, recovered itself, and, flinging up its head, struck her on the forehead as she bent over its neck trying to keep her seat.

I

Her hands released their grasp of reins and pommel, and, as the moon shone clearer, little Joe, who made a gallant attempt to reach his cousin, saw her head fall on her chest. Her balance went and the unfortunate girl fell backwards over the off flanks of her mare into the stream that swept her past, almost within reach of Joe's outstretched hand. Harlin saw it too. Saw, too, in horror, that Mabel's horse was plunging with her into the wash-out. Just in time to save her by driving the spurs rowel deep, he dragged the girl from her saddle across the pommel of his own, and reached shallow water in safety. Then the two boys ran scrambling through the scrub cooeying and calling to Bess. But all in vain ; there came no answering cry, only the roar of the river as it swept relentlessly on its way. Abandoning the search, the boys returned to the ford, and when the horses were caught Mabel rode back, shivering and crying, with Joe to break the news to her aunt, while Harlin faced the river again and started on his gallop to Grimsby Farm.

Mabel and Mrs Toland were now at Scott's doing their best to comfort the bereaved mother and the other children. The eldest boy was with his father, feeling a dreadful interest in the proceedings, less conscious of grief for his sister than of the melancholy prominence he and his family had attained amongst the neighbours. Then his eye fell on the dray, driven slowly up and backed down to the river, with their old draught horse in the shafts. He saw a straw mattress with a great sheet folded upon it, and burst into a torrent of boyish tears as he realised more vividly the dreary result of success so complacently looked for by the men scraping and prodding the river bed with the grappling-hooks and barb-headed poles.

Toland had early left the crowd and made his way down stream, forcing a path through the scrub, and peering with expectant dread into holes where the current eddied round logs and rotting heads of trees. Looking once across the river, he saw on the other bank the schoolmaster, with men from a neighbouring farm, engaged on a similar quest. His thoughts went back vividly to the arrival of the news on the previous night, and he tried to realise what it would mean were Mabel instead of Bess lying in those cold depths. He could not bear it as Scott was doing, he felt sure. He was almost angry with his brother-in-law for accepting help from all these meddlesome, well-meaning fools. He would not allow one of them about him were Mabel in the river. He told himself he would drive them all away, and she should stay there until he could find her and bear her home in his own arms; and probably, but for Squatter Harlin's son, there would she be, side by side with his poor little niece. He remembered with shame his snarling curse on the boy as the bearer of bad news. The conversations with his wife and Conyngham—all the experiences of the past night came home to him. They seemed psychological mile-stones marking stages on roads he must travel no further—crossing of his dear wife's wishes—growing bitterness towards his fellow-men and exaggeration of his own small ills at their hands. The long-cherished grudge against the Harlins had grown too strong to be suddenly uprooted, but he could cease to think bitterly of them by not thinking at all, and if he told himself every day that he was grateful, perhaps in time he would become so. At least he would cease to weary Ruth with his complaining; he could be more tender and forbearing. The look almost of fear which he had surprised once or twice on her face pained and shamed him, so that tears of pity for her, and anger against himself, stood in his eyes. He knew that with her dying breath she would declare him the kindest and best of husbands; and the newly-awakened consciousness of how lamentably short he had fallen in each day's possibilities, putting quite aside his long-ago ideals, kept him company all through his journey down the river bank.

When he began to retrace his steps early sunset had left the dark pools more forbidding; all light and colour had receded to the inaccessible hilltops, and to Toland's mood it seemed symbolic of life—bright things always in the distance and the sombre close at hand. By the time he reached the crossing dusk was drawing on and the river banks were deserted. An hour before the body had been found, beneath a great blackwood, which had caught the girl's hat in its overhanging branches, where they dipped in the swollen stream, and the searchers had dispersed to their homes. Toland looked about him and concluded that a cooey he had vaguely heard, while still wending his way downwards, had been meant to announce the sad news of success. He heaved a sigh of pity for poor Bess, of gladness that he had not been there to see, and then unbuckling the reins from a sapling in the wattle grove, he mounted his horse and rode across the river. Beached in a gravelly nook he saw the boat, and it was still light enough to distinguish wheel marks made by the dray on the sandy track through the scrub. He followed them at

a walking pace, not wishing to overtake the procession with the body, and it was late when he
reached the outer gate of Scott's farm and saw the
twinkling lights of the homestead. There he realised
with wonder how little true sorrow he was feeling.
Had he become so self-centered that no disaster,
unless it touched him personally, could really stir
the emotions that responded fiercely to even a distant
echo from a stranger's defeat in the battle to make a
home?

There was something uncanny, almost prophetic,
in the ascendency which he now realised one theme
of thought and aspiration had insidiously gained over
all others in his consciousness. The conversation
with Conyngham had brought it home to him and
made it seem not quite so noble. His selfish inability to feel real grief for this young life, snatched
senselessly from one to whom it was bright and dear,
made him angry and ashamed. He knew that the
John Toland of ten years back would have been
stirred to the depths of his nature by the pity
of it.

A light was burning in the great shed where Scott
kept his waggon, his binder and smaller farm implements. Toland looked in through the half-closed
door, unseen. At the carpenter's bench, in one
corner, Scott was at work. Several Murray-pine
boards stood beside him. He relit his pipe, sighed
heavily, and then with a tradesman's touch ran his
carpenter's pencil across the line, marking the length
of a head board for the coffin.

Toland changed his intention of entering and turned
away with a shiver of repulsion. But after all, why
not? Someone must do it. Scott was a carpenter

by trade—and he always liked to save money when
he could.   A few moments later Toland knocked
softly at the kitchen door.   There was no answer, but
he thought he heard a sob and entered the room.   No
fire was on the hearth ; a single candle on the dresser
showed Bess seated at the bare table, her hair in
disorder, her still comely face buried in her hands, in
the utter abandonment of grief.   She looked up at
her brother, years older, it appeared to him, than
yesterday.

'Oh, John !' she whispered,

'Poor Bess lass !'   He held out his arms, and as she
sobbed on his shoulder his capacity for sorrow returned to him.   That he had a sister whom he dearly
loved, and that he was a man of flesh and blood apart
from any spot of earth he trod, were truths into which
old meanings came crowding that he had not known
for years.

Presently Bess put her hands on his shoulders and
pushed herself away from him.

'John,' she said in a dreamy voice, looking into his
eyes, ' I am glad it wasn't Mabel.   I'm a woman and
can bear it, but you're only a man—and you—you'd
have gone mad.'

And this was the character he had looked down
upon with affectionate half contempt !   His 'Thank
God !' of the night before, when the news came that
one had been taken and the other left, echoed mockingly in his ears.   He almost fiercely forced her head
down to his shoulder that he might not see her eyes.

'For pity's sake don't, Bess !   You will send me
mad now.'

Ruth heard the voices.   She and Mabel were comforting the children in the antimacassared parlour,

appropriated to the dignity of grief. She looked into the kitchen with a wife's pang of jealousy at brother and sister drawn so close together. It would be sacrilege to disturb them, and, touching the corners of her eyes with her apron, she withdrew as softly as she came. She could not go back to face the crying children. There was more peace and company in the bedroom, where she went to snuff a guttering candle beside the bed on which little Bessie lay.

CHAPTER V

'MAB, I want you to take the lunch to your father. Here are some scones for him and a piece of plum duff for Joe.'

Mab took the basket containing the 'lunch'—a bush term for any refreshment between meals—and made her way through the wheat crop to the latest piece of clearing, where Toland and Joe were hard at work trying to get the last of the maize sown before night. Joe was dropping the seed into the furrows ahead of his father, who was harrowing, and for some time his glance had been frequently directed homewards, as, boylike, he looked forward to the break in his monotonous work.

When Mab appeared round a clump of trees he walked over to his father.

'I'll take the horses, father, while you have your lunch.'

'All right, my boy, keep them going, and don't let the harrows get foul.'

Joe took the reins and Toland joined Mab, who had seated herself in the shade of a blackwood on the unploughed headland. He spent but a few minutes in having a cup of tea and filling his pipe, and then Joe took his place.

'What have you got, Mab? Anything worth eating?' he asked, throwing himself on the grass.

'Oh, there are some scones for you.'

'I say, what rot! We always have scones. You might make a chap some brownie sometimes. Hullo! what's that you're keeping in the basket for yourself?'

'Only some plum duff mother sent for you.'

'By Jove! mother's a good sort, isn't she, Mab?' said Joe, helping himself to his favourite indigestible. 'You wouldn't have thought of me like that.'

'I don't suppose I would have thought you worth bothering about,' said Mab, smiling good-naturedly.

'Oh, no, of course you wouldn't; but if Rupert Harlin had been having lunch with me you would have bothered all right—like the day we went out kangarooing together and I got such a doing from the boss for not telling him. Why, the feed you put up was worth the row, and Rupert Harlin said I was lucky to have a sister like that—and I said he might have you for the asking.'

'Joe, I'll box your ears,' said Mab, blushing.

'And we always have a tip-top spread when Mr Conyngham's here, but when it's only me you don't bother.'

'I don't believe you care for anything but eating and drinking, Joe,' said Mab.

'Yes, I do.'

'And what is it, then?'

'Teasing you, Mab.'

'Come on, Joe,' shouted his father. 'Are you going to stay there yarning all day?'

'Oh, I'm full of this,' said Joe, enigmatically, as he yawned and went off to his work. When he had got a short distance he turned round and called out, 'I say, Mab, don't take on about what I've been saying. You're not bad for a girl.'

Evidently much relieved in mind, Mab laughed,

and, having packed up her basket, returned to the cottage.

That evening Toland came up from work seemingly in high spirits.

'The last of the maize is in, missis,' he said as he threw himself into a chair. 'There's a hundred and eighty acres of wheat and oats, and twenty odd of maize. We ought to make a fortune this year.'

'I hope so, dear,' said Ruth, smiling.

'Do you know what I was thinking on the way up?' continued Toland.

'How to get rid of the rabbits?' asked Ruth.

'No, hang the rabbits! I was thinking that when I got home I would find a little wife with a pale face who has been married for eighteen years and has never had a single jaunt away, and who has toiled and slaved all that time without a murmur; and I said to myself, "there's a few pounds in the bank, a big harvest to be reaped—in a couple of months' time we'll have a trip to Melbourne to see the Cup run." What do you say?'

'I ought to say let us wait till the harvest is reaped and our fortune made, but I just can't, John, dear, for I should so like the change.'

Toland saw his wife's eyes were bright with anticipated pleasure and felt elated.

'Then it is settled we go,' he said, getting up and pacing the room. 'What shall we do with the children?'

'Oh, can't we take them too?' said Ruth, pleadingly; 'it would be such a treat and do them so much good.'

'Well, I suppose we might manage it,' said Toland, beginning to get almost boyishly excited at the idea of his first holiday. ' There will be cheap fares about that time and we needn't stay away long, and I have some bullocks that should be fit for market if we spend too much. I wonder what they'll say.'

At supper-time the subject was broached to them.

' Mother and I,' said Toland, ' are going for a trip to Melbourne at Cup time. Would you like to come with us, Mab?'

Mab beamed with delight and was about to reply, when she caught a glimpse of Joe's face as he held his knife and fork in mid-air and stared at his father.

' Will Joe be coming too?' she asked.

' I don't suppose he would care to,' said Toland, with pretended seriousness.

' Oh, I say, dad, what are you giving us?' broke in Joe. ' I'd just peg out if you left me behind. Rupert Harlin says it's great. They went in a four-in-hand, and the old man won a thousand on Blue-bottle in the hurdles—he carried thirteen stone and won in a canter. You'll make dad take me, won't you, mother?'

Ruth smiled at the boy's outburst and his want of tact in mentioning the Harlins' method of attending the great racing carnival.

' Oh, I think,' she replied, ' after your working so hard at that maize crop he'll have to take you.'

' All right, Joe,' said his father, ' we'll take you—but it won't be in a four-in-hand.'

So it was arranged that Mick should be secured to take charge of the farm and that a start should be made in ten days' time.

Those were busy days for Ruth, who had to get the family outfits ready. The aid of Bess was invoked and willingly given, and Mrs Harlin, hearing of the intended trip, sent a little present to her godchild.

Toland rode to Tongalong ostensibly to attend the local stock market, but in reality acting under instructions from Ruth, his destination being the tailoring department of the store at which he dealt.

Such a hitherto unheard-of thing as a farmer taking his family on a pleasure trip to Melbourne created quite a stir in the district, and many heads were shaken at the extravagance of it. Most of the selectors were so used to the round of never-ending toil and sordid hardships that they resented the idea of one of their number setting out in pursuit of enjoyment.

Scott was specially annoyed at the folly of it and had not a good word to say for the Tolands whilst preparations were being made for their departure. He even begrudged his wife the time she spent assisting Ruth, but this did not impede matters in the least, as Bess was too warm-hearted to sympathise with his churlishness, and paid no attention to his grumbling. He was particularly indignant with his brother-in-law for taking Joe, as he considered it was not only harmful to the boy, but also setting a bad example to Jimmy, who, instead of contentedly sticking to his work, could do nothing but chatter about trips to Melbourne. However, despite his disapproval and prophecies of evil, the start was made at last, Toland and Ruth feeling quite young again under the influence of the wild excitement of their children. As they drove through the cultivation paddocks Toland remarked to Ruth that he felt anxious about the crops since there had been no rain that month; but, once on the main road, he forgot everything in connection with the farm. He whipped up the horses and started singing to the accompaniment of the rattle of the trap. The children joined in, and then Ruth, smiling at her own lightheartedness.

But she easily excused herself. It was glorious to have left the farm with its drudgery and worries behind and to be setting out for a new world. It was spring-time too; the sun was warm; a cool south wind blew, driving here and there a fleecy cloud across the blue sky; green crops relieved the sombre colours of the forest. God seemed to be smiling on the land and bidding His children rejoice. Great, indeed, was the excitement of the next few days. All was so wonderful to the bush children, and much of it to their parents. The train journey from Tongalong, the city with its magnificent buildings and crowded streets, the mighty throng at the Cup, the roar that went up from seventy thousand throats as the winner flashed past the post, the theatre, and the myriad lights at night. Then there was the sea, which brought her childhood's days back to Ruth, and filled the children with amazement, not untinctured with chagrin, for the great lagoon on the Tonga, of which they had been so proud, seemed now but a puddle. A week was spent in sight-seeing, and then Ruth began to find her thoughts reverting, amid the din of the city and the stench of its by-ways, to the little home in the forest, and a yearning came over her to return there and rest. To Toland the new scenes brought varying moods. At one time he felt exhilarated by the rush of life around him, at another depressed by the contrast between wealth and poverty. He watched the carriages roll by in Collins Street and wondered if their owners had worked harder than the farmers. He saw fat old dowagers reclining on the cushioned seats trying to appear like aristocrats at ease, and he thought how much better his wife would look than they. On the other hand, he saw for the first time in Australia men begging for food, women sunk to the lowest depths of degradation, ragged children earning stray coppers in the streets. His individuality, he felt, had vanished in the alien throng ; he was a nonentity whom nobody knew or gave a thought to. Sometimes a passer-by would turn in the street to glance at the powerful form that towered over the average townsman, or to smile at the group of country visitors, but friendly recognition he had from none, and he found the loneliness of the city greater than that of the bush. There were problems, too, that puzzled him sorely. Where does the wealth come from ? Why are they so rich and we so poor ? were questions he constantly put to himself, and which he left unanswered with the reflection, ' I'll talk to Conyngham about it when I get home.'

One incident of his visit deeply impressed him. He was walking along Bourke Street, admiring a great wool warehouse, when he was attracted by a crowd on a vacant allotment that graces with a heap of jam tins and other rubbish the centre of the city. About four hundred men, sullen and hopeless-looking for the most part, were listening to the speech which was being delivered from the vantage ground of a heap of road metal. The speaker was a thin, wiry, nervous-looking man, undersized in stature, harsh in voice, but in whose eye the fire of fanaticism glowed. Toland's attention was riveted by the first sentence he heard. ' They said,' shouted the man, as he waved his clenched fist, 'that they would make this land a paradise for the working man, but they've made it a hell. They said every honest man would be able to earn a living, but instead we are starving. They brought us here to make homes, but we're digging our graves. They tell us now to go to the country to look for work, but those who collared the land will only throw a man some scraps and tell him to clear. So all that's left is to tramp the roads and keep on tramping, for if a man stops to rest or to die he'll be run into gaol. This is our paradise, friends, and the monopolists are the gods that made it! So down with them, I say, down with them to hell!'

Quivering with passion, the man sprang from the stone heap whilst a murmur ran through the crowd. Toland, who was moved by the fierce earnestness of the speaker, whose every tone seemed to tell of a wrong endured, turned to a policeman who was standing next him.

'What's the meeting about?' he asked.

'It's the unemployed; they come here every day to do a bit of spouting.'

The next speaker was inaudible from where Toland stood, so he turned away and resumed his walk, troubled in mind and dispirited, for he felt that another nail had been driven into the coffin he saw slowly but surely being prepared for the hopes of his early years. Not in this land then, after all, neither in town nor in country, was the prophecy to be fulfilled which he had laid to his heart, and he muttered sardonically to himself as he walked along :—

'For a' that, and a' that
It's coming yet for a' that,
That man to man the wide warld o'er
Shall brithers be, for a' that.'

After they had been in the city a week they all began to long for home, not excepting the children, who were jaded with excitement, and whose feet were sore and limbs weary from walking on the pavements. Joe especially wanted to get back and grow quickly big enough to become a mounted trooper, the Governor's escort at the Cup having determined his future career. It was, therefore, decided to return forthwith, and next day, as the sun was sinking, the little party drew near their home.

'Isn't the air delicious after that of the town?' said Ruth.

'It is indeed,' replied Toland, drawing into his capacious lungs a great draught of the cool night air, fragrant with the scent of the blossoming gums. ' I don't know how men can live in those filthy streets; I should die of disgust in a month.'

'I shouldn't like it either,' said Ruth, 'so you needn't worry any more about my being shut up in the bush. After all, there's no place like home.'

'Out you get, Joe!' said his father, a minute later, as they drew up at the gate of the cultivation paddock. 'It's dark to see properly, but, by Jove! I don't like the look of the crop; it wants rain badly.'

When they reached the cottage they found old Mick ready to receive them; a welcoming light shone through the kitchen door, and a fire roared up the chimney.

'Good evening, Mick! No rain yet.'

'Good evening, sor! Divil a drop, and the crops needing it bad.'

'My pup all right, Mick?' burst in Joe.

'He is that, but I'll not be answering for the fowls he has kilt.'

'The boy's no good, Mick,' said Toland, as he lifted Ruth down ; 'he wants to be a policeman.'

'And that's what they're all wanting to be,' said Mick. 'The lads are all for rushing off to the town and the vanities of it. Miss Mab'll not be running off though, I'll be bound.'

'No, Mick,' replied Mab, with a merry laugh. 'I don't want to be a policeman, but I want the cob in the morning, though, to have a good ride round with father.'

'All right, miss ; he's nice and handy, and I've been giving him a bite in the stable whilst you've been gone.'

'That was good of you, and I didn't forget you, Mick ; I have brought you a pound of tobacco, and I hope you'll like it.'

Mab gave the old man a parcel, and then ran into the kitchen to help her mother and escape his thanks. That night when husband and wife were alone, Toland said,—

'Well, missis, what do you think of it all ? '

'I've enjoyed it very much, dear, and it was very good of you to take me, but I feel as if I didn't want to go again. I like the peace of our home, and I never knew how beautiful it was, or how fond I had become of it till I went away. I am afraid I have been discontented, but I promise to turn over a new leaf.'

'You discontented ! Why, you are the most patient little body in the world, and the best wife man ever had. I'm glad to be back too. Not that I like peace myself. I like strife. I hate a sluggish life, and it's I who have been discontented. But life in the town wouldn't content me. I wouldn't

K

like to be one of that sickly-looking lot, each one
hurrying along to swindle someone else. I used
to feel that with my back to a wall I could take
a dozen of them. Yet they're much cleverer than
us bush folk. They despise us for being stupid
fools. They make the laws and ride on our backs
and live on us, so Conyngham says, and I believe it's
God's truth. But I'd sooner toil in the sun and sleep
under the stars than be one of them and fill my lungs
with the stench of their filthy streets. Why farmers'
sons are rushing off into their factories, and to serve
behind their counters licks me. I'd despise a son
of mine who'd do it.'

Ruth smiled at her husband's outburst.

'It's just as well, John, you don't want to live
in the town, for I'm sure you would always be
getting into trouble—especially if you had Mr
Conyngham to make you want to fight everybody
about everything. I think I'll have to warn him
of the bad effect he has upon you.'

Toland laughed good-humouredly.

'Oh, Conyngham's all right, and has got as soft a
heart as anybody, though he tries to hide it more
than most. He's made a failure of life somehow,
and if he didn't gird at things with his tongue, I
believe he'd go mad. I know I should if I were
in his shoes.'

'Yes,' said Ruth, sympathetically. 'I feel very
sorry for him when he comes and sits by our fire-
side, and no doubt wishes he had one of his own.
It's miserable, too, when he goes out in the night
for his long ride to the Scotts.'

'Mother,' called Joe, from his little back room, 'I
want to speak to you.'

'Very well, I'm coming. Good-night, John, dear. I think I'll go to bed, for I'm tired. Don't sit up brooding, like a good man.'

'No, I'm coming as soon as I've finished my pipe. And there's nothing to brood over. It's grand to see you looking better. Go and have a good sleep, for it's work again to-morrow. I'm afraid we left our trip too late, little mother; we have got to be like a horse that is used to the furrow and is no use out of it.'

Ruth smiled and kissed him—for they were lovers still—and passed out.

'What is it, Joe?' she asked, as she put her head in at the boy's door.

'Mother, how long will it be before I can be a mounted trooper?'

'Go to sleep, dear, and don't be a stupid,' she replied, and went to bed, leaving Joe to dream of a fairyland in which, clad in blue cloth, white corduroys and resplendent helmet, and mounted on a prancing steed, he protected Her Majesty's representative from the too close presence of the multitude at the Melbourne Cup.

CHAPTER VI

WHEN Toland rode round his farm with Mab the morning after their return from Melbourne, his heart sank within him, for he saw that, without heavy rain in a few days' time, the crops would be a failure. Already, though the flag was not a foot high, here and there an ear of wheat could be seen—a fateful sign. The oats, being a later crop, looked more hopeful, but were beginning to go back from lack of moisture. The maize was above the ground, but, instead of being dark green, was tinged with yellow. The grass was rapidly drying up, and all round were signs that summer had set in a month too soon—a small thing to some, and yet threatening widespread ruin throughout the land.

'It's a bad lookout,' said Toland, as he glanced across the drought-stricken crop. 'If it doesn't rain soon it won't be worth cutting even for hay.'

'Oh, father, wouldn't that be dreadful? And there is no sign of a change.'

'None; it looks as if it would never rain again.' He turned his horse's head and rode back towards the cottage, followed silently and sorrowfully by Mab.

Nevertheless, Nature, animate and inanimate, seemed full of rejoicing. The great heat had not yet come, though the haze was beginning to dim the outline of the distant hills. The sunshine had a delicious warmth, and there were cool puffs from a changeful breeze, while fleecy clouds drifted aimlessly across the blue sky. The days of the summer silence, broken only by the skirr of the locusts, were not yet. Magpies sang with full mellow notes, jays chattered and shrieked in the creek timber, and flocks of parrots tinged the orchard with scarlet. It was spring without the refreshing showers, come like a lovely wanton to wither and destroy.

When Toland and Mab reached the cottage they found Ruth waiting on the verandah to hear their report.

'Well, how do the crops look?' she asked as they dismounted.

'Not very splendid. They want rain badly,' replied Toland, in a voice that was intended to be cheerful, as he had determined to save Ruth as much as possible from anxiety.

'I'm so sorry,' she said sympathetically; 'it would be too disappointing if they failed.'

'Don't you worry, little woman,' he replied. 'Even supposing they did fail we'd survive all right, though I must say I'd like to see a couple of inches.'

Day followed day without a rain-cloud appearing in the oft-scanned sky, and then, at the end of a fortnight, a change took place. From daylight clouds gathered on the horizon to the north and gradually rolled up the valley before the wind, growing darker and sinking lower as the day passed. The air was sultry and full of dust, borne along in mighty volumes. All sounds of life were hushed and the stillness that betokens an impending convulsion lay on everything. Toland and Joe worked hard to get in some potatoes before the rain, whilst Ruth and Mab busied themselves in planting vegetable seeds. About four o'clock black thunder-clouds massed themselves to the north and began an onward march in force. In an hour's time they had wholly overspread the sky, and then the battle of the elements began. From east to west a flash of lightning zig-zagged its way and a distant peal of thunder sounded a deep warning. Toland and Joe ran up to the cottage to escape the deluge that seemed to be at hand, and joined Ruth and Mabel on the verandah. Nearer and nearer drew the artillery of the storm, while in the darkening sky black clouds rolled over one another in charging squadrons. Then a splash of rain fell, and the drops were red like blood from the dust overhead that had been whirled up five hundred miles away. In a few seconds it ceased and there was a dead silence. Then right across the north darted a swift gleam of flame, followed by a thunderclap that made the little party shrink. Flash followed upon flash, peal upon peal; the forked lightning ran here and there, slashing the black pall with sword-strokes of fire ; the skies resolved themselves into one wild turmoil ; below, the wind howled with increasing fury.

'Hurrah! here it comes!' shouted Toland, above the roar of the storm, as a torrent of rain descended.

Ruth framed a silent prayer of thankfulness. Mab and Joe rushed inside to fasten the banging doors and windows.

For about ten minutes the rain pelted down and then suddenly ceased, while at the same time the wind dropped.

'Hang it!' said Toland, 'I hope that's not all we're going to have.'

'Oh, it can't be,' replied Ruth. 'Why, look at the sky!' Almost as she spoke a puff of wind blew off her hat.

'The wind has changed,' he said as he picked it up. 'We were sheltered before. If it goes round to the south it will be over.'

Husband and wife anxiously watched the progress of the storm. Every moment it seemed as if a deluge must fall, and at the same time they feared to see the clouds driven back from the south, the quarter from which rain never came. The wind for a while veered towards all quarters, and at last it seemed to make up its mind and blew steadily from the south. It increased in fury till it whistled and howled through the tree-tops and round the cottage. The advance of the rain-clouds from the north was checked, and then turned into a rout. At first they were driven back in mass, but, when the fierceness of the onslaught increased, they were dispersed in all directions and hurried from the sky in thunder-growling fragments. Blue sky appeared here and there and everywhere, and in an hour not a rain-cloud was to be seen. Then the south wind, having done its work, sank to a cool and pleasant breeze.

'By Jove! that's hard luck,' said Toland, in bitter disappointment, as all hope of rain and salvation from loss disappeared. Ruth felt inclined to cry and took his arm affectionately.

'It may rain before long, dear ; one never can tell.'

'This sort of thing is the sure sign of a big drought. It's all up with the crops now,' replied Toland, gloomily.

'Come to tea,' called Mab from the kitchen, and, with little inclination to eat, they went inside and sat down to the evening meal.

A week later Toland announced to Ruth that he was going over to the station to see if he could buy some sheep off the shears to fatten.

'But what are you going to fatten them on?' she asked.

'I'm going to turn them into the cultivation paddock. I've given up all hope of cutting any crop this year.'

'Oh, John! Is there no hope?'

'None at all. A foot of rain would do them no good.'

'I suppose it can't be helped, but how are we going to live and pay our debts?'

'Oh we'll pull through all right somehow or another—don't you worry and make yourself ill. That's what I'm afraid of. It's worse to see this pale face than the withered crops.'

'It's kind of you to think of me as you do, dear, when you have so much to trouble you.'

'No, it isn't. Don't you see you're something pleasant to think of. Now promise not to work too hard just because things look a little blue.'

'Of course I won't. I've quite an easy time now with Mab to help me. Couldn't you take her with you? The poor child never gets any enjoyment.'

'I think I'd rather not,' he replied; 'she'd better stay with you.'

'Very well, dear,' said Ruth, reading the unexpressed thoughts in his face, 'perhaps she might be in the way.'

When Toland rode off Mab put down the book

she had been reading and joined her mother, who was topping and tailing gooseberries in the verandah in the shade of the vines.

'Mother,' she said, 'I don't like going for the mail nowadays.'

'Why, dear?' asked her mother in some surprise.

'I hate that man Mallock. He will talk to me if he possibly can, and of course he gets the chance when I ask for the letters.'

'Does he ever say anything you dislike?'

'No, not exactly, but he tries to be very fascinating, and asks after you and father as if he were a friend of the family, but all the time he has such a horrid look in his eyes.'

'I can't bear him either,' said Ruth, shivering.

'I've always hated him,' continued Mab, 'since a long time ago when I was a little thing staying with Aunt Bess. I went for the mail, and Mallock offered me a big packet of lollies if I would give him a kiss, and then he said he wouldn't give me the letters unless I did. I was so frightened that I ran out and got on the pony and rode off. When I told Aunt Bess she gave Mallock a talking to, but he only laughed and said something with a sneer about her having to come to him on her own business some day that frightened her.'

'He's a horrible man,' said Ruth, 'and you must go to the store as little as possible.'

'I don't want to go at all if I can help it. I went one day with that little wretch, Jimmy, and when we came out he said, "Isn't it a joke old Mallock making eyes at you?" I would have liked to box his ears.'

'That was very wrong of him,' said Ruth, glancing in fond admiration at her daughter, thinking how much she resembled her father when her eyes flashed in anger. 'You mustn't go there any more. But you must say nothing to your father. Half what you have told me would make him kill Mallock.'

'I'd almost like to see him do it,' said Mab. 'How he would crush him in his great arms!'

'Mab, my child, don't say such things. I'm always afraid of what your father might do if put into a passion by some wrong. You must promise not to make him hate Mallock more.'

'Of course I won't, mother dear,' replied Mab as she kissed her. 'I'll go for the letters sometimes so that he won't have any suspicion; and anyhow Mallock can't eat me.'

'No, you mustn't do that,' said Ruth, stroking her daughter's soft hair. 'We won't talk of it any more, but I'm glad you told me.'

Though Toland spoke very confidently to his wife before starting on his ride to the station, his later thoughts scarcely confirmed the hopeful views then expressed. Like his neighbours he lived on what he was going to make. After each harvest accumulated liabilities were more or less paid off and a fresh career on credit started. Such had grown to be the recognised business understanding between the farmers and the storekeepers, whose assistance alone enabled men with insufficient capital to make a start upon the land. Consequently Toland deeply cursed the misfortune that had befallen him which seemed to render inevitable what he had striven so hard to avoid, namely, an increase of the mortgage on the farm. Further hard work, care and disappointment he felt he could face as directly affecting himself, but the bitterness came when he thought of those dependent on him. More especially when he thought of Ruth, his comrade and mainstay, and saw in the future no hope of escape from the toil, monotony and anxiety that were beginning to tell upon her. Then, when he left the road and crossed the flats on Kumbarra, he fell to musing once more on social inequalities and to wondering why Harlin's wife should have every luxury that wealth could procure, whilst his own had to bear the scourge of poverty. How could Ruth, he asked himself, have suggested he should bring Mab with him? Now that he was going down hill he must be more careful to see that they did not come to be regarded as pensioners on the bounty of the Harlins.

The shearing shed was about a mile from the house and now easily to be located by the shouting of musterers, the barking of dogs and the bleating of sheep. When Toland reached it he found operations in full swing, and not seeing Harlin about, he stood for a while and watched the busy scene. Twenty-five shearers were hard at work and the short, sharp clip of their shears filled the shed with sound, notwithstanding the bleating from a thousand throats. Each man worked as if for dear life, the 'ringer,' or highest tally man, for honour and glory as well, while the heat of the iron roof, the stooping position, and the hot bodies of the panting sheep bathed the shearers' faces and limbs in sweat. No one spoke, except to curse a tarboy or rouseabout for not being at hand when wanted, and for thereby causing the loss of a valuable minute, or to mutter an oath as the boss of the board passed by with a caution for a gash or a second cut. Penners-up bustled along the sheep with wild yells; rouseabouts hurried up and down the board, bearing away the fleeces; skirters tore at them on the table with eager haste, for the classer was doing his work with but a glance and tug at the staple. The press squeaked and groaned as two sinewy giants swung on the lever; and a few seconds later there was hammering at clamps, and yet another bale rolled out on the floor, to be branded and started on its trip round the world.

After a while Toland asked one of the pressers if Mr Harlin was anywhere about.

'No, but there's M'Intyre,' he replied, indicating Harlin's factotum, who was walking towards them.

Toland went up to him.

'Good-day; I want to see Mr Harlin.'

'Well, you'll not see him to-day,' said M'Intyre, looking at him suspiciously as one of those infernal cockies who had helped to spoil the run.

'Isn't he up at the homestead?' asked Toland.

'Yes, he's up there,' replied M'Intyre after a moment's hesitation, 'but he doesn't want to be bothered to-day. Is there anything I can do for ye?'

'No, thank you. If he's up at the house I'll go and see him, and I don't care a damn if he wants to be bothered or not. I've come to see if he will sell some stores off the shears, and don't want to come again.' So saying he turned and walked out of the shed.

M'Intyre followed him.

'Look here, Mr Toland,' he said, 'I think I might fix that for ye, and I know Mr Harlin will not be wanting to see ye, not feeling well this morn.'

'Well, he can tell me so himself,' replied Toland, annoyed at M'Intyre's manner. 'Why shouldn't he? Has he become such a great man as all that?'

'Have ye no understanding, ye great galoot?'
said M'Intyre, irascibly, as Toland prepared to mount
his horse. 'D'ye think a mon that's drinking his
bottle o' whisky a day can do a deal in sheep?'

'Good Lord! You don't mean to say that Harlin
drinks like that!' exclaimed Toland in surprise.

'That's aboot it,' replied M'Intyre; 'and excep' that
I wadna hae ye go to the house and the missis have
the turnin' awa of ye, it's nae a word I'd hae telled ye.
Ye may as well get back and I'll send word if Mr
Harlin will sell. Keep your mouth shut, as the boss
only goes fair off his head once in a whiles and the
missis don't like it known.'

Toland's thoughts on his homeward ride were very
different from those in which he had indulged so
shortly before. Too generous-minded to rejoice in
the knowledge of any man's failing, his thoughts
centred themselves, not upon Harlin, but upon his
wife.

In an instant she stood transformed in his eyes.
She appeared no longer the haughty, purse-proud
woman, raised above his own wife by the witchcraft
of fortune, but as a sufferer who also bore her burden
bravely in solitude. He could now understand there
being a bond of sympathy between Mrs Harlin and
Ruth, and he began to reproach himself for churlishly
hindering its expansion. When he reached home he
found Ruth lying down, as she often had to do from
sheer exhaustion during the great heat of the afternoon. He sat down beside her and said quietly,—

'Why didn't you tell me that Harlin was a
drunkard?'

'Oh, you didn't see him like that, did you? Poor
Margaret!'

'Why didn't you tell me, when you knew I judged her wrongly and thought she only wanted to patronise us? She has her trouble and leads a lonely life on account of it, and I've helped to make it a little harder by keeping you away from her.'

'She told me the secret she has kept for so long, and I promised never to tell a soul. She has been very lonely since Rupert went to school and her little daughter died of diphtheria, and once she said she envied me.'

'I owe her gratitude on account of Mabel,' said Toland, gloomily, 'and have paid her in different coin. I'm sorry, but it can't be helped. I'll try and think a bit more kindly of her and hers.'

'She's a noble woman,' said Ruth.

'It's a pity she's a squatter's wife, and that we're only what they call "blasted cockies,"' said Toland, somewhat coldly, as he picked up his hat and walked out of the room.

CHAPTER VII

DECEMBER, that should have ushered in the ripening summer, differed only in its longer days of shimmering heat from the preceding month, credited by the calendar to a never-existing spring. The sun shone perhaps a little hotter, a few early wheat-fields yellowed rapidly with starved heads of pinched grain, but cattle were grazing most of the sowed paddocks; and very few reaping-machines left their sheds to be put in gear for harvest.

Toland bore his losses philosophically, and to Scott, who grumbled all day long at disasters less severe, it seemed curious, and in a measure a personal affront, that his brother-in-law should be in a more equable frame of mind than he had been for several past years. Analysing neither his own feelings nor Toland's, Scott did not recognise that buffets from Fate and Nature had called forth from Toland a grim fortitude, not always proof against social wrongs; and he would have learnt with surprise that he himself had long derived a soothing sense of superiority and blessedness from comparing his good crops and good temper with Toland's smaller yields and increasing bitterness.

'Cleaned up' for tea, he leaned on the garden gate in his shirt sleeves, watching the last crimson of a fiery sunset fade from the sky. 'Another cursed scorcher to-morrow,' he muttered, and turned his eyes upon a pair of riders cantering down the dusty road towards his gate.

Bess came out from the verandah and slipped her arm through his.

'That'll be Mabel and Joe,' she said. 'I thought likely they'd be here for tea to-night.'

'It seems to me you might think it likely any night and not be far wrong,' answered Scott, surlily.

'You're surely not grudging them the bit they eat?'

'Of course I'm not,' replied Scott, a little ashamed, 'and it's not that they come after. Isn't young Harlin coming to-night to see Mr Conyngham?' he added with a cunning grin.

Bess bunched the cornflowers she had gathered into a satisfactorily compact mass and laughed.

'You're very clever, but you've got the cart before the horse. Mabel didn't know Rupert Harlin was coming, but I'm not saying that he didn't guess she was. And what's the harm?'

'Who talked about harm? But it's a bit of dashed nonsense all the same, and you know John wouldn't like it.'

'There's many a good thing John doesn't like— John's queer, but I must say I've not seen him so quiet and reasonable-like for many a long day.'

'Quiet enough,' assented Scott, with an irritated laugh, 'but I'm hanged if I see how he's so reasonable. Wasn't he going about with a long face talking about his stolen rights and fool talk like that, cursing and damning every well-to-do man in the neighbourhood when things was going right enough with him? And now, though I'll have a bag or two of wheat for every bushel he sees, you'd think from his happy face that he was an angel with a ten-bag crop.'

His pipe went automatically into his mouth after this long deliverance.

'Don't smoke now—tea'll be directly,' said Bess, taking the plug from his hand. 'So you're cross with poor old John for getting a bit contented.' She smiled rather sadly and sighed. 'It's a blessed thing for poor Ruth. Time was I set myself above her, but since little Bessie went—'

'None o' that,' interrupted Scott, with a roughness that stood for sympathy. 'Jack's right enough, but why the dickens don't he growl when he's got something to growl about? That's what I'd like to know.'

His problem was unanswered, and he gave Bess no time to consider the matter.

'Joe, you young vagabond!' he bawled in salutation to the pair just arrived within shouting distance. 'If you bring that pack of mongrels down here again I'll kick you off the place. D'ye hear?'

Joe heard, but his reply was fortunately inaudible, and a second later, dismounting and taking his sister's horse, the boy walked off to the stable-yard.

Mabel flicked the dust from her riding-skirt as she went, and strolled up to the garden gate, followed by four kangaroo dogs.

'It's not Joe's fault; they are my dogs, uncle,' she said, laughing. 'And if you call them mongrels again I won't come near the place, do you hear that?'

She kissed her aunt and shook hands with her uncle, whose face showed that her at least he was pleased to see.

'Don't shut the gate,' she advised him. 'They will only jump the fence and do more harm to your flower-beds, and really, if you shut up all the cats I don't see that they can get into much mischief.'

L

'You're a cool hand, Mab, but I'm glad to see you, my dear—dogs and all—dash 'em!'

Scott was fond of his wife's pretty, high-spirited niece, though he often suspected she was making fun of him, and sometimes she openly ruffled his dignity. But his displeasure was never long proof against a penitent speech, when she would show nothing but the long lashes of her grey eyes, avoiding his small peering ones lest she should hurt his feelings by laughing again in the midst of her apology. He compared her mentally with his daughter Bessie, whose loss he felt as much as he could feel anything, but admitted to himself that Bessie would never have been Mabel's equal. His wife, too, took Mabel closer to her heart now that her eldest daughter was gone, but if she ever compared the girls, it was not to find her idealised Bessie inferior. However, on another point she was clearer sighted than her husband, and knew that his hopes of making a match some day between Mabel and her cousin, Jimmy Scott, were doomed to disappointment—a fact which she regarded with resignation in view of other and more romantic imaginings for Mabel's future.

She encouraged young Harlin, who had discovered many knotty points in his vacation studies to visit the house and consult upon them with Conyngham. Scott was pleased to see the squatter's son, since, in conversation with his neighbours, there was a pleasing sound about such casual remarks as, 'When Rupert Harlin was at my place last night,' or, 'as I was saying to young Rupert at tea,' and others of the kind, conveying an impression of familiar relations with Kumbarra.

Harlin was not at tea that evening. Scott refused

to put on his coat for Mabel, who wasn't a fine lady—yet—he said meaningly. Joe and Jim wrangled, occasionally getting in a satisfactory kick at one another's shins, and four smaller Scotts, constituting a later crop, giggled and smeared themselves with treacle at the end of the table. Mab sat next Conyngham, answering his questions concerning her home affairs in the intervals of talk with her aunt and uncle, with a pause now and again to eat a mouthful.

By-and-by the springs of Scott's humour were loosened by beef and scones and he turned it upon Joe.

'Have you got your handcuffs about you, Joseph, my lad? No? Perhaps you've got a baton stuffed under your waistcoat, then—or is it only pudding and potatoes?'

Jimmy laughed disagreeably, and Joe, flushing, intimated *sotto voce* that he was quite equal to bashing his cousin's head in without the aid of a baton.

'Joe doesn't want handcuffs and batons,' said Mabel, scornfully. 'He's going to be a mounted trooper with a revolver and sword.'

'Why don't he stick to honest farming work instead of meddling with such things? That's what I want to know.'

'That is his business, isn't it—and father's?'

Joe went on with his tea, feeling that his battles were safe in Mabel's hands. Scott laughed and said he was only having a bit of fun, and Conyngham changed the subject by asking Mabel if she had read the novel that he had sent to her mother.

Joe and Jim who, though quarrelsome, were fairly

good friends, went off after tea to fish in a deep reach of the Tonga where perch and cod bit well on the warm nights. Rupert Harlin arrived before the boys started, but declined, after some hesitation, to accompany them. It would be very jolly, he said, but he had come to ask Mr Conyngham to construe a difficult passage in Virgil with him. Mab suggested that there would be plenty of time for the translation when he returned from the river, whereat he grew red but stuck to his point, and Conyngham good-naturedly interfered, saying that he should be writing later on but that he would be glad to spare half an hour for the Latin if Harlin came to his room at once.

Mabel got up when Harlin and the schoolmaster were leaving the kitchen, saying that she believed she would go down herself to see what sport the boys were having, and Conyngham smiled at the cloud of anger and disappointment he saw cross Harlin's expressive features.

Rupert Harlin, at twenty, was a fine-looking fellow, tall like his mother, with her dark eyes and clear skin, and his lithe figure showed to advantage in the dark coat with boots and riding-breeches that he wore. He was a lover worth tormenting, Conyngham reflected, and Mabel was a fortunate girl to have the doing of it. That Harlin was, or would be, in love with Mabel, and that she would take advantage of the fact to hurt his vanity and make him miserable in a dozen ways, it never occurred to Conyngham to doubt. In his philosophy all properly-constituted young men of twenty fell in love with the prettiest girl of their acquaintance—sometimes with two or three—and if Mabel had

denied emphatically that she knew Harlin admired
her, or that her determination to go fishing was
designed to disconcert him, he would have accepted
the assurance and put the incident down to sub-
conscious feminine cerebration, working true to type.
Human nature interested him. His thoughts were
upon it more than the Latin, in this case with a
kindly bias towards the particular examples of it,
which he condemned as unphilosophic ; and Harlin,
with his thoughts on the mosquito-haunted river
bank, was cursing Virgil and trying to think hard
things of Mabel.

'Ah, yes! The moods in those indirect questions
are sometimes puzzling,' said Conyngham, closing
the book with a yawn when the farce had continued
for ten minutes. He looked at Harlin with a
quizzical smile. 'I believe you might catch them
now, if you ran fast enough and are not too proud.'

Harlin met his glance with surprise, and reddened.

'I don't know what you mean,' he began with an
attempt at haughtiness. Then he laughed and
corrected himself. 'At least I do—but I think it's
rather rough on a fellow to rot him like that, you
know—and I won't run after anybody. I'm going
home. Good-night, Mr Conyngham.'

'Good-night! As a type you are perhaps commonplace. For you, individually, I confess to interest—
almost to sympathy. Come again.'

He got up and gravely opened the door for the
puzzled boy, who passed into the yard, uncertain
whether to be amused or angry. Conyngham went
back to his armchair, and, clasping his hands behind
his head, gazed at the damp-stained ceiling.

'Ah, Youth, Youth!' he sighed. 'How important

you are, and how eternally the same! She goes fishing to avoid you now. Ten years hence you will go fishing, and she will cry and think you do it to avoid her—whether you do or not.' Conyngham felt for his pipe while his thoughts wandered from Mabel's and Rupert's affairs to his own ; and he found himself patterning a face—with some of the features like Mabel's—too distinctly on the canvas overhead. ' This won't do,' he muttered, checking himself. ' Old fools are as bad as young ones—and not so honest.'

Meanwhile Harlin, in an injured frame of mind, walked round the house from the schoolmaster's room towards the kitchen to say good-night to the Scotts.

Bess was putting the younger children to bed, and Mabel looked up with a smile at Harlin's bewildered expression as his eye fell on her sitting at the end of the table playing draughts with her uncle.

Without a moon it was too rough a track that led through thistles and bracken to the river, she explained, so she had changed her mind about the fishing ; and Rupert had just presence of mind to change his before betraying his intention of immediate departure. He brought a chair to the table, and was silently happy, in spite of a snub he received for suggesting a move to Mabel, who won the game with three kings to spare.

Scott grumbled, gave several convincing reasons why he should have won, and then turned his attention to Harlin, questioning him about his parents and the station affairs with a mixture of familiarity and deference which grated on Mabel, while the scarcely-veiled distaste with which Rupert answered them put her further on edge.

The Toland blood in her resented the difference, to which she could not blind herself, between the tone and station of her relative and his visitor.

'Do stop talking about droughts and sheep,' she said at last. 'I get so tired of them at home.'

'It's the first time I ever heard you had any sheep at home, my dear,' rejoined Scott.

'There are lots—getting thin in our best wheat paddock, and we have enough drought to make up, at anyrate,' she laughed. 'Come and play me draughts, Mr Harlin—I'm almost sure I can beat you; and the winner can give uncle another beating.'

Harlin knew nothing about the game, but as he was not anxious to win that was of small importance, and he willingly took Scott's seat. They were arranging the draughtsmen when the dogs roused themselves and rushed barking out to the gate.

'Another visitor!' growled Scott. 'It looks as if the whole country was coming down on me to-night.'

Mabel's and Rupert's eyes met in a smile of sympathy.

'Isn't that nice for you, uncle?' she said sweetly, holding black and white men behind her back for Harlin to choose from. 'Are you going to see who it is?'

Scott had already gone, and Harlin was nervously congratulating himself on being alone with Mabel, wondering what use to make of such a boon, when it was snatched from him by the re-entrance of Mrs Scott, bearing marks of the final tussle with recalcitrant bed-goers.

'They'll be the death of me!' she sighed. 'And Georgie's really getting too big to bite.'

'You surely don't bite him, aunt!' exclaimed Mabel in astonished tones.

'Mercy, no! The idea! I mean for him to be at such tricks—seven years old, you know, and with teeth like—oh, get along, Mab! You're always making fun with that solemn face.' Bess laughed, joining in a merry peal from Mab and Rupert, and pulled down the sleeve she was rolling up to evidence Georgie's dental atrocities.

'I beg your pardon, Aunt Bess. It is a shame to tease you,' said Mabel. 'It's your move, Mr Harlin; it always is your move.'

Bess took her work-bag from a shelf and inquired what had become of her husband when he and the just-arrived visitor entered the room together.

'Here's Mr Mallock has just dropped in as it were to give us a look up,' said Scott, announcing his guest with an embarrassed attempt at heartiness.

'That's kind now. I'm glad to see you,' joined in Bess, hospitably mendacious, shaking hands and dusting a spotless chair for the visitor.

'Thank you, ma'am,' said Mallock. 'I hoped you'd take it that way. I thought to myself to-night, "It's small use having good neighbours like Mr and Mrs Scott if you don't sometimes drop in, and better late than never!" So, as it was a fine night, with not much business doing, I just saddled my horse, and here I am.'

Harlin glanced with surprise at Mabel, who had swept the draughts off the board and risen from her seat at the far end of the table.

'Beast!' she muttered, with an angry gleam in her eyes.

'Steady,' whispered Rupert, admiringly. 'He'll hear you.'

'I don't care if he does.'

It did not seem that Mallock had heard. He appeared to have only just become aware of the young people's presence, and came towards them with outstretched hand and the thick red lips parted in a wider smile.

'Well, I *am* in luck,' he said. 'Who'd ha' thought to meet Miss Mabel and Master Rupert here? It's bringin' a lot of pretty young birds down with one stone and no mistake.'

Mabel vouchsafed an unwilling 'good evening,' but coldly and deliberately ignored the hand he offered, keeping both her own behind her back. Harlin, with less dignity, dived beneath the table in search of an imaginary draughtsman, remaining there chuckling to himself till the danger was past. He would have readily cut Mallock in the open, but had some scruples about adding a knock-out blow to Mabel's, when the man was a fellow-guest, however unwelcome, in another man's house.

Mallock, however, was not disconcerted. He had heard that Mabel was at the farm, and to see her was the purpose of his visit ; but he was aware she did not like him, and, reckoning on some day making her change her tune, he choked a sudden impulse of rage and turned, smiling still, towards Mr and Mrs Scott.

'I am going home, aunt,' announced Mabel, calmly.

'Gracious, child ! it's not after nine yet, and Joe won't be home for an hour.'

'I don't care. I must set the bread or mother will do it. Mr Harlin will see me home—won't you?'

Rupert nearly jumped with delight as she turned to him, but he managed to say fairly soberly that he would be very pleased, and started off to get the horses.

'I will go with you to the stables,' said Mabel, 'if you wait half a minute.' Her cap was hanging on the wall. Her farewells were short. Bess was flustered, Scott angry, Mallock inscrutable and self-contained, not risking a second snub. Scott blunderingly suggested that Toland might not like Mabel riding home alone with a young man. Mabel blushed furiously, but managed to laugh.

'It's very kind of you, uncle,' she said, 'to take such an interest in father's affairs, but really he can manage them for himself.'

'Much chance you give him,' muttered Scott with some justice as Mabel left the room, and Mallock, chuckling, said girls would be girls, and he liked a filly with a bit of devil in her.

'I hate him—I can't breathe in the same room with him!' said Mabel with a long sigh when they got into the open air.

'You certainly let him see pretty straight what you thought,' laughed Harlin. 'He's a bad man to offend, though.'

Mabel sniffed contemptuously. 'I'll offend who I choose,' she said.

In a minute or two they had started on their ride, and talked of indifferent subjects for a time, Rupert despairingly watching mile after mile of his longed-for opportunity go by without venturing to say anything the whole world might not hear.

'Why do you hate Mallock so awfully much?' he asked at length.

'For every reason.' The darkness hid her blushes. She felt impelled to tell Rupert, and she continued, after a pause, 'Most of all, I think, because I believe he actually wants to make love to me.'

Rupert's horse gave a sudden bound, the victim of a vicious stroke of the spurs intended in fancy for Mallock.

'The old blackguard!' he said. 'I can scarcely even imagine him daring.' Then, with a nervous gulp, 'You wouldn't hate everyone who fell in love with you, would you?'

'No one else ever has,' answered Mabel, non-committingly.

'Yes, they have. I have,' he said boldly, the words coming freely enough now, 'ever so much and for ever.' He reined his horse closer to Mabel's and tried to see into her face, which she kept turned away. She laughed softly, but said nothing till Rupert broke in again hotly. 'Will you only laugh? Am I not even worth answering?'

'I only laughed because it seems so queer,' she said. 'I like you very much, but it's silly to talk about—like you did, you know. You are only a boy.'

'I am twenty.'

'Well, that's not very old. You're the dearest boy I know, Rupert, but that's because—'

'Never mind why—say "and always will be,"' broke in Rupert, catching her bridle hand in his fingers, 'and I will be satisfied.'

'But how do I know?' she laughed.

'Just say it, and I will trust you to know.'

'And always will be,' she murmured in a rather tremulous voice. 'I don't know—you are silly to make me say it,' and, snatching her hand away, she whipped her horse into a canter.

There was no chance to say anything more for a time, and Rupert, in a glow of happiness, felt that having gained so much it was wise to be content.

When their horses fell into a walk again, Mabel herself returned to the subject, and her quiet, womanly voice, in spite of his three years' seniority, almost overawed Rupert.

'Uncle George was right,' she said. ' Father will be angry at your riding home with me—and would be angrier still if he knew what we had been saying.'

Rupert made a gesture of impatience.

' I don't myself think parents or anyone else have a right to stop people liking each other if they are nice,' she continued, ' but '—with a sigh—' it's not only my father and mother.   There are your people—they might only laugh now, but you know how angry they'd be if you were a little older and you told them you liked me.'

'Not mother,' he answered with assurance. ' Dad, perhaps—but poor old dad, you know—or at least you don't know—'

' Yes, I do,' she said softly ; ' and I'm sorry. That's another reason you oughtn't to offend him. You must promise me not to say anything like this—oh, for ages to come.'

' I promise,' he said, ' and I couldn't for a long time, except in letters, because I'm going to England next week.'

Mabel's cheeks suddenly lost their colour and, in spite of an effort to prevent it, her voice trembled.

' Why didn't you tell me before ? ' she asked.

' Because I wasn't going to come trying to sneak you into liking me because I wasn't there and it wouldn't be much trouble,' he answered, with a meaning clear enough in his own mind, which Mabel seemed to grasp.

She made no comment but thought her own

thoughts for a time and then broke her own
compact.

'I expect when you see all the girls in England
and everywhere you'll forget all about me.'

There followed a torrent of protestation which she
had no excuse to stop, and which was at least exciting and flattering to hear. She told him how
longingly she envied him the delights of travel and
university life before settling down upon the station,
and he said there was no need for envy, for some day
they should go again and see all that he had seen
together, and after all he was only a child—as she
had herself said—and would not appreciate it yet.
Mabel tried to make him understand that it was
his youth she had been insisting on ; and, in light-
hearted, laughing dispute the miles flew by like
one.

Harlin said he would ride back to Scott's and spend
the night there, and Mabel felt with a new bitterness
that only misconceptions and narrowness prevented
her from offering him the hospitality of her own
home. In an hour's ride so many individual rights
and claims seemed to have sprung into existence.

Rupert rode with her to the harness-room door to
take the saddle off her horse. He knew it would
be fatal to ask permission—he guessed she would
be angry—but, deciding it worth the risk, when she
gave him her hand to say good-night, his other arm
went round her neck, and raising her face to his he
kissed her.

'Good-bye, dear Mab,' he whispered ; and leaping
on his horse was gone before she could reproach him
or protest.

CHAPTER VIII

DECEMBER, January and February passed with molten skies from which the sun blazed down in all-consuming wrath, so that it seemed as if the world must shrivel up like paper drawn through flame. Grass became innutritious straw, creeks turned into hot shingle beds, bottoms of dams and water-holes baked hard with sun-cracks which divided them into little squares. Even the song of the Tonga was still. Its loud murmur could no longer be heard in the hush of evening or the silence of night ; for where once the river flowed in exuberant mirth, there was now only a chain of water-holes growing green with slime. The forest trees dropped and exotics died. Men became sapless, but still worked on, fated to toil everlastingly, heedless alike of summer blaze or wintry storm.

March came, and the air turned sultry and more oppressive, and life was even less endurable.

At least, so thought Ruth as she sat in the shade of what leaves the locusts had left on the elms, and wondered if the sun would ever go down behind the hills and relief come from the fiery torment. So she sat and thought for an hour with some needlework lying untouched on her lap, when diversion came in the person of Conyngham, who rode up, attended by a vast and persistent convoy of flies, which he tried in vain to swish away with a piece of wattle branch. He tied his horse in a shady spot and entered the little brown garden.

'Good-day, Mrs Toland. I see you haven't aban-
doned hope of keeping cool.'

Ruth gave him a welcoming smile. 'Well, it's
almost hopeless. I'm just waiting for the sun to go
down. Won't you get yourself a chair? I think
this is the coolest spot to be found.'

'This will do, thank you,' he replied, as he sat on
the ground facing her and leant against the trunk of
the tree. 'Where is your good man?'

'He is away, poor fellow, with Joe. They've gone
to drag a bullock out of a water-hole where it got
bogged and hadn't strength to move.'

'What hard luck! Have the stock become as
weak as that?'

'Yes; they seem to be nothing but skin and bone.
It's dreadfully sad to see the poor brutes standing
with their heads down and the crows hovering over
them. John is afraid they will nearly all die during
the winter if they live till then.'

'It's hard luck, and no mistake,' reiterated Conyngham. 'I suppose he's very cut up?'

'He must be,' replied Ruth, 'but he says very little
about it, and is much more cheerful than I thought
he would be. He just works as if nothing particular
were happening, though he is more silent than
usual.'

'You may be sure that whatever happens he will
fight it out to the end,' said Conyngham, pensively,
crushing a bull-dog ant that had crawled upon his
boot.

'Yes, he would make a good soldier,' said Ruth.

'Oh, I don't think much of a soldier's bravery.
Trumpet and drums, honour and glory, excitement
and desire to kill make an ordinary man fit to do

anything. But no ordinary man can fight the fight in the solitude of the bush without a murmur.'

'Yes; it is hard,' said Ruth, looking pleased at her husband's commendation. 'Yet, all the same,' she continued after a pause, 'I think it must require some bravery to be a soldier.'

'Some, perhaps,' assented Conyngham, as he watched a smoke ring rise from his pipe; 'but I can almost imagine myself, when intoxicated with the devilry of it all, being so foolish as to rush into danger on a battlefield, whereas, if I were in your husband's place, I should just sit down, light my pipe and let the place go to—well, what it is very like at present, with the thermometer at a hundred and four in the shade.'

'I don't think that,' said Ruth, smiling. 'You would not like the idea of failing in what you had attempted; it is a matter of pride as well as courage.'

'You think not?' Conyngham replied with a tinge of bitterness in his tone. 'I am afraid that you flatter me and that I am a very complacent failure as it is. Fortune dealt me one hard blow, and I turned and fled until I found a spot where not even the faintest echo could reach me from the battlefield—where I couldn't even hear as a murmur "the shouting of the captains and the men-at-arms."'

'Do you never repent it?' asked Ruth, looking up from her needlework into Conyngham's face.

A cynical reply came to his lips, but he raised his eyes at that moment and met her sympathetically-questioning look.

'Sometimes.'

'Then why do you not return?'

He looked at her and smiled.

'That question requires a little self-analysis to answer. In the first place, I am indolent and hate change; in the second, the bush holds me in its thrall. I came to rest for a breathing space, but it looks like lengthening out to include my life. Sometimes I think I'll go, but get tired of the idea before giving effect to it. I know I am weak—weak as a woman who shuts herself up in a nunnery to escape the strife of the world. But after all it's of no consequence. Excuse so long an explanation over so small a matter, but I had to find some excuse for not ridding you of me when you seem to think I should.'

'Don't say that, Mr Conyngham,' said Ruth, deprecatingly. 'You know we should miss you dreadfully if you left. Talking to you is about the only pleasure John has—though I'm afraid sometimes you put dangerous ideas into his head.'

'Those dangerous ideas are prompted by his heart, and at most I help to show how they are supported by the head.'

'And then there is Mab. She wouldn't know what to do with herself if you didn't teach her to take an interest in many things. The daughters of the farmers about are all trying to get employment in Melbourne as domestic servants or factory girls, and after all, considering the lives they lead, one cannot blame them for wanting to leave their homes.'

'Well, Mab will never be a domestic servant or a factory girl,' said Conyngham with a smile, as he thought of his fascinating and masterful young pupil. 'I prophesy some fairer fortune for her.'

'I don't know how it is to come to her, poor child,' sighed Ruth. 'The lot of a selector's daughter isn't a very happy one. Mab's is better than most, of course,

M

since she doesn't have to slave at milking and things of that kind. Her father says he doesn't want women farm-hands. But still there are no amusements, no social intercourse and no light-heartedness anywhere.'

' That's true,' said Conyngham, ' and the education provided by the State is just sufficient to make them discontented with a purely animal life without supplying a fund for the mind's self-support. It enables them to read of the pomps and vanities of the wicked world beyond the little clearing, and naturally, having inherited the spirit of their parents, they want to be off to where they fondly believe fortunes are to be won and some happiness to be obtained.'

' Don't you think that if they had altogether the spirit of their fathers they would stay ? ' said Ruth.

' No, I think not. It would be demanding more of the children than was required of the fathers. Things are changed since the days when the pioneers settled in the land. They did so, flushed with hopes of independence and prosperity. Those hopes have largely vanished now, but the never-ending, joyless toil remains. This is the heritage the children find themselves born to ; and no wonder they are eager to relinquish it for the first mess of more highly-seasoned pottage with which they are tempted.'

' You do not encourage me much as to the future of my children,' said Ruth, with a sad smile. ' Do you include them among the others ? '

' Not altogether. Joe may be true to his juvenile intention of becoming a trooper, but I have greater hopes for Mab.'

' What are they ? Do tell me.'

' Well, you are imposing on me a distinctly

feminine task, and making me avow speculations that are incongruous in a gloomy misogynist, but I must admit that I have foreseen the possibility of Mab's being one day the mistress of Kumbarra.'

Ruth dropped her needlework and pondered, looking at the far-off purple hills.

'Do you think there is anything in that, then?' she said presently. 'I mean that Mab and Rupert Harlin are in love with each other.'

Conyngham meditatively enveloped himself in a cloud of smoke, seeming to gain inspiration therefrom like a priestess of Apollo. It was a habit with him, whenever he spoke on any subject dealing with human emotions, to enshroud himself in tobacco smoke and his thoughts in verbiage.

'Now you ask me a question that I find difficult to answer, because I cannot possibly conceive the essentials of that condition. Nor would I dare to affirm that, given they were in love with each other, as you term it, that they would consequently marry. My chief experience in such matters has been of a woman in love with one man marrying another. Consequently, you must acquit me of the foolishness of deducting matrimony from the premise love. I prefer to leave love out of the question, as neither here nor there, and find the probability of what I have suggested in the often-observed result of environment, contiguity and natural proneness to folly in the young.'

Ruth smiled as she gradually unravelled his speech, and came to the conclusion that it all meant nothing.

'Well,' she said, 'I never really thought of it as probable, and hope it is not the case; for her father would be furious if he thought Mab had encouraged him.'

'That I am sure she has never done. In fact, I fancy she has considerably reduced the young gentleman, for whom I have a great liking, in his own estimation. He's safe in England now, but he has a steadfast sort of nature, and I shouldn't be surprised if you have to get your husband to abandon his resentment for the sake of his daughter.'

'I'm afraid I never could—at anyrate not without your assistance.'

'My services as a matrimonial agent are always at your disposal. I see your husband coming and will go and meet him.'

Conyngham rose and looked at Ruth for a moment while her eyes were searching for her husband. '*Toujours votre serviteur, madame,*' he said in an undertone, as he raised his hat. Then he turned and walked away in his customary long stride, with his eyes fixed on the ground.

Ruth watched the retreating figure for a few seconds.

'What a strange man and what a ruined life!' she said musingly, as she remembered how every now and then in their conversation a grief, repressed and crushed out of sight, had almost revealed itself through the mists of expression. Then her thoughts wandered on to what Conyngham had said of Mab and Rupert, and, in spite of the barriers in the way, she could not help feeling glad, as Conyngham had intended she should, and she hoped that he might be right.

There was no time to think of it further, for Toland and Conyngham were walking up from the stable to join her.

When they were some distance off she saw the former stop and point to a far-away range.

Wondering what it was that interested them, she rose and looked in the same direction. Toland, however, was only pointing out to his companion a pillar of smoke that had been rising for days past from the Wallaby Table Lands.

She knew there was nothing to fear as her husband had told her it was fifty miles away at least. She would not have felt so satisfied if she had heard the conversation.

'It draws a little closer every day,' Toland was saying. 'I'm told it is off the Table Land and has started to make its way down the ranges towards the valley. We shall have to do something before long.'

'Well, John, dear, have you had a very miserable day?' she asked, as the two men approached.

'Not too pleasant,' he replied, mopping his head.

'You didn't find any more dead ones?' she asked anxiously.

'Only five.'

'How dreadful!'

'I suppose it's no use selling stock now,' said Conyngham.

'At the last market,' replied Toland, 'sheep sold for a shilling a head and steers for a few shillings. The graziers on the table lands are killing their stock for the hides and the farmers on the plains have to cart water thirty miles.'

'It's a bad lookout certainly,' said Conyngham. 'This is March, and we've only had a shower since the beginning of October.'

'Well, let's hope things will be better after the day

of humiliation and prayer I see the Government has appointed,' said Toland, sardonically. 'For my part I'd rather be cheered up than humiliated any more ; and as for praying, I find more relief in cursing. How long will it be to supper, missis?'

'Mab is seeing about it now, and as the sun is down I'll help her to get it at once.'

'Come and have a wash,' said Toland, as Ruth left them. 'There's only stagnant water in the creek, but the well is still going. By Heaven, it was beastly work pulling that rotting carrion out of the mud. The stench turned Joe up. It's a great thing to be a farmer, and no mistake!'

At supper Conyngham entertained them, as he was in the habit of doing, with news of the outside world culled from the papers and magazines. He took a delight in starting a general discussion and in summing up with some startling dictum contrary to all sane views held on the subject. It amused Toland and always annoyed Scott, who liked every-body to be practical and unoriginal. Mab enjoyed it too, for she dearly loved making fun of everything herself, and knew that this was Conyngham's way of doing it.

After supper the two men went out on the verandah to smoke, and later on Ruth joined them. Just as she was going to sit down something caught her attention.

'Look, John!' she exclaimed, pointing towards the range. 'There is the fire ; we can see it now.'

Toland and Conyngham turned round.

'By Jove!' exclaimed Toland, 'so we can. This is the first night we've seen it. It must be coming down the range.'

'What a spread it has,' said Conyngham, as he looked at the thin line of flame that ran mile upon mile along the brow of the distant hills.

'Twenty miles at least,' said Toland.

'Oh, I hope it won't come down on to the river,' exclaimed Ruth, fervently. 'It's dreadful to think of its drawing closer and closer every night.'

'We'll have to stop it before it does that,' said Toland.

'Perhaps we shall have rain soon,' suggested Conyngham.

'I do hope so,' sighed Ruth; 'but I'm almost beginning to despair of ever seeing rain again.'

'Don't worry, missis,' said Toland, laying his hand on her shoulder. 'Come and sit with us while we smoke and yarn, and we'll forget about droughts and fires.'

Meanwhile Mab and Joe played cribbage.

'Fifteen two, fifteen four, fifteen six, fifteen eight and a pair, that makes ten. I'm out and you're licked again, Mab.'

'You do have luck, Joe, but come on, I'll play you again.'

'Not now. I'm going to set possum traps in the orchard. Come along with us.'

'I hate you to set traps for the poor old possums; it's so cruel to leave them all night when they're caught.'

'Well, they shouldn't come and steal our apples— and anyhow, it isn't so bad as having your eyes picked out alive by the crows like the bullocks when they get down. As you're so mighty particular it's a good job you didn't come out with dad and me to-day.'

'I'm glad I didn't, but you needn't tell me about it. That would be worse.'

'Five of 'em. They'd have come out on their own hook if they'd been left much longer, although they were dead.'

'Don't be disgusting, Joe,' said Mab, putting her fingers in her ears.

'Come on,' he said, pulling her hands down. 'I'll make you a muff of the best skins I get.'

Mab yielded to the temptation, and as they went the sound of their voices and merry laughter helped Toland and Ruth to forget for a while their gathering misfortunes.

CHAPTER IX

THE day that followed Conyngham's visit to the farm deepened the feeling of anxiety in Ruth's mind, for that night showed the long line of fire closer. Now, too, a flaming area could be seen after the sun had gone down, thousands of acres glowing red on the hillside.

The wind was blowing from the fire, and dense masses of smoke rolled down and settled in the valley below. The sun was obscured and looked like a red toy balloon hung aloft. Darkness fell upon the land so that nothing could be seen beyond a couple of hundred yards.

The hills were blotted out, the birds never sang, and all sounds of life were hushed. The smoke made the eyes smart; its pungent smell never left the nostrils; it caused a feeling of suffocation in the lungs; in the cottage it filled the rooms. So gradually the fire crept down the range; but as yet nothing could be done, for it was coming before the wind. Then at last the wind blew from the south, and word was sent round that a 'break' would be burnt at night to head off the fire from the farms in the valley. So long as it was confined to the hills and the green timber, where there was no settlement, it could do no harm, but it was rapidly approaching the farming area below, where, amongst the ringed timber, it would become uncontrollable as the tides of the ocean.

Toland set out before sundown for O'Brien's selection at the foot of the ranges, the appointed place of meeting and the first farm threatened. When he arrived he found about twenty men at supper in the kitchen. He was surprised to find neither Scott nor Conyngham present, but learnt that they were with a party burning a break lower down.

O'Brien gave him a cordial welcome and explained the proposed plan of operations. An advance guard of the fire was making its way down a spur in front of the main body and it was imperative to head it off before the wind changed again. As the farm ran to the foot of the ranges, it was necessary to climb for a few hundred yards before starting the break, so that in case of the fire getting away it could be beaten out before it reached the land on which dead trees stood close and dry kangaroo grass covered the fallen timber.

When the party reached the spot selected for a start, branches were cut from saplings and the leafy boughs bound together for the purpose of beating out the flames. Then O'Brien gathered and lit a bunch of dry bracken, and ran with it trailing in the grass. When he stopped another did the same ahead of him, and immediately a line of fire blazed up for fifty paces. The beaters rushed in and thrashed out the slow advance down the hill against the wind, whilst flames rolled away before it, leaving the ground, between the great fire and the farm, burnt and bare.

When that section had been secured the trail was run on again, and the fire again beaten out. At first the work was easy, for the ground was stony, with little grass, and the wind blew steadily from the south. But soon the trail, which was run as nearly as possible parallel with the bush fire, passed into long grass and bracken, and then the work began in deadly earnest. The undergrowth flashed into flames that leapt up ten feet or more, and each beater could only rush in and make a few strokes before being compelled to fall back. Sometimes, too, the wind changed and blew the smoke and flames towards the men ; but nevertheless the fire had to be beaten out before it escaped beyond control ; and beards were singed, shirts burnt into holes, and lungs filled to suffocation with the smoke.

Scarcely a word was uttered except when the boys were cursed for not being at hand with the water buckets, or someone shouted in desperation to the fire-runners for a spell. As the trail extended in length men were left behind to patrol the work already done, in case some smouldering embers should break into flame and send the fire sweeping down the range. Sometimes a cooey was heard from the watchers, betokening that such a break-away had got beyond control, and others ran back to assist.

Deep gullies had to be crossed, where a foothold was scarcely obtainable by men well nigh dropping from exhaustion, and belts so dense and inflammable that only a few yards could be fired at a stretch. By midnight two miles had been run, but the need to press on was now more urgent than ever. Ahead the great fire could be seen beating down the range, and the trail had to be run quicker still to intercept it. So the fight grew fiercer, and the men, now black as stokers, fought like devils amidst the flames of the Inferno. The sight was magnificent. Behind the forest lay dark and glowing where not lit by the lurid light of towering flames. In front and stretch-ing for miles the fires raced to meet each other. In the long grass and bracken they burned savagely. Green scrub crackled and flashed ; the flames ran up huge dead trees to their topmost heights and turned the trunks into pillars of fire, while the branches crashed down amid showers of sparks. The noise of the conflagration was terrific. Trees fell with a loud boom, and the swirl of the flames in the wind was accompanied by a hungry roar. For another mile the trail was continued, and then, the bush fire being headed, it was run into a gully with water at the bottom of it, and work was suspended for the night. The men threw themselves down in the grass for a while, and the first light of dawn was in the sky when they tramped wearily back to O'Brien's.

It was after six o'clock when Toland rode away. The sun had risen, the heat was already overpower-ing, and his brain reeled with exhaustion, so that he wondered vaguely if the world was going to be dis-solved in flames. The day passed wretchedly away, and that night no one went to bed at the farm, for it was useless to try and sleep while sweltering in a temperature of a hundred degrees, below which the thermometer never sank. Ruth and Mab sat in easy-chairs on the verandah, while Toland and Joe stretched themselves on the floor. No one spoke, but every now and then one of the little group rose to get a drink from the canvas water-bag hanging up on the verandah post. Want of sleep, inability to eat, the smoke in the lungs, and the sinking feeling in the pit of the stomach, caused by physical collapse, all went to cause an insatiable thirst. Toland, who was completely prostrated, felt he did not care what happened. All he knew was that in a few hours' time he would go out again and fight the fire. The eyes of the little group were fixed in one direction across the narrow gulf of darkness to the hell on the range. Mile upon mile the cordon of fire stretched away to the north. Forty miles it had now advanced from its starting-point on its march of desolation, leaving in its track but smouldering ruins of forest, farm and homestead, with here and there little white heaps of ash that betokened where a living creature had melted into flame. That night more than ever its grandeur was apparent, and in the rising north wind it appeared as if enraged that its progress had been barred by the efforts of puny men. From the base to the tops of the hills the bank of fire rose a thousand feet, the topmost flames appearing to leap into the lurid clouds on the skyline.

Mab and Joe wondered if the end of the world was approaching, and thinking of the fate of Sodom and Gomorrah, added a suitable prayer to their customary ones. Ruth, when she gazed at the mighty furnace, thought of the brave, overwrought men fighting in its face for the preservation of their homes, and remembered with a dread that in a few hours' time her husband would go to a worse fight still, when the blazing sun would make the work a long-drawn agony. About two o'clock she and Mab went inside to lie down, leaving Toland and Joe on the verandah, where they remained till dawn. At six they had breakfast together, and at nine Toland set out again to take his place in the relief of the fire-fighters of the night. By that time the north wind was sweeping in terrific gusts down the valley, scorching hot from the torrid deserts of Central Australia and from the fires it had passed in its course. It heated and shrivelled the lungs, dried the skin and the saliva from the mouth. It howled through the ringed trees wild with hot, ravening rage. Its voice was that of an avenging fury crying woe and desolation to the land. It tore along as the harbinger of destruction—the proclaimer of ruin at hand. Great now was Toland's fear lest the fire should break from the forest on the hills, where it had so far been retained, on to the ringed country in the valley. He could not see the position of the fire, for the smoke, swept along in mighty volumes towards him by the wind, obliterated everything further distant than one hundred yards. Showers of burnt and scorched leaves were falling around the cottage like flakes of black snow, and a charred piece of bark that he picked up was still hot. By the constant dropping the cultivation paddocks, which at one time were white with the trampled straw of the ill-fated crops, had been turned to a dun colour.

At first Toland rode slowly, but gradually anxiety possessed him, and he spurred his horse into a canter. A mile from the cottage he passed on to the main road and slackened pace, so that he might fill his pipe. Then he heard the sound of a horse galloping towards him, and a second later a man rode out of the smoke haze. He was beside Toland before they recognised each other.

'Conyngham! What's the matter?'

'Bad news, old man. The fire has broken away. It's in the rung country. It has swept away Thomson's and is travelling towards us like hell on wings.'

'Have you been in it?' asked Toland, as he saw

Conyngham's shirt had been burnt in half a dozen places.

'Very near it. It's on the road not a mile from here. There's no time to lose.'

'Is it any use going forward?'

'None. It's flying from tree to tree, taking leaps of a hundred paces. Gallop back and save your family; that's the most you can do.'

'The house ought to be safe,' said Toland, as he turned and spurred his horse. 'I burnt a break round it some time ago.'

'It's useless, with the dead timber round. Thomson's house was fired from a tree a couple of hundred yards away. You can't leave them there.'

After that the two men galloped on in silence, turning their heads every now and then to see if the advancing line of fire were yet visible.

Soon they reached the cottage, where they found Ruth and the two children in dread and expectancy watching the wall of darkness grow nearer. As Toland and Conyngham galloped out from it into sight—safe and unharmed—a great wave of thankfulness flooded Ruth's heart. Toland quickly told her what he knew. The smoke each moment grew denser. Everything was enveloped, and for all they could tell the fire might be only a hundred yards away. The men flung themselves from the horses. At a word from his father Joe led them away to the creek, and Toland turned to Conyngham. 'The cottage is not safe,' he said, pointing at the dead trees close by. 'Ruth, you and Mab must go down into the potato patch and stay by the creek till the fire has passed.'

'What are you going to do? You must come too.'

'Not yet. I must stay here and see if I can save the place.'

'I'll stay with you,' said Conyngham.

'Go at once, Ruth,' said Toland. 'It can't be far off—and keep Joe with you. If I want him I'll call.'

Ruth longed to stay with her husband, but she knew she could help best by obeying him, and taking Mab's hand she drew her away from the cottage.

Toland and Conyngham carried some of the furniture and most. precious belongings out of the house on to the bare ground in front, and then hurried away to the bark shed, whence they dragged out the cart and buggy and the reaper, as they would be safer anywhere than under the inflammable roof. It was too late to do more, for the fire was upon them, and they retreated to guard the cottage. They could see the line of fire now as it swept forward, crackling and roaring in the straw and dry grass and blazing up every here and there into red pillars of flame. On it came to within thirty paces and then was checked by the fire break. Round the little clearing it swept, till it had surrounded it on every side, and then rushed onward and away. Toland and Conyngham lay with their faces on the ground and gasped for breath in the agonies of suffocation. The heat was intolerable, but as the inflammable matter on the ground quickly burnt out, their condition improved. But the real danger was now beginning. Already the great forest trees were blazing from butt to topmost limb, sending down cascades of sparks. Up other trees, hollow in the centre, the wind and fire roared as through a funnel, carrying red-hot ashes high into the air. They fell in showers upon the clearing, and the two men gazed at the bark roof in dismay, knowing that the first spark that lighted there meant the destruction of the home. Then Toland got a ladder and mounted on the ridge of the roof, and Conyngham drew buckets of water from the well and handed them to him to dash upon the bark. They had hardly begun when smoke rose from the roof of the shed, and a minute later the whole structure burst into flames. Nothing could be done. Only Conyngham worked harder hauling water from the well, blinded with smoke and sweat though he was, and almost fainting from exhaustion. Relief, however, came to him from an unexpected quarter as Joe suddenly made his appearance.

' I'll give you a hand, sir,' he said, gasping for breath.

' What are you here for? Why did you leave your mother?'

' They are all right—in the creek—and I was not going to be out of the fun. Isn't it awful, though?'

' You'd better carry the buckets to your father.'

' Let me draw, sir. The old man can't see me here, and he might send me back if he did.'

But even Joe's valuable assistance was not to be of much avail. A hollow tree not forty yards away had caught fire and was belching forth showers of sparks right over the cottage. Again and again the roof began to smoulder, and Toland, nearly blinded and maddened by the smoke, each time drenched the spot with water. Once he had just emptied one bucket, and the second had not been handed to him, when a spark fell on the roof a few feet below. Immediately the bark began to smoulder, but before it could burst into flames he lent over and crushed it

N

with his hand. A Berserker rage was upon him. He intended to save the home he had built with his own hands—which was endeared to him by a thousand ties. So he clenched his teeth, and, heedless of the agony in his scorched hands, smoke-laden lungs and tortured eyes, fought like a demon in his element.

Conyngham and Joe were staggering with exhaustion when the end came. A limb broke from the tree and a flight of sparks soaring into the air was carried by the wind over the cottage. In a second the roof smouldered in half a dozen places. Toland threw what water he had here and there, but a spot burst into flames just below him. He had no water left, and, ferocious with despair, he tore at the sheet of bark, thinking to remove it from its fastening and throw it to the ground. But the great sheet was immovable, and the flames licked the hair from his arms as he tugged, and the smoke made him groan. Along the roof the fire sped and in a second he looked as he knelt on the ridge like a martyr at the stake.

Conyngham shouted to him to come down before too late, while Joe burst into tears. But he either did not hear them in the roar of the wind and the flames, or heeded not, for he only groped here and there with his hands but did not move.

Conyngham rushed to the ladder and carried it to the side of the roof that was not yet in flames, and, running up, seized Toland and dragged him down. The latter did not utter a word and seemed too dazed to help himself, whilst his burnt hands were incapable of holding the rungs of the ladder.

Conyngham steadied Toland as he slid down the roof, and as the eaves were only seven feet from the ground he was able to let him down without injury and lead him a few paces away. And none too soon, for the roof was now blazing from end to end and the whole cottage enveloped in flames.

'Come farther away,' shouted Conyngham.

Toland put out his hands in front of him and staggered towards the flames.

'What are you doing? Do you want to be burnt alive?' cried Conyngham, pulling him back.

'Give me your hand,' said Toland, hoarsely. 'Can't you see I'm blind?'

Conyngham took him by the arm and dragged him away, followed by Joe.

'We'll go to your wife,' he said.

'Is it all over?' asked Toland.

'Yes.'

Then he turned and let Conyngham lead him across the smouldering track of the fire to the potato patch at the creek side, where Ruth and Mab were waiting in an agony of sorrow.

When Ruth saw her husband's fire-blasted face she found it hard to control a frenzy of grief, and hung upon him, sobbing.

'It's nothing,' he said. 'It was a good fight. I'll be able to see soon.'

Conyngham, too, assured her that men's eyes recovered from the smoke blindness, and, there being nothing further to be done, they sat down together in silence whilst the wind howled by and swept the fire on to complete the work of desolation.

After weary hours had passed, Conyngham suggested that Mab and Ruth should mount the two horses and that they should all make their way through the burnt area to the Scotts, who, he thought, had escaped, being well to the north of the point at which the fire had broken away. Ruth and Mab were put on the horses. Conyngham led Toland, and Joe piloted the way amongst the burning timber.

When they passed the cottage Ruth felt almost glad that her husband could not see, for a few smouldering logs were all that remained of the home consecrated by happy memories. The smoke seemed to rise as from a funeral pyre on which a loved one had perished, and she wept as she passed. When they got to the road they found it almost impassable for the fallen timber, and their progress was slow amongst the ashes, smoke and flames.

Late in the afternoon the sorrowful pilgrimage came to an end and they found shelter at the Scotts.

CHAPTER X

FOR days after the fire Toland's thoughts scarcely dwelt a moment on the wreck of his material prospects, for he was living in a fever of alternate hope and despair of his wife's recovery from an illness brought on by the shock and strain of the bush fires, winding up with the terrible hours of the refuge in the creek. The chill which she made light of at first could no longer be resisted when it developed into inflammation of the lungs, and the doctor from Tongalong informed Toland he must be prepared for the worst, as his wife was thoroughly run down and had no reserves of strength to draw upon. There seemed indeed no hope, and for hours at a time Toland would refuse to leave the room, scarcely aware of the presence of Mabel or Bess, who were unremitting in their care as nurses, nor of Mrs Harlin and the doctor when they visited the sick chamber. He had eyes only for the pale face, and his ear heard nothing but the quick, loud breathing that evidenced the struggle of the body to keep life within it.

Sitting by the bedside with his eyes fixed on those that for long periods in the height of the fever gave no gleam of recognition, Toland was scarcely a reasoning being, and for the first time for years he prayed, not humbly, nor with great faith in the efficacy of prayer, but almost fiercely, contemptuously of himself and his weakness, as a measure of despair.

From the night of the fire the Toland family had

been quartered on the Scotts ; and much as Toland disliked the arrangement, he knew that any other would have greatly offended his sister, who was the soul of sympathy and kindness, while, after Ruth's prostration declared itself as serious illness, no considerations of pride or independence would have induced him to separate himself and the children from her.

Mrs Harlin drove down every day from the station to the Scotts, usually bringing medical luxuries for the invalid, and Toland saw her come and go with a sullen feeling of jealousy that she of all strangers should intrude upon his grief. Then one day, when the crisis was at hand and hope almost gone, the doctor had ordered him to leave the room for a few minutes, and, walking with bowed head into the garden, he nearly ran against Mrs Harlin.

Hearing a sob, he looked up wonderingly, and their eyes met. She dabbed a pocket-handkerchief on hers and greeted him with a sad smile.

'Do you cherish your friends as you do your injuries?' she asked.

Toland wrinkled his brows and shook his head with a dazed look. He scarcely took in her words and was in no mood to deal with psychological problems.

'Walk with me to my buggy,' she went on, and he found himself mechanically obeying the softly-toned command.

As he opened the garden gate she stopped and rested her fingers for a moment on his arm.

'I won't force my sympathy on you,' she said, 'but you must not grudge me my own grief. Remember that before she was your wife she was my friend, and that I loved her dearly.'

Toland raised his head with a frightened look in his eyes. Her unconscious use of the past tense sounded like a death sentence. He clenched his nails into his palms, suppressing an impulse to curse or cry.

'Oh, for pity's sake don't!' he exclaimed pleadingly. 'I know she loves you, and I—I grudge you nothing.'

Mrs Harlin could not forbear giving expression to her pity for herself and him. She clasped his strong fingers in her gloved hand.

'Mr Toland,' she cried, 'I am so sorry for you. And you must pity me and give me your sympathy —even if you will not have mine.'

Toland's mood softened at the touch of her hand; and this appeal from a sorrow-stricken woman to a man in like sorrow rose above all considerations of class and dimmed the memory of real or fancied wrongs.

'I *am* thankful for it,' he said with an effort; 'and I suppose it makes it easier to bear that someone else feels it something the same.' Then, gripping her fingers fiercely as she was withdrawing them, he turned a searching gaze on her face.

'Tell me, Mrs Harlin, do you think there is any hope?'

'There is always hope,' she faltered. 'Have you prayed for her?'

'I think so,' replied Toland with a bitter laugh. 'I've said, "God—if there is a God—let this woman get well. If You do I'll believe in You. I'll thank You, I'll try to love the Harlins and all my enemies —if You don't let her die. If You do I'll try to believe in You that I may hate You and curse You." I've said that—and things like that—cried them with my whole soul for hours and days together. Is that praying?'

'Hush!' said Mrs Harlin, gently. Toland had raised his deep voice and was quite unconscious of the wonder the strange scene and conversation were exciting in the mind of the man holding Mrs Harlin's ponies only a few yards away. 'If prayers count that come from the heart,' she went on with a smile, 'yours will be answered. And—please Heaven—so will mine.'

'You are a good woman. I—I believe I trust you more than the doctor,' muttered Toland, huskily.

He turned his back abruptly and, without another word, Mrs Harlin slipped away to her buggy, calling out, as she took the reins in her hand, 'Good-bye, and keep up your spirits, I shall be back again for news in an hour.'

Toland leaned on the gate and watched till the vehicle was out of sight. She was as unhappy as he, and her pride was as great as his own—and of a finer kind, he supposed, since she employed it to hide the skeleton in her cupboard, and wore a smiling mask over the great misery in her life. Had it not been for an accident he would never have discovered the secret of Harlin's weakness, with which only Ruth had been entrusted. If Ruth recovered there were happier days in store. And she must recover, for there were wrongs that he must set right. Still he leaned upon the fence, not daring to go back to the house for a later bulletin, lest it should dash the hopes that unaccountably were growing, when he heard a step behind him and a strong hand rested on his shoulder.

'Toland, old man! The crisis is past and she will recover.'

The voice was Conyngham's. He was boarding at Mallock's shanty now and had ridden across through the paddocks to ask for news. Approaching the back of the house, unseen by Toland, he had just met the doctor as he left the sick chamber, and had hurried away in search of his friend.

No words were adequate, but the men could read each what the other would express in the silent hand grip, when suddenly Toland looked from Conyngham's trembling arm to his face and felt a momentary, almost jealous, surprise at the depth of the emotion he saw written there.

Then consciousness of everything else was swallowed up in the over-surging joy of Ruth's return to him.

The doctor stood by the verandah step drawing on his gloves and talking to Bess, and he smiled as Toland, forgetful for the moment even of Conyngham's existence, hurried towards him, demanding almost fiercely full confirmation of the good news.

'My dear Mr Toland, I am not omniscient and I can promise nothing,' he said deprecatingly. 'But the fever has left her, and with the care of such nurses as your sister and daughter here—provided there is no relapse—I see no reason why Mrs Toland should not be up and about again in a fortnight.'

'May I see her?' asked Toland.

'You had better not to-day. Miss Mabel is with her, and the fewer people about the sick room the better. Ah, there is my buggy at the back. My congratulations to you, and good-bye!'

The doctor stepped briskly to the gate, settled himself on the driving seat and rattled off, leaving Bess and Toland together. Bess had had a satisfactory cry before her brother's appearance, and contented herself now with kissing him affectionately.

'He is a real clever man,' she said, nodding towards the departing buggy. 'You've got to thank him—and God that made him an instrument—that we've got Ruth with us to-day.'

'And where do you come in?' he asked, resting his hand lovingly on her shoulder.

'Oh, me?' she laughed happily. 'What on earth have I done? Here's Mr Conyngham wants to wish you joy too. Come on, Mr Conyngham! You'd best interrupt John and me before we get downright silly.'

Conyngham was approaching, rather hesitatingly, down the path beside the house from the front garden, where Toland had left him.

'I'm afraid you'll have to do without my restraining influence,' he said, smiling—'if there is any reason not to be silly—for I have come to say good-bye.'

'I am sorry we are keeping you out of your quarters and driving you back to that beastly shanty,' said Toland. 'However, all being well, Joe and I will be back at work on the farm again in a day or two.'

'I hope so,' answered Conyngham, deliberately ; 'but, as a matter of fact, you are not keeping me out of my quarters, for I am not likely to be back here for some time. I have to go to Melbourne on business, and I expect the next time I shall see you will be at the tea-table, presided over by your wife, on the new Grimsby Farm—risen Phœnix-like from the ashes of the old.'

'That is sudden, isn't it?'

'Not very,' said Conyngham, holding out his hand. 'You will give my warmest congratulations to Mrs Toland on her recovery?'

'Yes,' said Toland, wondering.

'And to you they are beyond expression — you know that. Good-bye, Mrs Scott. I hope you haven't found my absence so great a relief that you will be unable to give it up in a month or two.'

Toland watched him ride away, with his mind reverting, in spite of himself, to the thoughts of half an hour ago.

'Well, well,' sighed Bess, 'he's a queer chap. You never know rightly how to take him.'

'I don't believe you do, Bess,' answered Toland, with a half smile; 'but take him any way you like, he's a fine fellow and a good friend. Can I see Mabel?'

'I think you'd best not. It might disturb Ruth if she left the room.'

'Then I'm going to smoke and think. I don't believe I've had a pipe for days.'

He took himself off, and for the rest of the day and the night obediently kept out of Ruth's room, avoiding Mrs Harlin when she called again, also Scott and the family, feeling equal to no other companionship than his pipe and his thoughts.

On the following day he saw Ruth for a minute or two only, and he scarcely dared to speak, lest the fierceness of his joy in her promised recovery should carry him away in some outburst of feeling that would excite her and check the feeble current of returning strength.

Then he went back to the farm, camping with Joe amid the ruins of his home, when he put all his pent-up energy into clearing the ground of fallen trees with which the fire had strewed the blackened paddocks. No other work was possible since, until heavy rains came, post holes could not be sunk for new fences, nor the baked ground be turned over by the plough.

He had not the heart to put his own labour into the building of a second home. In any case ringing and clearing had put an end to the old days when slabs could be split and bark stripped a few chains from the door; so, with the bitter-sweet memories of those years ago when he and Mick felled corner posts in the forest, he watched the weatherboard cottage, for which he had contracted, go up on the desolate site of the old, rough dwelling he had loved so well.

Money had to be found to pay doctors' bills and make a new start in life. From a relief fund liberally subscribed to by neighbours and people throughout the district, whom the fires had spared, Toland refused to accept a penny, angrily tearing the forms for particulars of loss sustained and aid sought sent to him as a matter of course by the secretary of the Relief Committee. He had not sunk so low as to accept charity! In any case it would have been but a drop in the bucket; and the alternative was a further mortgage on which—at eight per cent.—Macnamara, of Tongalong, let him have eight hundred pounds.

Every evening, often taking Joe with him, he rode down the river to see his wife, and Scott showed practical kindliness by lending him mounts, as the daily pilgrimage was too great a strain on horseflesh for Toland's resources.

Scott's sympathetic conduct all through Ruth's illness induced in Toland a more cordial feeling towards him than he had entertained for years, and he began to wonder if he had attached too much importance to idiosyncrasies of character, and overlooked the good heart underlying them, which was wrung so much by his relatives' misfortunes that, in a mood of expansion, Scott would have made any sacrifice to help them, provided it did not involve the undisguised expenditure of cash.

Toland's mind, in fact, after this great crisis in his affairs, underwent a kind of moral spring cleaning, during which he cleared his brain of much lumber in the way of bitter humours, and found occasion to revise his estimate of other people besides Scott.

For his wife there was no higher place than she had always held in his esteem, but she returned to him from the brink of the grave dearer if possible than ever. Bess, too, had regained almost her old childish place in his affection and regard; but, apart from its crushing effect upon his material fortunes, disguised at first by the stimulant of the mortgage money, the most important result of the fire to Toland was the changed relations it indirectly brought about with Mrs Harlin. Not till Ruth was well on the way towards convalescence did he meet her again, when, riding down to Scott's from Grimsby Farm, he found her on the point of leaving after a visit to his wife.

Both felt the constraint resulting from their unwonted display of feeling when they had been face to face with life as fellow-partners in sorrow, and there was an aloofness, greater even than usual, between them; but Mrs Harlin had encountered him with a purpose which she would not leave unattempted. She wanted Mabel in a week's time to go and stay with her till the family should be settled in their new home.

It was the old, old bone of contention, dragged

anew from the hole where it lay buried, and it was long before Mrs Harlin could conquer Toland's unreasoning obstinacy; but when she begged it as a favour, saying, in a voice that trembled, she was lonely, his heart smote him for dragging such a confession, of which he understood the truth, from the lips of this proud woman.

'Thank you,' she said. 'I cannot say that you have given your consent graciously, but I thank you for giving it at all.'

Toland remained silent with his eyes on the ground. No one could guess what a wrench to his cherished independence the consent had been.

She hesitated for a moment. Then, with a little angry colour in her cheeks and a haughty ring in her tone,—

'I suppose I must make allowances for your pride, Mr Toland. I asked a favour and you have been generous enough, however grudgingly, to grant it; but I should admire you more if I thought you had the generosity to accept one.'

Toland reddened. The last blow was feminine. It was delivered from a social distance; but it was aimed true, and he did not reply.

And thus it was settled that Mabel should go to Kumbarra.

BOOK III

CHAPTER I

THE rattle of the binder, now loud, now faint, from the wheat paddock's furthest limit, had sounded through the cottage since the first streaks of dawn, ceasing only at long intervals when the hard-worked machine creaked a request for more oil or the twine drum was replenished by another ball.

There were two hundred acres to cut, threatening to shed the grain under the blazing heat of December's last few days, and Toland had hired a couple of draught horses to keep two teams going without a rest from daylight until dark.

At twelve o'clock Joe's eight hours' day on the driving seat was over, leaving him free to rest for an hour or two before taking his turn at stooking in the absence of other tasks.

Mabel moved about the verandah room getting ready his dinner. She brushed from the cloth the crumbs left from her father's just finished meal, and picked a faded rose out of the bowl on the table.

' Now, that looks neat and appetising,' she said to herself, critically surveying her work. ' Poor old Joe! He must be tired and sleepy.'

Father and brother laughed at Mabel, but secretly were not sorry to give way to what they called her fads. She had put her foot down on kitchen meals, urging with plausibility that since the cool bark roof had gone, and the whole house was like an oven beneath the iron, there was no sense nor comfort in choosing the hottest spot to eat in, merely because their neighbours were foolish enough to do so. In the two years since the bush fire Mabel's voice had become a power in the house, and her parents more and more deferred, in the world of little things, to the whims and wishes of the beautiful, headstrong girl of whom they felt so proud.

In a cheap print, almost white from frequent washing, brightened in lieu of vanished pattern by a crimson belt, for without colour of some kind Mabel could not exist, with glossy hair brushed back from a broad low forehead, a bright face and a figure slim and erect, Mabel Toland presented a grateful vision of coolness very different from that which greeted most harvest labourers in the valley when they went in to their meals that day.

And Mabel was not altogether unconscious of the fact. Without much vanity she was proud of her good looks and did what she could to enhance them. They were one of the refinements jealously treasured for their little household, which, she told herself with girlish vehemence, should never sink under any poverty to the level of others, where frowsy fringes and ill-cooked food, on dirty tables, gave the men every excuse to be ill-mannered savages. Joe chafed sometimes under Mabel's tyranny. He considered it unjust that ingrained dirt should be regarded as an aggravation rather than as an excuse for the crime of soiled hands.

'Anyone would think I was going to be a bloomin'

dook, instead of a policeman, from the way you fuss me,' he would grumble ; but he always gave in to Mabel's commands if not to her argument that, for all he knew, he might have to arrest dukes and that kind of people some day, and the least they could expect would be to have the handcuffs put on them by policemen with clean hands.

The tramp of wearied horses led her on to the verandah. The team, relieved from work, with bowed heads and sweat-blackened collar marks, were making their way in single file to the little creek by the stables, where sheaves of wheaten hay flung out on the banks awaited them. Joe slouched along behind, not looking cheerful or alert. His tanned face was furrowed with little perspiration rills in the layer of dust and dabbed here and there with cakes of oil-mud, acquired when his head was beneath the machine among the cogs and bearings requiring lubrication. The effect was grotesque when he smiled at his sister, who nipped vine shoots on the trellised wires and waited for him.

' Got anything decent to eat, Mab ? ' he asked, tramping on to the verandah and pretending to embrace her.

' Yes,' she said, recoiling and laughing. ' Cold beef —junket—and raspberries—much too decent for you as you are now. Go and get clean.'

' No,' he said calmly, flinging himself down with his back against a verandah post. ' That's worth waiting for, and I'm too beastly hot to enjoy it.'

' Well, have a drink.'

' Of what ? ' he asked, looking up with a half-suspicious expression of hope, armed against disappointment. Mabel sometimes prepared pleasant surprises, but she also sometimes played tricks and was quite capable of saying 'water.'

'This.' She brought out a jug and a cup from the table.

'You're a trump, sis,' he sighed, after swallowing half a pint of lemon water at a gulp, and wisely checking an impulse to rub the back of a variously-blackened hand across his mouth. 'I believe you know what will do a feller good better than any farmer's daughter on the river—though you do look so horrid clean.'

'So I am clean,' she said with dignity. 'Do fix yourself up for dinner, like a good boy, because I've waited for you. Where's mother?'

Joe rose, stretching himself, and laughed. 'Watching dad. He's cutting out a little bit all turns—and there she sits under an umbrella in the blazing sun, against a stook, an' admires him an' the machine. He tells her to go in and shams he don't want her there, an' I swear he'd be awfully disappointed if she took him at his word. It's rum how fond those old people are of each other.'

'They're not so very old,' returned Mabel. 'Mother at least can hardly be forty.'

'Oh, well! They're older than me anyhow,' yawned Joe. 'I'll be back in a jiffy.'

Getting a towel from his room he went to the creek and a few minutes later was in the parlour again with the shine and smell of soap on his face to testify his thoroughness. Neither very tall nor very broad, Joe had not the physique of his father and would not attain it, though he had some time to grow yet, but he was a strong, wiry lad with a well-knit figure when he straightened it, as he sometimes did; and in his face, which suggested the same plan as Mabel's, more carelessly executed, there was keenness and humour in a measure not possessed by either of his parents.

Mabel felt satisfied with his upper end at least, where only brushed hair and clean white coat were in evidence, while heavy grey boots and blue dungaree trousers were out of sight beneath the table. Her mind dwelt that day more than usual on the social position of her family, for only on the previous morning Mrs Harlin had told her that Rupert was expected home in a week or less. He had been absent just three years now, and she had neither seen him nor heard from him since the evening he had kissed her by the old harness-room door, and in the meantime he was grown into a man with the capacity for giving weight to petty things that nobler-minded childhood treats with fine disdain. She understood better now their difference in position and wealth, and he perhaps laughed if he remembered his boyish protest of life-long devotion ; but she scarcely believed so. There was a message for her in his last letter to Mrs Harlin which meant very little, perhaps—nothing without the key forged on their moonlight ride and grown rusty with disuse—but she blushed suddenly when Mrs Harlin read it to her, and that lady intuitively grasped at least a part of Mabel's carefully-guarded secret, kept it to herself and pondered.

Joe was hungry, Mabel preoccupied, so there was little conversation during their meal to interrupt the monotonous buzz of the big flies and the distant rattle of the binder, but when it was finished Joe pushed his chair from the table, and with a wink and a 'Don't split, Mab,' produced a cherry-wood pipe from his pocket.

'Joe! You don't mean to say you smoke!'

'I don't mean to say it just yet awhile—but I do it—when I get the chance,' he drawled, shaving off the corners of a dark plug of 'Two Seas' with a novice's deliberation.

'Father would be awfully angry.'

'That's just why I don't let him know.'

'But it's not honest.'

'That's so like a girl! I'll bet there's lots of things you keep dark—or would, only girls are generally fools enough to tell other girls an' get peached on for their pains.'

Joe's random thrust, quite unjustified so far as he knew, for Mabel was singularly frank, nevertheless got home since, compared with her great secret, Joe's smoking was as nothing.

'But you've just told me,' she objected inconclusively.

'Girls split on girls—not men. Anyway, sisters don't count.'

'Not boys' sisters?' she asked, with a mischievous smile.

'Don't nag,' said Joe, loftily, 'but come down to the creek and have a yarn under the wattle tree before I go back to that beastly stooking.'

The wattles had grown rapidly after the fire, clothing the devastated creek banks again in greenery, but the beloved elms were gone, and the vines springing vigorously from the roots remained almost solitary survivors of the Tolands' old plantation.

When she had made the eatables safe from cats and flies, Mabel took some sewing with her and

joined Joe beneath the trees, announcing her arrival
by dropping a pebble into the pipe bowl sticking out
from beneath the slouch hat pulled over his face.

'Oh, stow it, Mab!' he grumbled, sitting up.
'Can't you let a feller alone?'

'Well, can't you give a "feller" room to sit—you're
sprawling all over the only bit of shade that's any use.'

Joe collected some of his limbs and Mabel sat down.

'I've been thinking, Mab,' he said presently. 'I'm
going to sling the farm as soon as I'm old enough to
be a trooper.'

'Then that old joke is going to be a reality. They
haven't laughed you out of it?'

'No, I don't get laughed out of things,' said Joe,
with something of his father's expression. 'It's a
kind of life I should like—I'm the right weight and
cut for it—and I believe a fellow could get on.'

Mab put down her work and stared across the
creek at the hills. 'It's awfully rough on father,' she
said. 'Have you thought how cut up he'll be?'

'Yes, poor old dad. I know he will feel it, but I
can't help that.' Joe spoke seriously, and the pipe,
which required attention still, was flung aside. 'But
you know, Mab, it's no use my sticking here. We
are just going to the dogs as fast as we can go, but
father's so determined to pull through that he can't—
or won't—see it.'

'I know the fire and mother's illness and all cost
a lot of money, but I thought we were picking up,'
said Mab, incredulously. 'And isn't this going to be
a grand harvest?'

'Not too bad. The wheat might go four bags all
round.'

'Well?'

'Well, what's the good of that?' queried Joe, contemptuously, 'with wheat at two bob a bushel in Tongalong? Suppose we have four bags—say seventeen bushels. That's one pound fourteen shillings an acre, which sounds like money on two hundred acres. But when you take off—oil and twine, two shillings—bags, two shillings—thrashing, three shillings—carting and stacking about two shillings—carriage to Tongalong, ten shillings—commission, I suppose, another bob—there's not much in it, is there?'

'I don't know,' said Mabel, wearily. 'I can't follow all your figures.'

'They sing-song themselves through my head all the time I'm on the binder, and they're not far out. Anyway, that means there's only about fourteen shillings an acre left to pay for dad's work and mine, and horse feed, and meet a bill on the reaper and binder—and it won't do it—let alone pay interest and allow us to go on living.'

Joe's grasp of the position which she had unthinkingly supposed to be improving was a revelation to Mabel.

'I had no idea you thought about it like that. Have you said anything to dad?'

Joe shrugged his shoulders. 'No; what's the use? He could know it just the same as me if he would, but he won't go into it because he wants to be cheerful for mother's sake, I think. And it's just as well, because he couldn't do anything different if he did, or save one penny of the expense.'

'I could help with the stooking, couldn't I? and—and drive a cart?' said Mab, knitting her brows into a frown as she racked her brains vainly for possible economies.

'You just suggest that to the old man and see
. what he thinks,' laughed Joe. 'But all the same you
know it's just those mean little things that do make
farming pay—a crowd of overworked, half-starved
kids—living on nothing but salt junk—going a bit
slow on soap—makin' beef of a beast with lumpy
jaw, and working a man sixteen hours a day for ten
bob a week till he jacks it up and you pick up
another poor devil out of a job that reckons he can
stand it for a time.'

'The Scotts are getting on pretty well, aren't
they?' asked Mabel.

'I think so—but they have a picked bit of land
with ten miles less cartage than us—and look at
Uncle George! Isn't he as mean as they make 'em?
When does Jimmy get a holiday? And the other
kids, poor little beasts! have to work like niggers
out of school-hours in the cowyard, for all Aunt Bess
can do to stop it.'

'If farming can't pay except by doing things Uncle
George's way, I don't want it to,' said Mabel,
decisively.

'Well, you take it from me—it can't. Not dad's
way anyhow—paying fair wages when he must have
a man, and treating me and you and everyone else—
except himself—like human beings. No; it's not a
white man's game, and I'm going out of it.'

'But what will father do?' reiterated Mab.

'I'll be able to send him a pound a week—almost
enough to pay the interest—and a darned sight more
than I'm worth to him here — with nothing for
myself.'

Joe had common sense on his side, and Mabel sat
silent, grieving over sentimental aspects of the

separation which she knew would sink into her father's soul, but felt it profitless to urge on Joe.

'But that won't be for a bit yet,' he said after a pause; 'and in the meantime I'm going to keep my spirits up, and you keep your mouth shut.'

'Of course!' she said with indignation.

'And about this—it's no use to annoy the old man.' He took up his pipe again and felt for a match. 'By the way, I wonder what Rupert Harlin's got like, and if he'll look at us now since he's become a University man and a travelled monkey and all the rest of it. He came back yesterday.'

'Yesterday?' Mabel was startled into a little cry of surprise. 'I—Mrs Harlin told me yesterday morning he wouldn't be home for a week.'

'Perhaps the old man's playing up worse than usual and they've telegraphed Rupert from Sydney. Anyway, he is home, because Jimmy Scott was up to borrow a couple of balls of twine this morning, and he told me he saw him in Tongalong yesterday.'

Mabel was bending attentively over her work again, and Joe kept one eye on her as he relit his pipe.

'You seem fluttered, old girl,' he said sympathetically. 'I know he was a bit sweet on you when we were kids, but—come on! You might as well tell us all about it now I've spotted you.'

'You haven't spotted anything,' said Mab, blushing.

'Oh, all right,' he laughed; 'but I know you're dying to tell somebody.'

It was true; and, thus encouraged, with judicious excisions and refusals to gratify Joe's outrageously inquisitive interest on some points of detail, Mab told him the story of the ride to Grimsby Farm.

When she had finished Joe suddenly burst into a mocking peal of laughter, and Mab got up with flashing eyes and flaming cheeks.

'You are perfectly disgusting,' she almost sobbed. 'After sneaking me into telling you, too! Let me go!'

But Joe hung on to her skirt to its imminent danger.

'Don't go, sis,' he exclaimed. 'I'm awfully glad. But isn't it beastly funny you being so holy about my smoking on the quiet? "It isn't honest, you know."' He mimicked her to tone and manner, and Mabel sat down again, laughing too.

'It's different,' she said.

'Of course it is—and about a million times worse. I'm ashamed of you.'

Then they fell into serious talk and discussed the matter with brotherly and sisterly freedom.

'Rupert's a jolly fine chap and I hope neither of you have changed your minds,' said Joe, summing up the situation. 'Anyway, unless he's a fool he hasn't, for he wouldn't find a girl like you if he looked in half a dozen Europes.'

'You've travelled such a lot—haven't you, Joey?—and know all about it,' she asked, laughing.

'I know enough to bet on,' he answered, 'and,' with a sudden twinkle in his eye, 'just a little bit more than you.'

'What do you mean?'

He was on his feet leaning against the wattle trunk, and after another glance towards the house looked down at her with a mocking smile.

'Never you mind, but just let me know when you're going to tell dad, so that I can hide his boots and take to the hills for a week. By Jove, I forgot to bathe that borrowed horse's shoulder!'

Joe swung suddenly off towards the stables at a pace that surprised Mabel, who sat to muse for a little in the shade before going back to the hot house and washing up.

Presently she heard Joe's step again and turned round ; but it was not Joe, and she jumped to her feet with a rosy face as Rupert Harlin stood before her.

'Mabel!' he exclaimed, holding out his hands.

'Rupert!'

Then she did not know exactly what she said. The consciousness that they had parted as children and met again as man and woman was at first embarrassing, but it soon passed away ; and when Mabel went back to the house half an hour later, the sight of a pair of her father's boots made her laugh nervously and think of Joe.

CHAPTER II

KNOWING her father better than Rupert, Mabel did not think it wise to stop him, hot and tired in the midst of his work, to drop on him such a bolt from the blue as the news of her engagement, and she insisted that nothing should be said of it in her home till the Harlins had been told. She welcomed this excuse for delay, which Rupert chafed at, for his mind was so filled with the beauty of their romance that there was no room for contemplation of its possible obnoxiousness to others, and he could see no reason, he said, for sneaking away from the farm as though he had done something to be ashamed of.

Mabel laughed and said that if she was worth having she was worth sneaking for, since her comfort and her father's would be secured by his doing so. She insisted that he should have it out with his own parents before approaching hers. Unwillingly obedient, in a rather injured frame of mind, Rupert Harlin rode away, passing Toland reaping in the distance ; and, on the way home, trying to realise his new happiness, he smiled occasionally to himself as he recognised landmarks on his last ride to Grimsby Farm when mile after mile of his longed-for opportunity had gone by without a word.

His mother was lying on a sofa in the drawing-room, with her thoughts less on her novel than on the heat and the weariness of life in general, when

Rupert Harlin entered. He had changed his dusty clothes for a light suit of flannels which seemed to bring comfort and coolness with them.

Mrs Harlin sat up and welcomed him with a smile of pride and pleasure.

'I am so glad you have come, Rupert,' she said. 'I have been intolerably hot and bored.'

'I am afraid I can't make you any cooler, mother— unless there may be a breath of air here in the draught from the fireplace. Come and try it.'

'Thank you ; I think that is better,' answered Mrs Harlin, settling herself with a sigh in a cushionless wicker chair that Rupert placed for her. She looked at her son, who had selected another, and, with his long legs stretched out, and his hands behind his head, leaned back gazing thoughtfully at the ceiling.

'Do you know, I believe you are getting quite handsome, Rupert?' she said, laughing.

'That is crushing from a mother who I thought always considered me an Apollo. But to change the subject to the beauty of lesser mortals—do you know who I think is absolutely the prettiest girl I have seen in the last three years?'

'You must have seen so many whom I have never met.'

'But you have met this one—Mabel Toland.'

'Oh?' exclaimed Mrs Harlin, interrogatively, yet not altogether surprised. She studied her son's face for further information. He was still looking with half-closed eyes at the ceiling, and a smile flickered about his mouth.

'You have seen her since you came home, then?'

'Yes, this afternoon. In fact, I have just come back from Grimsby Farm.'

'Mabel is certainly a very pretty girl,' assented Mrs Harlin, waiting in nervous apprehension, albeit with interest, for further developments; 'but I should have thought in England you would have found higher standards of beauty. Will you ring the bell and let us have some tea?'

Rupert straightened himself in his chair and looked at Mrs Harlin. 'If you don't mind waiting a few minutes for your tea, mother, I have something I want to tell you first.'

'Certainly, my boy—I can wait.' She raised her eyes to his with a rather sad smile. 'Shall I guess what you are going to tell me?'

'If you like, and if you can.'

'That you are in love with Mabel Toland.'

'I am in love with Mabel, but that's only a small and unimportant part of it. I've been that for years. I am engaged to her. Won't you congratulate me?'

Mrs Harlin gave a start of surprise and disappointment. She had known there was danger and guessed at Rupert's feelings without any idea that things had gone so far.

'I thought you would be surprised,' he continued. 'Don't you think I am a very lucky man?'

'Yes, dear. I think you are fortunate indeed in having such a nice girl as Mabel Toland to love you.' Mrs Harlin's voice trembled a little. As Rupert got up from his chair she rose too and kissed him, with a variety of feelings, kept under for the moment by a mother's sympathy, and unwillingness to chill his happy enthusiasm.

'It is very sudden, isn't it?' she asked presently.

'It is—and it isn't. I told her how I cared for her before I left three years ago, but I couldn't tell if she had forgotten me. I never saw her or heard from her since that till this afternoon, and it all happened then.' Mrs Harlin waited tactfully for further confidences and he went on to tell with due reservations just how things stood now between himself and Mabel.

'It is a risky experiment, Rupert,' she said at length. 'Her father and yours will do all they can to stop the marriage; and I am not sure that they will not be right.'

'Why?' he asked combatively.

'Why?' she repeated with a little shrug of her shoulders. 'I am afraid I should only make you angry if I tried to explain—further than that, on general principles, marriage between people of different classes, especially when parents on both sides disapprove, is a mistake.'

'But general principles have nothing to do with it. Individuals can't sacrifice their happiness to effete class prejudices. Mabel is Mabel, and I am I.'

'And you are both young and in love, which puts an end to argument and makes you deaf to anything an old woman might say, even if she had the heart to say it.'

'I wish you would not treat me like a child,' said Rupert, loftily. 'I think it is rather insulting to my common sense to suppose I should not be willing to listen to any criticisms on my conduct.'

'To declare them out of date and absurd,' she said smiling, and resting her hand lightly on his shoulder. 'No, Rupert, dear; don't let us quarrel. I tell you frankly it was not what I had hoped for you. But accept my congratulations, and believe that I think Mabel is a very nice, sweet girl, and trust that you will be very happy.'

But Rupert was not satisfied. His egotism demanded approval complete and absolute, and the offer of anything less seemed an injury.

'Thank you, mother,' he said grudgingly. 'I know you wish me happiness, but I think you might at least tell me why you think I have gone an idiotic way to get it.'

'Rupert! I did not say I thought anything of the kind.'

'Well, you implied it.'

Mrs Harlin smiled at the sullen cloud gathering on his face. 'Nor did I imply it,' she sighed. 'You young people are so impracticable.'

'We want to be treated like reasonable beings.'

'Which, when you are in love, you are not,' she laughed. 'But seriously, Rupert, if you insist upon a little lecture from me you shall have it, though I know it is wasted words. I confess I am disappointed in a way at your engagement, because I had hoped that you would marry some girl of your own station in life. At anyrate, you are too young to marry now. And I should have liked to keep you to myself a little longer. You are my only child.'

'Now you will have two—Mabel and myself,' interrupted Rupert.

'Perhaps,' she went on with an affectionate glance at her son, who leaned against the mantelpiece in front of her. 'Perhaps I shall ; but it will be different. As for Mabel herself, I am very fond of her. She has been with me much since you went to England, and I have learned to know her. And if her family and relations were different I should not have a word to say.'

'I don't marry her relatives,' he interjected grandly.

'That shows how young you are. Do you suppose no one has pride but yourself? Can you imagine yourself allowing all the tribe of Scotts to make themselves at home at Kumbarra? Can you guess at the sore feeling it will cause if you don't—even though your wife should agree that it won't do? And besides, Mabel has the deepest love for her father.'

'Quite right too. I think that he is a very fine man.'

'There is no need to tell me she is right. And I agree that he is a fine man, but one quite impossible for you or me to get on with. He is embittered against us already—an old sore, not to be healed, that had its origin in the dummying of Kumbarra more than twenty years ago, when he and your father had hot words. This will make matters worse— alienate Mabel to some extent from her father, and make things harder than ever to bear for her mother, who was a very dear friend of mine, and has become almost a stranger to me since her marriage—for a woman can keep no friends who are her husband's enemies.'

'But I have no enemies who are Mabel's friends,' argued Rupert.

'But you speedily will have. Her relatives will call you stuck up and proud. They will transfer their dislike to Mabel, and she will feel the bitterness of it. Don't ask me to say any more,' she said wearily. 'Perhaps I was unwise to say so much. Come and give me a kiss, and tell me you forgive your old mother.'

Rupert kissed her and laughed. 'There is nothing to forgive, but I am going to marry Mabel and be very happy.'

'Of course you are,' she answered, surreptitiously brushing away a tear. 'Ring the bell now, like a good boy, if you are content to argue no more.'

Rupert's hand was on the bell when the door opened and his father came in, bringing with him an atmosphere of the drafting yards and whisky and tobacco.

'What are you two discussing so earnestly?' he asked.

'We were just having a little talk,' answered Mrs Harlin, with a warning glance at her son. 'We are going to have some tea.'

'Rupert seems to spend all his time in tea and talk,' sneered Harlin, throwing himself into a chair and wiping a shining forehead that merged itself in a wilderness of baldness. 'Why weren't you down with us at the yards instead of loafing about indoors?'

'I had something more important to do,' answered Rupert, curtly. He still stood by the fireplace looking down at his father, noticing how the once well-cut features had been marred and the whole face prematurely aged by dissipation. Woman's loyal conservatism he thought was certainly an extraordinary thing. His mother had married in her own class— and yet she was an enthusiastic advocate of such a course.

The heat and the sheep had not improved Harlin's temper. His furtive blue eyes, which could not now meet others for a second, had detected Rupert's calm scrutiny, and he resented it.

''Pon my soul, Rupert,' he said testily, 'I don't think your trip to England has improved your habits or your manners. What the deuce are you staring at?'

' I beg your pardon,' answered Rupert, with a start.
' I did not mean to stare. I was thinking of my
own affairs.'

' Then you have some affairs to think about ? I'm
glad to hear it, for you seem to take deuced little
interest in mine.'

' Rupert has not been long enough back to get
into the routine of the station work yet,' interposed
Mrs Harlin. ' Will you have any tea, Tom ? '

' No, thanks. You know I never drink tea.'

Rupert placed his cup beside him on the mantelpiece and waited till the servant had left the room.

' I don't know that I ever shall be particularly
interested in the station, except as a means to a
living,' he said. ' But would you like to hear what
I have to tell you ? '

Harlin grumbled an affirmative, and in disregard
of his mother's frown of warning, Rupert thrust his
hands into his pockets and looked again at Mr Harlin.

' I am afraid it may not please you, father,' he said
with a slight nervous tremor in his voice, ' but I hope
you will let me judge what is for my happiness. I
am engaged to Mabel Toland.'

' What ? '

The shock of surprise and anger brought Harlin to
his feet as he almost bawled the question ; and before
the roughness and menace of his tone, all Rupert's
hopes of conciliation vanished.

' I thought I spoke plainly,' he answered with his
lips parted and slightly-heightened colour. ' I am
engaged to Mabel Toland.'

Harlin sank into his chair again and laughed
angrily. ' Then be good enough to break the engagement off immediately.'

'Is that all you are going to say about it?'

'Yes—unless you want me to add that I won't have it; that I will not leave you a penny if you disobey my wishes; and that I refuse to let my son marry the daughter of a sullen blackguard who has had nothing but black looks and bad words for me ever since he and a few precious mates of his sneaked on to my land.'

'Your land! Who made it yours?' queried Rupert, with a sarcastic laugh.

'The law—and my good money—not a penny of which you shall see if I hear any more of this nonsense.'

'Look here, sir,' began Rupert, with rising temper. 'I may owe you respect, but I am of age, and I refuse—'

Mrs Harlin rose hurriedly from her chair, and laid her hand pleadingly on his arm. She had sat in silence up till then, hoping in vain that the storm would pass by without her interference.

'Pray don't quarrel with your father,' she begged. 'Go away now and discuss the matter again when you have both thought it over.'

'I have given the subject all the thought it deserves, Margaret, and he has my answer,' exclaimed Harlin.

Rupert turned to his mother.

'Don't worry about us,' he said soothingly. 'I know what I am doing.'

'No! no! You are both angry and excited, and I can't let you dispute and say things you will regret.'

'I am not a boy, mother—I must manage my own affairs. Please go away for a few minutes and leave us alone.'

Mrs Harlin hesitated, astonished by a tone of command in the voice which she had hitherto been accustomed to hear in protest against, or in acquiescence with, her own. Then, as he urged her again, and almost led her to the door, she gave way; and Harlin saw with uneasy astonishment his wife obey her son's quiet order where she would have ignored his own, however emphatically expressed.

Rupert closed the door and, returning to his place by the mantelpiece, reopened the conversation.

'Look here, father,' he said, 'I am truly sorry my wishes are distasteful to you, and I don't want to say anything disrespectful; but please do not speak of Mr Toland, who is as honest and in every way as reputable a man as yourself, as a sneak or a blackguard.'

Harlin winced. He sat angrily twisting his moustache, with Rupert standing above him, taking the tone of reproof that should be his, and became aware that in this son there were reserves of violence as great as his own underlying the mother's quiet manner.

'We will keep each our own opinions of Mr Toland,' he said with a sneer. 'I suppose you have become imbued with this new democratic foolery at Oxford. However that may be, I forbid you to marry Mabel Toland.'

'Why?'

'Because she is not a fit match for you, and I don't choose that you should disgrace the family and make a fool of yourself.'

'Please drop personalities,' said Rupert, flushing. 'I presume that you have nothing to say against Mabel—not that I should listen to you if you had,' he added hastily.

'You may set your mind at rest on that score. I think her rather a pretty and—considering her station and her brute of a father—quite a remarkably nice girl. But you shall not marry her.'

'And I say I shall.'

'Very well. Your allowance from me ceases and you get nothing under my will. By God, I mean what I say! Do you hear that, sir? I refuse to support an undutiful, idle prig of a son who forgets he is a gentleman and plays the fool with a blasted cockie's daughter! I have done with you.' Harlin had worked himself into a passion, and he stamped about the room.

Rupert's eyes blazed with anger too and his face went very white. 'A gentleman!' he sneered. 'What example do you set to me?'

'You—you young viper!' spluttered Harlin. 'Get out of my house and go to your Tolands!'

'Very well,' answered Rupert, with a twinge of conscience. 'I know you have been a good father to me, and I regret having said anything to hurt you.'

Harlin's only answer to this advance was a contemptuous snort and Rupert continued, 'I am sorry, and I apologise for what I said in the heat of temper. But all the same I am old enough to be my own master and I intend to have my own way.'

'Then have it and be damned to you! But don't ask me to help you.'

'I shall not. But, as you know, there is money of mine in the station payable to me now under my mother's marriage settlement.'

'Well?'

'I must have that money out, or a portion at least, as you can afford it. This is not a threat but a necessity, as I have no profession, and, except what you have allowed me, nothing to live on.'

Harlin thought for a second or two, calmed by this practical drawback to a quarrel, and Rupert watched him. It would be a squeeze to realise the sum in hard cash, but suddenly his rage returned, getting the better of caution.

'Take it,' he said, 'and go to hell with it!'

'Thank you,' said Rupert, smiling in spite of himself. 'Have you anything to add?'

'Nothing—except go quickly.'

Harlin strode angrily out of the room, leaving his son to ponder over the delights of his engagement.

CHAPTER III

MRS HARLIN found Rupert in his room, angry and crestfallen, but more obstinate than ever. He was refilling a half-unpacked Gladstone bag amongst his just-arrived baggage, preparing to shake the dust of his father's house from his feet, and to take up his abode in Tongalong till he could see Mabel and tell her of the crisis in their affairs. His mother's entreaties, however, induced him to give way, and not to bring the eventful day of his engagement to quite such a melancholy close. If he left the house in anger it would break her heart she said. She smiled at his indignant query how it was possible for him to accept his father's hospitality after what had passed between them. All things, she thought, should be possible in the way of conciliation from a son to a father, whose deepest prejudices he had opposed, especially a father who up to now had been so generous and indulgent as his had been. She did not for one moment ask him to give up Mabel, or to surrender anything that he thought was right, but only to keep silence on the vexed question and remain for a few days at Kumbarra, after which he might go up to the New South Wales station while she fought his and Mabel's battles at home. He would show the truest generosity by subordinating his pride a little to the family peace, besides which, she was sure that he would be sorry to aggravate the quarrel and cause indelible bitterness by forcing his father to find the money, which had really gone into the station as an investment for him.

Being unwilling to embarrass his father, and attached to both his parents, Rupert had already cooled down and succumbed to Mrs Harlin's arguments when, womanlike, she could not forbear adding to their cogency by throwing in a little bribe. On Sunday she promised she would get Mabel to spend the day at Kumbarra, and early on Monday morning, if she could be persuaded to stay the night at the station, Rupert should drive her home.

That was Thursday. Rupert obeyed his mother's wishes ; and, with the greatest difficulty keeping away from Grimsby Farm, lived in a fever of expectation till the longed-for Sunday came.

In the meantime, he again saw his father, who, doubtless owing to Mrs Harlin's influence, seemed a little ashamed of his former violence. He was ready to meet Rupert half way, so that a peace was patched up between them, on the understanding that nothing more should be said at present of his intention to marry Mabel ; that he should go shortly to spend a few months at work on Harlin's New South Wales property; and that if he was still of the same mind the question might be re-opened on his return.

Rupert declared with some warmth that delay or absence could make no manner of difference to his feelings. This nearly provoked another outburst from his father, who checked himself, however, merely saying grimly that fools sometimes exaggerated their own folly, and that Rupert had better not run his head against a wall earlier than was necessary.

Mrs Harlin had said nothing to her husband of Mabel's expected visit, and Rupert salved his conscience for likewise keeping silence by the reflection that he had made no promise not to see her, and that he was not to sit in judgment on his mother's tactics, which were admirably designed for the convenience of Mabel and himself. He more than suspected that an idle impulse of his father's towards a visit to a neighbour the other side of Tongalong was fanned into activity by Mrs Harlin. At anyrate his father drove away on Saturday afternoon, and early on Sunday morning Mrs Harlin sent her buggy and ponies to bring Mabel to Kumbarra.

Mabel blushed and looked inquiringly from Rupert to his mother when the latter welcomed her and kissed her affectionately, without, however, making any reference to late events.

It was an awkward moment for everybody concerned, but Mrs Harlin put an end to it by a sudden recollection of orders concerning lunch, which would be ready in half an hour, and she begged Mabel to excuse her.

'Does she know?' was the girl's almost breathless inquiry, with anxious eyes turned on Rupert, as the door closed behind her hostess. She stepped back a pace and with a little commanding gesture kept him from her till he had answered her question.

'Yes.'

There was a sigh of relief; her lips parted in a smile that showed a flash of white teeth, and her eyes fell before Rupert's which were worshipping everything about her with admiration he fondly believed to be critical, triumphantly vindicating his constancy to the boyish ideal, which, in the short hour of three days ago, he had only half discovered to fall so far short of the reality.

To a man more experienced and less in love than
Rupert the picture that Mabel presented would
indeed have been fair to see. A half-petulant little
frown and pouting of the lips, at the readiness of her
undemonstrative lover to obey the lapsed command to
keep away, gave an added piquancy to her bright
young face ; and Rupert was so engrossed in the
æsthetic pleasure of studying her that he subdued the
impulse to take her in his arms and, with a smiling
suspicion of its cause, watched the frown deepen.
Her foot tapped impatiently and he looked down at
it. Unable to persuade himself that it was extra-
ordinarily small, he noted with satisfaction that it was
well shaped and neatly booted. Good looks, allied
to innate good taste rising superior to limitations imposed by rigid economy, made her faultlessly dressed
in Rupert's eyes, and, though he could for a moment
concentrate his attention on some single detail to approve it, a grateful impression of brightness, coolness
and grace summed up his perception of Mabel. A
woman would have told him that the pink print was
cheap and fading ; the straw sailor hat last year's
shape ; the Suède gloves cleaned more than once, and
would have probably felt injured that such grave facts
should weigh so little, but Rupert saw only a sweet
picture harmoniously framed. Her clear olive skin,
that defied sunburn, showed the red beneath, intensified
a little by the excitement she felt and the drive in a
north wind that had blown loose a lock or two of
brown hair, giving a pleasant relieving touch of un-
tidiness. Her tall, slight figure had the grace that
comes from constant exercise, never degenerating
into toil beyond the strength of healthy young limbs ;
for it was a jealously-guarded article of her father's

faith that no necessity justified the imposition of other than woman's work on woman's shoulders ; and the charm of Mabel's lithe shapeliness was his complete justification.

As Rupert still showed no disposition to speak, Mabel was obliged to break the silence.

'You don't seem to have much to say to me,' she ventured.

'Haven't I, though?' he laughed, kissing her this time without other protest than a slight blush. 'I have so much to say that I don't know where to begin— and you're so good to look at, Mab, darling, that it seems a pity to leave off even to kiss you.'

She glanced up at him with a bright smile.

'It's nice of you to be so silly, but I want you to be serious now and tell me all that Mr and Mrs Harlin said.'

'Well—I don't think I'll exactly do that, you know,' drawled Rupert, with humorously-raised eyebrows, as he recalled his father's violent language. 'But I'll tell you the long and the short of it. The mater considers us young and foolish, but approves— your being here is the best proof of that.'

'Yes—and your father?'

'He considers us still younger and more foolish— and he doesn't approve—somewhat emphatically.'

'Why not?'

Rupert laughed a little uneasily, but Mabel's eyes demanded the truth, and he saw that the question could not be evaded.

'Because,' he began, casting about for euphemistic words, 'because he and your father are not friends, you know—and I think he wants to choose my wife for me.'

A combative smile hovered about Mabel's lips.

'And he thinks a selector's daughter is not good enough for you?'

'Come here and don't talk nonsense, Mab,' he exclaimed, trying to put his arm round her. 'Or at least, if my father has ridiculous squattocratic notions, don't visit his sins on me.'

'There, you have admitted it,' she said pettishly, but smiling in spite of herself, and making only a feeble effort to escape the hand on her waist. 'I don't want anyone thrown away upon me.'

'Then you should have said so before. See here, darling!' He held her by the arms; and Mabel, looking up into his face, felt that parents' wishes counted for very little while that expression was there. 'You must be fair, Mab, to my father as well as to me. Yours thinks you are much too good for a beastly squatter's son—he's right, to be sure — but that's your fault, not his. And in his way he is just as cranky and unreasonable as my old dad.'

'I suppose he is,' sighed Mabel.

'Of course he is!' Rupert clinched the argument with a kiss. 'So let's make the best of our respective father's idiosyncracies and show them that love has no time to bother about little things of the kind.'

'That is all very well, but—'

'But nothing—this is Sunday, and I'm not going to argue.'

'I don't care whether you argue or not ; but you're going to listen. Sit down there and hear what I have to say.'

Rupert drew a chair up opposite hers and leaned forward with his elbows on his knees, staring at her solemnly. 'Go on, Goddess of Wisdom. I am all ears—except a little bit of eye that tells me you are very beautiful.'

Mabel haughtily ignored the interruptions.

'It is not exactly the same for us. I know my father has just as much pride as yours,' she began hesitatingly; 'but I do know, too, that our positions are different. You are a gentleman's son, and I—'

Rupert half rose with an impatient gesture.

'No ; let me say it,' she went on with a somewhat disdainful smile curling her lips. 'Don't think that I am humble—I am not. And it is just because I am proud, and our social positions—' This time Rupert refused to be silenced or to keep his seat.

'Look here, Mab,' he said almost sternly, standing over her and imprisoning her hands with his on the chair arms. 'You are not to think. I don't care two-pence whether it is your pride, or humility, or position or any other nonsense—you are not to have it. We belong to each other and that's all about it. Do you hear ? '

'I ought to — you are emphatic enough,' she answered, looking up with a laugh.

'I have to be when you are so obstreperous. No, I am not going to let you go yet. Pride is rot some-times. I have pocketed mine by staying here in the old man's house after a row with him. I have pro-mised to go up to New South Wales for a few months and not to make our engagement public, or say any-thing to him till I come back, because more row now would mean money worries to him and grieve my mother. You see he hopes—or pretends to hope—that we will think better of it ; but we know that is nonsense. Your people, if you like, need not be told anything till I am home again and my side of the business settled once for all. Will that do ? '

'I think it will,' she said meekly.

'Well, let this be a lesson to you. Be good another time. You may go now.' He smiled at her affectionately and released her hands.

'But you may not,' she said, clasping one of his. 'I am not going to argue or dictate—I am not violent enough to have a chance against you—I only want to know something.'

'Anything you like.'

'Are you sure—quite sure—that you are not making a mistake? Is it worth all the quarrelling and everything for a girl you scarcely know?'

'Is it the girl who was boasting just now of her terrible pride?' He shook his head at her mockingly. 'I am surprised at you, Mabel.'

'Pride has nothing to do with it,' she said with a happy sigh. 'You are sure—that is all I want. I am very fond of you, but it seems wonderful that you should care so much—though I thought of you always and somehow expected you would, and I should have been ever so unhappy if you had forgotten what you said that night.'

'It was the only thing I really remembered. Ever since I was a boy I have never cared for any other girl like you. And I used to think—' Rupert stopped suddenly as he heard a step in the passage. 'I'll tell you all about that some other time. Now I have got you, and I'm not going to give you up. That's mother coming, so I'll clear out and give her a chance for a five minutes' yarn with you to put things straight before lunch. Don't funk it.' He stooped down and kissed the hand holding his, just as the door opened and Mrs Harlin came in with a smile of comprehension to take Mabel to her room.

CHAPTER IV

'Do you know what I have been thinking of, Ruth?'
said her husband as she kissed him good-night.

He had been sitting brooding over the fire for
hours, whilst the wind howled and the rain rattled
on the iron roof.

'How to make farming pay?' she asked with a
smile.

'No, not to-night. For once I thrust that away.
I was thinking of the days when you helped me
among the maize. We were not married then, and
there were no grey hairs amidst the brown. Ah,
lassie! I never thought to drive furrows across your
face.'

'Hush, you mustn't say such things. No one is
proof against time. Let us think of that day
together. I shall never forget it. It's long ago, but
it seems like yesterday. I feel now as I felt then.
Do you, dearest?'

He pressed her closer to him for reply, and like two
lovers they sat gazing at the glowing embers whilst
the ticking of the clock alone broke the silence in the
room.

Then Toland spoke in a deep, low voice full of
suppressed emotion.

'How I misled you! I lured you with a picture
of the future painted in bright colours. Fate has
daubed it all over and made it real,'

' You did not mislead me. You promised to love me—that was all I wanted, and I have got more than I ever hoped for.'

They were silent again whilst a gust of wind struck the cottage and made it shake to its foundation, breaking round it with a shrieking sound like a spirit in distress. Then there followed a muffled roar, as a great tree, not far distant, crashed to the ground.

Ruth gave an involuntary shudder and drew closer to her husband.

' Everything seems to fall,' he said enigmatically.

' But some can rise again,' said Ruth, interpreting his thoughts.

' Ruth, there is something I should tell you,' he said after a pause. ' I have been keeping it to myself. Things are in a bad way with us. The mortgage falls due shortly. If I cannot get it renewed God only knows what will happen to us.'

' I knew something was worrying you, dear. Why did you not tell me before ? '

' I couldn't,' he replied with something like a groan. ' I want to bear it all myself; and yet the misery is that if things go wrong you must suffer too.'

' I shall only suffer because it will make you miserable.'

' Not suffer ! Why, what would become of you if we were driven from our home to tramp the roads and become vagabonds on the face of the earth ? '

' I should be like the Ruth of old, " Wheresoever thou goest I shall go." But all the same I am sure everything will yet turn out for the best.'

' For years I thought so, but failure follows upon failure. At the start I was full of hope, and no work seemed too hard ; but nothing seems to prosper, and sometimes now, when I'm out, I feel inclined to throw away the tools and go and drown myself. I know now what it is that drives men to the shanty. It isn't the brutishness of their nature but the hopelessness of their lives.'

Ruth took her husband's hand in hers and looked at him with compassionate eyes from which the lovelight had not faded.

'You will not fail, John, dear—and you will not fall. All will come right. I know it will.'

'We will hope so, little mother. There is nothing to do but to fight on. It's a shame of me to worry you about it, for that can't do any good. You must try and not mind if sometimes I'm a bit of a savage—for somehow or another strange fits come upon me now.'

Though that was precisely what Ruth did mind, and which crushed her loving nature more than any prospect of misfortunes to come, she replied sweetly,—

' I will try and not mind, for I know how much you feel it all, but you must promise to tell me all your worries.'

'Well, we will not talk about them any more to-night. It's late, and I must send you to bed. Do not lie awake thinking of them.'

'You must come soon too,' said Ruth, as she rose. 'You are always so very late now that it seems to be near morning. Mr Conyngham will be here tomorrow night and you are sure to sit up talking, so do get a good night's rest.'

'I won't be long. I'm glad Conyngham's coming. I want to have a yarn with him.'

When Ruth had gone, Toland sat brooding for a while with his elbows on his knees and his head

Q

between his hands. Then he began to pace the
room, a prey to the thoughts that would not let him
rest. At first there was a gentle look upon his face
as he thought of Ruth's unfaltering love, but gradually
it departed and he grew to look stern and morose.
Round and round the table he strode, with his hands
clenched behind his back, his head bent forward
and his great shoulders stooping. Then he felt
cramped by the limits of his cage and passed on to
the verandah. There he felt more in his element ;
for as he marched up and down he was buffeted by
the wind, and the noise of the storm at once soothed
and exhilarated him. After a while he threw himself
down on a bench, and his iron frame being inured to
all weather, he did not heed the piercing wind. He
was just beginning to doze when he was startled by
a voice close by him.

'Father !'

'Yes, Mab,' he replied, springing up. 'What's the
matter ? '

Mab stood by him, shivering in a wrap thrown
over her nightdress, and with her brown hair tossed
in the wind.

'Father, you're not cross with mother, are you ? '

'No, child. Whatever made you think so ? '

'I heard she was not sleeping, and went to see and
found her crying. She pretended nothing was the
matter.'

'I will go and see,' he said, and went inside while
Mab crept back to bed, thankful that her father had
at last gone to rest and that her vigil was over.

Next morning the members of the little household
were very quiet and subdued. Toland, now ashamed
of the emotionalism of the previous night, was stern

and moody. The affection even that he had exhibited towards his wife seemed in the light of day a betrayal of weakness.

What right, he asked himself, had a man on the verge of shame and ruin to think of such things? Henceforth he would steel himself against all softening influences and meet the buffet of fate in armour of iron. He remembered being told when a boy how in the cold North his forefathers had been known as fierce, relentless men, who went their own way in spite of blood and tears. So would he go his, untrammelled and alone. Ruth could have the children to comfort her. He was getting on in years, and the time had passed to think of love. With back to the wall he would fight against impending ruin. If it conquered him, what then? When he thought of it the blood seemed to surge through his brain and a whisper was there which, though vague and inarticulate, he feared, knowing in his heart of hearts that it was a prompting to destroy.

Ruth was sad, for she felt instinctively her husband's revulsion of feeling, and knew that he had shut himself up in himself again. She did not love him the less for it, but pitied him and herself the more. Even in his blackest moods he had always been gentle to her. She had never had to suffer a harsh word, though she would almost have preferred that to his terrible silences. Nor had she the consolation Toland supposed, in being first in Mab's affection, for she guessed that place was reserved for her lover. So the day wore drearily away, the routine of the farm seeming even more monotonous than usual, and all were glad when evening came and the advent of Conyngham relieved the tension.

During supper the conversation of the schoolmaster led their thoughts into impersonal channels; and under the spell of Mab's contagious merriment and Conyngham's good-humoured repartee to her attacks, even Toland forgot for a while his gloomy forebodings. Once, however, an unfortunate subject was touched by Conyngham.

'Did you see the announcement in the last *Banner*,' he asked, 'of Harlin's intention to cut up the estate into farms and let them by tender?'

'No,' replied Toland; 'but I heard there was some talk of his doing it.'

'Yes, I know. But I refer to the paper's announcement. It is very amusing. I have it here, and with your leave, Mrs Toland, will read it.'

'Yes, read it, if it is amusing, by all means,' said Ruth.

'It is headed in big type "A Patriotic Undertaking. Settling the people on the land," and the editor goes on to say,—

'" In these days when inability to procure an acre of land on which to pursue their calling is driving our farmers' sons into Melbourne factories and sweating dens, it will be learnt with gratification that it is the intention of Mr T. Harlin to cut up the Kumbarra Estate into small farms, which will be let at an annual rental to be fixed by open competition. The great fertility of the soil assures a rush of applicants, and doubtless Mr Harlin will be well repaid for his far-sighted and patriotic endeavour to advance the prosperity of the district by enabling it to retain its rising generation—" and so on.'

'What do you see in it that is so amusing?' asked Mab in tones slightly suggestive of resentment.

'Oh, I m amused at the introduction of the rack-renting system into the district being so highly eulogised, when, by the cablegrams in the same paper, we read that Irish landlords who have but done the same thing are being potted by their tenants from behind convenient hedgerows. However, perhaps I should not be amused. It will doubtless be a good thing for the district; and Harlin will make more out of men than sheep—that is, if there is any difference.'

Toland gave a grunt and asked for another cup of tea in tones of such unnecessary acerbity that Conyngham felt he had broached a topic better avoided, and turned the conversation.

When supper was over Toland asked his friend to come into the kitchen and have a smoke.

'I always feel more as if I could let out over the fire in the kitchen than in the sitting-room,' he said, as he placed a couple of chairs in front of the hearth and threw his coat on the table.

'Yes; it's more comfortable,' assented Conyngham, proceeding to fill his pipe. 'How are things going?'

'To the devil,' replied Toland, laconically.

'A very fit and proper place on a cold night like this,' commented Conyngham, as he kicked the logs together. 'Have you got all the crop in?'

'Very nearly. I'm not putting in so much this year.'

'How's that?'

'Wheat at one and sixpence a bushel in Tongalong does not encourage one much, and the fact that the mortgagee will probably reap the harvest still less.'

'Surely things are not so bad as all that?'

'My mortgage falls due in a month's time, and unless I get a renewal it will be all up with me.'

'By Jove, that is serious!' said Conyngham, now deeply concerned. 'Who is your mortgagee?'

'I got the money from Macnamara in Tonga-long.'

'A bad man to deal with,' commented Conyngham.

'I had to go to him. At the time I didn't know anyone in Melbourne, and I knew lenders there would not look at a security so far from a railway—at least, that's what I was told.'

'But surely you can get the mortgage renewed?'

'That's just what I'm afraid about. When I borrowed prices were high and there was a boom on. Since then land has fallen in value. Macnamara pressed me to take more than I intended at the time, and like a fool I did, thinking I could go in on a larger scale. Everything seems to have gone to pot since. Bad seasons, low prices, rabbits, have kept me down. I've had a terrible struggle to pay the interest; and now there's something worse coming.'

'It's serious,' said Conyngham; 'and I would advise you to go to Tongalong at once and see Macnamara about a renewal. Don't wait till it's too late to do anything.'

'Yes, I was thinking of that, and may go to-morrow. But, my God, Conyngham! isn't it a come down for a man? After all my years of labour, clearing the bush and making a home, I may be ruined and sold up and have to tramp the road for work—and be a slave till I die.'

Conyngham nodded his head in acquiescence, not being able to frame a consolatory remark.

'How we have all been fooled!' continued Toland. 'Man after man among the neighbours has been sold up, and, except Scott, I don't believe there is a single one left of those who selected at the same time as myself.'

'And they came to the colony to better themselves!' said Conyngham.

'Yes, to better themselves,' repeated Toland with a hoarse laugh as he got up and stood with his back to the fire. 'To be independent men and have land of their own to hand down to their children. Don't I remember the old gags I have spouted, and don't I see now the whole fraud of the thing? The old-world curse is on the new; there is no such thing as independence for the poor.'

'Things may come right yet,' said Conyngham, though he knew Toland had not exaggerated the seriousness of the position.

'I hope they will, for, mark you, Conyngham, this life of debt is driving me mad. When I look at my wife I think of her driven from her home to beg for shelter! I see Mab in a Melbourne sweating den! Would to God such things did not happen, but they do so every day.'

'That's true,' said Conyngham, bitterly. 'They have become so common that no one takes any particular notice of them.'

'There must be a remedy,' said Toland, pacing the room; 'and if I were as strong in brain as I am in muscle I should find it out and make this a world where there would be some other reward for honest toil than starvation and slavery.'

'It would be a mighty task, my friend,' said Conyngham, humouring him.

'Yes, and I'll never see it done. I thought to once when I left the old country, but the attempt here to better things has all proved a failure and a sham.'

' I don't know that there ever was any real attempt,'
said Conyngham, contemplatively. 'And whatever
endeavour was made was conceived in ignorance
and executed in fraud. It's the same the wide world
over, ever was, and ever will be. It was only in a
dream that the lean kine swallowed the fat. It's
always the other way in reality.'

' And no one cares—no one lifts a little finger to
cause justice to be done! ' burst in Toland, his eyes
flashing beneath eyebrows contracted with passion.
' How I long for that which oppresses me to take
form! If it were a man I'd seize him in my arms
and crush him to death. I'd throttle him till the
blood gushed out between his teeth. I'd bury my
teeth in his throat like a wild beast! But instead I
must sit down and wait, and hope for the best, and
pray like a pious hag that I may not end my days as
a vagrant in gaol—for they haven't even got a poorhouse in this accursed country.'

Conyngham looked at Toland with alarm, for the
fury of his outburst deepened a suspicion he had held
for some time that his friend, from constant brooding
over his troubles, was becoming a monomaniac.
This thought troubled him all the more because, a
pessimist himself, he felt disqualified to relieve the
mental sufferings of another.

' Yes,' he said after a slight pause. ' You might
even come to be no better than a vagrant schoolmaster.'

The remark was a fortunate one, as it instantly
directed Toland's thoughts from himself to his companion. He dropped into his chair with an exhausted
look, and both men sat for a while gazing into the
fire in silence, each wondering where the current

of the other's life would reach that ocean of eternity.

Presently Toland rose and said,—

'I'm not a pleasant mate nowadays. Come and have a game of crib with the wife.'

CHAPTER V

NEXT morning Toland started before daybreak for Tongalong, and in the afternoon Mallock rode up to the cottage at Grimsby Farm. He tied his horse to the fence, and looking about him with an air of complacent interest, knocked at the door that opened off the verandah into the sitting-room. Ruth came to see who was there, Mab being away with Joe, who was shifting some stock. She was dumbfounded on recognising Mallock, and felt a tremor run through her at the thought of a *tête-à-tête*.

'Oh, it's you, Mr Mallock,' she said hesitatingly, as she held the door half open without asking him to enter.

'Yes, it's me, Mrs Toland, and how are you?' With an air of uneasy familiarity he held out his hand and Ruth touched it unwillingly, thinking how clammy it felt.

'Quite well, thank you,' she replied.

'I want to talk over a little business with you,' Mallock continued, edging closer to the door and looking into the room.

'With me?' said Ruth, in tones of astonishment.

'Exactly! And I reckon no one else will do.'

'Come in, then,' she said, and, going back into the room, she resigned herself to the inevitable and sat down.

Mallock took a seat facing her, and with his hands on his knees leant forward and stared at her closely.

'Mr Toland's gone to town,' he said after a pause.

'Yes. Did you want to see him?'

'No; I reckon he's gone on mighty unpleasant business.'

'I don't know,' said Ruth, frowning. She knew the man was being insolent, but felt powerless to rebuff him.

'Well, I do,' said Mallock, with a malicious grin; and if you like I'll tell you what his particular business is. He's gone to try and get an extension of the mortgage, so he won't be sold up and turned out of house and home.'

'You seem very well acquainted with our affairs, Mr Mallock,' said Ruth in a vain attempt to snub him.

'Well, I do know something about them—a deal sight more than your husband does. And the funny thing is he might have fixed up his business nearer home than Tongalong, if he knew where he was.'

'How is that?'

'You see, he wants to get a renewal from his mortgagee.'

'Yes.' Fear was beginning to mingle with Ruth's indignation.

'Now, *I'm* his mortgagee.'

Ruth gave a little cry and turned deadly white.

'You!' she gasped. 'No, I know you're not. My husband got the money from Mr Macnamara.'

'Who got the money from me and transferred the mortgage to me,' said Mallock, triumphantly. 'You see ladies don't understand business. I, so to speak, bought the deed from Macnamara, and so your husband owes the money to me. That's why I was saying it was so funny him going to Tongalong when he could have fixed it up closer.'

'But how is it my husband doesn't know this?'
asked Ruth, trying hard not to believe.

'I daresay he does by now. I told Macnamara he
could let him know.'

'Then our farm is mortgaged to you?' Ruth
spoke faintly, slowly realising the horror of it. Then
Mallock's jarring voice startled her from her thoughts.

'It is. But that's nothing; we can fix it up all
right—never you fear. It wasn't about that I came
to talk to you. That slipped out promiscuous like.
What I wanted to talk about is something more
interesting to a lady. See here, Mrs Toland, I'm a
rich man. I'm worth thousands and thousands of
pounds. I own thousands of acres. Half the district
is mortgaged to me. Well, I'm getting on in years.
I don't want to see it all slip away, so I'm thinking
of getting married.'

'Indeed?'

'Yes, Mrs Toland—and what's more, I'm thinking
of marrying your daughter Mab.'

'You can't mean that!' cried Ruth. It sounded
like a disgusting joke, and she flushed angrily, feeling
inclined at once to laugh and to cry. Mallock was
too absorbed in his scheme to notice her.

'I just do,' he went on placidly. 'She'd suit me
first rate, and I reckon my money would suit her, and
suit you all. I tell you there's lots of it for all. Why,
I own half Tongalong.'

'If that's all you have come to see me about,' said
Ruth, rising with a quiet dignity but trembling from
head to foot, 'it is no use your staying longer.'

'It is, though!' said Mallock, angrily. 'Perhaps
you think I'm too old; I tell you there's plenty left in
me yet. My sort never get old—can't afford to.'

Ruth began to move towards the door.

'Perhaps you don't like the idea of your daughter marrying a man that keeps a public-house, but I tell you she can live in Toorak with the best of them—or the worst of them—for I'm told they're a pretty hot lot. Money'll do anything. Doesn't a draper have the Governor to breakfast? Isn't the son of a bullock-driver one of the cocks of the walk? And can't I be the same? Why, haven't I been asked to put up for the Upper House, and couldn't I ruin any man that opposed me? I tell you, people don't know what I've got, and every day I make more—for thrift's the thing to get a man on.'

While Mallock spoke in a tone of fierce earnestness Ruth sank back into a chair. When he had finished she spoke in a rather more kindly tone.

'Don't say anything more about it, Mr Mallock,' she said, 'you must know it is impossible.'

'But I say it isn't impossible,' insisted Mallock, striking the table beside him. 'Nothing has been impossible for me. Didn't I learn to read and write by the light of a lantern in the stable when I was working for Cobb & Co.? Didn't I start with only a few shillings, hawking with a pack on my back? It's no use telling Nick Mallock anything he wants is impossible to get.'

'Do you suppose my husband would consent?' asked Ruth.

'No,' said Mallock, with a short laugh, 'but that wouldn't be necessary.'

'Or my daughter?'

'I could make her see things in the right light. There's nothing like money. And ain't it better to be wealthy than a pauper any day?'

'You are insulting,' exclaimed Ruth, incensed with herself for having allowed Mallock to argue the matter.

'I beg pardon, I didn't mean it. I was thinking she'd jump at me when I told her of the nice little present I'd give her on her wedding-day to do what she likes with. Here it is! It's the mortgage on her father's farm. That would square that little business nice and satisfactory to all, now, wouldn't it?'

Mallock drew a deed out of his pocket and laid it on the table before Ruth.

'There it is, you see. That's Mab's the day she marries me. Now, what's it to be? Will you stand by me or not?'

Ruth got up from her chair.

'Mr Mallock, will you kindly go?'

Mallock was utterly astonished, for his experience of women had been confined to those whose favours were in the market. His anger for the moment was kept under by surprise.

'I don't want to offend,' he said. 'It seems to me a straight and fair way of doing things.'

'Go!' said Ruth, pointing to the door. 'I'm only sorry that my husband is not at home to see you about the matter— No—I'm glad he's not for he'd kill you if he knew. Be careful, Mr Mallock, when he hears about the mortgage.'

The speech, made in desperation, was an unfortunate one. Hatred and rage flashed in Mallock's eyes, and he shook with passion. He rose hastily, knocking over his chair.

'At home!' he spluttered. 'You're glad he's not at home! I tell you, in a month's time he'll have no home. Didn't I on purpose tell Macnamara to lend more on the place than it was worth, so he wouldn't get it from anyone else when it was due? He'll never raise the money to pay me off. He's a ruined man—he's in my power. In a month he'll be tramping the roads, and you and your precious daughter begging a lodging. His home! Why, damn it! it's my home and he'll have to come and beg on his knees to be allowed to live in it! Now, Mrs Toland, what have you got to say to me—who's not good enough for your gallivantin' daughter?'

Ruth tried to speak, but words failed her. She had swiftly grasped the fact that the position was hopeless, and that her husband's ruin was assured, and she felt more inclined to burst into tears for him than to upbraid Mallock.

'Well, I'll leave yer to think over it,' he said, picking up his hat and moving towards the door. 'You can let me know on the quiet within the next few days. But bear in mind, Mrs Toland, Nick Mallock's a man of his word. Good-bye.' He held out his hand, but Ruth did not see it, and with a sneer he walked to the door. His hand on the knob, he turned. 'You've got a nice little place, Mrs Toland—a very nice little place, and well worth keeping.' Then, chuckling to himself, he walked out.

Ruth's eyes followed him till he disappeared.

'Oh, John!' she cried, and sank into a chair. A moment later she slid down upon the floor and fainted away.

Just at the time Ruth wailed for her husband a man left Macnamara's office at Tongalong with his hands clenched and his face convulsed with passion. A few minutes later he galloped out of the town on a powerful horse that plunged along with a fresh, free stride. A mile on and the township was no longer in sight, while the level road stretched out in front as far as the eye could reach in the gathering shades of a dying winter day. Mile after mile sped by. Night fell. Misty exhalations rose from the ground and wreathed themselves round the great gums that fringed the road. Still the rider drew not rein, but pressed on, with his head thrust forward and his fierce eyes seeing far other sights than any disclosed by the deepening gloom. Though the road was lonely, yet he was not alone. Voices of spirits that thronged the air were calling to him. Ever and anon they yelled in chorus, 'Kill! Kill! Kill! Kill!'—keeping time to the hoof-beats of his horse. Sorrow and care were now things of the past, and again and again, as he drove the spurs in, he laughed in exultation. For the shock of finding himself body and soul, wife and child, in the power of Nicholas Mallock had been too much for John Toland's overwrought brain. To-day he had found the man on whom to be revenged. To-night he would clutch him by the throat and strangle him to death.

Mallock sat over the fire after supper in the bar-parlour, smoking and considering his interview with Mrs Toland. On the whole he felt fairly well satisfied. If, on the one hand, he was not going to obtain Mab with her parents' consent, on the other hand he was enjoying a sweet revenge. He had always hated Toland, not altogether without reason, and had determined if possible to get him into his power. Fate proving no kinder to his enemy than to the farmers around, who one by one had fallen into the hands of the mortgagee, this was easily accomplished. The frequent visits that Mab was obliged to make to the store had given Mallock the opportunity of seeing her develop into radiant womanhood, and in an evil hour he thought how good it would be to possess her. To desire with Mallock was to attempt, and an undertaking determined on, one accomplished. Puffed up by the coarse, overweening pride of the self-made man, living amongst those more or less poverty-stricken, he regarded his neighbours with contempt, and their less prosperous condition with brutal cynicism. Knowing him to be an insolvent, Mallock considered that Toland should jump at the chance of marrying his daughter to the richest man in the district. Reckoning him to be a fool, he guessed he would not do so ; and consequently had judged it best to leave him out of the question and to put the question to his wife. As he pondered he determined, if nothing came of that, to tackle Mab herself. She might give herself airs, but he would quickly bring her to her senses. After all she was only the daughter of a beggarly cockie whom he had in his power. She couldn't want a price which he couldn't pay if he liked. And he did like. He was going to have her. If as his wife, well and good—if not . . . So his thoughts ran on, getting more brutal as he meditated on the realisation of his passion. One thing he felt certain of, namely, success—not immediately, perhaps, but in good time. Had he not always succeeded, he asked himself? Sitting by the fire, in shirt and moleskins, he ran over the rising scale of his life's achievement. Stable-boy, hawker of illicit spirits, shanty-keeper, dummy-agent, storekeeper, landowner, mining speculator, prospective millionaire and member of the Legislative Council of Victoria. He felt the adulation he received in some quarters was but his due. He was one of the self-made men to whom the disciples of the doctrine of thrift pointed as a shining example of what a man who chose to work could accomplish in the colony. He was one of the sturdy pioneers who had changed a shilling into a fortune, certainly not the man to whom a pauper would refuse his daughter. Mallock found his reverie most entertaining. The world looked well for him. He had just had a heavy meal. His beard was reminiscent of the fried chops he had eaten, and, blinking like a gorged beast, he chuckled every now and again as he thought of his latest venture. His thought even became too entertaining and jocular to be silenced.

'By God! I wish I had her sitting by me now! I wouldn't want no fire to keep me warm.'

As he spoke he started.

'Hullo! There's someone on the road.'

He listened a moment. The far-off hoof-beats of a galloping horse could be heard. Mallock felt annoyed at his amorous reveries being interrupted by a traveller. He went into the bar and, leaning over the counter, listened again. Yes, he had not been mistaken; there was a horseman on the road. Who would be returning by night? he wondered. He had seen no one ride down. Then a recollection flashed across his mind—'John Toland!' But if so, why was he returning now, and making a two days' journey into one? Had his interview with Macnamara anything to do with it? Then Mrs Toland's warning occurred to him, and at the same time he heard the hoof-beats draw nearer. Beads of perspiration broke out on his forehead. He determined at least to be prepared, for there was no man on the place, and his only servant was in the detached kitchen. Opening a drawer in the bar counter he took out a life-preserver, which he slipped on to his right hand, so that a narrow band of iron, padded beneath, lay across his knuckles. He was afraid of no man now. Then he listened again. The hoof-beats were close at hand, and he scarcely had time to mop his forehead when the rider pulled up at the door. A moment later heavy footsteps sounded on the verandah, and Toland reeled into the bar. He stopped in the centre of the floor and stared at Mallock, with murder and madness in his gleaming eyes. For an instant the two men glared at one another in silence which Toland was the first to break.

'You dog, I've got you now!' he hissed between his teeth.

'Clear out of this, you drunken fool!' retorted Mallock.

'I'm not drunk—I know what I'm about. I've come to kill you.'

'Oh, you have?' sneered Mallock, adjusting the iron bar below the counter. 'Start away and do it now—the sooner you're hanged the better.'

Without a word Toland sprang upon the counter, but before he could get over, and as he knelt upon it, Mallock struck him a fierce blow between the eyes. With a terrible cry, half roar, half moan, Toland threw up his arms and crashed down upon the floor. As he lay huddled up and motionless Mallock ran round and pulled him over on his back to see the result of his blow. There was a great gash on the forehead, from which blood was trickling over his face and disappearing in his beard. To all appearances he was dead.

'By Heaven, it looks as if I had done the killing!'

muttered Mallock, as he slipped his hand beneath Toland's coat to see if the heart still beat. He felt it faintly, and dashed the contents of the water jug over his victim's head. Then, fearing someone might come upon the scene, he half dragged and half carried Toland through the bar-parlour into a small room opening from it, where he laid him on a sofa and poured some more water over him. Presently Toland showed signs of returning consciousness. His limbs moved and he moaned heavily. Mallock began to fear that he would come round and resume the attack, for he knew the nature of the man. Then it occurred to him to treat Toland as he had treated many a drunkard whose violence he feared. He hurried into the bar and brought back a glass containing a powerful dose of laudanum which he poured down Toland's throat. Then he waited and watched. But there was no longer cause to fear, for the limbs ceased to move and John Toland slept the sleep of the drugged.

' He'll be all right till morning, anyhow,' muttered Mallock as he left the room and locked the door behind him lest his prisoner should be discovered. Then he put out the lights and went to bed, though, as it proved, not to sleep. Having a drugged man on the premises was nothing so unusual as to be a cause of sleeplessness, but what kept Nicholas Mallock awake and tossing on his bed through the night was the weaving of a web wherein to entrap Mabel Toland.

CHAPTER VI

AT breakfast, the morning after Toland's departure for Tongalong, Mab announced her intention of riding to meet him.

'I told him I might when he left,' she said; 'and I think poor old dad would like it.'

'You had better not go further than the gap, then,' said her mother. She hated the idea of Mabel even passing the 'Morning Star.' Mallock's visit she had not mentioned to her children, fearing their questions as to its object.

'Very well,' replied Mab, cheerfully. 'I'm longing to hear dad's news. Joe, you've finished your breakfast. Do go and get the cob, like a good boy.'

'All right, but he's sure to be looking over the fence in the furthest corner,' grumbled Joe, good-naturedly. 'What a nuisance sisters are!'

'Well, you get the cob, and I'll ride away and leave you in peace.'

An hour later Mab was gaily cantering along the road, singing snatches of song, and thoroughly enjoying the bright sunshine and keen, frosty air. It had been a practice of hers from childhood to ride and meet her father on his return from occasional visits to Tongalong, and she felt more than ever desirous not to neglect any little act that might gratify him. His lot, she knew, had become hard to bear, and she longed to be able to cheer him when he fell into his gloomy moods. She idolised her father, believed he could do no wrong, and wished she were a man to help him out of his difficulties. Then she thought of Rupert, and sighed to think how unsatisfactory was the condition of their love affair. But Rupert and she could wait for one another, she decided, and after all, it was necessary for many people's sake that they should be separated for a time. So, singing, and dreaming and thinking by turn, Mab soon found herself at the foot of the gap. As there was no sign of her father, she dismounted and found a comfortable seat for herself. An hour passed, and as he still did not appear she grew impatient, and determined to ride along the road till she met him. She struggled up the steep incline on foot to ease her horse, and stopped half way to get her breath and indulge in an old amusement of her childhood, of throwing stones off the causeway to see them strike and rebound fifty feet below. She remounted on the top of the slope, and a few minutes later cantered past the ' Morning Star.'

Mallock saw her ride by from the bar, and went out on to the verandah to watch the retreating figure. He guessed her purpose, for he had frequently seen Mab ride to meet her father; and he chuckled to himself as he thought how fruitless was her errand, and how accident was assisting designs he had formed. He knew she would soon return alone, and his brain ran riot with hot imaginings, part products of the waking dreams of the night before. In order to steady his nerves and help him to decide on a course of action, he tossed off a nobbler of brandy. Then he went to have a look at Toland, to whom he had given another dose that morning. He found him seemingly unconscious, but in order to make sure, he shook him and called him loudly by name. There was no response, and, fully satisfied, he returned to the verandah to wait for Mab. As time went by, Mallock grew more and more impatient, and began pacing up and down. Now and again he laughed to himself as he thought how fortune was ever on his side. He had said he would succeed, and here was success coming to him almost unsought. He wished the girl would come quickly, as, between excitement and brandy, he was feeling shaky. Soon he saw Mab returning, and as she drew near, he went out into the road and signalled her to stop.

'Good-day, Miss Mab! I thought you might be looking for your father,' he said, putting his hand on her horse's neck.

Mab looked down with disgust at the blear-eyed face turned up to hers.

'I was going to meet him, but he must have been detained,' she replied curtly.

'Well, then, he hasn't,' replied Mallock.

'How do you know?' said Mab, in surprise.

'I happen to know because at this moment he's over in the hotel.'

Mab looked astonished.

'If he is,' she said, 'kindly tell him I am here.'

'It wouldn't be no good, Miss Mab,' said Mallock with a shake of the head.

'What—he isn't dead!' cried Mab, conjuring up horrible visions of accident.

'Yes,' replied Mallock, laconically. 'Dead drunk!'

'It's untrue! A horrible lie.'

'If you'll step inside I'll show him to you. You needn't believe me. It don't matter to me.'

'I wouldn't go on any account. I know it's not true.'

'Then you'd better go home and get Joe to come down for him, before I have to hand him over to the police. Good-day.'

Mallock moved away. Mab rode on a step or two, then pulled up and turned round.

'Mr Mallock,' she said simply, 'I'll see if it is true for my father's sake.'

She sprang off her horse before Mallock could touch her and followed him into the bar-parlour. Toland lay in the next room ; and in the wall between the two there was a trap-door, used for passing glasses from one room to the other. Mallock went to the trap-door and drew it on one side.

'Come here and see for yourself,' he said, turning to Mab with a sinister smile.

Mab looked through and gave a cry of horror, for there was her father, stretched apparently lifeless on his back, blood stains alone relieving the ghastly pallor of his face.

'What is the matter with him?' She cried in anguish, 'Father! father!'

Toland did not stir. Mallock, breathing heavily, watched her and said nothing.

'Let me go to him at once,' she demanded imperiously. 'Ah, there is the door!' She ran to it. It was locked. 'Open the door this instant!' she cried.

'Not yet, Miss Mab. You don't believe your father's here, do you?'

'Unlock it—at once, I say, or I'll get someone to make you.'

Mallock smiled sardonically, and Mab rushed to the door by which they had entered. It too was locked.

She turned on Mallock, quivering with wrath.

'What do you mean by locking me in here? Let me out at once.'

'Not yet.'

'Then I'll scream for help.'

'There's only a woman on the place—and she's not within call.'

Mab was beside herself and rapidly becoming hysterical.

'What does it mean?' she moaned, dropping into a chair. 'My father! What is the matter with him? Is he dead?'

'It means this, Miss Mab,' said Mallock, drawing closer. 'In the first place you needn't be afraid about yer dad. I can bring him round right enough for you. He's only a bit off his head over this mortgage business.'

'Why don't you let me go to him, though?' said Mab, with a measure of relief at hearing that at least her father was alive.

Mallock did not answer immediately, but took a chair opposite Mab, who leant with her head between her hands and her elbows on the table, striving to stifle a fit of sobbing.

'Because I want to explain matters a bit first,' he said. 'You see it's all this mortgage business has upset your dad. I'm real sorry I should be the cause. But you see money lent must be returned.'

'What do you mean? What have you to do with it?'

'Don't you know? I'm his mortgagee. He owes the money to me.'

'To you!' cried Mab, incredulously.

'Yes; he got my money through Macnamara. Here's the mortgage deed, you see.' Mallock placed the deed on the table.

'Poor old father!' cried Mab, jumping up and running to the aperture. 'I don't wonder now. Mr Mallock, you must open that door; I won't wait any longer.'

'No, no, not yet. I have a little proposal to make first. See here—this business is killing your dad. What I say is this. Marry me, and take the mortgage.'

Mallock stepped forward, and Mab recoiled in horror.

'Marry you!'

'Yes, that's it—and save your father. I love you too—by Heaven I do.'

'I'd die first.'

'Won't you think over it a moment? Wouldn't I suit you, Mab?' he said with a semi-drunken leer.

'It's revolting,' she gasped. Disgust almost choked her utterance.

'You're so much better than I am, are you, my fine lady?'

'Open the door! open the door!' cried Mab, frantically.

A malevolent smile played on Mallock's flushed features.

'And how shall I tame my little bird if I let her out of the cage?' he asked brutally.

Mab ran to the trap-door again.

'Father, help me! Wake! wake!' she called piteously.

Mallock laughed, amused at her helplessness.

'It's no use, little one. Nick Mallock's the only man to help you. By G—d, I must have you, my beauty.'

He seized her hand. She jerked it away and screamed. Mallock laughed again.

'Don't cry, my pet. I only wanted a kiss. Look here, Mab, I'll give you this mortgage for a kiss.' He held the deed out, his hand shaking violently.

Mab made no reply, but stood spellbound, trembling with fear and repulsion.

'Then I must have it for nothing.'

He ran towards her and caught her by the waist. There was a shrill cry quickly stifled.

'Keep quiet!' he hissed. 'You'll be glad enough to marry me yet. Let go, you vixen!'

Mab, for a moment, held him back, but she quickly felt her strength relax and his thick lips draw closer to hers. His spirit-reeking breath beat hot on her face.

'Father, help me!' she shrieked for the last time. An awful fear came to her. She could struggle no more. Then the room swam round. It came crashing down with the sound of splintering timber. She heard a hoarse voice. The sound of a fall and a heavy groan. With a start she returned to full consciousness, and saw Mallock stretched on the floor, and her father, with his knee on his chest and his hand on his throat, strangling him to death despite his struggles. Mab gave a cry of joy, which was quickly succeeded by one of horror, as she realised that murder was being done before her eyes. She threw herself on her knees beside Toland and tried to loosen his grasp.

'Let go, father, dear! You're murdering him!' she

cried. But Toland was unconscious of everything around, unconscious even of what he was doing. His face was set; his muscles were rigid; his eyes stared vacantly at the floor. Mallock was being done to death by the hands of an automaton. Mab, finding her efforts useless, rushed to the door to summon help. It was locked. She rushed back for the key and found it on the floor by Mallock's side. Then she ran, crying for help, through the bar into the verandah, and almost into Conyngham's arms.

'Good heavens, Mab! What's the matter?'

'Come quick or you'll be too late. He's killing him!' she gasped.

They rushed back together into the room, and not a moment too soon, for blood and foam were oozing from Mallock's lips, and he had almost ceased to struggle.

'Let go, Toland,' said Conyngham, authoritatively, as he seized his wrists.

Toland's grasp immediately relaxed. His head fell forward on his chest, and if Mab had not caught him he would have fallen on the floor.

Mallock lay for a moment gasping for breath, then he struggled to his feet, and, moaning horribly, staggered out of the room. At the same time Toland drifted back into complete unconsciousness under the returning influence of the drug; and, being placed on the sofa by Conyngham and Mab, lay there inert and motionless.

CHAPTER VII

'ASLEEP at last,' said Conyngham, entering the parlour and gently closing the door of Toland's sickroom behind him. 'He is sure to recover now.' He glanced with an expression of solicitude at Ruth's weary, sorrow-worn face, for the moment lit up by a great thankfulness. 'But why are you not lying down as you promised, Mrs Toland? We shall have you ill yourself, and that will not do.'

She smiled gratefully and sank into the chair he placed for her.

'I couldn't,' she said. 'I tried, but I couldn't sleep. I was afraid to hear him struggling again with you and Joe.'

'That is all over,' he replied confidently. 'And now you really must remember that it's selfish not to think of yourself a little—for your husband's sake, you know.'

Ruth looked indeed in need of care, and the smile faded from Conyngham's face as he noticed the dark lines under her unnaturally bright eyes, and the fragility of the figure emphasised by her black dress, which also made the pale face look paler.

'Then how you must need rest!' she said. 'You have not left him for two days—two days!' she went on musingly. 'It seems like as many years since you brought him back to me.'

'Don't think of them,' said Conyngham, soothingly.

'They are over now, and when he wakes I am sure he will be himself again.'

Ruth stared at him anxiously, hanging with hope and dread on every word.

'Yes,' he continued, standing with his arms resting on a chair-back before her; 'I feel certain of that. But he will be very weak—and his mind a blank probably since the time of his accident. I think I would just tell him—about the fall from his horse, you know—and how he was carried to the "Morning Star," when Mabel and I found him and brought him home.'

Looking into Ruth's trusting face Conyngham could scarcely bring himself to deceive her, but he knew that falsehood was merciful, and the truth would be infinitely cruel. It was his most fervent hope that Toland would indeed remember nothing.

'Don't let his mind dwell on past events more than can be helped till he is strong. And now, Mrs Toland, I should only be in the way, and I am going to say good-bye.'

Ruth sprang impulsively to her feet; and, disregarding the hand he held out to her, laid her fingers on his arm. 'Oh, you must not go yet!' she cried. 'Wait at least till he wakes and can thank you.'

'I need no thanks—and if I did I should value them at least as much from you.'

'Well, you have them—true friend,' she said tremulously, placing her hand in his.

A flush passed over Conyngham's sallow face, and he checked an impulse to raise her fingers to his lips.

Then there was a faint sound of movement from the next room, and, forgetting Conyngham, Ruth tip-toed swiftly towards it.

'Wait! I thought I heard him stir,' she whispered, with her ear against the panel; and then, opening the door, passed into the other room.

Joe was sitting there with his head between his hands, gazing into the fire, utterly tired out. During the time of Toland's delirium Conyngham had insisted that the women were better away and that he and Joe would make the most efficient nurses.

Ruth went to the bed and leant over her husband. He still slept peacefully. The morose look had left his face, and she was reminded of the John Toland of other and happier days. Tears filled her eyes as she thought of him waking to the cares he had for a time forgotten, and she bent and kissed him gently. Then she left the room again to say good-bye to Conyngham but found that he had gone.

On the way to the stable for his horse, Conyngham met Mab, who, being unable to sleep or rest, had spent the last two days wandering about a prey to almost unendurable misery. No one knew what she had gone through in the parlour of the 'Morning Star,' and she had to support alone the nightmare of shame and horror. She wished to die, to blot out the thought of her humiliation and end the agony of her morbid grief. She felt desecrated in mind and body by Mallock's brutal embrace, and could scarcely refrain from tearing the flesh where his arms had wound round her. In the turmoil of hysteria she found herself almost wishing that her father had killed Mallock, and that he himself would never regain consciousness. It was hard enough to endure alone, but she could not bear it at all, she felt, if another soul should know. If her father remembered from what he had rescued her, she knew that he

would kill Mallock with his returning strength, and
then the world would have the whole sordid story.

Conyngham startled her from a reverie with his
cheery salute.

'Well, Mab,' he said, 'don't be so doleful. I
have good news for you. Your father has fallen
asleep and we believe that he will wake all right.'

Mab was silent a moment, struggling with con-
flicting feelings.

'It's a dreadful thing to say,' she ventured hesitatingly, 'but I feel glad chiefly for mother's sake. I
believe it would have been happier for him if he had
died, or lost his reason.'

'And for you, miss?'

'Oh, I—' Mab stammered and hung her head,
suddenly aware how little of her real thought she
could explain to Conyngham.

He regarded her meditatively. 'That's a very
gloomy way of looking at it,' he said. 'Life and
sanity are generally regarded as essentials of a happy
existence.'

'And money to pay debts,' added Mab, hurriedly,
glad to have the discussion shifted on to a more
impersonal basis.

'Yes, that is true. But I think you worry too
much over that aspect. I've never cultivated a
hopeful turn of mind myself, but I don't think you
should be quite so ready to consign your father to a
nice quiet grave, or to a strait waistcoat in a
lunatic asylum, merely because of a deficiency of
cash. I don't wish to appear unsympathetic, but I
think you will all have to pull yourselves together.'

'I know you are right,' said Mab, with something
approaching a smile, as she realised how cold-blooded

her hastily-voiced avowal must have sounded. 'But nobody nowadays expects to be happy—and it's sometimes so consoling to be miserable.'

Conyngham looked at the spirited face, half turned from him, as she plucked a chrysanthemum to pieces and gazed with an expression he could not read at the hills. Mabel did not look like a creature to surrender, without a struggle, the bright things of life.

'That is a paradox I am afraid I have not time to stay and unravel,' he said at length, smiling.

Mabel turned quickly towards him. 'Why, you're not going to leave us, are you?' she exclaimed. 'It will be worse when we are left to ourselves.'

'I'm not wanted any more. Your father will be himself when he wakes, and then your mother will be his best nurse. If by any chance I should be wanted, send for me, and I will come at once.'

'I know you will. You've been very good to us.'

Her eyes spoke all the thanks her voice could not utter, and Conyngham smilingly wondered at the strength of the narrow browned hand that clasped his as he said good-bye.

She went restlessly back to the house, and Conyngham started on his lonely ride, musing upon the irony of fate that made him a consoler of the unfortunate.

The remainder of the day passed wearily, Joe going to rest and Mabel sitting, in the intervals of necessary and welcome tasks, with her mother, who never left the sick-room.

Late that night, when Ruth was watching by his side alone Toland, woke.

'Is that you, little wife?' he murmured dreamily.

S

'Yes, dear,' she replied, with a great throb of joy that the delirium had gone.

'What's the time?'

'After twelve o'clock.'

'Why are you not in bed, then?' he asked wonderingly.

'I have been watching you, dear.' She affectionately smoothed back the hair from his bandaged forehead and touched his face with her lips.

Toland turned with an effort to her. 'Has anything been the matter with me?' he asked. 'I feel very strange.'

'You have not been well,' replied Ruth, hesitatingly, dreading what was to come.

'Tell me what has happened? It makes my head ache trying to think.'

'Don't worry over it now, dear. Try to go to sleep again.'

'No, I don't want to sleep,' he said, with more decision. 'Have I had an accident?'

'Yes, dear, you had a fall from your horse. Mr Conyngham found you and brought you home.'

'I don't remember anything about it. Where had I been riding?'

'Don't ask all these questions now, dearest. It is not good for you. Do wait till the morning,' she entreated, feverishly wanting to gain time and dreading the cross-examination so merciless to himself and her.

'I can't,' he said fretfully. 'I might sleep if I knew all about it. Everything seems a blank, and it makes my brain ache puzzling it out. Where had I been riding, Ruth?'

There was a demand not to be gainsaid in his voice, weak as it was, and Ruth trembled, feeling herself on the brink of a precipice. 'To Tongalong,' she said faintly.

'To Tongalong? What did I go there for?'

'I—I—I don't know. That is—I think on business. Oh, John, my darling husband, do go to sleep again!' she cried piteously.

He stared for a moment with knitted brows into her agonised face; and, clasping both her hands in his, he raised himself against the pillows.

'On business! What business?' He pressed one hand to his forehead. 'Yes—let me think—I begin to remember—oh, my God! The mortgage!'

He fell back again and closed his eyes, scarcely conscious that Ruth was bending over him.

'Don't think of it now. I beg you not to!' she whispered imploringly, laying her head against his on the pillow. 'You have been ill, but you are going to get well again, and I am here beside you. Only think of that to-night.'

Toland seemed not to hear her. Weak from long delirium, his mind was feebly feeling its way through the darkness.

'I remember seeing Macnamara, but nothing after. Did I have the fall on my way back?' he muttered presently.

'Yes, dear. You fell on your forehead and were stunned.'

For a while he lay in silence, and Ruth did not stir, praying fervently that he was dropping off to sleep again. Suddenly he clenched his hands and Ruth caught his wrists in dread.

'I remember now!' he moaned hoarsely. 'I'm in the power of Nicholas Mallock!'

Then he raised himself on his elbows and stared

about him, fiercely at first, and then with a look of dull despair. Ruth feared that he was going to throw himself from the bed.

' Lie down again, dearest, if you love me ! ' she cried as she flung her arms round his neck and pressed him gently back. Toland sank again on the pillow, and with a deep groan turned his face to the wall and lay in silence. Ruth stood a minute leaning over him ; and then, as he did not stir, gently withdrew her arm from beneath his neck ; and, taking a chair by the bedside, sat with her head bowed down on the counterpane, sobbing as if her heart would break.

Soon Mab stole noiselessly into the room ; and Ruth, feeling a sympathetic touch on her shoulder, looked up and checked her crying.

Mab's eyes were sparkling with terrified curiosity.

' Is he awake ? ' she whispered.

' Yes, dear ; at least he was.'

' And better ? '

' Yes ! quite himself again.'

Trembling all over, Mabel looked at the silent figure by the wall. Then she turned to her mother.

' Does he remember anything ? ' she asked with an effort, in a voice she scarcely recognised as her own.

' Nothing after leaving the lawyer's office in Tongalong.'

The room swam before Mab. The tension had gone, and she could scarcely see the couch by the window to which she falteringly made her way. She sank upon it, hiding her face a moment in the curtain folds. ' Thank God ! Thank God ! ' she sighed beneath her breath, realising the immensity of the dread that had loomed before her for the last two days. Now it was gone she understood more clearly the less selfish grief that weighed her mother down, and saw with a pang of conscience how pale and wan she had become.

'Oh, mother dear!' she said, going over and kissing her fondly, 'you look so tired. You must go to bed and let me stay with father now.'

Mrs Toland was touched by Mab's strangely softened mood. She would not go to bed, however, but insisted that Mab should do so. No one need sit up, she said, as she was no longer anxious, but she would lie down on the couch, where she would be at hand if the invalid should need anything. So Mab stayed for a little with her mother, and then went to her room, thankful that her own cup of bitterness had not been filled quite to overflowing.

Toland woke in the morning, clear-minded, but very weak; and, though gradually regaining strength, he remained nevertheless utterly broken in spirit. The violent, wrathful moods had gone, but in their place a gloom that never lifted settled upon him. He wandered about, scarcely ever attempting to help Joe with the work through the day, while at night he sat for hours gazing into the fire. No memory of his ride and after events returned. The story of his accident he accepted without question, and he never alluded to his trip to Tongalong; but as soon as he had sufficiently recovered to attend to business, he wrote, at Conyngham's suggestion, to the Tongalong agent of Messrs Owen & Smith, a Melbourne firm that did a large money-lending business in farming districts. In reply to his request for an advance, the firm's valuer came to inspect, with the result that an

offer of £700 was made—£300 short of the amount
required to pay off the mortgage. After that Toland
seemed to entirely abandon hope, and, with folded
arms, to wait the falling of his doom.

But not so Ruth. Distressed by her husband's
silent apathy more than by the stormy resentfulness
which it succeeded, she did not give way to despair,
but summoned all her latent energy to fight against
disaster. She recognised that her husband's mind
was unhinged and incapable of warding off the fate
that day by day drew nearer ; so she felt that hers
must be the active part in the struggle to prevent
their home going from them. She wrote, herself, to
Macnamara, and to other money-lenders, without
result ; and then as scheme after scheme fell through,
she determined to apply to Scott. She knew he had
some money saved, and if he could be prevailed upon
to lend it to her husband, with the amount offered by
Owen & Smith, there would be enough to pay off
Mallock and avert the sale.

Scott hummed and ha'ed a good deal when she
went to him, but his regard for Ruth, and sense of
family ties, stronger than his friendship for Toland,
which was more the creature of circumstance than
sympathy, finally drew from him a guarded promise
to see what he could do. Ruth offered good interest
on his money, and the season promising splendidly
made it almost certain that she could pay it, and with
any luck, soon return a portion of the principal as
well.

Accordingly, he promised Ruth that he would go
that afternoon to see Mallock and warn him to take
no other steps since the mortgage money would be
paid. There and then he called Jimmy to finish the

last land which he was ploughing, and returned to the house with his sister-in-law, who forgave him the advice and homilies with which he entertained her for the genuine kindness prompting his action. Her heart was too full to say much in thanks, but if Scott was at first disappointed, he was finally overwhelmed, and tempted for one mad moment to say something about foregoing interest on the loan.

There had been silence for a moment when they reached the gate, and Scott looked down at her sad, gentle face with a sudden flow of compassion.

'We'll get him out of this mess, never fear, Ruth. And don't you worry any more. I'm real glad you came to me,' he said. 'Mallock knows me, and I'll make it right straight away.'

Ruth looked at him, and, overcome all at once by the kindly concern in expression and tone, she smiled with her eyes full of tears.

'Thank you, George,' she said. 'As much almost for your sympathy as your help.' She held out her hand, which was swallowed up in his. 'I am almost tempted to kiss you,' she said, with a half-hysterical little laugh. 'That would express all the thanks I can't say. I think Heaven will reward you for this.'

Scott drew back nervously, reddening with surprise, pleasure and a sense of shocked propriety. It was then that he felt tempted to refuse interest on the loan, but Heaven does not offer seven per cent., so calmer counsels prevailed, and he contented himself by muttering something incoherent and escaping to 'clean' himself for his journey. Ruth went into the house, where she had left Mabel and Bess, who looked curiously at her, but asked no questions, for beyond the fact that she had gone to speak to Scott on business, and as her face showed that it had been satisfactory, neither of them knew anything.

Scott soon reached Mallock's hotel and found Mallock in the bar, leaning lazily over the counter, picking his teeth appreciatively as he glanced at the day's paper spread before him.

'Good-day, Mr Scott. Crops lookin' well?' he said, with interrogative vagueness. It was not mail day and he was puzzled as to what brought his visitor.

Scott quickly let him know, with a mixed feeling of importance and self-reproach for his fatuous act of brotherly charity; and Mallock, still leaning on the counter, listened attentively with a scowl on his face at the first mention of Toland's name, which gave place to a pleased leer as Scott unfolded his scheme.

'This here business, it strikes me, wants a bit of private discussion, Mr Scott,' he said affably. 'If you would be so kind as to step this way—' He lifted a hinged board in the bar counter and led the way into the parlour.

'Take a seat, sir,' he said, when he had closed the door, politely handing a chair to Scott, who took it, a little overcome and yet gratified by the publican's deference, 'and excuse me for one minute.'

Scott watched him in silence fumble in a safe among a bundle of papers, from which he presently selected one and scrutinised it with knitted brows.

'Ah! That's what we want,' he exclaimed cheerfully, seating himself at the table with the paper under his hand. 'Now, Mr Scott, I understand you want . me to hold things off a bit in Toland's little affair, seein' that you can give him what he's short to make up what's owing to me?'

'Yes,' said Scott, airily. 'It's just a matter of three hundred pounds, which I can make up—with a squeeze, you know—with a squeeze,' he added in deprecation.

'Well, you're a blamed fortunit' man,' drawled Mallock, with a grim smile; 'and I congratulate you, Mr Scott, on being able to put your fingers on such a sum—squeeze or no.' He checked some disclaimer from Scott and went on: 'I congratulate you on your good fortune and your charitable heart—more'n on your good judgment—for I say it straight —no offence to you —that same Mr Toland's a bloody dangerous rascal I'd like to see out of decent society.'

'He's my relative, you know,' protested Scott, reddening. 'It's a duty, you know, and I don't want to hear—'

'Of course you don't! And I'm—not—blamin'— you,' said Mallock, with slow, indulgent emphasis. 'Blood's thicker than water, they say, and if you want to stump out three hundred pounds on his account—why, I've nothing to say. But first of all, what about settling your little business with me?' He lifted the paper from the table and looked from beneath his beetling brows at Scott.

Scott changed colour, and rising from the chair approached the table.

'What? What business do you mean?' he asked nervously.

Mallock rose too, looked at his bewildered face for a second, showing all his yellow teeth in a grin of admiration, shook his head, and clapped Scott on the shoulder.

'By God, Scott, you're a deep 'un and no mistake!' he said with a chuckle. 'Sit down here and tell me if you know that 'ere signature.' He pushed the unresisting Scott into a chair and spread the paper before him, jamming his thumb down on it beside the queerly-scrawled 'George Scott,' which the writer nevertheless recognised as his performance.

'What—what is this?' he gasped faintly.

'A transfer of your land to me for twenty-five pounds cash, bearing date, November 19th, 1863— the day it became yours, and that others that did their dealin's with Mr Harlin only got ten pound each for lots as good—but I liked the looks o' you and was a bit generous.'

'I—I swear before God I never signed any such thing!' cried Scott, in amazement, staring blankly at the tell-tale document.

'Now, what's the good of you sittin' there perjurin' yourself like a blasted infidel, with your signature staring you in the face?' asked Mallock, persuasively, with his hand on Scott's shoulder. Then, as Scott gave no answer but a groan, he leaned over and picked up the transfer. 'A joke's a joke, Mr Scott,' he said sternly ; 'but I tell you I don't like it carried too far. Why, you might take it into your funny head to tear up this little paper here.'

'I must have been drunk,' said Scott, feebly.

'That's your business,' rejoined Mallock, coldly. 'As far's I remember you were sober enough when you signed, but did get mighty drunk afterwards with my money, and broke up my home considerable. I'd have sued you for the damage, only the dummies burnt your little smash with the rest of the place about my ears. Ask your friend Toland if he didn't have to carry you home.'

Mallock left this view of the ballot night to sink

into Scott's bewildered brain, and presently began in a more friendly tone. Of course he would take the three hundred pounds on Toland's behalf, he said, but he thought maybe if Scott had ideas of fighting an action he had better keep it himself. He gave Scott a full and fanciful account of the circumstances leading up to the transaction. He had not cared to press for rent while the pioneering work was going on. In fact he had often thought of selling out for a mere trifle to Scott. Now, he admitted, the fact that he had slept upon his rights so long—which he had done out of mere good-heartedness and regard for Scott—might give the latter a kind of dog's show in fighting an action if he should be so unscrupulous as to make one necessary. But that, he said, would cost a lot of money—hurt them both, and merely gorge the lawyers. To show his good faith, and that he really had a friendly eye for a good farmer and a thrifty man, he would propose a compromise.

Scott dismally pricked up his ears and found spirit enough to ask what it was.

That he should give Mallock a hundred pounds—draw a cheque for it there and then—and that there and then Mallock should tear up the transfer and say no more about it.

Mallock watched his visitor with stealthy amusement. He had long ago given up all hope of doing anything great with the forged transfer, as involving too much risk for a man in his position, but still he had kept it by him for possible use in emergencies; and suddenly, on Scott's arrival, the brilliant idea had struck him of using it as a lever to move Scott from his charitable intent, and perhaps to squeeze something out of him as well.

Scott had been dazed at first, but his misery became less acute as he realised that, at the worst, the disaster was not illimitable, and with his memory courage returned, making him hope for entire escape.

'Well, what's it to be, Mr Scott? Shell out or fight?' Mallock asked at length, lovingly fingering the transfer as Scott remained silent. 'I reckon you'll find this bit of paper cheap at a hundred.'

For a moment the little man became only a red-faced, spluttering mass of indignation. He jumped up and made as if to snatch the document from Mallock, who put it into his pocket and pushed him gently aside.

'Now don't you get fightin' me, Mr Scott,' he said suavely, 'or the missis will be saying you don't look pretty.'

'I'll not give you a penny. And you'll find your-self in gaol before long, Mr Mallock, if you press this infamous claim,' he blustered. 'Oh, I know all about it! I have a better memory than you think. I had to sign a paper for Mr Archer, hadn't I? I wasn't hocussed, was I? Oh, I remember!'

Mallock lay back in his chair and laughed.

'Well, I tell you straight no one'd ha' thought, to look at you that night, that you'd remember much. You didn't appear like rememberin' anything when you was dancin' and singin' with those girls of mine, and makin' a damned noosance of yourself with my money. Let's hear what you do remember and what gives you the notion of putting me in gaol.'

Scott was somewhat taken aback by the levity with which Mallock received his threats. Visions of such scandalous tales of his behaviour reaching Bess's ears rendered him almost speechless. However, he detailed with indignation, but less confidence, his recollection of events at the shanty, and Mallock listened quite pleasantly.

'Um,' he said, lighting a cigar, 'a very pretty little tale! I'll tell mine in court, and you'll tell yours. The judge will decide—and us and the lawyers will have a nice pleasant trip to Melbourne together—at our expense.' He rose as if to end the conversation.

'But I have witnesses. I tell you you can't take my land,' exclaimed Scott, excited and frightened.

'Now, look here,' said Mallock, with a scowl darkening his face. 'I don't want to argue this matter except in court. You have your friend Toland, I know—he'll swear anything. But s'pose — I say, s'pose—your tale should be true? You know Nick Mallock's a fighter. And do you think you'll get much help from the evidence of a man that's three parts mad and tried to murder me?'

'I can't consent to pay you any money,' said Scott, weakening.

'That was my friendly suggestion. I'd have lost money on it, and I don't press it. Now, we'll leave your affair to the proper time. What about this mortgage of Toland's? Are you going to square it up?'

Scott pondered a moment. Ruth's face rose up before him. Her tearful thanks echoed in his ears. But he might be engaged in a costly suit to keep his own home. He had his children to think of—and the voice of prudence was the louder.

'I—I don't see my way,' he said glumly. 'With this action hanging over me I don't see as I can do more in that matter—in justice to my family, you know.'

'That's a sensible view to take. You're a real man, Mr Scott, that don't shirk his responsibilities, and a rare plucked one. If we fight, we fight fair and friendly.'

The friendliness of the combat seemed, from Scott's face, to afford him poor consolation, and with a searching glance Mallock added,—

'And I tell you this straight. That action has hung a goodish bit now, and, so long as you don't meddle in affairs that don't concern you, it might hang a blamed long while yet. Have a drink?'

Scott gave a feeble refusal.

'Nonsense, man! It'll do you good.' Mallock leaned his hand affectionately on Scott's shoulder, and led him to the bar again, where he succeeded in swallowing a glass of brandy that nearly choked him.

'Here's you health, Mr Scott! This quite reminds me of old times,' said Mallock, raising his glass. 'And remember,' he added significantly, 'while you shut your mouth like an oyster—and your purse too —Nick Mallock's your friend, and me and you ain't likely to quarrel.'

Scott thanked him incoherently and left the shanty, scarcely knowing how he would face Ruth, and wondering at the strange means Heaven had chosen to reward him for his new-born desire to help lame dogs over stiles.

CHAPTER VIII

THE time of Rupert Harlin's exile passed with irk-some slowness, whether spent in hard work on the station or in unsuccessful attempts at gaiety in Sydney, whither he often restlessly wandered. In his mother's letters the hope was constantly expressed that his father would eventually consent to the marriage with Mabel. Only in the meantime, she said, he must do nothing to widen the breach, and she begged him to stay a little longer and possess his soul in patience until she should advise him that it was wise to return. In any event, she hoped that he would not, except in case of absolute necessity, withdraw his money from the station, as it would be a great strain on his father's resources to find the cash at the present time. She had managed to pay. into his account a thousand pounds from money of her own, and could let him have another thousand shortly, which he might treat as a loan until the difference with his father should be ended or a definite rupture come, when he would either not need the money or have means of his own to repay it.

The position was very trying for Rupert, and only love for his mother, and the affection which, in spite of everything, he felt for his father induced him to suffer it in the hope of eventual reconciliation.

Toland and Mrs Toland were still in ignorance of the engagement. From Mabel, Rupert had received

only one letter assuring him of her affectionate hope
that everything would come right, but stating in
emphatic terms that nothing must be said to her
parents till things were definitely settled with Mr
Harlin. She had kept the secret from her mother,
not wishing to worry her, and had spoken to Mrs
Harlin, who agreed that one family complication was
enough to have on their hands at a time.

So matters stood when Rupert, arriving in Sydney
one morning, found two letters, several days old,
waiting for him at his hotel. One was from his
mother, and his spirits fell as he glanced over it.
Things had been going well, he read. Mr Harlin,
mollified by his conduct, was becoming more reconciled to the idea of the marriage, when, looking
through the paper, he had seen a notice that in a
month's time Toland's farm would be offered by the
mortgagee for sale. This, coupled with a report he
had heard of some discreditable fracas at Mallock's
hotel in which Toland was involved, had re-awakened
all his prejudice and antagonism, and Mrs Harlin
could now hold out very little hope of ever obtaining
his consent; and—the letter concluded significantly—
he was not at present in a state to consider the matter
reasonably at all. She did not know what to say.
Apparently the only choice lay between defying his
father or giving up all hope of marrying Mabel, at
least for a long time to come. That was a matter
on which he must consult his own heart and
conscience.

Thinking to himself that a decision would not be
difficult, Rupert tore open the second letter, which
he found to his surprise contained some advice.
It was from Conyngham. Rupert had vaguely

thought the handwriting familiar without recognising it as he looked at the address.

Like Mrs Harlin's the letter contained news of the forced sale of Toland's farm. Now, it went on to state, things were in a very bad way at Grimsby Farm. Toland's troubles and his hostility to Mallock weighed so much upon his mind that Conyngham feared he was practically a monomaniac. Not even his wife and daughter could rouse him from his moody hopelessness. Mrs Toland was miserable, Mabel's nerves completely unstrung by the fight between Mallock and her father which she had witnessed. Joe had left the farm and gone to the west. His father called it desertion, and spoke with unmeasured anger of Joe, but Conyngham thought the lad right, as he had obtained the offer of work which would enable him to send at least a pound a week, and perhaps more, to his parents. However, it was of Mabel he had most to say to Rupert; she would not write herself, but she was quite broken down and pining to see him. It was eminently no business of his, Conyngham admitted, but he had learned from Mabel how matters stood between Rupert and herself, he could see that she was fretting her heart out, and, while it did not seem that things could be made worse, they might possibly be improved by his immediate return to Kumbarra. Therefore, with surprise at his officiousness, and a full recognition that it was quite as likely as not the most mischievous advice in the world, he advised Rupert to come home and see Mabel without delay.

After his mother's letter Rupert scarcely needed such a spur to action, but it increased his impatience

T

to get away, and that evening he took the Melbourne express from Sydney.

It was noon of the following day when he left the train at Tongalong and, avoiding such acquaintances as he met on the platform, he hurried to the livery stables, where he procured a buggy and good pair of horses and was soon clear of the township.

The roads were heavy and slushy with winter rains, but Rupert rattled his horses along, finding a soothing music in the plashing of the hoofs. He passed the Kumbarra entrance-gate, just catching a glimpse of the white-painted roof glistening in the sun among the distant trees. Long strips of rich soil were turned over in the old sheep paddocks by ploughmen whom Harlin's new policy of subdivision had brought on to the land. Rupert wondered vaguely if it would ever be his, with Mabel installed as mistress in the station homestead. He did not believe in his heart that, however his father might rage and bluster, his anger would survive many years or carry him to such lengths as willing the property away from his only son. Excited and eager for action, Rupert could not concentrate his thought on any detailed plan. He only knew that he was going to have it out with Toland, and claim his right to Mabel, in spite of parents on either side, leaving circumstances to decide what he should do or say.

Near the gate of Toland's farm the plough stood at the end of an unfinished land. Trace chains and swingle bars lay on the ground before it, but gathering rust on the mould boards showed that it had not been used for days. There was a melancholy suggestion of hopelessness in the idle plough and the grain bags still lying at intervals where the jays were feasting on a patch, sowed but not harrowed, further from the road. Toland's spirits must be low indeed to suffer such things, Rupert reflected, as he drove through the paddock towards the house. There a like air of neglect and desertion enveloped everything. All the yard gates swung open; there seemed no one about the place; not even a barking dog greeted his arrival as he splashed in through the mud and pulled his horses up at the stable door. Flinging the traces over their backs he put the pair into empty stalls and, with a nervous presentiment of evil, made his way towards the house. Entering the garden unnoticed, he walked on to the verandah, wondering if the house was quite deserted, and knocked at the sitting-room door. He heard some-one stirring within; the door opened and Mabel stood before him. She had been crying and she had been asleep; her hair was in disorder rare for her. Marks of tears and of the chair on which her head had rested lined her cheeks, her old grey dress was worn and shabby. Blinking from the glare of the setting sun in her eyes, she stared in astonishment at Rupert. To him she seemed as beautiful as ever. Feeling the glow of a knight-errant's pride, he knew that he had never loved her so much as now when he stood there to relieve her distress. Forgetting all caution, he caught her in his arms and kissed her again and again, while she felt too much the joy of having someone to love and care for her to do anything at first but passively and happily submit.

Soon, however, it occurred to her to ask how and why he had made this mysterious appearance, and leading him into the sitting-room she gave him a chair, choosing another for herself at safe conversational distance. Rupert told her as clearly as he could of the letters he had received and his instant departure from Sydney, concluding by asking where he should find Mr Toland.

'Then you did not know I was alone?' she said.

'Alone? No, I had no idea of it. I came to tell your father that he must give his consent to our marriage—and also to ask him if he would allow me instead of Mallock to be his mortgagee.'

Mabel laughed nervously, though on the verge of tears. The picture of such a meeting with Rupert, with her father as a possible witness, struck her as grimly ludicrous.

'What are you laughing at? What have I done?' asked Rupert, puzzled and frowning.

'Nothing,' she answered. 'Father and mother have driven down to consult the Scotts and see if anything can possibly be arranged. There is no one but me in the house.'

'When will they be home?'

'Any time,' answered Mabel with a frightened glance at the clock. 'Not later than an hour, or an hour and a half at anyrate.'

'Then I shall wait and see your father.' Rupert settled himself back in his chair for a good long look at Mabel. 'Don't be worried, little girl. We can have a talk first and then I'm sure I shall be able to persuade him. If you'd rather be out of the way I will go and meet them on the road.'

Mabel sighed and shook her head.

'No. Don't do that.'

'Shall I stay here, then? Say that you are glad I have come.'

Mabel went over to him and somehow found her head on his shoulder. 'I am gladder than I can say to see you—I was utterly miserable five minutes ago,' she said; 'but it is not the slightest use to do anything.'

'Why?'

'Because my father will refuse to allow us to get married.'

'And if he refuses?'

Mabel pressed her hands over her eyes. 'I—shall obey him,' she said, stifling a sob.

An exclamation of impatience from Rupert caused Mabel to raise her head, and she looked at him reproachfully.

'Don't be ungenerous, Rupert,' she sighed. 'You can't understand. · If you only knew what my poor old father had been through you would never ask me to be cruel to him just because we love each other. Try to help me instead of persuading me to be selfish and disobedient.'

'My darling girl, I would do anything to help you —only tell me what?'

Mabel shook her head hopelessly.

'There, you can suggest nothing. The one thing I won't do is leave you here to be miserable. I know from Conyngham something of what you've been through.' He felt the tremor of a smothered sob, and a nervous pressure of his arm, confirming what Conyngham had said, encouraged him to go on. 'I would disobey my parents for your sake,' he argued persuasively; 'and if people are unreasonable I don't see that we owe them obedience.'

Mabel smiled through her tears. 'You were always obstinate, and I believe as much as anything, dear, you want your own way.'

'I want you, Mab—and I'm going to have you—with our parents' consent or without. Anyhow, it can do no harm to ask.'

'Don't—don't,' she cried. 'I simply can't let you speak to my father and be refused with such a storm of anger as you don't know—you can't imagine. He is so changed—morose and almost fierce. I should be ashamed and—and frightened—I would rather run away.'

'Run away!' echoed Rupert, softly, a gleam of hope dawning on him. He left the chair beside Mabel and stood thinking for a moment, scarcely aware of her frightened, questioning gaze.

'How much money does your father want to save the place from being sold?' he asked suddenly.

'A thousand pounds.'

'And you don't think there is any chance of his taking it from me as a loan?'

Mabel shook her head. 'Not the slightest.'

'And from you?'

'What do you mean? From me? Where should I—'

Her eyes met his and she lowered them, blushing.

Rupert stood over and caught her hand. 'Mabel, dearest, listen to me,' he cried. 'You spoke just now, as a wild possibility, of running away. But there is really nothing else to do if you won't let me speak. Truly, I had never thought of it. I came to honestly tell your father that I love you, and if he were here I would do so in spite of anything anyone could say.'

'You would be mad then,' she interjected.

'Well, as he is not here I can't try. Anyhow, you

think it useless ; and see how Fate has played into our hands. It is only your father's misfortunes that have made him hard and bitter, so you must marry me and put an end to them. If he would not take a loan from me, at least from his daughter he surely would. Come with me and send a cheque—your own cheque—for a thousand pounds to your father as soon as you are my wife.'

Mabel trembled all over and her heart beat furiously. She dared not look at Rupert, but she felt her power of resistance giving way before the mingled command and pleading in his tone and the strong clasp of his hand. The temptation was overwhelming. First, there was her strong love for Rupert. Then with a stroke of the pen to free her father from all his troubles! To do it herself—she who had never possessed a sovereign of her own in all her life! It was scarcely imaginable. Salvation for her parents if she yielded — for herself, freedom from sordid worries and fears—escape from the memory-poisoned surroundings she had grown to hate. She loved her father as she had always done, but of late her presence seemed to give him no pleasnre—only to add poignancy to his regret—while she could not conceal from herself that there were times when she positively feared him.

Then there was the other side of the picture—her father's fierce anger, her mother's blank dismay should they return to find her gone.

She looked at Rupert in dumb appeal. He saw that she hesitated and pursued his advantage.

They might travel together, see some of the great world that she had so longed to see, and return again when her parents had made the best of it, as they were sure to do, and all was forgotten and forgiven. Mrs Toland would be glad to see her married ; Mabel had admitted that her mother knew of the engagement and was pleased with it. Only yesterday she had told her. Could she doubt, Rupert demanded, that in time Mrs Toland would succeed in bringing her father over to their side? That was to say when his mind was free from the great trouble oppressing it. If she stayed at home saying nothing, and the farm were sold, his mind might never recover from the blow.

Rupert pleaded his cause well. Mabel's love for him and her own personal longing for happiness were his champions, and finally they triumphed for a time over fears and scruples.

She got up and, flinging her arms round his neck, buried her head on his shoulder.

'Yes, I will go with you,' she faltered. 'It may be wicked. I don't know what it is, but I can't bear the strain any longer. Life is terrible here and I must go —I simply must !'

Rupert was triumphant.

'It's not wicked at all, but common sense,' he laughed, kissing her. 'Everything will go right now, you will see.'

She looked into his happy face, trying to absorb some of the confidence she saw there. Then the last slanting sun ray vanished from the room as the sun dipped behind the distant hills and she was seized suddenly with a new fear.

'No, no! It is too late,' she cried, breaking away from him. 'They would meet us on the road. They may be here any moment. You must go away and leave me. We can only wait and hope.'

It was nearly six. Rupert had not thought of the hour, and he was staggered for a moment, but quickly recovered himself and made up his mind.

'No, Mab, darling. You have promised, and you won't go back on it,' he said, holding her by the arms.

'But suppose my father should meet us? It would almost send him mad.'

'But he won't meet us if you are quick,' he said confidently. 'Go and put up what things you want. Write a note to say what you have done, and I will bring the buggy to the house.'

'Oh! Is there nothing else we can do?' she asked despairingly.

Rupert kissed her again. 'Nothing,' he answered promptly, 'except to stay to bring misery on everyone. You will trust me, won't you?'

Mabel answered the question with a look that satisfied him.

'Don't waste any time, Mab,' he said, hurrying away to the stables. His pulse beat fast. He would have preferred not to sneak away, but there was compensating excitement and a glow of triumph in purpose accomplished. All now depended on good luck and good speed. As he led out his tired horses for their long journey he almost welcomed the need for haste, with all its disadvantages, since, with more time to think, Mabel might have faltered from her eminently sensible resolution. Practical in spite of his excitement, he thought of his horses and stowed half a bag of chaff in the buggy to feed them on the road.

Meanwhile Mabel, feeling faint and giddy, leaned her head on the mantelpiece for a moment's thought. Then she pulled herself together. There was time only for action, and fear of her father's anger,

looming larger than anything else, gave her speed.
She scribbled a few hasty, tear-smudged lines to her
parents, saying what she had done. They looked
bald and heartless, but there was no time to put on
paper the justification, excuses and protests of affection that rushed pell-mell through her brain. Then,
going to her room to pack a few things into an old
portmanteau of her mother's, she saw her reflection
in the looking-glass. It gave her quite a shock. A
sleepless night had made her fall away from the high
standard she held of what a woman owes to her
appearance. She had not dared to go to bed till the
droning voices of her parents in the next room had
ceased early that morning, but now a few seconds
must be spared to wash away all traces of tears and
put on her smartest dress to face the world and
troubles in a woman's strongest armour. Things
looked brighter then, and she had almost finished her
small packing when she heard the rattle of wheels
and Rupert's voice, with an undercurrent of impatience in it, calling from the garden gate.

'In a minute,' she answered. She paused with a
lingering look round the little sitting-room as she
passed through. She saw with a new pang of conscience that the fire was out. The lamp was un-
trimmed, the table was not laid. She had not left
even a materially comfortable house for her parents
to return to.

Rupert called her again, and she hurried out, half
fearing to see the other buggy appearing over the
hill. He stowed the luggage beneath the seat, helped
Mabel in with a sigh of relief that she had come at
last, and started his horses away at a gallop.

Anxiety and, on Mabel's part, remorse at the step

she was taking, kept them almost silent till long
after the white gate of Grimsby Farm was left behind.
Then the novelty, the excitement, and the prospects
of the new life coming gradually shook off the spell
of the old one left behind. The moon had been high
in the sky before the twilight had gone, and there
was little chance of passing Toland unrecognised if
they should meet him on the narrow road. Rupert,
therefore, made all the pace he could, and began to
hope that they might pass in time the turn where the
cross road came in from Scott's. He had only half
a mile to go, and was walking his horses up a sharp
pinch some six miles from the farm, when a distant
rumble of wheels sounded on his ear. Mabel heard
it too and clutched his arm in fear.

'They are crossing the bridge,' she whispered.

Rupert nodded. 'I think we can do it, dear,' he
answered, and whipped up his pair. In a minute the
white schoolhouse by the corner gleamed ahead
through the trees. Mabel gave a long sigh of guilty
relief as they passed it, and Rupert, reining his
horses down to a slow trot, pointed to a buggy just
emerging from the moonlit lane.

'It was a narrow squeak,' he said. 'It is your
people, isn't it? I'm glad we did not meet them on
the track.'

Mabel turned her head and looked where he
pointed. She recognised the grey horses; then her
father's voice reached her, commenting on the strange
buggy on the roads. There came suddenly a great
revulsion of feeling.

'Oh, Rupert! I can't leave them. Let us go
back!' she cried imploringly.

'It is too late, Mab, darling. It would be only folly

now.' He called to his horses again, and in a few seconds the rattle of the buggy driving up the road they had come died away in the distance.

Mabel was silent for a long time torturing herself by picturing phases of the old folk's surprise and dismay when they arrived at the deserted house. Rupert left her alone. Though young, he was not devoid of sympathy ; and with tact beyond his years understood the occasional value of silence.

After a time he roused her to interest in their immediate plans. They would drive slowly through the night, not to Tongalong, but to the next roadside station, where they would not be known, and catch a train at daybreak. Then she should go to a cousin of his mother's, an old maiden lady, who would undoubtedly be shocked, but who was devoted to Mrs Harlin and very fond of him, and whom he could trust to take care of her until they were married on that day or the next.

' And then what ? ' asked Mabel.

' Then, as soon as you hear from your mother that she has the cheque and all is right, first boat to England with six months free from jawings and rowings, to give all the old people time to forgive us.'

His confidence was infectious, and Mabel found great solace in the thought of her mother's joy on receiving that wonderful cheque, which should make life at Grimsby Farm smooth and unmortgaged again. Surely then her father would forgive her, and, with returning mental health, admit that she had acted for the best.

By-and-by the pale light of Mallock's shanty lamp showed its glimmer down the road.

Mabel shuddered as she thought of the last scene

enacted there and demurred at first when Rupert asked her to hold the horses while he entered. But she could not account to him for the depth of her repugance and conquered it, since Rupert said that he must change a cheque or be stranded penniless on the railway station. It had also occurred to him that Mabel would need refreshment to keep up her strength on the long night drive ; and here he might get biscuits and wine.

He still retained something of a mischievous boy's pleasure in taking a neat fall out of an enemy. Therefore he greeted the shanty-keeper pleasantly when Mallock entered the bar wondering greatly at Rupert's presence there, his purchases, and his anxiety for cash in exchange for the cheque which he offered. Then as he left the house Rupert turned smilingly on his host.

' Well, good-bye Mallock,' he said ; ' I won't see you for some time as I'm off to England. I suppose you've heard that Miss Toland and I are to be married.'

' What the hell do you mean ?—Mabel ? ' gasped Mallock, astounded.

' Miss Toland, I said,' replied Rupert, quietly. ' Don't swear, my good man, as she's in the buggy outside. We're driving to Tongalong now, you know— and, by-the-bye, my wife will send you a cheque in a day or two to square off that little mortgage business of Mr Toland's.'

Laughing to himself, Rupert jumped into the buggy and drove off, leaving Mallock staring after him and uttering curses so heartfelt and foul that it was well they had no audience but the trees.

CHAPTER IX

AT other times Toland might have noticed in such moonlight the fresh wheel marks at his gate, but his thoughts were turned inward. Even the empty feed boxes in the stalls, which he had left with chaff in them that morning, failed to arrest his attention, and he scarcely heeded his wife's exclamation of surprise at the darkness enveloping the house. She would not go in as he told her to, but remained talking at his side until the horses were unyoked and fed and the old buggy, dating from before the bush fire and associated with many happy holidays, had been stowed away under cover.

The familiar routine seemed to bring a keener realisation to Toland, and he paused, looking at the buggy as he slung up the pole in the loop of fencing wire.

'We've had our last ride on those old wheels, Ruth,' he said. 'I wish it had gone in the fire with the rest of the things we had when we were young, instead of being laughed at and knocked down for a pound or two this day fortnight. My God! to think that two weeks from to-day you'll have no home, and like as not I'll be a debtor still.'

'Don't think of it,' she said, drawing him away. 'I have a sort of feeling that something might happen yet, and at anyrate you've done your best, and your wife and children are proud of you.'

Toland laughed bitterly as he put up the buggy shed rails and turned towards the house.

'Surely my wife and children are not such fools,' he said. 'Not Joe, at least. Mighty proud he is, when he'd run away and leave the sinking ship! Sensible maybe, but—' He checked himself and shook his head in a way that suggested a crowd of whirling thoughts he could not or would not put into words.

'Joe only went to fight our battles further afield,' ventured Ruth. 'You must not be hard on the boy.'

'I know—I know—I'll try—but don't speak to me about it.' His hand was on the garden gate and he waited for his wife to pass through. 'What's Mabel doing, I wonder, that she's got the house in darkness? Poor little girl! We shouldn't have left her alone.'

Mrs Toland was trembling. The dark windows had filled her with apprehension ever since she had stepped from the buggy, but she had not dared mention them, nor enter the house alone.

Now they were at the window of the sitting-room, which stood ajar, with the moonlight streaming in, revealing the black, cheerless hearth, a symbol of desolation. Ruth's heart stood still, fearing she knew not what.

'Mabel! Where are you? Mabel!' called Toland in a voice gruff and stern from an endeavour to conceal his fears. The call was repeated, but no answer came.

'Don't be frightened, little mother. The girl's worn out and gone to sleep,' he said kindly. 'You'll find her in her bedroom.'

It seemed possible. Mrs Toland pressed her husband's hand and hurried towards Mabel's door when a scrap of white paper fluttered from the mantelpiece as she passed.

'Ah, what's that?' she cried, snatching it in feverish haste from the floor. She strained her eyes and held the paper where a moonbeam fell upon it. 'Mabel's writing! What can have happened to her? Quick, John! A light. Oh, let me see what she says!'

Toland stood beside his wife, and, looking over her shoulder, held a match, throwing its flickering light on the few lines of Mabel's message. He had seized their import even before she did, and, dropping the light, stamped heavily upon it. He laughed again fiercely, making Ruth shudder.

'And this is the daughter who is proud of me! Like Joe, runs away—curse her, I say! Curse her!'

'Hush! Oh, for Heaven's sake, John, hush!' Ruth clung to Toland and tried to place her hand over his mouth, but he wrenched himself away.

'Yes, curse her, and the low puppy thief that has stolen her. Are you going to turn against me too?'

Ruth had fallen into a chair where he could scarcely see her in the dim light. She sobbed almost inaudibly, but with a violence that shook piteously her slender frame. Her silence only seemed to add fuel to his fury.

'Land and children,' he laughed bitterly; 'what I pictured as the joy of my life—and would to God I had neither to be the curse of my old age. Well, I won't have the land long, and I'm glad of it—and the children will never enter my doors again. If that Harlin—that blackguard cub of a drunken rogue—comes across my path I'll strangle him, by God I will!'

Mrs Toland rose with an effort. Dry-eyed and composed, though she was deadly pale and could scarcely breathe, she caught her husband's coat-sleeve with a trembling hand.

'John, are you not ashamed of yourself?' she asked in the sternest tones her gentle lips had ever framed. 'Remember me and have mercy, if you have no forgiveness for our poor children, nor respect for your God or yourself.'

Astonishment sobered Toland for a moment; there came a temporary revulsion of feeling, and, catching her in his arms, he strained her to his breast.

'At least *you* are not afraid of me, little woman,' he cried. 'You love me and will not run away, and I love you more than I ever did, because you are not one of those cursed cowards.'

All Ruth's strength had gone again with her husband's words and his caress, and almost happy in spite of everything, she could only cry and cling closer to him.

He had been silent for a moment, when his eye fell on the scrap of paper at his feet, and releasing himself he stooped to pick it up with the fierce mood creeping on him again.

'Bring a light, Ruth. Where are the lamps?' he muttered, going to the doorway, where he stood crunching the letter in his fingers and gazing with knitted brows over the clear sweep of the hill paddock. Ruth's hand shook and the lamp-chimney rattled against the brass clips as she tried to place it over the wick.

Toland turned from the window to the light. Then, changing his mind, with an impatient gesture he flung the crumpled paper into the fireplace.

'Why should I read it again?' he exclaimed. 'She's
gone. That's all I want to know—gone, she said, to
catch the train to Melbourne and marry him to-
morrow.' He watched Ruth go to the hearth and,
picking up the letter, smooth out the creases, with
difficulty repressing an impulse to knock it from her
hand.

'That was the strange buggy, then,' he broke out,
clenching his fists. 'Do you remember, Ruth?
Passed within a chain of us at the corner. Oh, my
God! Why didn't I know it then, so that I might
have dragged him out and smashed his head on a
fence rail Stop reading that wicked child's scribbl-
ing and listen to me, Ruth. Do you hear? Listen
to me!'

The paper that she had already read again in a
devouring glance was slipped almost defiantly within
her dress, and sinking into a chair, she turned dull
eyes on her husband striding angrily about the room.

'I think I hear, John. What is it?' she asked with
a faint, quivering smile.

'I say that like a fool I missed my chance,' he
almost shouted. 'I had the sneak at my mercy to
wring his wretched neck and I let him go— Could
I catch him now?' he went on, more to himself than
to Ruth. 'There is no train till daybreak. The
old horses might do it, and it's the last and best thing
they'll do for their master if they let me get my hand
on his throat. By Heaven! I'll make them try.'

Toland snatched up his hat from the floor where
he had thrown it, but before he was through the door
Ruth had caught him and was dragging him back
with an effort of strength that raised astonishment
for the moment above all else in his sick brain.

'John, my dear husband!' she cried. 'Don't do anything so foolish and so wicked.'

'Why wicked and foolish?' he asked, giving way with something like a wild animal's sullen obedience and standing still in hesitation.

'Sit down and let me speak to you.'

He almost smiled at his wife's gentle endeavours to force him to a chair, and allowed himself to be pushed into it. She sat down upon the arm with one hand resting on his shoulder, but she looked past him into the moonlight and with a silent prayer nerved herself to an effort.

Her voice sounded strange and far away to Toland.

'It would be foolish to go after Mabel and Rupert Harlin,' she began, 'because you know that with those horses that have travelled so far to-day you could never reach Tongalong in time—and it would be wicked because you would be going with only fierce, evil thoughts in your heart. What good could it do if you found them? You would only commit some rash violence that would ruin Mabel's happiness for ever and fill you with remorse. Oh, if you knew how thankful I am to Heaven that you did not re-cognise that strange buggy on the road to-night.'

She paused, wiping a mist of tears from her eyes, and Toland moved uneasily. 'Maybe it was for the best,' he said grudgingly. 'I couldn't but have laid hands on him. But you're not going to make ex-cuses for her, Ruth—the daughter I trusted would stick by her parents whatever other folk did.' He passed his hand wearily through his hair. 'It's cold, let me make you a bit of a fire. The child didn't leave us even that,' he said with a mirthless laugh and made as if to rise; but Ruth leaned against him, imprisoning him in the chair, and his arm slipped round her. 'Ah, well! Life must go on,' he sighed. 'I'm a little mad, Ruth. There's the savage in me coming near the top. Give me time, wife—give me time. Let me alone and we won't speak of her to-night—I can't forgive her, but I'll try to forget. But no excuses—there are none. Come, get up, Ruth, and we'll have the night like old times alone together.'

Ruth did not move, however, but kept a restraining hand on his arm, pressing it closer to her. 'I must make excuses, John,' she said bravely, 'even if it hurts you I must, for there are true ones.'

'You're not wise—not to-night,' he muttered.

'To-night or never. You'd not think I would willingly hurt you, John?'

For answer his great brown hand slipped over hers and raised it to his lips.

'No, you could not think so. And yet I must, for I'd rather you blamed yourself a little than her too much.' Her words came in a nervous rush. 'Poor child, you know how you love her, and that she loves you. But, John, dear, you've been cold and rough lately. It's our misfortunes, I know. But you've made her afraid—she thought she was no help to you. She loved Rupert Harlin for a long time, and she dared not ask for your consent, though he wanted to. You—Heaven knows what you would have said— But you'll forgive your daughter—John— Say you will forgive her—not to-night perhaps—yes—now—- to-night!'

He looked into her face for a moment, hesitating; then threw aside her hand and brushed past her roughly as he rose to escape her pleading touch and tones.

'Never,' he said hoarsely. ' I can't do it. Are all
my children cowards?'

'Am I?' sighed Ruth.

'You? No—but you're not afraid of me, Ruth.
Good God! am I going mad? Don't tell me
you're afraid.'

'Not now—but I have been.'

If her white face told the truth the time was
scarcely past. Toland stood staring at her for a
moment incredulously. Then, staggering to a chair,
he flung himself down on it, and leaned upon the
table with his face between his hands.

'Tell me,' he said. ' I'm learning that there's worse
things than having the roof sold over your head.'

Ruth's heart beat furiously, but she was determined
to get her confession over, and met her husband's gaze.

'I knew,' she faltered—'I knew that Mabel was
engaged to Rupert Harlin.'

'When?'

'I had guessed it for weeks. Mr Conyngham
suggested it long ago. Yesterday she told me.'

'And you didn't tell me because you were afraid of
me—afraid of my violence, eh?'

His calmness frightened her more than any
violence now. 'Ah! forgive me!' she cried longingly,
going to him with outstretched arms. 'Forgive me,
John!' but he pushed her away and laughed, striking
a chill to her heart.

'I'm a little madder than I thought—that's all.
Don't let us worry over it. The children run away
from me. The wife doesn't trust me—the land
is going this day fortnight, and I'll not be long after
it. Then they'll have no one to frighten them—
Cheer up, Ruth, girl! There's a good time coming.'

Neither of them had heard the step on the verandah. Ruth was clutching the table for support in an agony of fear, and Toland, throwing up his head in mad merriment, swung on his chair when the partially-closed door opened wide, and as Toland's voice died away, husband and wife turned their eyes to see Conyngham's tall figure framed in the doorway.

Toland sprang to his feet and stretched out his arm pointing. ' Look, Ruth ! ' he cried. ' I told you I was going. Oh, there's a good time coming. Here is a protector for you. He has no land to lose and you will never be afraid.'

Conyngham strode into the room. He glanced at Toland, but all his eyes were for Ruth ; and Toland, panting for breath, ceased to laugh and glared from one to the other.

There was a fateful moment's silence. Conyngham, hearing of the elopement from Mallock, had ridden straight away to see if he could offer any comfort or assistance. He had thought Toland's reason tottering in the balance, and now it seemed that it had kicked the beam.

Those surely were a madman's eyes. His own sought Ruth's. His arms moved from his side in an involuntary movement of protection, and her lids dropped before his glance. To Toland came back suddenly the memory of years ago when Ruth was ill, memory of the suspicion since laughed at and forgotten. The jealousy his sane, generous mind could never harbour sprang suddenly into monstrous existence. He stepped in front of Conyngham, struggling against a mad impulse to grasp his throat, with a great effort of restraint keeping his hands

from creeping up the arms which they clutched like
a vice.

'Get out of my house,' he said huskily. 'Get out,
before mischief happens. You don't know what you
are doing—coming here to-night.'

Conyngham stood firm and motionless, leaning
forward to passively resist Toland's weight. He
looked at Ruth, and the issue of a tragedy hung
on a glance or a word from her.

She was terrified, but loyal love and hope prevailed over fear. In a moment she was at her
husband's side, with her fingers resting lightly on
his arm.

'John, dear, don't push Mr Conyngham out,' she
said, trying to force a laugh, while her teeth chattered.
'But you must not think me rude, Mr Conyngham,
for begging you to leave us. My husband and I are
terribly upset to-night.'

A beseeching glance which was unseen by Toland
decided Conyngham, in spite of his fears for her.

'I am sorry I intruded so unfortunately,' he said
quietly. 'My best apology will be to go at once.'

Toland had insensibly allowed the grip of his hands
to slacken. As Conyngham withdrew himself he
turned to look at Ruth; and almost before the retreating figure had passed the doorway, she flung her
arms round her husband's neck, overwhelming him
with kisses and tears.

Outside the little house Conyngham waited long
in the shadow. He was no eavesdropper, but however
wrong his love, and however brave the woman, he
dared not leave her alone in the power of a madman, even though it was at her command.

Again and again he told himself he was a weak

fool, as he began to realise the strength of the feeling
that had grown in silence, that was to be always a
secret, and had kept him in spite of many resolutions
anchored in the Tonga Valley year after year. Only
now did he fully comprehend what his life had missed
when he witnessed the loving trust with which Ruth
had thrown herself into her husband's arms—and he
stretched out his own in an uncontrollable gesture of
hopeless longing.

All seemed quiet within. Though only a few yards
away he could scarcely hear the voices, and almost
hating Toland, with a new insistent jealousy of
which he felt ashamed, Conyngham told himself
that he was utterly forgotten, and that Ruth's
gentle influence had triumphed, securing Toland's
threatened reason at least for a time.

And so it seemed was the fact. With a heart full
of thankfulness Ruth had felt her husband's arms
close round her, quivering ; she had looked into his
face and seen his eyes grow soft, as for months she
had not known them ; and when he brushed his hand
across them suddenly, and, going to his easy-chair,
drew her gently towards him, she left him to break
the silence, feeling that the dawn was coming after a
hideous nightmare which had tortured them.

Toland did not speak for a long time. When he
did his voice was deep and resonant with sane
emotion.

' You saved me, Ruth. My reason was going, and
nothing but you and your love could have brought it
back again. How can you care for such a brute
as I ?'

' Don't,' she whispered softly.

' Yes, I was mad,' he went on, ' but never again,

Ruth—never while you are near me.' He paused and looked slowly round the room filled with Ruth's and Mabel's handiwork. 'It's hard to have to leave the old place, but I'll try to bear it like a man.' He stroked her hair and smiled sadly. 'No. That's not much after all—like a woman—like you, Ruth.'

She had no voice to speak, and she would have kissed his hand but that with a sense of shame he wrenched it away.

'Then there's Mabel.'

Ruth started and clung to his arm, but his voice was quiet and even. 'Don't be afraid. I—I've learnt what I am. No wonder the girl was frightened of me. I wouldn't like to see her—not yet a while, but some day—some day I'll forgive her.'

One look of dumb gratitude flashed from Ruth's eyes; then the long-resisted strain had its way and she cried uncontrollably as if her heart would break. It was long before Toland could soothe and scold her back to control of herself once more; and the emotional experience he went through in the time was a healthful one for him.

Conyngham, still keeping his vigil in the garden, heard the tones of soothing and appeal—not those of the same man who had saluted him in the doorway so shortly before. Then his own name caught his ear, and with the blood mounting to his face he stole softly away to where his horse was tethered. There was no reason for him to wait longer. When husband and wife could begin to discuss him quietly together, the wife had no need of his protection, he thought, with a bitter laugh at his wasted championship. It was intolerable to think that he had betrayed himself, and that the woman he had loved, and her husband, were talking of him not with anger, perhaps, but with pity—possibly amused by his infatuation, as they had a perfect right to be—and saying to himself many hard things of Ralph Conyngham, the schoolmaster rode away from Grimsby Farm.

CHAPTER X

MEMORIES of the long journey, the arrival in Melbourne, and the marriage so different to any that her fancy had ever pictured, were already dreamlike and far away to Mabel Harlin a few days after she had left her father's farm. Even the excitement and the strangeness would not stifle thought. Amid her happiness in Rupert's devotion and the new pleasure of spending money with what seemed reckless extravagance on the dresses that her husband insisted she should have, there intruded sharp pangs of conscience, and always as an undercurrent was the longing for news of her parents in the old home.

Rupert understood her anxiety and did his best to allay it. All would be well, he assured her, when Mrs Toland received the money. To that chance Mabel also pinned her faith. Her hand trembled so when she wrote specimen signatures for the bank, and later, when she filled in the cheque under Rupert's directions, that he laughed, declaring that no one could possibly read such a scrawl; and then she spent hours on the letter to her mother for an answer to which she feverishly waited.

Her hurried note of farewell, written at Grimsby Farm, had omitted to give any address, and hence the silence from home, which had hitherto oppressed her, might after all, she kept repeating to herself, have no sinister meaning.

Standing before the long glass one evening she re-arranged the lace at her neck, thinking how deep beneath the surface went the changes effected by dressmakers and a few days. Gowns that she in-stinctively knew men admired and women envied gave her confidence, amid her strange surroundings in a fashionable hotel, that nothing else could have given. It seemed quite natural that a pearl necklet, Rupert's gift, should be gleaming on the throat that had never known anything before but a string of beads or a silver brooch. It was scarcely strange that she and Rupert were going to dine at the *table-d'hôte*, and afterwards spend the evening at the theatre, of which her only experience was the childish visit to the upper circle years ago. If only her parents would make perfect by their sympathy her joy in the new life, stretching out in kaleidoscopic hues before her! In time they must. Her father could not fail to see what a fine fellow Rupert was and to accept their help, because she longed so ardently that it would happen so.

Rupert was late. She could hear now and then the *frou-frou* of silks in the passage, and laughter and footsteps on the stairs that led to the great dining-room, and wondered what detained her husband, when presently he entered. He begged for time to recover from the shock of his wife's new magnificence, and then kissing her, praised her beauty and the dress she wore in words that brought a blush to Mabel's cheeks and made her almost as proud as he.

'Then you don't think the black velvet is too old for me?' she asked, turning slowly round before him like the millinery figures in the windows.

'You are a Spanish princess from a picture and

you would make anything look young. The dress and that lace affair suit you right down to the ground.'

'If you are pleased that is all I want.'

'Pleased?' The emphasised interrogative assured her that he was, and smiling happily, she threw an opera cloak over her shoulders. Neck and arms showed a little fairer beyond the sun line of her active country life. Otherwise one would scarcely guess that she was a stranger to cities, and nothing suggested that this was the first evening gown she had ever worn. She knew instinctively how to carry her unaccustomed finery without awkwardness, and the black velvet and pearls suited her fine carriage and her colouring. Only the appropriate dressing of her abundant hair she felt at present beyond her skill, but for this occasion a hairdresser had overcome the difficulty, so on that point too she felt at ease.

She had forgotten home troubles completely for the moment when Rupert recalled them to her.

'I'm sorry I'm so beastly late, Mab,' he said; 'but it suddenly struck me that there might be a letter at the Wanderer's Club—and there was.'

'Well?'

He smiled at her impulsive movement towards him.

'Good news as far as it went. Your people don't know where we are. But Mrs Toland had been to the Scotts—'

'And they wrote to you?' she asked in astonishment.

'Good Lord, no! It was Conyngham. He's a trump and a regular old uncle to us, Mab. Mrs Scott told him that there had been no end of a row, but that your father and mother were taking it well at present and longing for further news of you.'

Mab drew a long breath of relief and raised her arms in a gesture almost of thanksgiving, while her eyes filled with happy tears. 'Oh, how thankful I am that you got that letter!' she sighed. 'Perhaps everything will really be right now. Mother must have my other letter by this time. I'm actually beginning to be glad I married you, Rupert.'

Her pale blue opera cloak had slipped from her shoulders.

Rupert picked it up and handed it to her with a proud glance at the queenly young figure, thinking he had no cause to regret his part of the contract. He laughed at the glow of delight that brightened her face and belied the tears glistening on the long eyelashes.

'You are kind,' he said, 'and I am deeply flattered —but it doesn't occur to you to wonder what my old people think of our performance.'

She looked at him remorsefully. 'Oh, Rupert, what a selfish wretch I am!' she exclaimed, laying caressing fingers on his coat sleeve. 'Have you heard from them too? There was no room in my thoughts just now for anything but what you told me.'

Rupert kissed her again, laughing. 'Nonsense, darling!' he said. 'My affairs are all right. Much better than I expected. I'll tell you about them at dinner.'

He had gone to dress before Mabel could question him further, but later on she learnt that things were not much changed at Kumbarra. Mr Harlin was angry and still uttered threats of cutting Rupert off with a shilling, but Mrs Harlin, who had written him a letter of mild rebuke, believed that her husband would accept the position with better grace now that

he could in no way alter it. She would write in a
day or two, she promised, to scold and congratulate
Mabel.

Though she might have indignantly denied it, Mrs
Harlin was in her secret heart not greatly displeased
that Mabel and Rupert had run away. She knew her
son too well to have had hopes of preventing the
marriage, and the elopement disposed of the unpleasant prospect of a bourgeois wedding where class differences—and the Scotts—would be much in evidence.
Harlin said bluntly that since Mabel had shown her
good taste by clearing out from the family, and
Rupert some glimmerings of good sense by not
mixing himself up in functions with a common
crowd, in which it would be an insult to ask him
to join, he did not so much mind him making an ass
of himself. Mabel was a pretty girl, and he should
not wonder if she were smart enough to pass as a
lady among people who didn't know her father or
her uncle.

Thus the Tolands and themselves were the only
people to whom the young couple's elopement was
fraught with gravity, and Rupert could, with some
show of reason, congratulate himself that he had
taken the wisest course. Mabel listened to his enthusiastic appreciation of his own foresight, smiling,
suspending judgment till the reply which she dreaded
yet longed for should come from Grimsby Farm.

At last it arrived. On the breakfast-table one
morning she found a letter waiting—the first one she
had seen addressed to Mrs Rupert Harlin—and in
her mother's handwriting. She snatched it up with a
beating heart. She could not trust herself to read it
in the presence of other inmates of the hotel, scattered

about at adjoining tables, and the waiter who was at her elbow for orders got no intelligible answer, but she shook her head and ran upstairs.

There she was able to be alone with her letter. Rupert, having business to attend to, had breakfasted earlier and left the hotel.

Mrs Toland had written very little of their return to the farmhouse on the night Mabel left, but there was enough to let her know there had been a scene— that her father had been bitterly incensed, and was only gradually becoming reconciled to her absence. Then came thanks for the cheque, which Mabel was to convey also to Rupert, and she cried to herself as she read. She felt in a way ashamed, and yet happy, at receiving thanks of such a kind from her parents, or rather from her mother, who wrote on behalf of both. She was at the Scotts'. There she had got Mabel's letter and immediately written the reply; for Toland, who was in Tongalong trying to get rid of some unmortgaged stock, would not return till the following day, and for another week there would be no mail from Mallock's post-office. However, Mabel's idea of going for a voyage to England with Rupert was approved of, and even urged by Mrs Toland. She would dearly like to see her daughter again before she sailed, but though she could not bear to say so, she believed it would be wiser not to wait. Her father's affection needed only time to cure his displeasure. Her absence would in itself be a help, and Mrs Toland trusted that at the end of the year Rupert and Mabel would find a happy, loving welcome from her parents in the old home.

Gentle chiding, forgiveness, advice, affectionate, good wishes, Mabel read again and again with a full heart, till she knew almost every line of the long letter. It left her with only a slight sad strain running through her triumphant happiness, that by a bold stroke her husband and she had been able to save the dear old people, in spite of themselves, from heart-breaking ruin. With that to think upon, and preparations for leaving Melbourne for England by the next mail steamer, breakfast had little chance in her thoughts, and, with a bright glow on her cheeks, she was still writing to her mother when Rupert returned.

On the following evening Mrs Toland and her husband were seated together by the fire in the house that only for a few days more should be their home.

At least so thought Toland. As the time came near he found it very hard to bear, but the experiences of a week before had a lasting effect, and at the worst, moody silence replaced the fierce outbreaks which he controlled with increasingly painful effort for his wife's sake. She knitted tranquilly, pausing sometimes as if about to speak, and then checking herself with a smile to wait a favourable opportunity. It came at length, when Toland took his pipe out of his mouth and studied her for some time in silent wonder.

'I can't understand you, Ruth,' he said presently. 'You don't look like a woman who has been brought to beggary by her husband and will be turned out of her home three days hence.'

'What if I am not that woman in any particular?' she asked, still smiling.

'I am in no mood for riddles, dear,' he answered, with a tired, questioning look.

'Then here is the answer.'

She took Mabel's letter from her pocket, and hand-

X

ing it to him, put down her work and watched every
movement of his countenance. He glanced first at
the enclosure, his thick eyebrows contracted and his
lips set close. Then he perused the letter slowly
and carefully, and when he had finished stared im-
passively into the fire without comment or a glance
at Ruth.

'Well?' she asked, resting her hand on his knee.

Toland seemed to start from a reverie. 'That
letter is well meant,' he said coldly. 'I believe
Mabel really is fond of us in spite of what she's
done — maybe even she persuaded herself that she
was doing right; and young Harlin seems to have
some generous impulses. But—' he sighed heavily
after a pause, 'it makes no difference, Ruth.'

'Why no difference? Why can't we pay off that
mirerable mortgage and be free?'

'This is why.' Toland's teeth were clenched. He
did not meet Ruth's questioning eyes, and she had
not grasped his intention till he had taken the
cheque in his fingers and torn it into fragments,
which he tossed upon the burning logs.

She watched them go. She let her knitting drop
on the floor; then leaning forward, with her head
buried in her hands, she fought against this great
bitterness and struggled not to cry aloud.

'Oh, John! You don't know what you've done,'
she said at last. A piteous note of despair in the
almost whispered words roused Toland and brought
him to his feet.

'I do, Ruth,' he cried. 'I have put self-respect
above ease. I have refused to accept our home as
the charity of people I have hated. The signature
to that cheque was Mabel's, but you know as well

as I do that the money was Harlin's. I have refused
to sell him forgiveness for his theft of my flesh and
blood!'

Ruth had risen too and stood listening with an
expression of utter weariness, almost scornful.

'You have sacrificed your daughter's happiness to
pride,' she answered slowly. 'You have lost the
opportunity for the noblest action of your life. You
have made us homeless indeed, and—you have disappointed me!'

She could say no more. It was too hard to bear.
Her head shook backwards and forwards; her lips
moved without uttering a sound; and only when
Toland, thoroughly alarmed and cut to the heart by
her words, came nearer, did she find voice again.

A gesture of her hands kept him standing away
from her, abashed. 'No; don't touch me now,' she
faltered, with a smile. 'I'm sorry if I was cruel, dear,
but I'm upset. I will go to bed.'

Toland watched her leave the room without a word.
There was absolutely nothing to say. For the first
time in their lives there had come a deep irreconcil-
able difference where no compromise was possible,
and only the utter abandonment of the position on
one side or the other could ever bring them together
again as they had been through all the years that
ended five minutes ago.

She would not yield. He had seen it in her eyes
and felt it in her tone, and all without finding a word
of protest or defence. Then could he? Or must
this barrier, worse than a dozen evictions, remain
between them, darkening all the brightness that was
left in life? He almost regretted that his maniac
violence had gone. Where his wife was concerned,

at least, there was no longer even refuge from thought in the fierce intoxication of despair. He was just utterly unhappy, while love and every other impulse fought against his pride, and he felt that all that made life worth living would be destroyed by the victory of either. Estrangement from Ruth and homelessness as fruits of the defeat of love by pride— loss of the independence, treasured even above the home which was almost part of himself, as the fruits of its victory.

Leaning forward in the chimney with his head in his hands, he sat till the fire was out, and still the fight went on. There had long been silence in the next room when it was broken, and through the thin partition Toland heard restless tossing on a pillow, and then a heart-broken sob. Suddenly the fight was ended and Toland stood up with his brain reeling.

'Ruth!' he cried.

'What is it?'

'I—I will write to Mabel and ask her for another cheque.' He had forced the words out in spite of devils striving to hold him tongue-tied, and he waited for the guerdon of his victory.

The answer came with a pent-up torrent of tears. 'It is too late. She will be on the seas on her way to England.'

All that her words meant was at first incomprehensible, and he could not go to Ruth till he had thought it out. He had conquered his pride—he had kept Ruth—kept his independence, too, in spite of his willingness to surrender it—and he had lost his farm. Above everything stood out the fact that fate had refused to make him Harlin's pensioner.

It was hard to regret that repentance had been

tardy, and not till it came vividly before him that, with the home which belonged to both of them, his tardiness had sacrificed Ruth's dearest hopes, was he able to go to her bedside and on his knees beg forgiveness.

Ruth granted it before it was asked.

With her husband's repentance new hope sprang up in her brave contriving mind. It kept her wakeful far into the night, and with the bright frosty morning it gained strength. It was not to be thought of that they should tamely submit to ruin when salvation had been driven from their doors by a mere accident and was surely still within their reach.

Might she drive the buggy to Kumbarra? she asked. She would return to the Scotts in the evening, and he could understand that there were many things which she wanted to discuss with Mrs Harlin.

Toland gave his permission with unusual readiness, for he was anxious to do all in his power to make amends, and early after breakfast he drove with her to the gate. Ruth urged the old horses in a way that astonished them from her, and wasted no time on her arrival in telling her troubles to Mrs Harlin. She showed her Mabel's letter and told her of the fate of the cheque and of her husband's subsequent sorrow for what he had done.

Mrs Harlin waxed wrathful and sarcastic, but Ruth's pale face and quivering lips checked her even more than her remonstrances ; and she listened with futile longing for power to grant the request when her friend asked for the loan of another thousand pounds which Mabel would repay.

With a lump rising in her throat Mrs Harlin shook her head 'If I had it, Ruth, dear, nothing

would give me so much delight, but every penny I
could lay hands on has gone to Rupert, for otherwise
he must have asked for his own money and embarrassed his father.'

Ruth's face fell with this last grand castle in the
air, and she sat in hopeless silence, trying to be
brave. Mrs Harlin sought vainly for words of comfort, but none came. At last she rose impatiently
with knitted eyebrows. 'Oh, something must be
done!' she exclaimed. 'It is too wicked! too
absurd!' She looked doubtfully at Ruth. 'I might
be able to get the money from my husband.'

'No, no! not that!' she cried nervously. 'John
would be too angry, and I feel no good would come
of it.'

'It would be just a temporary loan.'

Ruth rose wearily and held out her hand. 'No,
Margaret. Don't talk about it any more. You have
been very kind and I am glad I came to you, but
I don't think I will stay longer now. Good-bye.'

Mrs Harlin kissed her, smiling enigmatically.

'You must not go yet,' she said; 'we have a great
deal else to talk about, and don't be downhearted,
dear, something shall be done.'

'Not what you said.'

Mrs Harlin laughed at the new anxiety in Ruth's
face. 'I believe you are as prejudiced as your husband,' she said kindly. 'But trust me, mine will
not be asked to pay the mortgage or provide any
money for a loan to you or Mr Toland. And all
the same, I feel confident that you will not lose that
farm. Do you trust me?'

'I can't help doing so,' she answered gratefully,

puzzled by the pleased mystery in Mrs Harlin's face, and yet rendered hopeful by it.

'That is right,' said Mrs Harlin, gaily. 'Ask no questions, but when you go to sleep to-night, dream of happier times. Now try not to think of those things for a little, but let me show you a letter from Rupert. He is very much in love.'

Nothing more was said of the mortaged farm. It was the first time the women had met since Rupert's and Mabel's love affair developed, and they spent a long afternoon together talking of the young people, Ruth almost forgetting her own troubles in picturing their delight in each other and in life.

She drove away much more cheerful than she came. She had never known Margaret break a promise; and, utterly unable as she was to guess how or whence help was to come, the words, ' Trust me; you will not lose that farm,' kept ringing in her ears, and she believed them.

CHAPTER XI

THE morning of the sale had arrived at last, and Toland rose early from the kitchen floor, where he had passed the night rolled in his blankets. No persuasion could induce him to stay at Scott's, though his brother-in-law pressed him to make the farm down the river his head-quarters until he could find a job. He had even, with tactless well-meaning, thrown out hints about himself giving Toland employment if he could find an excuse for sacking a man who was doing a bit of clearing for him—as he pointedly mentioned—very cheap.

Sympathy, especially Scott's sympathy, was more than Toland could bear, but he was not sorry that Ruth should be with Bess, and after the sale was over he scarcely knew what he himself should do.

As the sun was rising he tramped from one to another of the empty echoing rooms, stripped of their furniture which lay piled in lots for the sale, while some of the more precious personal belongings of little monetary worth had been carted away to Scott's to meet there some future fate.

Only the previous afternoon had he and Ruth paid a last visit to spots enshrined by a sad or tender recollection in their memories, and bade a farewell together to the old home. Then Toland had driven his wife to Scott's and read with her Mabel's happy

letter, written just before she sailed, returning in the
evening to spend the last few hours on the spot of
earth that was almost his handiwork, and face the
music on the morrow like a man.

Ruth had bid him good-bye with brave, loving
words. She had even managed to smile through
her tears, and, standing at the gate watching him
drive off, had once made as though to call him back.
He pulled up, she hesitated, made a step towards
him and stopped again. No word had come from
Mrs Harlin and things seemed hopeless indeed.
She could not comfort him with her shred of hope
in her friend's promise, but for her the age of miracles
was not past, and hope was living still.

' It is nothing, John,' she called softly. ' I—I only
wanted to tell you that I have a presentiment—a
certainty almost—that you will be happier this time
to-morrow than you are to-day.'

'Bless your superstitions! Go on believing in
them—and in me while you can,' he muttered ; but
she only saw him smile and wave his hand, and went
back to the house impatient for their next happy
meeting.

Now Toland wondered why he had come. It
seemed impossible that he should be driven out of
his home like a dog. He felt madly inclined to
stand in the doorway with his gun to shoot down
anyone who dared approach, and then in hand-to-
hand fight hold the place against rogues and lawyers
till he was overpowered by weight of numbers. Or
he would put a match to the walls and watch the
new house burn like the old one from the scrub
thickets by the creek.

Other lunatic fancies came crowding while he

pursued his aimless, mechanical round, and he laughed bitterly as with an effort of resolution he cast them aside—only for Ruth's sake he told himself. Were it not for Ruth he would embrace the jolly temptations of insanity and make the sale day of Grimsby Farm one long remembered in the neighbourhood.

Going back to the kitchen he rolled up his blankets. With the billy beside them they seemed emblematic of his future life as a tramp and an outcast. He wanted no breakfast. If he were hungry later on, would there not be the sale luncheon with whisky flowing, and no doubt he would be allowed a share.

He lit his pipe and looked over the hill, starting at every sound that his ear deceived him into thinking was the rattle of buggy wheels. It was early yet, but an hour or two hence all the vehicles in the district would be driving through his open gates, their inmates holding high holiday, coming with jests and laughter to tramp about his house, moralise on his downfall, and burst into loud guffaws at the auctioneer's witticisms on his poor little household gods. No—he could not bear it. It might be necessary to see the salesman on some matters of business, but he could creep back in time for that when the desecration of his lares and penates was over and all the careless crowd had gone. If he stayed to witness it he should make a fool of himself, or worse.

Then a new idea came to him. It was so deliciously absurd that he laughed long and loudly as it crossed his brain. But it was a good one and he determined to act on it. Joe was doing well in West Australia and might get him a job. If the daughter could give him a thousand pounds for nothing, surely the son might put his old dad into some work about the mine that would bring him in a pound or thirty bob a week. Anyhow, if he were going to tramp the roads, he would rather do it as far as possible from scenes and faces he knew. There and then he found ink and paper and scribbled some grimly humorous lines to Joe, stating clearly enough, however, what it was he sought. If he posted the letter at the township post-office that morning it would go at once and a whole week would be saved, and he would be away from the farm when a tap of the auctioneer's hammer broke to fragments the materialised result of his enthusiastic young dreams.

He went mechanically to catch his horse in the little paddock, when he suddenly remembered that it was no longer his. Every animal was on the catalogue for sale that day, and a ride might involve him in a prosecution. Anyhow, he preferred to walk. Then he could hide himself in the scrub by the roadside, and avoid the eyes and the sympathy of neighbours gathering for the sale. With a nervous dread of being discovered in the open, he left the house deserted, and striding across his cleared paddocks where the early crops gave ironic promise of bounteousness, he was soon travelling at a swinging pace down the scrub-bordered road to Kumbarra.

It was not long after his departure that the auctioneer and his clerk arrived in a smart Abbot buggy, behind a fast-trotting chestnut, first upon the scene. Calling brought no one to his assistance. The brown gloves, worn presumably to protect his hands from the stain of professional dirty work only, were slipped off with a curse on people generally for not coming out to take his horse, the just-lighted cigar was laid aside, and Mr Salaman helped his clerk to unharness, sulky because his small vanity had not been gratified in impressing a single soul by his arrival. But the first comers were not far behind the auctioneer, and soon, in buggies, spring carts, and on horseback, the visitors arrived by dozens. There were drays too, brought by far-seeing ones, who meant to buy pigs, harness or the like, and taking delivery on the spot to combine business with pleasure and avoid the loss of another day.

The sun shone bright and genial. The wattle on the creek bank just bursting into bloom, the cheerful whistle of the magpies, and a mystified chattering from all the birds of the air, each had their part in lightening hearts and loosening tongues, to an extent of which the most exigeant pleasure-seekers at the sale could not complain. Everything was as it should be, and jollity, irresponsibility, brutality reigned supreme. Toland's little garden was soon a flowerless wilderness of heavy foot-prints strewn with broken plants; Ruth's spotless floors a sea of saliva, with here and there an island not entirely submerged. The crowd elbowed one another through the rooms and passages. Young women blushed and old women laughed at coarse jokes bandied carelessly in their hearing. Females fingered the house linen with muttering and shaking of heads over darns and iron mould. The elderly of both sexes leaned lovingly by the pigstyes, chaffing and betting about the weights, and mentally turning pounds of live pig into bacon at so much per pound. There was a mighty din in the poultry-

yard, where a hot, plum-coloured woman with a green
umbrella pursued fowls to test their age and fatness,
with an admiring crowd of onlookers adding their
cackling to that of the hens. Little groups of men
told one another what was wrong with Toland's
plough, and knowing ones with many winks and
grunts divulged the true age of his horses—contradicted now and then by a man who remembered
such and such an animal's foaling. A large woman
shaped like a cottage loaf, threatening to rise and
burst the black watered silk, made frequent captures
of a small toothless husband who had got at a whisky
bottle that morning just after she had made him
passably clean; and now and then wrenching his
coat collar free of the detaining hand of his breathless, red-faced spouse, he dived into brief liberty
among the legs of the delighted crowd.

Scott and Jimmy Scott were early at the farm, to
represent Toland, on whose account some goods were
going under the hammer, in addition to the land and
stock, both sold by order of the mortgagee.

There was not much demanded of Scott but he did
the little that he could in Toland's interest, giving
information where he thought it would lead to better
sales, withholding it where the effect would be contrary; and now and then ordering the too roughly
curious to keep their paws off the household goods
which they pulled about and soiled. He was not
imaginative or sentimental, but he felt an undefined
sympathetic anger with all the laughing throng, and
surprised his friends by snappy answers to their
greetings. Now and then a flash of what it would
be to have such visitors on his farm crossed his mind,
and he understood Toland better than he had done

since the long ago days when they were one in hope
and indignation by the camp fire at Kumbarra.

Once Conyngham touched his arm in the crowd.
The schoolmaster had insisted that he would not
bother the Scotts while the Tolands were with them
and had found temporary lodgings at another farm.
He had seen neither husband nor wife since the evening Mabel left, and did not wish to do so yet.
Probably they would soon bid good-bye to each
other and the valley for ever, but he could not pass
Toland without a word if he should meet him now.

There was less indulgence than usual in his
habitual half sneer for mankind in general and
himself in particular to-day.

'Good morning, Scott,' he said. 'Have you seen
anything of Toland?'

'No. I scarcely reckoned he'd be here, though he
said something about seeing it through. I'm attending to his business for him.'

'Well, he's better away. He would scarcely find it
so amusing as you or I do.'

'Amusing?' Scott stared at Conyngham, dimly
suspicious of sarcasm. 'I'd like to wring half a
dozen of their b—— necks for 'em—especially the
women's and the auctioneer's!'

Conyngham laughed. 'Do, like a good fellow,' he
said. 'I see your brother-in-law's business is safe
with you. I can't stand any more of this, so I'm
off. Good-bye.'

He sauntered away towards the long row of horses
tethered to the nearest fence, and Scott sulkily obeyed
the auctioneer's beckoning to join him among a knot
of loud-laughed toadies.

It was twelve o'clock. The sale had been ad-

vertised for eleven, and Mr Salaman was anxious
to begin. Scott, he understood, represented the
vendor. Scott said he did, and a move was made
to the big kitchen to put up furniture, house linen
and crockery. The land itself and the stock were
to follow in the afternoon, when food and alcohol
had roused combativeness and loosened purse-strings.

Mallock had no fear that the upset price of the farm
would be reached, and he trusted his beer and whisky
to put ten times the value of the stuff consumed on to
the price of horses and cattle, which secured other of
Toland's debts that he held.

The disposal of Toland's effects did not take long.
The property collected bit by bit in the course of
years, talked over and saved for, almost articulate
with associations, went in a few minutes tó a running accompaniment of auctioneer's *facetiæ* in an
atmosphere of stale tobacco, moleskins, dress stuffs
and humanity, with scarcely a soul in the room but
Scott even dimly remembering that the farce they
shrieked or chuckled over was really a poor little
tragedy.

Then came the luncheon on trestle tables outside
the house; and after it, raised voices, more daring
profanity and doubtful jokes, a decrease of elderly
feminine squeamishness to vanishing point, and an
alcoholic exhalation from every knot of men, gave
promise to Salaman's experience of brisk bidding
for the horses and cattle.

First, as a matter of form, he had to offer the land
for sale, which he prepared to do, feeling some
wonder and a little disappointment that Mallock
was not present—not on Mallock's account, but on
his own, since he could not curry favour by con-

gratulations as he practically presented the mortgagee
with the unsold farm.

The bell rang once more, and mounting a chair in
the crowded sitting-room, Salaman gabbled through
the conditions of sale—Terms, a third cash, the
balance payable by promissory notes at six and
twelve months respectively. The property to be
passed in if the reserve of £1070, covering money
lent, interest due, and expenses incurred by the
mortgagee, should not be reached.

The onlookers listened silently, scarcely understanding the legal jargon, which indeed was rattled
through at an unintelligible pace; but the great
central fact that the home one man had created was
being offered by another man for sale touched them
to the quick, and there rippled through the room a
little wave of sympathy for Toland. The force of
the abstract words, ' Right, title and interest,'
reached their hearts, which were unresponsive to the
more delicate pathos of the lovingly-mended lace
curtains and the two well-worn, old easy-chairs—
' one for the big bear, one for the middle-sized bear.'
They could laugh at the auctioneer's poor wit, applaud
his affected astonishment that the little bear Tolands
had not any ; but there was no laughter now that
another farmer was going and the hated Mallock
once again laying field to field.

' Who'll give me a bid for it ? It goes at one
thousand and seventy—as tidy a little farm as you'll
find on the river, with twenty years of a good
farmer's work and sweat in it—worth more than
twice the money. Come on, you moneyed squires
and Crœsuses ! '

His ivory toy poised in the air, the auctioneer

paused and curled his moustache with one hand, looking patronisingly down on the upturned rough faces, knowing not one of his tantalised hearers to be good for fifty pounds cash if it were to purchase a proved gold mine.

'No offers? You astonish me. Where's all the money gone?' he resumed tauntingly. 'Only a third cash—only ten hundred and seventy! At less money she's passed in. Is there any offer?'

The hammer was already descending, and he was nodding to his clerk, when a man near the door held up his hand and everyone turned to look at him in wonder.

'You might have been a bit smarter, my man,' called Salaman, acidly; 'but I'll take your bid if you look alive with it.'

'Eleven hundred pounds. Wasn't that good enough to wait for?' answered the stranger, calmly.

There was a loud hum of astonished applause, and the auctioneer had to raise his voice.

'Name, please?'

'Mrs Rupert Harlin.'

Salaman beckoned impatiently to the stranger to come forward, and he elbowed his way through the gaping onlookers, ostentatiously pulling out a roll of notes as he did so.

Scott recognised the purchaser then as an old servant of the Harlins whom he had seen on the station years ago. Ruth's faith was justified at last. Mrs Harlin had racked her brains for a means of saving the farm, and a visit to her Tongalong bankers had confirmed the hope that had sprung into her mind when Ruth was with her at Kumbarra. To raise the mortgage money was beyond her means, but she had overdrawn to meet the deposit, and not a penny of it was Harlin's.

Scott could not resist having a slap at the auctioneer. 'More money than you thought after all, Mr Salaman,' he said. 'Mr Mallock will be glad to make a sale of it, I suppose—and Mrs Rupert's a good mark too, eh?'

'Um! Damn his theatrical waste of time, I say. By the way, where the hell is Mallock?'

Others were asking the same question. Scott wondered where Toland was, and for the first time wished him present; but soon the stock sales engaged his attention and he remained till the close of the day at Grimsby Farm, getting a statement of accounts from Salaman and expecting Toland at any minute to return.

However he put in no appearance. The sun was almost down when Scott and his son passed last of all through the gate of the wrecked and deserted home, in haste to see Ruth and gladden her ears with the great news. The purchase of Grimsby Farm was the absorbing topic of talk and speculation in the home-going buggies, and the opinion was freely expressed that Mallock must have got wind of Mrs Rupert's intention and stayed away to conceal his mortification. Toland, it was evident, could have known nothing or he would not have absented himself and missed the fun.

Even though the sale was over Toland was not on his way home. Waiting by the roadside in the morning, he had seen the auctioneer—the undertaker of his dead hopes—drive past, with difficulty subduing a desire to spring out and grip the horse's bridle.

Then he resumed his tramp, thinking, or rather
with disordered thoughts rioting uncontrolled through
his brain.

'It is your fault! it is your fault!' one voice kept
singing. 'If you had trusted your daughter's love you
would be at home to-day.'

'But there is no fault!' he cried almost aloud. 'I
have my independence—I am not a pensioner.'

'Fine independence!' sneered another voice in his
ear.

He stopped and started, staring all around him.
Who had said that? Surely there were voices. He
could swear he heard them. They contradicted one
another; and one laughed. Perhaps he was only
thinking—but he could not think so loud, nor so
many things at once. No, there were voices calling
in his ears; and he laughed too as he listened to
them and trudged on. 'You loved your wife and
you yielded for her sake. You are a brave man and
independent,' sounded one.

'That's true,' thought Toland, complacently,
throwing up his head; but then came the other
voice again.

'Fine independence! You're an independent
pauper—you're an independent tramp—your independence will break your wife's heart. You're an
independent madman—that's what you are!'

Toland stopped dead, with fear-stricken eyes, and
pressed his hand to his forehead. 'Ah, God! no!
not that! Not that, for Ruth's sake!' he exclaimed
aloud. 'I'm tired—it's the sun—my head's queer—
I must rest a little.'

The sun was already hot; he groped his way to
a shady bank of spring grass beneath a spreading

peppermint, and flung himself down. Two or three buggies and some horsemen went past while he rested, and he watched them stealthily, with the mocking voices silent for a time. He remembered that he was faint from want of food. He had eaten little on the previous day—nothing at all in the evening—nothing that morning—and constant smoking, though it dulled hunger, could not repair the nervous waste.

He lit his pipe again and fixed his thoughts resolutely on the future. He was a young man yet, with twenty years work in him, and he would make a start in the arid West, where there was only gold and sand—no green leaf or tree tempting men to the folly of making homes. The letter in his pocket was the passport to a new free life in which he could take his master's money and throw up a job when he chose, with all his worldly wealth upon his back. Yes, the mercenary in the battle of life was the only free man; and the independent pioneers were fool slaves of the soil. Strange that in his first letter from the valley, he should have boastfully asked his sister to come and share his bondage, and that in his last he should be humbly begging his son to set him free.

The buzz of insect life, the chattering of birds, and the smell of the spring flowers gradually soothed him, and thinking of the camp by the creek on the night he wrote to Bess, Toland at last dropped off from sheer weariness to sleep.

Vehicle after vehicle passed him by unnoticed and there was no human creature near when he suddenly awoke and looked round bewildered. Remembrance came all too quickly, and springing to his feet he looked cautiously up and down the road.

Deep wheel ruts in the drying mud showed him that the holiday-makers had passed in numbers. The sun was high and he bethought him of his letter. If he did not hasten it would not be posted in time. So he resumed his walk, growing more weary at every step, afraid to think lest thought should run away with him and the dreaded voices come again.

Pictures of the farm filled with people—of Ruth crying, or perhaps praying all alone—of Mabel in happy ignorance, possibly writing to them at sea—such would spread themselves before him, but whenever he heard the buzzing in his ears and felt the madness creeping in, he clasped his hands over them and talked to himself of his letter. ' I must post my letter. I must hurry or I shall be late. It must go to-day—it must go to-day.' In a dull, monotonous voice he repeated the words over and over as a charm.

There was only a mile or two left to cover. He had scarcely taken note of the familiar land-marks, but he was trudging up hill and knew, without raising his eyes, that he was on Mallock's gap. A cutting through the hill summit lay ahead. On each side of him were the steep slopes of an embankment, in the one passable opening of the range through which the Tonga flowed away westward. He paused a moment and looked over into the deep gully down which water trickled through the culvert at the embankment's base, wearing great ruts in the dray track of the old days, now lumbered with logs and clothed with grass, trees and budding, bronze-tipped

scrub. Down far below him Mick had piloted the
way when he drove his cart first to Grimsby Farm.
Now the road hugged one slope on a side cutting
till the gradient became too steep, when it crossed by
an embankment to the other. It was a steep pinch
still, and hundreds of times had he traversed the gap,
walking his straining horses up the hill and holding
them hard on the down grade as he came and went
from the post-office.

This was the last time, and never again should he
rattle his buggy down it, homewards, with screech-
ing brakes and the horses' shoes ringing on the gravel.

Memories roused by the old track were dangerous,
and leaving the causeway behind he climbed on up
the red hillside road. Soon he was nearing the
highest point. In another half minute he would be
in the cutting, and beyond it, only a mile away, lay
the post-office on the gentle fall to the plain. The
sound of wheels fell on his ear, and stopping still he
looked up. A buggy and pair were coming over
the hill and just beginning to gather way on the
slope.

In a moment they would be upon him. His first
impulse was to hide himself, but there was nowhere
to do it. He heard the brake grind on the wheels,
recognised the turnout, and with his brain madly
whirling stood rooted in the middle of the narrow
road.

It was Mallock's buggy with Mallock in it going
to the sale. Mallock gathered his reins tighter and
jammed his foot harder on the brake.

'Get out of my way, you scoundrel, or I'll drive
you down!' he called.

Toland scarcely heard the words. With no thought

or intention, powerless against the impulse that urged
him, he clutched at the off-side horse's rein. Mallock's
whip lash whistled through the air and curled round
Toland's face and neck. A rough laugh sounded in
his ears. With blood dripping down his cheeks—
with every drop in his body on fire—he released the
horse's bridle. Mallock called to his horses and
drove on ; but he had not gone ten yards before an
arm was thrown round his neck, hot, fierce breath
was on his cheek, and some words, inarticulate with
passion, were hissed in his ear.

Toland had sprung into the buggy from behind as
it passed him and had gained absolute happiness at
last, for all the devils in him were stiffening his
muscles to strangle Mallock, with no one in the world
to interfere.

Mallock was strong, no coward, and fond of life.
Though his face grew blue and he gasped for breath,
hand and foot kept their hold on reins and brake.
With his right arm he struck out blindly, and forcing
his chin down, buried his teeth in Toland's wrist
His throat was suddenly freed, but he was caught
again by the shoulders and could almost hear his
spine crack as he was bent back over the low seat.
The reins dropped, and a look of grey fear came into
his face when he saw Toland's eyes glaring down into
his.

The horses were galloping now. The swingle bars
rattled on their legs, the collars flopped about their
ears and the red slope flew by.

Toland released Mallock for an instant and looked
before him, laughing. Danger brought Mallock's
dazed senses back, and feeling himself free, he made
a frantic effort to lean forward and catch the long

trailing reins, for the buckle was still within reach, caught in the ironwork of the dash - board. But Toland seized him again and forced him back to his seat with overpowering strength, and Mallock's courage gave way.

'Good God, man! you'll kill us both,' he screamed. Toland hugged him a little closer and laughed.

The brake was free. Every buggy bolt was rattling. Sparks were flying from the gravel, and the causeway lay across their path only a hundred yards ahead. Toland's arms crushed the life out of Mallock's final convulsive struggle for freedom.

'I will give you back your farm,' he gasped. There was no answer, but a fierce grip, and they were at the embankment's edge. The horses bravely tried the sharp curve ; but the buggy, crashing on their quarters, flung them forward, and on the old road, fifty feet below, locked in one another's arms, the mortgager and mortgagee of Grimsby Farm found eternity together.

THE END

www.ingramcontent.com/pod-product-compliance
Lightning Source LLC
Chambersburg PA
CBHW020423030726
47495CB00006B/1632